THE
LOST
TEN

HARRY SIDEBOTTOM

ZAFFRE

First published in Great Britain in 2019 by
ZAFFRE
80–81 Wimpole St, London W1G 9RE

Copyright © Harry Sidebottom, 2019

Map © Bonnier Zaffre Art Department

A CIP catalogue record for this book is
available from the British Library.

Hardback ISBN: 978-1-78576-560-5
Trade paperback ISBN: 978-1-78576-789-0

Also available as an ebook

1 3 5 7 9 10 8 6 4 2

Typeset by IDSUK (Data Connection) Ltd
Printed and bound in Great Britain by Clays Ltd, Elcograf S.p.A.

Zaffre is an imprint of Bonnier Books UK
www.bonnierbooks.co.uk

Harry Sidebottom was brought up in racing stables in Newmarket where his father was a trainer. He took his Doctorate in Ancient History at Oxford University and has taught at various universities, including Oxford. His career as a novelist began with his *Warrior of Rome* series.

Also by Harry Sidebottom

Fiction
Fire in the East
King of Kings
Lion of the Sun
The Caspian Gates
The Wolves of the North
The Amber Road
Iron & Rust
Blood & Steel
Fire & Sword
The Last Hour

Non-Fiction
Ancient Warfare
The Encyclopedia of Ancient Battles
(With Michael Whitby)

To Michael Dunne
16th December 1958–17th August 2017

The Roman Empire
in AD265

·············· Provincial borders

1. ZEUGMA   5. HATRA
2. BATNAE   6. NINEVEH
3. CARRHAE   7. ZANDRAKARTA
4. RESAINA

CHAPTER 1

The Castle of Silence

NO ONE HAD EVER RETURNED from the Castle of Silence.
The dark tower, with its tall outer wall, was set on a narrow crag, high in the Elburz Mountains. The remote fortress-prison was impregnable. A prisoner who passed through its gates was never heard of again. Even to mention his name was a capital crime. The Greeks called it the Place of Forgetting.

Barbad the eunuch studied the horrible scene. At first, in the foothills, they had journeyed up through forests of beech and oak. Deer had grazed in the glades. The convoy had shared the road with shepherds driving their flocks to the upper pastures in the spring sunshine. Now they were in a different world. The only trees were stunted junipers, the only living creatures the buzzards that rode the chill winds that scoured the jagged grey precipices. In the distance, the highest peaks were still capped with snow.

Barbad sat back, let the curtain fall on the window of the cart. The cold cut into his aged skin, made his old bones ache. He looked across at Prince Sasan. The boy sat upright and still. His dark eyes betrayed no emotion. Barbad was proud of him. The boy had been raised to ride and shoot and abhor the dark Lie of faithlessness. Nothing had prepared the boy for this. It was not his fault. No blame should have attached to his father. Prince Papak had not been faithless. Barbad knew the truth. Barbad had been there, seen everything with his own eyes.

The hunt had been far to the south, on the borders of the great marsh by the Persian Gulf. The court had been staying in Babylon. When Shapur the King of Kings went hunting it demanded the preparations of a military expedition. Thousands accompanied his progress. There were kinsmen and dignitaries, courtiers, priests, the royal harem, scribes and entertainers, foreign envoys, soldiers, innumerable servants and an army of huntsmen.

The hunting ground was spacious and well stocked. It teemed with geese and ducks. Wild boars rootled in its thickets. But the Master of the Royal Hunt had promised Shapur a lion – the king of beasts for the King of Kings. Not just any lion, but a huge, scarred and wily old male. The beast was said to have killed two royal slaves.

Barbad did not hunt, not since he was cut all those years before. His place was with the other eunuchs and the women. As Chief Scribe to Prince Papak, a brother of the King of Kings, Barbad had joined the royal harem. They were stationed on a low rise. It was shaded by trees, but commanded a fine view. Shapur, flanked by his brothers and some of his many sons, had taken his stance just below them.

The King of Kings was gorgeous in purple and gold. As he had laughed and drunk with the princes, his kohl-lined eyes and very white teeth gleamed. Only slightly less elegant, his kinsmen, Papak among them, had shared his good humour. Their cup-bearers and fan-bearers and those soldiers carrying their weapons had waited with silent deference.

From far off came the sounds of the beaters working their way through the undergrowth in a great semi circle, driving the game towards the royal party.

Even in the shade, it had been hot. There was no wind, and the air was close. Spring came early this far south. Barbad had seated himself on a folding stool. At his age, it was a trial to get up from a rug spread on the ground. Around him the eunuchs and concubines drank cool wine drawn from great barrels packed with snow transported from the distant mountains. They ate sweetmeats, and chattered. Clad in bright silks, they resembled a flock of exotic yet domesticated birds.

Barbad had watched his master Prince Papak for a time, then he had dozed.

A terrible noise startled him awake.

The deep-throated roar of a lion caused the women and eunuchs to give shrill yelps and squeals of alarm. The guards had tried to quiet the harem. There was a net backed by spearmen at the foot of the hillock. They were perfectly safe. Barbad had ignored the commotion around him, concentrated on the hunters.

Shapur, bow in hand, had stepped ahead of his kinsmen. Tall and straight, arrow nocked, he looked the essence of majesty. Alone and brave, calmly facing the onslaught, this was what it meant to be a king.

Prince Papak had been a couple of paces behind, slightly to one side. A slender hunting spear with a crossbar at the base of its long blade was in his hands. Some of the other royal kinsmen had spears, more held bows. None would intervene unless it was absolutely necessary. It was the right of the King to take the first shot. The king of beasts was not the quarry of other men. It was reserved for the King of Kings, and Shapur's skill with a bow was legendary.

All the attention of the hunters was on the cover. Barbad had followed their gaze. Fifty paces beyond Shapur was a wall of reeds. Although there was not a breath of wind up on the low hill, here and there the feathery heads of the reed bed shifted.

Barbad found he was on his feet, straining forward, like a hound in the slips.

The lion roared again. The ascending vibration reverberated in Barbad's chest, had seemed to shake the air. And then the reeds parted.

It was a mature male lion, tawny, lithe and young. The feral stench had reached those on the hillock. A eunuch whimpered.

The beast looked back at the undergrowth. The beaters must be close. Their shouts, and the rattle of spears on shields, put up wildfowl at no great distance.

The lion turned to those who blocked his path. Its blank eyes focused on the man that stood nearest and alone.

Shapur half drew his bow.

The lion gathered itself, roared a third time.

The King of Kings pulled the bowstring back to his ear, aimed.

For a moment all was still. The noises of the beaters, the clatter of the wings of the flighting birds, seemed far away.

Shapur's arm trembled slightly with the strain.

The lion launched itself forward. Almost quicker than the eye could follow, Shapur's arrow had thumped into its chest. The beast staggered, but bounded again. The second arrow caught it in the windpipe. This time it crumpled on landing. But this was a fierce lion. A bloody pink froth bubbling from its mouth, it crawled on its belly towards the figure that had caused it such pain.

Shapur handed the bow to one of his sons. The King drew his long, straight sword. With graceful steps, he walked to the lion. The beast's lifeblood was fast draining away, its muzzle red with gore. Its roar of defiance was now a choking cough.

Straddling the back of the lion, Shapur turned to face his entourage. He flourished his blade, then, with the skill of long practice, plunged the steel down between the shoulder blades in the killing blow.

'*Hail the Mazda-beloved Lord Shapur!*' The high-pitched cries of the harem joined the deep shouts of the hunters.

As Shapur basked in the applause, Barbad noticed the tips of the reeds moving.

'*King of Kings, descended from the Gods, famed for his courage!*'

Against all courtly etiquette, Papak rushed forward towards the King.

'*May the Gods . . .*' The chanting had faltered.

Again the reeds parted.

This lion was old, slab-shouldered and powerful. A long white scar ran down its flank from its mane to its haunches. In its eyes was the cunning of a man-eater.

Unaware of the threat, Shapur half turned, affronted, as Papak darted past.

With no preliminaries, the man-eater leapt. Its acceleration defied its enormous bulk. At the third bound, it was on Papak. There was no time to take the proper stance, but the Prince somehow thrust out his spear. The momentum snapped the shaft, flattened Papak, sent him tumbling like a child.

Thrashing and sliding, the lion crashed to the ground almost at the feet of the King. Curling, the lion tore at its own hide with teeth and claws. It ripped jagged wounds in its own flesh as it struggled to get at the white-hot agony embedded in its vitals, at the steel which was robbing it of life.

The face of the King of Kings was a mask as he looked down at his brother, bruised and battered in the dirt. Without a word, Shapur had sheathed his sword, and stalked away.

The hunt was over.

The evening was mild. A gentle breeze blew through the tamarisks and trees. The stars were clear in the vault of the heavens. Yet in the pavilion of Prince Papak the atmosphere had the tense stillness before thunder.

Barbad attended as his lord was bathed, and his wounds tended. There were two gashes and much bruising, but Papak was not seriously injured. There was little talk while the prince was served his dinner, less while he was put alone into his bed. No one, not even young Prince Sasan, had talked of the lion. No one voiced the question in every mind. Would the King of Kings reward Papak for his bravery, or punish him for his presumption? Like the rest, Barbad kept his opinion to himself.

The answer had not been long in arriving.

With his advancing years, Barbad slept little and badly. In the middle of the night he heard the tread of the boots of the guards surrounding the tent. Barbad had retired still wearing a tunic. Now he tied a sash around his waist, pulled on slippers and a cloak, and hurried to his lord's bedchamber.

As was to be expected, Prince Papak had awaited his fate with a calm fortitude. He summoned his son, and the senior members of his household. In the soft lamplight, he spoke to them quietly. Not words of reassurance, but of courage and faithfulness. Respect the will of the Gods and abhor the Lie.

When the soldiers entered, Barbad felt his heart pounding in his chest. Wherever he looked was steel and leather, bearded and cruel faces. Yet it was done with respect – no violence or insult was offered. They shackled Papak with chains of silver, as befitted his princely status.

And then the officer had read out the decree of the King of Kings.

Even then Prince Papak retained his composure. Looking into Barbad's eyes, he had spoken quietly to his eunuch. 'Do your duty. Serve my son until the end.'

Barbad had bowed his head.

That very night young Prince Sasan and Barbad began their long journey to the distant province of Hyrkania and the Castle of Silence.

The final ascent was steep. Some of the outriders got down to put their shoulders to the wagon. When it reached the gate, they put wedges under its wheels.

Barbad and Sasan were ordered to get out.

The wind fretted at Barbad's cloak. All around were dizzying cliffs. The only sound was the thin mewing of the buzzards overhead.

The captain of their guard called up to a sentry on the battlements. His voice was small in the immensity of the mountains, the words almost snatched away by the wind.

One of the sentries left. Another told them to wait. The gate remained shut.

Chilled to the core, Barbad felt his courage failing. The Greek doctors at court claimed that the heart of a man shrank as he aged, ended up no bigger than a child's. Barbad was very old. In the summer he would be seventy-five. If he survived that long. A eunuch was not expected to have the courage of a whole man.

Noticing Barbad shivering, the boy touched his arm reassuringly.

Rallying, Barbad smiled back. Sasan was only ten. A brave boy.

Turning his head so Sasan would not see the tears in his eyes, Barbad studied the fortress. The outer walls were of dressed stone. The masonry was close fitted and smooth, its surface impossible to climb. On the journey, Barbad had entertained thoughts of escape. They had been nothing but fantasies. The guards had been watchful. Like his father, Sasan had been shackled with silver chains. In any case, how could an elderly eunuch and a young boy hope to escape? Where would they go? To the savage nomads of the northern Steppe? To the Romans far off in the west? Without money or friends, they would reach neither.

At last the gate opened. It was heavy, bound with iron.

As Barbad and Sasan walked into the dark gatehouse, the boy took Barbad's hand. His skin was warm and smooth in the old eunuch's grip.

Shafts of light from holes in the ceiling penetrated the gloom. The clomp of the draught horses' hooves and the squeal of the wagon wheels followed them, echoing back from the walls. Another gate was open at the far end, and they passed into the light of the courtyard.

The castle was larger than it appeared from outside. The curtain wall ran in a rough oval, following the irregularities of the crag. There were buildings against the inside of the wall: barracks to the right, stables and storerooms to the left. Directly ahead a smaller postern stood opposite the main gate, wedged between the barracks and the inner tower. The latter was circular, four storeys high. It had no openings at ground level. Higher, the few windows were small, little more than arrow slits, too narrow for a grown man to fit through. Stone steps were built against its face, climbing from right to left up to a door on the first floor. At the top of the steps, the warden of the Castle of Silence stood waiting.

Naduk, the zendanig, was a huge man with a broad red beard that spread across his chest. Barbad had seen him before at the royal court. As befitted his gloomy occupation, Naduk always wore dark clothing. No zendanig was ever loved, but such was the air of menace that hung about Naduk, even in the entourage of the King of Kings, men shrank from his presence.

Barbad and Sasan ascended the steps. The boy went ahead, walking calmly, holding himself straight. Again the young prince's courage threatened to rob Barbad of what manliness the knife had left.

'Welcome, Prince Sasan, son of Prince Papak, of the House of Sasan.'

The warden's eyes were cold and black, like pebbles in a stream. His words were polite but there was no compassion in his voice.

'Your accommodation is on the upper floor.'

'You are most kind,' Sasan replied.

Naduk turned and led the way. The guards brought up the rear.

By the time they reached the top of the tower, Barbad's old legs were aching, his chest tight.

A heavy door, bound with iron like the outer gate, stood at the head of the stairs.

'Your food and drink will be brought.' Naduk gestured them through. 'Your fetters will be removed.'

The door closed behind the boy and the eunuch. They heard the key turn in the lock.

There were two main rooms: a day chamber and a bedroom beyond. A tiny privy, built into the wall, opened off the living room. The rooms were well furnished: rugs on the floor, hangings on the walls, braziers burning, the furniture almost opulent.

The boy opened the shutters. Fresh masonry showed where iron bars had recently been embedded across the slit window. Sasan looked out.

The cold mountain wind whistled in, made the braziers glow.

Barbad unpacked their meagre possessions: some clothes, slippers, a book of poetry, Sasan's favourite toy – a stuffed lion. They had not been allowed to bring cosmetics or medicines, or writing materials, nothing sharp. Their belts and laces had been removed. The rooms contained no cutlery; none of the hangings had a sash.

Against all etiquette, Barbad sat on a divan unbidden and considered.

The warden had been courteous. He had used Sasan's name and title, those of his father as well. The silver fetters would be removed from the prince's wrists and ankles. Perhaps the future was not without hope. Perhaps the King of Kings would show mercy.

Humanity and pity were the kindly sisters of the virtues. For an individual of quality, if the offence was not heinous, it was not unknown for a King of Kings to order the cloak of the miscreant to be whipped instead of his body. The executioners might cut off the tassels of his headgear, not his ears. They might sever his turban, not his head.

But Shapur was not known for his clemency. At the siege of Arete, the Roman prisoners had been blinded with boiling oil. Barbad had seen a rebel sent back to his city tied to a maimed donkey. The man's ears, hands and feet had been cut off. At Ctesiphon, a traitor had been tied to a wheel for ten days. In the end his eyes had been gouged out, and molten brass poured in his ears. And then there was the even slower yet more horrible execution by the troughs. Barbad had witnessed that, many years before. That day was not something he wanted to remember, but something he would never forget.

Barbad would not let such a fate befall the boy. Men thought eunuchs contemptible and weak. They were wrong. To be sure, vicious horses, when gelded, ceased to bite and kick, but they remained serviceable for war. The same was true of bulls. When castrated, they lost their unruliness, yet retained their strength. After being cut, dogs became less savage, though were still just as useful for hunting or guarding their masters.

Barbad would do his duty to Prince Papak. He would serve his son until the end.

The warden had been thorough, even extending to measures such as the new bars on the windows, preventing the boy throwing himself to his death. The only thing Naduk had overlooked were the braziers. Swallowing the hot coals would bring death. The agony would be no better than that inflicted by the executioners. Still, it need not come to that.

Hidden in the sleeve of Barbad's tunic was a knife. Only about the length of a finger, and not more than one third as wide, it was intended for trimming nails. Yet it could serve another purpose.

CHAPTER 2

Rome

THE CAMP OF THE STRANGERS was a place of ill omen. Situated on the Caelian Hill, it was the headquarters of the *frumentarii*, the Emperor's spies and assassins. Political prisoners important enough to be transferred to Rome from the provinces were held here, awaiting execution, or further interrogation. The tortures were agonisingly efficient. Ordinary citizens kept away from the place. Some held that its appearance in a dream signified an evil future. Only informers, driven by greed or malice to denounce others, willingly crossed its threshold.

Murena had loved the camp ever since he had first set eyes on it years earlier. Entering its walls, immediately he had sensed its power. Here all the secrets of the empire were gathered together, all hidden plans laid bare. From here, nondescript-looking men rode out across the breadth of the imperium carrying letters that could put armies in motion or order the execution of their generals. Sometimes the writings they carried were a ruse to gain access to their target. Then their mission was direct and brutal.

Walking between the neat barrack blocks in the gloom of first light, Murena stopped at an apse that housed a shrine of Hercules. As was his habit, he placed his hand on his chest, and offered a prayer to the god. Hercules had travelled the world overthrowing tyrants, casting down evil. The deity was a fitting patron of the work of the *frumentarii*.

The demands of piety satisfied, Murena crossed the paved square in the centre of the camp. Ascending the steps to the commanding officer's building, he returned the salute of the two guards. One of them opened the door for him.

Inside, Murena stood motionless for a time surveying the plain, unassuming room. There was a desk, on it a stylus with other writing equipment, two lamps, and a pile of reports. Behind the desk was a chair, two more for visitors in front. Apart from a stand for armour in a corner, there was no other furniture. All the walls were lined with pigeonholes, each stuffed with documents.

As he did every morning, Murena regarded the scene with a quiet satisfaction. Four years previously he had arrived at the camp as a mere army scout. Seconded from the Fourth Scythian Legion, he had carried an important despatch from the east. Its news had been welcome. The generals Odenaethus and Ballista had turned back a Persian invasion, and a pretender had been killed. Enrolment as a centurion of the *frumentarii* had been Murena's reward. Now he was promoted to *Princeps Peregrinorum*, the *Leader of the Strangers*, commander of the *frumentarii*. If the Emperor's spies were imagined as a spiderweb spread out across the empire, Murena sat at its heart, pulling the threads, catching those who whispered plots against Rome or its ruler, luring those who even thought such things to their doom.

Murena liked to arrive early each morning. Recently appointed, there was much for him to master, and every day brought fresh rumours of sedition. His secretary had stacked the documents on his desk. Each was read and considered, some acted upon, all carefully filed. Hanging his cloak on the armour stand – the late spring dawn was still chilly – Murena sat down. He was eager to find new evidence, to uncover more of the alienated and malignant.

No sooner was he sat at his desk, the first papyrus unrolled, than there was a knock at the door.

'Come.'

'Visitor for you, sir,' the guard said.

A tall figure in a hooded cloak entered without waiting to be summoned.

Murena remained seated. His dignity might be slightly affronted, but he was unalarmed. Secrecy was the stock in trade of the *frumentarii*, and the guards would admit no one without authorisation.

The large man pushed back his hood to reveal a ruddy, broad face.

Murena leapt to his feet. 'My apologies, sir. I was not expecting you.'

'No apologies are necessary.' The weather-beaten man smiled. 'Do you have any warmed wine? Have them bring three cups. It is as cold as a witch's tit out there.'

As Murena went out to arrange the drinks, his heart was thumping. A visit from the Praetorian Prefect, unannounced and incognito, would not be undertaken without good reason.

By the time Murena came back into the room, Volusianus had thrown his cloak on the armour stand, and was seated behind the desk. The Praetorian Prefect waved Murena to one of the visitors' chairs.

'I have arranged a discreet meeting,' Volusianus said. 'The officer should be here soon. You will remain. As you know, in a few days I will leave with the imperial entourage for the north. The Emperor Gallienus is determined to cross the Alps and crush Postumus the pretender, who holds Gaul. Should anything happen to me, I want a trustworthy man to know what has been arranged.'

Murena acknowledged the compliment with a nod.

Volusianus said no more. He sat waiting, perfectly at ease in the silence.

As the leader of the *frumentarii*, Murena reported to the Prae-torian Prefect. Volusianus answered directly to the Emperor. Apart from the sacred majesty of the Emperor himself, no one was more powerful than the Praetorian Prefect. There was a ritual when a new prefect was appointed. The Emperor would take the prefect's sword. *If I reign well, use this on my behalf. If I rule badly, turn it on me.* The prefect commanded the Emperor's bodyguard. The Praetorians, the twelve thousand most highly paid troops in the empire, guarded the palace in Rome, and accompanied the Emperor on all his travels. Over the years the prefects had also acquired rights of civil jurisdiction, often presiding over court cases in place of the Emperor.

Such power was an evident threat to the Emperors themselves. To counterbalance the Praetorians there were other military units stationed around the capital: the Urban Cohorts in Rome itself, the Second Parthian Legion in the Alban Hills outside. Most Emperors maintained a personal bodyguard of German warriors recruited beyond the frontiers. To watch for disloyalty in each other, usually there were two Praetorian Prefects: Volusianus's colleague was currently in Milan gathering forces to cross the Alps into Gaul. To curtail their ambition, the men appointed pre-fect tended to be drawn not from among the senators, the highest social order, but from the equestrians, the second rank. The idea was that the senate would be reluctant to accept a man of lower status than themselves if a prefect murdered his ruler and aimed to take the throne for himself.

None of the carefully constructed checks and balances worked. Only one Emperor had been killed by the barbarians, but several had met their end at the swords of the Praetorians. Two Prae-torian Prefects had arranged the assassination of Emperors they had sworn to protect, and assumed the purple in their places. The danger remained. As the poet Juvenal had rightly asked: *Quis custodiet ipsos custodies? Who guards the guards?*

A tap on the door announced the arrival of the wine. Murena got up, dismissed the soldier, and served the drinks himself.

Volusianus took a deep swig, then warmed his hands around the cup. 'When I was young – serving on the Danube, the Rhine – I never felt the cold.'

Murena made a vague noise intended both to express sympathy and reject the implication that his superior was old.

'There was a frost the other night. It will have done the spring vegetables no good.'

Volusianus had never hidden his peasant origins. If anything, he drew attention to them. Some claimed it was vanity, to point out just how far he had risen. A personal favourite of Valerian, the previous Emperor, Volusianus could not have climbed higher: through the ranks of the army, admitted to the equestrian order, appointed Praetorian Prefect, granted senatorial status. The capture of Valerian by the Persians had not stopped his ascent. The Emperor Gallienus, Valerian's son, was said to rely upon him. Certainly Gallienus had confirmed him as commander of the Praetorians. Indeed, Gallienus had shown the former peasant the signal favour of holding the office of consul with Volusianus. For eternity, the one thousand and thirteenth year since the founding of the city of Rome would be known as the year when Gallienus and Volusianus were consuls. It was a proud form of immortality.

Loyalty and ruthless efficiency were the public qualities that underpinned the meteoric career of the Praetorian Prefect. Of course there were rumours. But, looking at that open and guileless rustic face, Murena found them hard to credit. There were always unfounded rumours. Anyway, Murena owed his own office to Volusianus.

Another knock at the door.

'Gnaeus Claudius Severus,' the guard announced.

The officer saluted as the door closed behind him.

'We will do what is ordered, and at every command we will be ready,' Severus said.

After the formal words of a soldier to his superior, no one spoke. Severus remained standing at attention. Volusianus regarded him closely, like some physiognomist trying to read his innermost soul.

Murena half recognised Severus. He had seen him before – years before. The stubby beard and short hair, the grey eyes, the slightly sticking out ears; all were familiar, but Murena could not place from where.

The silence stretched, was fast becoming oppressive.

Murena kept his face expressionless. What was this about? Was it the arrest of a traitor, the promotion of a deserving officer, or something altogether more sinister? There were no guards in the room, and Severus was armed. It was unlikely to be the detention of conspirator.

A horrible suspicion surged up, like a monster emerging from the depths. Was the man detained to be Murena himself? Would he be dragged to the cells and subjected to hideous tortures? In the twilight world of the *frumentarii* no one was above suspicion; innocence was no guarantee of safety. Murena pushed the thought back down into the darkness.

'You are Gnaeus Claudius Severus, son of Publius, an equestrian from Samosata in Cappadocia.' Without pausing for an answer, Volusianus continued. 'You have commanded the First Aquitanian Cohort in Britain, the Third African Cavalry in Germany, and the Second Thracian Cohort in Syria.'

That was where Murena had seen Severus. At the start of Valerian's ill-fated campaign, somewhere north of Carrhae, he had delivered a report to Severus and his Thracians. He remembered him now – a tough, experienced officer.

'Since then you have served as a procurator, overseeing imperial estates in the provinces of Arabia and Macedonia.' Volusianus had consulted no notes, but spoke from memory.

'Yes, sir.'

'Are you ready to return to the standards?'

'Ready, sir.'

With an energy that defied his age, Volusianus bounded to his feet. Smiling, he extended his hand. Severus shook it.

'Have a seat, Severus.'

The tension had gone from the room.

Pouring the officer a cup of wine, Volusianus settled himself back in his chair. He exuded the amiability of a farmer at a festival.

'Health, and great joy.'

They toasted each other.

'Am I right in thinking that growing up in the east, Severus' – somehow the name was pronounced as if to an intimate friend – 'you speak Greek, as well as a smattering of Syriac and Persian?' Volusianus was beaming like the sun.

'I do, sir.'

'Then you are the man that I am looking for.' Volusianus dropped his air of bucolic geniality with the speed and finality of a theatre curtain. 'Tell me what you know of the Castle of Silence.'

Severus narrowed his eyes with the effort of recall. 'A Persian fortress, somewhere in the mountains south-east of the Caspian Sea. They use it as a prison.'

'Quite so,' Volusianus said.

Murena wanted to add that for Persians it was a capital crime to mention the name of anyone condemned there, but he did not. A *frumentarius* must know when to hold his tongue.

'Prince Sasan, a nephew of the King of Kings, has been confined in the fortress.' Volusianus gave Severus a measuring stare. 'You will go and get him out.'

It was to Severus's credit that he received this order with the calm of a Stoic philosopher instructed to take his own life. The command amounted to much the same.

'What troops would be at my disposal, sir?' he asked after a moment.

'Ten men. The leader of the *frumentarii*,' Volusianus indicated Murena, 'will provide you with a squad of eight of his best soldiers, and a junior officer of equestrian status.'

Severus glanced at Murena.

'You will be disguised as a merchant caravan out of Antioch,' Volusianus continued. 'Murena here will arrange for mounts, baggage animals and suitable trade goods. Any questions so far?'

Severus frowned with concentration. 'When we have freed the prince, how will we return to the empire? After the rescue there will be a pursuit. Our subterfuge will be exposed. We will not be able to cross back into Syria posing as merchants.'

'You will not return to Syria,' Volusianus said. 'Murena, get a decent map.'

As he selected a recent map from one of the pigeonholes, Murena reflected on the confidence of Severus. *When*, not *if* he had rescued the prince. Murena doubted that the expedition would get anywhere near the Castle of Silence.

With the map spread on the desk, they stood looking down at the little depictions of towns, the lines representing roads, the imprecise drawings of mountains, rivers and seas.

Volusianus pointed to the great emptiness of the Steppes. His finger moved from north-east of the Black Sea to east of the Caspian. 'All this territory is ruled by Naulobates, King of the Heruli. Since the

THE LOST TEN | 21

mission of Ballista two years ago, the King has been recognised as a friend and ally of the Roman people. Naulobates will be informed of your coming.'

'Sir,' Severus cleared his throat, 'might it not be better to send a man known to this Naulobates?'

'I have other plans for Ballista.' Volusianus dismissed the idea. 'When you have the prince, you will ride due north, the Caspian on your left, until you reach the Heruli.'

His fate sealed, Severus nodded and turned to practicalities. 'Where will I rendezvous with the *frumentarii*?'

Volusianus jabbed at the map. 'At Zeugma on the Euphrates. There you will cross from Syria into Mesopotamia.'

Murena considered the small town on the wide, brown river. He had been born there, the son of a soldier with the Fourth Scythian Legion. As a boy he had seen the army of the Emperor Alexander Severus straggle back across the bridge from defeat at the hands of the Persians. As a man enrolled in the same legion, he had fought in the vast wastes of Mesopotamia. Although the towns there were now held by the Romans, most had been sacked at one time or another. When Zeugma itself fell, he had barely escaped with his life. Only the gods had preserved him when the Emperor Valerian had been captured near Carrhae. The bare countryside of Mesopotamia was a no man's land, subjected to endless raids by Persians and nomadic Arabs. Severus and his rescue mission would be lucky to get that far, let alone reach the distant Castle of Silence.

The Praetorian Prefect and Severus had turned to a discussion of the merchandise the caravan should take. As they talked, Murena mulled over the vital question that had not been asked. Why should Volusianus want to rescue Prince Sasan?

It was well known that the Praetorian Prefect had long urged the Emperor Gallienus to lead an expedition to free his father Valerian from Persian captivity. Gallienus had proved reluctant. If Prince Sasan fell into Roman hands, war would be inevitable. Even if he wished, Shapur would not be able to ignore the blow to his prestige as King of Kings. Gallienus would have to respond. Volusianus would get his desire. And his influence over the Emperor would be demonstrated.

But was Rome ready for another full-scale conflict with the Persians? The Roman forces in the east were understrength and ill-disciplined. This summer, Gallienus and the imperial field army were committed to cross the Alps to fight Postumus the usurper in the west. Volusianus must be gambling that the campaign in Gaul would be over by the autumn. It was a high-stakes bet. A previous invasion had proved indecisive.

Sardonyx and agate. Volusianus and Severus had settled on goods manufactured in the empire that were less widely available in Persia. Jewellery and carved cameo stones were small and expensive items. The former quality would account for the caravan consisting of only ten men, the latter that they would be heavily armed.

Murena wondered if Volusianus had ever served in the east. Perhaps, like many westerners, he considered the Persians no more than effete and cowardly Orientals. If so, Volusianus was wrong. They had defeated four Roman armies in pitched battle. Three of them had been led by Emperors. Gordian III they had wounded, Valerian they had captured, Alexander Severus had been fortunate to escape unscathed. Murena remembered the Persian warriors streaming over the walls of Zeugma. He had seen them cut down his own father. For all their kohl-lined eyes and perfumed silks, there was nothing weak or effeminate about them.

Murena prided himself on his loyalty. He owed it to Volusianus, but more so to Rome. A war with Persia now would be a disaster.

It was vital no pretext was offered to the King of Kings: this Prince Sasan must not be rescued. Murena could not openly go against the Praetorian Prefect, but nor could he approach the Emperor directly. If he warned Gallienus of this plan, Volusianus would be informed, and Murena would find himself in the dungeons of the Palace. It need not come to that. Most likely the mission of Severus would fail, but certainty was necessary. That should not be hard to arrange. Murena was the commander of the *frumentarii*. If he chose carefully enough, he could make sure the party would ride into the deserts of Mesopotamia, and never be heard of again.

CHAPTER 3

The Euphrates

O F ALL THE DUSTY EASTERN TOWNS through which Valens had passed on his long journey, Zeugma was the most depressing. Of course he was prejudiced. In the others he had spent only a night or two. He had been waiting in Zeugma for almost half a month now. Still, the wait was almost at an end.

It was the day before the *Kalends* of August, midsummer in Syria. It was hot, hotter than Rome. Valens had never left the west before, and Zeugma was hotter than anywhere he had ever known. To escape the stifling streets, Valens had toiled up the stepped path to the citadel. Below the temple and the palace there was an orchard. The young equestrian officer sat in the shade, back against an apple tree, hoping to catch whatever breeze might blow. At least it was quiet up here.

The fruit trees ran steeply down to a low, crumbling wall. Beyond, a jumble of red-tiled roofs descended the slope. The drop was vertiginous, and the houses seemed to be built on top of each other. Halfway down, on a flat shoulder of the hill, was an open space fronted by another temple, a monumental arch, a theatre and other public buildings. Valens cast a disparaging eye on these symbols of Hellenic civic life. The inhabitants of Zeugma might claim to be Greeks, but they looked Oriental. Some even had earrings, and many answered to Syrian names.

Far below was the Euphrates, and the bridge from which the town took its name. Valens let his gaze wander across the river to Apamea, the settlement on the far bank. Unlike Zeugma, with its narrow, twisting alleys, Apamea was laid out in a regular grid on its plain. Yet on both sides of the river there were abandoned dwellings, their fallen roofs and smoke-blackened beams like missing or rotten teeth in the lines of the streets. It was more than a decade since the Persians had sacked the twin towns. Before, these had been thriving settlements, rich from the endless caravans trading with the east. Now the stream of merchants had dried to a trickle, and the towns were shrunken and run-down.

Valens looked out to the east, beyond the walls that had failed to keep out the Persians. The land, shimmering in the heat, stretched perfectly flat to where a range of hills rose like a mirage. They were the foothills of the great high plains of northern Mesopotamia. Into that bare expanse, infested with predatory nomads and swept by raiding Persian horsemen, Valens would soon depart.

The disquieting thought made him glance at the military camp in the northern quarter of Zeugma. Even the base of the Fourth Scythian Legion had seen better days. Once, imperial expeditions had assembled there. The parade grounds would have been full of marching troops, bright with standards, loud with the call of trumpets. Now the legion itself was below full strength, with many men on detached duties, and only a handful of troops moved desultorily across the baked bare earth. Tomorrow, at long last, after the lengthy journey from Rome and this interminable waiting, Valens would report for duty.

The summons by the *Leader of the Strangers* had come like a peal of thunder from a clear sky, like a portent. Although the headquarters of the *frumentarii* lay at no distance from the camp of his own unit on the Caelian Hill, Valens had never set foot in the place.

No one in their right mind chose to go there. Like all members of the Roman upper classes, Valens both despised and feared the *frumentarii*. The secret soldiers were underhand spies and assassins. The Emperors used them to pry into the lives of the elite, to ferret out any hint of disloyalty. Dressed in civilian clothing, they were rumoured to be impossible to recognise. Nowhere was safe from them. An ill-considered word in a casual conversation at the baths, or at a dinner party, might lead to arrest. If evidence was lacking, the *frumentarii* were notorious for inventing incriminating details. Once in the hands of the torturers, you would confess to anything.

Murena, the *Princeps Peregrinorum*, was a vulgar little man, obviously promoted from the ranks. But he had been civil. Once he had established that Valens was indeed Marcus Aelius Valens, Deputy Tribune in the Imperial Horse Guards, he had been brisk and efficient. It was well known, Murena had said, that Valens was bored by garrison duty in the capital. Valens had agreed. He had not wondered how Murena knew. It was the sort of thing the *frumentarii* found out.

Another officer was introduced, a tall man in middle age, with a short beard and protruding ears. Gnaeus Claudius Severus was to lead a team of ten across Mesopotamia, and into Persian territory. Severus would claim to be a merchant, trading in jewellery. Eight *frumentarii* would act as the guards of his caravan. Valens would be second in command, and pose as Severus's nephew. The aim of the mission was to rescue a Persian prince named Sasan from a prison called the Castle of Silence, situated to the south-east of the Caspian Sea. Once they had freed the Prince, they were to travel north to the Steppe. There, the ruler of the nomad Heruli would convey them to the Black Sea, from where they would take passage on a ship back to the empire.

'Any questions?' Murena had asked.

Dozens jostled in Valens's mind: routes, logistics, money, weapons, above all the chances of survival.

'No, sir,' he had replied.

'Good,' Murena had said. 'You will report to Severus in the military camp at Zeugma on the Euphrates on the *Kalends* of August. You will travel there alone, not even with a slave.'

'Sir.'

'One last thing. You will resign your commission in the Horse Guards. You will not be formally transferred into the *frumentarii*. You will not be issued with the identity token of a *miles arcanus*. The others will hand their disks in at Zeugma. If you are captured, you are not a soldier of Rome. We will deny any knowledge of you, or the mission.'

'Sir.'

Murena smiled. 'Welcome to the world of the secret soldiers.'

Thinking back on the conversation in that insignificant office, Valens knew that he had had no choice. Once the mission had been revealed, he could not refuse. Murena would not have let him leave. Valens had no idea why he had been chosen, but it was true that he had been stultified by the round of ceremonial duties in Rome. All the efforts of securing a commission had not been undertaken just to stand guard on the Palatine, or parade in the Circus Maximus.

Valens had wanted action. He had been crushed when it was announced that he would remain with the detachment of the Horse Guards ordered to stay in the capital, that he was not among those selected to accompany the Emperor on the campaign in Gaul. Now, here in the east, there was no doubt that he would see combat. But this furtive, and probably suicidal, expedition – the whole idea was insane – this was not at all what he had wanted. He had envisioned leading men in open battle, riding at the head of a cavalry charge under the eyes of the Emperor. Not sneaking about like some filthy merchant, intent on cheating those foolish enough to buy his wares.

And there was the problem of the *frumentarii*. Valens did not trust them. How could anyone trust men whose trade was deception? They would all be veterans. They would realise his inexperience. Even under an experienced commander like Severus, commanding a squad of them would not be easy.

The light breeze had dropped. It was getting hot in the orchard. Valens thought he could do with a drink.

Severus was another cause for concern. The man was from a respectable equestrian family, but he had been taciturn, his attitude far from amiable. Perhaps on a dangerous mission behind enemy lines an officer of his long service might not welcome as his second in command someone he might see as a callow fop from the imperial guard?

Gods below, I really need a drink. But he could not get too drunk. It would not do to arrive in the camp tomorrow morning with a bad hangover. The baths down by the river were the answer: a massage, a cold plunge, have a couple of drinks listening to whatever philosopher or sophist might be giving a lecture. With luck, there might be a half-decent poet. Even in this backwater there were always one or two itinerant intellectuals haunting the public buildings, seeking an audience. As Lucian had written in one of his satires, it was easier to fall over in a rowing boat and not hit a plank than avoid being accosted by some down-at-heel man of words.

By the time Valens had negotiated the steps down to the town, he had changed his mind. There was a bar on the waterfront, close to his lodgings. It was nothing special, but it was dark and cool, and the wine was not too bad.

He stood for a moment in the doorway, letting his eyes adjust to the gloom. A bar ran along the right-hand wall. Across the back was a worn staircase, up which the customers might take which-ever of the serving girls was working. A door under the stairs led out to a privy in a small courtyard. The rest of the room contained four tables with benches. At one of them sat two stevedores. In the furthest corner was an extraordinary figure clad in yellow-and-green striped trousers and a blue tunic. His cloak, also sky blue, was folded neatly on the bench next to him, and a long ebony cane was propped against his table. The man had been a regular at the bar over the last few days. As ever he was eating fruit, and not drinking wine, but plain water.

As Valens entered, the man looked up. His huge domed head was entirely hairless, lacking even eyebrows. His oddly small features were those of a contented baby. He nodded to the newcomer. Valens nodded back. The man ate a piece of melon, then broke wind loudly, with evident satisfaction.

Taking a stool at the bar, Valens called for a jug of the best wine. The owner claimed that it was from Chios. Valens doubted that. He poured himself a drink, adding an equal part of water. Not wanting to get drunk, he took some coins from the wallet tied to his belt, and paid.

Valens studied his own reflection in the tarnished mirror behind the bar. Short haired and clean shaven, he looked younger than his twenty-five years. His tunic was plain, but of good material. He wore no jewellery, except a signet ring, the seal set in silver. There was nothing left of the dandyish gilded youth of Rome. His appear-ance fitted his role as the nephew of a moderately well-to-do pro-vincial merchant.

Two men came in from the street. Almost as if by prior arrange-ment, the stevedores got up and left. The arrivals were dressed as off-duty soldiers: boots, belts and swords. Yet the ornaments on their belts were not military, and their appearance was too slovenly for them to be serving under the standards. Most likely they were local toughs, hired as bodyguards by some town councillor or the like. Ignoring Valens and the bald man, they walked to the bar with the swagger of their kind.

A second jug would do no harm. Valens called the girl. She served him perfunctorily, eager to get back to the newcomers. Irritated, Valens half turned on his stool and studied them. One had a very long face. Its length was accentuated by a wispy pointed beard, an abnormally long nose, and high, receding forehead. The other made up for his companion's lack of hair with a bushy, square-cut beard, and thick ringlets falling to his shoulders. The latter wore a pearl in one ear. They talked to the girl in Greek with thick eastern accents.

Valens turned back to the mirror. Behind him, the bald man, having finished his eccentric repast, was writing in a small hinged book. The stylus and writing block looked miniscule in his big fingers. Valens focused on his own reflection. All the effort to obtain the post of Deputy Tribune in the Horse Guards – the letters of recommendation wheedled from family friends, the badgering of his cousin, the Senior Tribune – and he had ended up in Zeugma. Instead of winning glory beyond the Alps, or even enjoying dinner parties and recitals in Rome, he was drinking alone in this fly-blown town at the edge of the empire. He doubted he would have joined the army if disaster had not struck. His life would have been very different were his parents still alive. It was not that the gods were cruel, simply that they did not care.

The man with the long face brushed against him as he passed. Valens bridled. Smiling, the man apologised. His teeth were like those of a horse.

The girl met the man at the far end of the bar, led him up the stairs. She was better at feigning pleasure than the other girl who worked in the bar. Valens had tried both. Celibacy was bad for the health. No one blamed a man for taking what was offered, for walking down a well-used path.

Valens stared into his cup. He did not see the wine, but the empty expanse of the high plains of Mesopotamia. The tent-dwellers were fierce, strangers to the laws of humanity. It was said their pitiless nature often led them to torture those they captured. Instead of holding them to ransom, they staked them out to die slowly beneath the merciless sun. As for the Persians, they were infamous for the refinements of their cruelty.

Let us be men, the heroes encouraged each other in Homer. Literature was stocked with sayings to instil courage. *If your sword is too short, take a step forward.* Everyone knew what was expected. *Return with your shield, or on it.* Slaves and criminals faced wounds and death in the arena. They were a lesson in courage to the free citizens watching in the stands.

Although he had trained with weapons since childhood, Valens had never drawn a blade in anger. Veterans had told him that nothing could prepare you to stand close to the steel. Some men froze. Fear made the urine run down their thighs, as they stood, motionless and unresisting, waiting to be slaughtered. Others threw down their weapons, sank to their knees, vainly pleading for their lives. Many betrayed their manhood, and turned and fled.

A burst of ribald laughter brought Valens back to his surroundings. The long-faced man had returned. He was boasting of his prowess. The girl, behind the bar again, seemed unmoved.

Perhaps one more jug. Then Valens would go and sleep it off. He reached for his money. The wallet was gone.

Valens was on his feet, moving before he stopped to think.

The long-faced man turned as he approached.

'You stole my money.'

The man smiled, showing his equine teeth. 'Not me, friend.'

Valens grabbed the front of his tunic, hauled him off the bar stool. 'Give it back.'

'On the honour of my mother, that would be impossible.'

Valens shook the man, as if the wallet might fall from the folds of his clothes.

'You are really most uncivil.' The man sounded amused.

With no warning, the man brought both his arms up inside Valen's forearms. He snapped them outward, breaking the grip on his tunic. The sparsely haired head lunged. His forehead cracked into Valen's nose.

Reeling back, hands to his face, Valens felt the blood, hot on his cheeks, the iron taste of it in his mouth.

The serving girl was running out of the door at the back. In the corner the bald man was looking up quizzically, as if this was a mildly interesting, if unexceptional occurrence. The second ruffian remained on his stool.

'A puppy should not fight bigger dogs.' The first thug was actually laughing. 'Consider it a lesson cheap at the cost.'

Valens rushed at him, trying to get his hands around the man's neck. They grappled, staggering from side to side, like men on a ship in a storm. The long-faced man was the stronger. Valens was being forced backwards. With a move from the gymnasium, Valens got his left leg behind his opponent, twisted, and threw him to the floor.

'Give me the wallet.' Valens was standing over the man.

A movement in the air warned Valens. He went to turn. Too slow. The heavily bearded man's punch caught him in the left eye. Again, he lurched away. His back collided with the bar.

The two brutes, fists at the ready like boxers, were closing. Valens had no room to manoeuvre. *Hades, I am not going to take a beating from the likes of these common swine.* He yanked out his knife.

His assailants gave a pace.

'Not so brave now,' Valens panted.

The ruffians glanced at each other. The hirsute one shrugged.

'Your decision,' the other said to Valens.

Both drew their knives, dropped into a trained fighting crouch.

Be a man, Valens thought. *Nowhere to run. Just be a man.*

The yellow and green striped trousers were a blur of colour as the bald man crossed the room. For all his bulk, he moved soundlessly, with the grace of a dancer. The thugs did not hear him coming. Massive hands took them by the scruff of the neck. There was a sickening crack as their heads were slammed together. Then, as if they were no more than child's toys, the brightly dressed stranger tossed them both aside.

'You are fucking insane, Iudex,' the long-faced man shouted from where he had landed half under a table.

'And you are a thief, Zabda.' The man smoothed his blue tunic. 'The opinions of others are crosses we must all carry.'

Both ruffians began to scramble to get up.

The gigantic figure wagged a finger.

The men stopped.

'Zabda, give the officer back his wallet.'

Slowly, with the utmost reluctance, the long-faced man picked himself up, then tossed the leather bag at the feet of Valens.

'Now leave.'

Sheathing their knives, the two shuffled out of the bar. 'Fucking madman,' one muttered.

The oddly garbed man took Valens by the shoulders, sat him on a bench. The big hands checked him over, solicitously, like a mother with her son.

'You will have a black eye, but your nose is not even broken.'

The man bent and scooped up the wallet, handed it over.

Valens took it dumbly.

'You must forgive them.' The cherubic face beamed. 'They are unenlightened. It was their idea of playing a joke on our new officer.'

'You mean they are . . .' Valens did not say the word.

'I am afraid so. Our profession calls for the crudest of recruits.'

'And the stevedores?'

'As far as I know, they were just stevedores.' The grey eyes smiled. 'Come, Marcus Aelius Valens, let me take you to your lodgings around the corner. We must be on parade early tomorrow.'

CHAPTER 4

The Euphrates

VALENS WALKED UP THROUGH THE streets of the town. It was the second hour of daylight. This early it was no hotter than a spring day in Rome, yet Valens was sweating, and his head ached. He was unsure how much of the pain was due to the wine, how much to the fight. The barber who had shaved him had commented on his black eye.

The military camp at Zeugma, like most in the eastern provinces, occupied a quarter within the town. It was separated from the civilian settlement by no more than a low wall. In the west, legions, even detached units of auxiliaries, tended to be based in purpose-built fortresses on the frontiers. Civilian communities always sprang up outside their defences, but the troops were not exposed to the temptations of a big city. Baths and brothels, hippodromes and theatres, the seductive luxuries of urban life, were bad for discipline. No wonder the soldiers who kept watch along the Rhine and Danube had nothing but contempt for the fighting qualities of the eastern armies.

Of course, Valens thought, *the troops in the north are just as disparaging about my own kind.* The pampered officers and men who served the imperial household in the city of Rome. That the Praetorians and Horse Guards received extra pay exacerbated the dislike.

Valens puffed up to the open gate. Four soldiers stood at ease in the shade under the arch. The Capricorn symbol of the Fourth

Scythian Legion was carved above their heads. The legion had been based at Zeugma as long as anyone could remember. The vast majority of its recruits were drawn from Syria. The climate and life-style of the east had never been conducive to martial virtue.

The indolent and offhand manner of the sentries confirmed all the western prejudices of Valens. After he had stated his business, he was told that those merchants who were putting in a tender to supply hay were to report to the disused barracks, third row on the left, second building along. The sentries asked for no proof of iden-tity, and no one was detailed to accompany Valens.

Inside, the bright sunshine hurt Valens's eyes as he crossed the open space of the parade ground. The altars at one end were gar-landed, dark blood drying in the earth at their bases. From some-where out of sight came the smell of roasting meat. It was the *Kalends* of August. *For the birthday of the divine Claudius and the divine Pertinax, to the divine Claudius an ox, to the divine Pertinax an ox.* The time-hallowed festival would be held in every military camp in the empire. That Claudius had been a stammering fool murdered by his wife, or that the aged Pertinax's fleeting tenure of the throne had been ended by the swords of his own soldiers, made little difference. Anyway, few under the standards knew anything about the long-dead Emperors being honoured. A festival was a day of leisure, one of its keenly anticipated pleasures a communal feast. On such a day, with the promise of plentiful wine and beef, the sketchy discipline of the Fourth Scythian Legion would be fur-ther relaxed. It had to be granted that Severus had chosen a good date to avoid anyone taking an interest in the rendezvous.

Valens found the building easily enough. Outside he took a few deep breaths, and hitched his belt. Last night he had been a fool, but this morning he would make the best impression that he could.

The outer door gave onto a long corridor. It smelt of mice and long disuse. Motes of dust floated in the shafts of sunlight from the windows. A voice summoned him from a room at the far end.

Severus was standing with his back to the end wall of the sleeping quarters. Three men sat side by side on the lower tier of each of the bare wooden frames of the bunk beds on either side. To the right was Iudex. He grinned at Valens. His baby-like features looked unnaturally small set in his vast, hairless head. With him were Zabda and the other ruffian from the night before. They did not smile. To the left were three strangers.

'This is Marcus Aelius Valens, second in command of the mission.' Severus spoke without warmth.

None of the men said anything.

Valens remained standing.

Severus addressed him. 'I understand that you have already made the acquaintance of Iudex, Zabda and Narses the Persian.'

Valens nodded, keeping his eyes on Severus.

'These are Clemens the armourer, Quintus the navigator, and Aulus, our quartermaster.'

Valens glanced to his left. The eyes that met his held no warmth.

'Decimus, the horse master, is guarding the animals and the baggage at the inn of Antiochus by the bridge, where we will meet tomorrow one hour before dawn. The last member of the squad has not reported. Do any of you know the whereabouts of Hairan?'

A great sadness passed across the face of Iudex. He shook his domed head with sorrow. 'The man of Hatra is a slave to base appetites. Yesterday evening he went to waste the divine light, with which the Lord God entrusted him, on whores. Perhaps he is exhausted, perhaps he is dead.'

'Humour is out of place,' Severus snapped.

'I was not joking,' Iudex replied.

Severus stepped forward, dominating all the seated men and towering over Valens. 'Listen to me, and mark my words. You are *frumentarii*. I do not trust you, and I do not like you. *Frumentarii* forget they are nothing but common soldiers. I am here to remind you of that fact. By the authority of our Emperor Publius Licinius Egnatius Gallienus Augustus, you are under my command. I have the power of life and death over each and every one of you. I will not hesitate to use it.'

Severus looked hard at first Valens, then the two easterners. 'There will be no fighting under my command. In future, if there is, the punishment will be death.'

Valens felt the colour rushing to his cheeks. He nodded.

'Do I make myself clear?'

Zabda and Narses dipped their heads in sullen acknowledgment.

'If Hairan is not dead, he will be punished.'

Severus stepped back. The tension relaxed.

'You all know our goal,' Severus said, 'but not our route.'

He unrolled a map. It showed the usual cobweb of roads linking pictograms of settlements, with scant indication of topography, and, away from the roads, only an inexact relationship with geography.

'We will take the road across Mesopotamia through Batnae and Carrhae. Beyond Resaina, we will leave the path and cross the desert directly into Persian territory.' Severus pointed to an ochre-coloured section of the map, completely empty except for the word 'Arbayestan'. 'Quintus will plot our course. He served with the fleet in the Mediterranean at Ravenna, and on the Rhine along the German border. He can navigate by the stars.'

For some reason that Valens could not guess, Iudex looked far from happy.

'When we reach Adiabene and the mountains of Matiane, Narses will act as our guide to the shores of the Caspian Sea, and on to the Castle of Silence.'

'Is that wise?' said Clemens.

Severus looked at the armourer.

'Orientals are not to be trusted. I should know, I served in the east for years. As for this Persian, is it wise to entrust ourselves to a renegade to lead us into the realm of the King of Kings? Blood is thicker than water. He will return to his own kind, and deliver us, hands bound, to their tortures.'

Narses leant forward, his dark eyes glittering above his beard. 'It is true I served the King of Kings Shapur faithfully. After the battle of Corycus, my lord Zik Zabrigan released me from my oath. At that place I took the *sacrametum* to Gallienus. For five years I have fought for Rome.'

Clemens snorted. 'You were trapped by the Roman forces under Ballista. You had no choice. Anyway, a man who has changed sides once finds it easy to do so again. Oaths are just words to you Persians. Deceit is in your nature.'

The Persian was half out of his seat. 'I was raised in the clan Suren; taught to ride, shoot the bow, and tell the truth. The god Mazda instructs us to abhor the Lie.'

Like a stern Roman of old, the lined and careworn face of Clemens expressed nothing but contempt for such foreign concepts. 'You fuck your own mothers, let the beasts eat the corpses of your fathers. The gods themselves avert their eyes from your crimes.'

'Enough!' Severus snapped. 'Every people follow their own customs. Our chances of success are slim enough. If we are divided among ourselves, we are doomed to failure. No matter the origins of a soldier, nothing is more sacred than the military oath. Here and now, before each other and the gods, you will reaffirm your vows.'

Narses was on his feet before the others. Right hand flat on his chest, in the Latin of the camp, he recited the *sacramentum*. 'By Jupiter Optimus Maximus and all the gods, I swear to carry out the

Emperor's commands, never desert the standards or shirk death, to value the safety of the Emperor above everything.'

One by one, the mismatched assortment of soldiers repeated the oath.

'Now you will give me the tokens that identify you as secret soldiers.'

Silently, the metal disks carrying the words MILES ARCANUS were handed over to Severus.

'Until tomorrow morning at the inn of Antiochus,' Severus said. 'Remember, from now on we have nothing but each other.'

CHAPTER 5

The Euphrates

B Y THE BRIDGE WAS COILED a large chain, ivy and vines growing through its links. It was said to be very old, from the original crossing of the river by Alexander the Great, or even the god Dionysus on his way to India. Whichever, the queue waiting to cross to the east bank had given Valens far too much time to contemplate its supposed antiquity.

'Not long now,' Iudex said. 'The ships have gone through, and the pontoons will soon be back in place.'

Valens studied the chain. It was remarkably free of rust for something claimed to be so ancient. Evidently the Persians had not thought it worth looting when they sacked Zeugma.

'This delay is nothing.' Hairan sat in the shade, his elegantly trousered legs crossed. 'Before the fall of Hatra, the street would have been solid with caravans. The warriors of my city kept the routes through Mesopotamia safe. The land between the two rivers was full of camel trains. Silks and spices, lapis lazuli and turquoise, transported from the distant east; sweet white wine and unguents in delicate alabaster from the west; the most beautiful concubines from across the world – all the good things in life flowed through Zeugma.' The young Hatrene gestured dismissively at those waiting to clear the customs post. 'These are no more than peddlers, or peasants bringing things to market.'

'How many years since Hatra fell?' Iudex asked.

'Twenty-five years since the evil fell across the land.'

Iudex was smiling. 'And you are how old?'

Hairan stretched like a cat. 'I was a child, but it is like yesterday. We men of Hatra have long memories. One day we will have our vengeance.'

For a time they sat without talking, listening to the *slop slop* sound of screws raising water into the town from the river.

Severus had crossed over before dawn, before the pontoon bridge had been opened to let the boats downriver. He would meet them at the first milestone beyond Apamea. It was beneath the dignity of a prosperous merchant to wait with the rabble in the street. He had left his *nephew* in charge of the caravan.

There was nothing to do but wait. The men had largely ignored Valens. The two easterners with whom he had fought – Narses the Persian, and Zabda from Palmyra – had looked at him with open malevolence. Only Iudex and Hairan had offered their company.

'Severus docked your next two months' pay for not reporting yesterday,' Iudex said.

Hairan snapped his fingers. 'That is all money means.'

'Yet you needed it to pay your whores. I thought you had a sterner morality. Do you Arabs not put to death those even suspected of adultery?'

'That may be the case among the primitive tent-dwellers.' Hairan twirled the ends of his luxurious moustache. 'We men of Hatra take full enjoyment of the pleasures of the flesh. We pride ourselves on our prowess. Not that we lack morals. Among us there is a law that anyone who steals a trifle, if only water, is punished with stoning.'

Valens glanced over at Zabda, the long-faced man from the bar.

'Yes,' Hairan said, 'that Palmyrene needs watching.'

'And boys?' Iudex had his notebook out.

'Never!' Hairan looked outraged. 'Be careful, brother. Beyond the Euphrates, if a man is accused of such intercourse he will take revenge, and not shrink from murder.'

Iudex wrote quickly. His head was bent over the hinged wooden blocks, the stylus, tiny in his big fingers, pressing neat characters in the wax.

'We do not share the tastes of ugly old Aulus.' Hairan nodded to where the quartermaster was fussing over the loads of the mules. 'Gauls like him are terrible pederasts. They see no shame at all in their infamy.'

As if at a secret signal, everyone waiting in the street got to their feet, checked their belongings, and began to close up, shuffling towards the bridge.

Conscious that he should assert his authority, Valens went to the head of the caravan.

There were only two customs men at the post. Goats and sheep bound for slaughter were driven towards one. Produce – olive oil and grain, animal fat and pine cones – presented to the other. There was much delay and argument. Everything had to be taxed and tempers became frayed. Peasants from the villages in the territory of Zeugma were exempt, and traders in goods like salted fish and rock salt, items most unlikely to be local, volubly tried to claim the exemption.

When the caravan finally reached the customs, things went no quicker. Even when Valens had persuaded the official that only two of the mules carried trade goods, the remainder being loaded with personal provisions not for sale, the question arose if a mule should be taxed as if a donkey or a camel. Eventually Hairan intervened, speaking fast, in what Valens thought was Aramaic. Some coins changed hands, and the mules were rated as low-tax donkeys. Further coins, more openly given, settled the tariff, and they were free to proceed.

They crossed the wide brown river, the hoofs of their animals clattering on the boards that linked the pontoons, and rode down the straight streets of Apamea to the desert gate.

Severus was waiting, sitting in the shade of a tomb in the necropolis by the first milestone. The caravan halted to be inspected. The men dismounted. With Decimus, the horse master, Severus went first to the line of short, stocky mules.

'You still think it was best not to use camels for the baggage?' Severus asked. 'Mules can never keep up with horses in a forced march.'

Decimus shook his head. 'None of the westerners are accustomed to camels. Me included, I have never served in the east before. Well looked after, a mule can go twenty-five miles a day, sometimes thirty.'

Severus gestured to the mare with a bell on her harness at the head of the mules. 'And that will announce our coming.'

The horse master smiled. No longer young, he was still a strikingly handsome man. A scar by his right eye added to his looks and his only disfigurement was a large wart below the scar. 'Mules are harder to manage without a bell-mare to follow. If we did not have one, it would look strange, and draw attention.'

As they checked the loads, Valens tightened the girth of his mount. All the animals – the ridden horses and the spares, as well as the mules – had been purchased by Decimus. The chestnut gelding assigned to Valens was small, not much over thirteen hands, and it was not young. Growing up around the stables on his father's villa, Valens knew horseflesh. He had checked its mouth, but after seven years the age of a horse can no longer be judged by its teeth. Valens was satisfied. A large horse needed more feed, and often lacked stamina, and a young horse could not take as much hard work. The only disadvantage of an older animal was the years made it less resilient to the cold and wet, and he could not imagine that they were going to be a problem in Mesopotamia.

The load on one of the mules had shifted. Severus, holding the beast's halter, told Narses to remove the pack and the harness. The officer looked around.

'Valens, help the Persian reload the baggage.'

For a moment Valens stood in disbelief. Was a man of the equestrian order to be treated like some common muleteer?

'Every man in the column must be able to undertake every necessary task,' Severus said.

By the time Valens had tethered his horse, Narses had stripped the packages and the rigging. The mule stood quietly. Narses placed the blind over its eyes and took his place on its off side.

Valens went to the nearside, abreast of the mule's shoulder. Narses had left him as the main loader. Valens placed the woollen pad on the beast's back, canvas side down, then put the saddle blanket on top. He aligned them carefully, a couple of inches further forward than the blanket would be on a cavalry horse.

Narses had placed the wooden and leather frame which would bear the weight the wrong way round. Valens turned it, so that the crupper was towards the rear of the mule. He hefted it above the mule, so that Narses could take the far side. Together they placed it several inches to the rear of its proper position. When Valens had bent the crupper, and fitted it beneath the mule's tail, they slid the frame forward.

Together they set about lashing the rigging tight. Valens's hands moved without thought. *Cinch – take – break.* If Severus had hoped to humiliate him with this task, the officer would be disappointed. There had been pack animals, as well as hunters, in the yard of Valens's father.

Take – cinch – tie.

As he worked, Valens looked over the mule's back at the tombs of the necropolis. Among the sculpted reliefs were portraits of the dead: men and women in respectable clothes, children clutching toys and pets. Here and there were carvings of the eagles that the pious hoped might carry their souls to a better place. The paint was peeling from many of the reliefs and some of the burials had been looted. Their doors gaped open, the interiors looming black in the sunshine.

This was an inauspicious place to begin the dangerous journey into Mesopotamia. Although the towns between the two rivers – the Euphrates and the Tigris – had changed hands more than once, for now they were held by the Romans. But the same could scarcely be said of the country between those walled settlements. It was rumoured to be a hard place, the landscape parched and unforgiving. Its inhabitants were lawless and cruel: bandits, nomadic tent-dwellers and Persian raiders. The gods alone knew what they would find in the mountains beyond.

To set out to travel hundreds of miles into enemy territory, to rescue a child from a well-guarded fortress, let alone to aim to escape across the wastes of the unknown Steppe, was madness. And those undertaking the desperate venture were not united. Yesterday had made it evident that Clemens the armourer loathed the easterners in the party. Today had revealed that Hairan despised Zabda the thief. And Severus mistrusted all those under his command, and had nothing but contempt for Valens himself. If he had still believed that the gods cared for humanity, Valens would have prayed.

CHAPTER 6

Mesopotamia

B Y THE TIME THEY LEFT CARRHAE, the fifth day out from the Euphrates, the caravan had settled into a routine. Severus was an experienced cavalry officer. They took the first couple of miles at an easy walk, then halted for a quarter of an hour, adjusted the packs on the mules, let the horses have some water, checked their feet and tightened their girths. After that they alternated between a trot and a walk to avoid the muscles of the animals becoming fatigued by the same gait. They would rest for a few moments on the hour, longer at midday. Decimus would go down the line, testing the cinching on the mules and making sure that none of the saddles had slipped. Too far forward was easier on the rider, but bad for the mount.

They had come down through Batnae. Until they reached the plain of Carrhae, the road had run through bare ochre hills. They had met a few other caravans, and from time to time passed a black-tented Arab encampment. The tent-dwellers were half naked, their animals and children thin. The adults had watched the riders, silent and grave-eyed, too proud or apathetic to beg.

Although they had encountered no danger, the riders proceeded cautiously. While their armour and helmets were stowed with the baggage, each man had a sword on his hip, and a bow case and quiver, as well as a small round shield, slung from the horns of his saddle.

Severus had set the order of march. On the first day, Valens had suggested putting out scouts. Severus had overruled him. They were armed merchants, not a cavalry patrol. Even so, the officer ordered Hairan, who knew the country, to ride a couple of hundred paces ahead. Often the man of Hatra was out of sight in the hills, hidden by the lie of the land. Severus himself rode at the head of the column with Iudex, Aulus and Quintus. The four spare horses came next, led by Zabda. Behind him the ten mules, roped together, plodded along in single file after the bell-mare. Narses went with the mule train, under the eye of Decimus. At the rear, eating the dust kicked up by the hooves, were Valens and Clemens the armourer.

To begin with, Clemens had made it obvious that he was disinclined to speak. But, with the passing days, he had become a little less reserved.

'What do you have against the easterners?' Valens asked, passing over a skin of watered wine.

Clemens took a swig, and handed back the drink without answering.

'They are soldiers of Rome, no different from us,' Valens added.

Clemens frowned. His face was square, as if carved out of a block of stone. Lined and weather-beaten, it could have been the bust of some stern Roman senator from the days of the old republic.

'Surely you do not really think they would betray us?' Valens persisted.

'They are not to be trusted.' Clemens wiped his small, stubborn mouth. 'I served out here, in Syria Palestina with the Sixth Legion, the Ironclad.'

'But Narses and the others have taken the military oath,' Valens said.

Clemens leant out from the saddle and spat. 'Narses is a renegade. The Persian has betrayed his own people. He would not hesitate to do the same to us.'

'Zabda?'

'You should know, the Palmyrene is a thief. If that madman Iudex had not intervened, most likely he would have killed you. Palmyra is a desert shithole. Without Persian trade, it would not exist. Zabda's countrymen serve in the armies of the King of Kings, hold office in the cities he rules.'

'Hairan seems sound.'

Clemens snorted. 'An exile from a destroyed city, a mercenary who sells his sword to the highest bidder, no family and no home to keep him loyal. Dresses like a Persian, speaks Persian, look at him.'

Ahead, through the dust of the caravan, Valens could see Hairan where the plain once again reached the hills. The bright colours of his loose tunic and wide trousers shimmered in the heat.

Clemens turned away, bringing the conversation to an end.

Like the mules, they followed the tinkling bell into the hills. The high country was bunched and cut by ravines. The surface of the track was white and powdery. It raised a fine grit, which worked its way into eyes, mouth and nose. The path twisted and dipped, crossed and recrossed dry watercourses. Naked slopes rose on all sides, shutting off the view. When they crested a rise, and the vista opened up, it revealed nothing but miles of yellowish-brown rock, turning pinkish in the distance with the heat of the afternoon.

When the sun was halfway down the cloudless sky, Valens began to think that it would soon be time to make camp. He was hot and tired. With fatigue the column had become stretched out. It was difficult to estimate how far they had travelled – about ten miles from Carrhae to the hills, after that possibly another fifteen along the track. Given the circuitous course of the latter, they would not have covered half so far towards the east.

Clemens was muttering under his breath. The armourer had given up swatting at the flies and was gazing around at the slopes. Perhaps he too was wondering how long before they would halt, was looking forward to a rest, and something to eat. It occurred to Valens that Clemens was no longer young.

'How long have you been with the standards?'

Clemens did not look at Valens. 'Twenty-four years.'

'What will you do when you are discharged?'

'I had intended to buy a small farm with my retirement bonus next year. Somewhere quiet, like Calabria or Apulia. Take my family out of the city.'

'You *had* intended?'

Clemens glanced at Valens. 'I do not think we will return from this mission.'

'We will do our duty.'

'*Dulce et decorum est* . . . I am not so sure it is sweet and fitting to die for your country.' A strong but unreadable emotion burned behind Clemens's eyes. 'You are right, we will do what is ordered, and at every command we will be ready.'

They rode on in an awkward silence. Clemens returned to studying the surrounding hills. One persistent fly buzzed incessantly into Valens's face.

'Look!'

Clemens reined in, and pointed.

Valens's eyes followed the outstretched arm, ahead and to the left.

A shadow moving down an incline. No, there were no clouds. Not a shadow. Men on horses, moving fast. There must be twenty or more. They were aiming for the head of the column. A fold in the ground prevented Severus and the others seeing their approach.

'With me!' Clemens booted his horse forward.

Caught unaware, Valens gathered his reins and pressed his mount to follow.

They overtook Decimus and the baggage train.

Hardly slackening his pace, Clemens shouted, 'Raiders! Circle the mules, tether the led horses inside. You three, stay and guard them.'

Narses and Zabda sat looking around for the threat. Decimus bellowed at them, and, long accustomed to obey, they sprang into activity.

'Valens, you follow me,' Clemens said.

The horsemen burst over the crest, not thirty paces from their target.

Although taken by surprise, Severus and his three companions did not hesitate, but turned their mounts and reached for their weapons. Without time to draw their bows, they went for their swords.

As the attackers thundered down, they hurled a volley of javelins. A Roman horse went down. Valens saw its rider jump clear. In an instant the two sides met, and the space was transformed into the wheeling confusion of a cavalry skirmish.

Clemens was about four lengths in front. Valens saw the veteran readying his sword and shield. Fool that he was, Valens had not thought to do that himself. He dropped the reins on the neck of his horse, and fumbled to free the laces that tied his shield to a horn of his saddle. The motion of the galloping horse, and his nerves, made his fingers clumsy. At last the knot came undone. Gods below, he nearly dropped the thing. Now they were almost upon the fight. Desperately, he yanked out his sword.

The enemy were circling around the outnumbered Romans. They stabbed down at the figure on foot. It was Severus. The officer twisted this way and that, defending himself.

The attackers saw the two riders coming and drew back. Clemens charged into the gap. Valens urged his mount behind. They clattered to a halt on either side of Severus.

For a moment they were the calm in the eye of the storm. The sounds of the others fighting came as if from a great distance.

'Good of you to join us,' Severus said.

The respite was temporary. Two riders surged at Valens. The leading one thrust from Valens's left with a javelin. Valens deflected it with his shield. The second swung a long cavalry blade at his right leg. Somehow Valens got his own sword in the way. The screech of steel sliding down steel. Training took over, and Valens rolled his wrist, forcing the attacker's weapon wide.

The assailants backed their horses. Fierce, bearded faces above stained tunics. The wicked glint of sunlight on the weapons in their hands. One had a number tattooed on his arm.

Wild eyed, the raiders looked at each other, communicating without words. Next time they would attack together.

Valens was not going to wait passively, like some sacrificial animal. He kicked his heels into the ribs of his mount. The chestnut was no trained warhorse. It shied and crabbed sideways as it leapt forward. Off balance, Valens braced himself against the horns of his saddle. Again the javelin jabbed from his left. He ducked forward, nose down in the mane of his horse. His assailant's momentum pressed them close together. Valens punched upwards with his shield. He did not make contact, but the man jerked back. A half-seen movement to the right. Valens dragged his sword up to block the attack. Too slow, the blade was within his guard. Valens winced from the impending impact, but the blow never landed.

Instead, the raider reeled in the saddle. From the ground Severus struck again, a controlled slash that cut the man's thigh open to the bone.

Valens hauled himself upright. There was no chance to thank Severus. The javelin man stabbed at his face. This time Valens leant back. The tip of the javelin sliced by in front of his nose. Again they were wedged together, too close for Valens to use his sword. He swung wildly with the edge of his shield. The wooden boards smacked into the man's temple. Dazed, he swayed, almost losing his seat.

A grunt of pain from the right. Valens twisted around. Instead of a threat, he saw Severus. The officer was staggering, blood dark on the back of his tunic.

A pounding of hooves. Two more riders were coming to support the man on Valens's nearside.

Getting the chestnut balanced, Valens prepared to face them. Odds of three to one. It could only end one way. To Hades with *dulce et decorum est*. Valens prepared to sell his life dearly.

As if summoned by a god, the bald, domed head of Iudex appeared next to him, the lined face of Clemens on the other side.

'*Ferrata!*' Clemens shouted. *Ironclad*, the war cry of his old legion.

At the sound, the raiders seemed to lose heart. A slight hesitation, then they spun their mounts and raced away.

Valens drooped in the saddle. He was panting, running with sweat. His limbs felt like lead.

'The commander is down!'

Valens did not know who shouted. He saw Severus, face in the dirt, not moving. Sheathing his unbloodied weapon, he slung a leg over the horns of his saddle. He staggered as he hit the ground, dropped the shield. Weary beyond belief, he tottered to his leader.

Gently, he turned Severus over. The officer's eyes looked into his. Kneeling, Valens cradled the mortally injured man.

Severus was trying to speak.

Valens bent close.

The words never came.

With a gasp, Severus breathed his last.

CHAPTER 7

Mesopotamia

'WE MUST GO BACK.'
Valens had been in command for less than twenty-four fours, and now he faced a mutiny.

At first things had not gone too badly. Although Severus was dead, no one else was even wounded. Apart from the officer's horse, none of the animals had been lost or harmed. The baggage was secure. After the ambush, Valens had sent pickets out in all directions. Beyond some hoof prints, there was no further sign of the raiders. Before long, Hairan was spotted cantering back from the east. Scouting ahead, the Hatrene had been unaware of the fight. He had found a good site to camp. A wadi, sheltered from the wind, just off the track, no more than a mile ahead. Best of all, it was tucked out of sight.

They had retrieved their war gear from the mule train, put on their helmets and armour. Despite the heat and the discomfort, from now on they would travel ready for combat. The corpse of Severus was tied face down across one of the spare horses.

The campsite was everything that Hairan had claimed. They saw to the horses and mules, before burying their commanding officer in a hollow a short distance away. They had worked in relays. The labour was hard, the ground stony. Sharp splinters flew when they struck with their picks, the vibrations jarred their arms. Everyone except Narses had taken their turn. The Persian claimed it was against his religion. Valens had laboured with the rest. In the end, having gouged out only a shallow trench, they piled a cairn of rocks over the grave to prevent wild animals digging up the body. Valens had put a coin in the mouth of the dead man – Severus would be able to pay the ferryman. They did not want his shade walking the Earth. Denied Hades, the unhappy dead haunted the living.

It was dark when they had finally laid Severus to rest and muttered the perfunctory ritual. *Dis Manibus. To the Gods Below.*

Too tired to light a fire, they had sat and eaten cold rations – hard tack and bacon – and drunk sour wine. No one had complained when Valens drew up the rostra of sentries. There were about eight hours of darkness left. Two men would stand guard, one on the lip of the wadi on either side. Each pair would be relieved after two hours. Three men would be on duty in the final session before dawn. Valens took the first watch with Iudex.

After the heat of the day, the temperature dropped fast in the hills at night. Valens was cold, clammy with the sweat from the digging. He had sat, swaddled in his cloak. He had removed his helmet, the better to listen, when a chill breeze blew. He would have liked to pull his hood over his head, but that would have cut down his hearing.

Slowly the vault of stars had wheeled across the sky. The myriad points of distant light made him feel small and alone. Severus was dead. Valens was in command. The weight of responsibility oppressed him. If the gods had been kind he would not have been here . . . But the gods were far away, as distant and uncaring as the stars.

From time to time, the cold and his aching legs and back had forced him to get up and move about. He stepped carefully, his senses alert, probing the darkness. It was quiet. Occasionally a mule had stamped or a horse whickered. A desert fox barked somewhere out in the desolation. There was little to see. If you stared too long at the surrounding slopes, you saw things that were not there. The men and animals were hidden down in the gloom of the depression. On the far bank, the bald head of Iudex gleamed in the light of the stars. The giant man sat motionless, as if lost in meditation.

At long last, a clatter of rocks slipping from under boots climbing the side of the wadi told the watchers that their duty was at an end. Before turning in, Valens had walked the horse lines. The animals had watched him. He paused to stroke their soft muzzles, savour their warm, sweet breath. If you put your face very close to that of a horse, breathe into its nostrils, it will relax and trust you. There was a comfort in animals that was lacking in other men.

Wearily, Valens had struggled out of his armour. It was near impossible to sleep in mail. He tugged off his boots. Using his saddle blanket as a pillow, he had wrapped himself in his cloak, checked his sword was to hand, and fallen asleep.

The trouble started in the morning.

The men must have been talking while Valens still slept.

Aulus, the quartermaster, was their spokesman.

'We must go back.'

Quintus, the navigator, nodded in agreement.

The others stood in a rough semicircle. Their expressions were impossible to read.

'We have our orders.' Valens wished he was wearing armour, or even his sword. He felt foolish and vulnerable barefoot, in just an unbelted tunic, with a piece of half-chewed bacon in his hand.

'Severus is dead,' Aulus said.

'A great loss,' Valens said, 'but he was only one man.'

Quintus stepped up. 'We have to go back, before we die in this wilderness.'

'You served in the fleet.' Valens attempted to sound confident, as if this was merely a discussion, not a direct challenge to his authority. 'If you can plot a course across the trackless sea, you can guide us home from anywhere.'

The flattery seemed not to have swayed Quintus.

'The mission has failed,' Aulus said. 'To go on is suicide.'

'You are a Gaul,' Valens said. 'I thought the only thing you feared was the sky falling on your head.'

'If we follow you,' Aulus said, 'you will get us all killed.'

The men stood, mulish and stubborn. A few had their hands on the hilts of their swords.

Mutinies were not unknown in the Roman army. Valens knew the stories of how others had dealt with them. Julius Caesar had dismissed entire legions with a word, just by calling the men *citizens*, not *soldiers*. That was hardly appropriate, and most likely Caesar had not been clutching a part-eaten bit of bacon. When rebellious troops had refused to return to duty, the imperial prince Germanicus had threatened to kill himself, had reached for his sword. A veteran had offered his own, saying it was sharper. This was no time for histrionics. No nonsense about going on alone. Humour and cajolery had failed and Valens lacked the means to punish – all that was left was a bare appeal to discipline and duty.

'*We will do what is ordered, and at every command we will be ready.* We all took the military oath again at Zeugma. Do you think the *sacramentum* is just empty words, a thing of no account?'

No one replied. Valens caught the eye of Zabda. Gods below, the Palmyrene had already tried to kill him once. Valens could not lose his nerve now.

'Severus was your commander. Severus is dead. Now I am your commander.'

Aulus and Quintus looked to the others for support. The silence stretched.

'*At every command we will be ready,*' Clemens said, 'no matter how insane the command.' A wry look flitted across his careworn old face. 'I have no doubt that Aulus is right, that none of us will return. But I am equally certain that Marcus Aelius Valens is the ranking officer.'

'True words.' Iudex, beaming like a baby, came and stood by Valens. 'And travel enhances a man. I have always wanted to see the east, observe their customs, converse with their wise men.'

'A man has to die somewhere,' Hairan said. 'One place is as good as another.'

It was over. Aulus and Quintus, deflated and anxious, looked at each other.

'Saddle up,' Valens ordered. 'We move out in half an hour.'

The death of Severus meant a change in the order of march. Valens now rode with Iudex and Quintus at the head of the column. He ordered Aulus to take his place at the rear with Clemens. Let the mutinous quartermaster eat and breathe the dust kicked up by the animals.

Valens considered posting outriders, but Severus had been right, it would remove any pretence of being a merchant caravan. And anyway, there were not enough men. Best they stuck together, kept the intervals short between the animals.

They had not long rejoined the road when they encountered a party of travellers coming the other way. There were about forty of them – men, women and children – most on foot. They stopped and talked. Valens told them of the attack. An old man thanked him gravely in oddly accented Greek. The route was known to be dangerous. That was why they travelled together. They had waited at Resaina until they had enough numbers to set out for Carrhae. The old man said there was a caravanserai some thirty miles to the east. Valens thanked him, wished them a safe journey, and they parted.

Valens pushed the column hard for the rest of the day. There was no grumbling. Although they would not admit it, doubtless the men were as keen as their new commander to spend the night safely behind the walls of the caravanserai.

Night came suddenly in the high country. One moment they were in scorching sunshine, then the sun dipped below the crests, and darkness welled up from the ravines, flooded up the slopes, and engulfed them. They rode under the stars burning cold in the heavens.

'I hope the tent-dwellers do not fall upon the camp of the old man.' Valens spoke as much to himself as the others. 'The travellers were ill-armed, and less than half of them were grown men.'

'It was not Arabs who attacked us,' Iudex said. 'They were too well equipped, too well mounted. The nomads go half naked.'

'Bandits?'

'Deserters among them. A couple had the tattoos of their old units.'

'They were like no bandits that I have ever encountered.' Quintus had been quiet for most of the day. Evidently now he wanted the morning forgotten, and to get into favour with his new leader. 'Once I was stationed south of the Danube. There are many bandits in the Haemus Mountains. Hunting them you get to know their ways. What bandits would make straight for four armed men, and ignore the baggage animals?'

The unanswerable question hung in the air as they rode through the darkness.

After a time the silence became uncomfortable. Valens gestured to the stars, asked Quintus to name the constellations. Glad to talk, the navigator pointed them out: the Little Bear, the belt of Orion, the Hyades.

CHAPTER 8

Mesopotamia

IT WAS LATE AND QUIET in the caravanserai by the time the mules had been unloaded and bedded down for the night, and now the others had finished seeing to their horses. He was alone in the stables. Standing well away from his horse, leaning his weight into the strokes, he brushed its coat, always following the natural direction of the hair. If grooming was neglected, a horse soon lost flesh and condition. Mange and lice were the sure and certain result of neglect. The other men were in the communal dining room. He preferred his own company.

Eventually he was finished. The hide of the animal gleamed like silk in the lamplight. He fussed its ears, looked into its great limpid eyes, spoke gently to it. The whiskers on its muzzle tickled his cheeks as it snuffled his face. *Until tomorrow, my friend.*

Taking the lamp, he stepped outside into the courtyard. It had already been the third hour of darkness when they had reached the caravanserai. The gates had been shut. The tall, blank walls dark and forbidding. They had shouted. The gatekeepers had been suspicious. The times were troubled. At long last, the bars had been lifted, the bolts drawn, the gates swung open, and the caravan had entered its nocturnal sanctuary.

He stood under the stars. Around him were the shadowed arches of the stables and storerooms. They were built against the outer walls. Above them a gallery ran around three sides of the upper floor, opening onto the rooms for travellers. He noted the two guards up on the flat roof. They were alert, pacing their rounds. The times were troubled indeed.

There were only two other trading caravans, neither large, and a small party of hardy voyagers cloistered here for the night. Their bales of merchandise and belongings were piled in the open, close by where their animals were stabled. The baggage and tack of his own group was neatly laid out. Valens had had the trade goods locked in a secure room.

Light and a muted noise spilled out from where the others were eating. With something akin to reluctance or distaste, he made his way across.

Inside it was smoky, smelt of roasted meat and stale wine. A couple of serving girls, their smiles false and resigned, moved around the patrons. Doubtless they would be busy later. Working in a place like this, they may as well go around with their skirts already hauled up.

Valens waved him over. With a gesture intended to be both polite and final, he declined, and walked to the bar. Ordering a big jug of strong wine, and a small plate of bread and cheese and olives, he turned and surveyed the room.

It was a tall, vaulted chamber. The only windows, shuttered now against the night, gave onto the courtyard and were overhung by the balcony. The place would be cool in summer, and the cooking fires would keep it snug through the cold Mesopotamian winter.

A thin, ascetic looking man was singing, unaccompanied in a corner.

> '*Blasphemy is a stealthy woman;*
> *she commits adultery in the inner room.*'

The words were in Aramaic. It was a local song, one designed to instil piety and morality. Beyond the Euphrates the hold of the

Olympian gods weakened. The land between the two rivers was home to many competing faiths. Some followed Zoroaster, others the teachings of Mani. The city of Edessa was said to be rife with Christians. In the *Island*, as the inhabitants called Mesopotamia, true religion and every degraded cult all flourished alike, bound together by mutual animosity.

The innkeeper brought his dinner. Ignoring the jug of water, he poured a generous cupful of wine. A drink to drown sorrows and warm a frozen heart.

It had not been hard to find the bandits. Every band of brigands relied on informants to tell them who was setting out on the roads. All it had taken was a few nights in the waterfront bars in Zeugma, some discreet inquiries, and a handful of coins. A lot more coins had been necessary to secure their services. The bandits had earned their pay. Two of them were dead, but so was Severus. For a moment, in the heat of the skirmish, he had thought they would fail. He had been ready to strike the blow himself, but the treachery might have been spotted, even in all the confusion.

He refilled his cup.

Initially, he had thought that the death of Severus would be enough, but young Valens had surprised him. This morning, during the abortive mutiny, he realised the job was not yet done.

Murena had told him that the mission must fail. Not just fail, but vanish from the eyes of men. Had they returned to the empire, Murena might judge that he had not carried out his orders. The consequences of that judgement would be awful.

He took another drink.

Gods below, he hated that bastard Murena. Almost as much as he loathed himself. Yes, he was a *frumentarius*, a secret soldier. He had spied, played on the trust of others. He had delivered messages that brought summary execution. Once he had killed an unsuspecting man in cold blood. But he had never yet betrayed his own kind.

That bastard Murena! If only a man could be truly solitary, a misanthrope like Timon of Athens, living alone, shunning all human contact. A brave man could face his own pain and death. But everyone loved someone – parents, wife, children, some woman or boy. No man could endure the torture of a loved one. Once his beloved had been simply discovered, the threat had been more than enough.

The brigands had killed one man, not the mission. The gods knew, he did not want to, but now he must find other means.

The jug was empty. He called for another.

I was born as nothing
Shall be again as I was;
Humanity is nothing. Pour out
The pleasurable drug of choice, the wine
That is antidote to all our miseries.

CHAPTER 9

Arbayestan

Two days out of Resaina they left the road, and set out east into the wilderness. This was Arbayestan, the land of the Arabs; a harsh place of sand and rock, inhabited by no one except the nomadic tent-dwellers.

With no clear path to follow across the flat emptiness, they were guided by Quintus the navigator. On the second day, mountains loomed in the distance to the south. The Singaras range was a sudden wall of grey rock, fissured and cut by deep ravines, running parallel to their progress. Clouds hung over the crests, bringing a promise of rain that was never fulfilled. Away to the north, a hint of green along the horizon would have been taken for a mirage, if wildfowl had not marked it as wetlands. Where they journeyed, between the mountains and the marshes, there was nothing except bare rocks and rippled sand, dotted with desert shrubs blanched by the merciless sun.

Over their armour, they wore loose robes, bought in Resaina. Even so, the sweat ran copiously under their mail. The straps and fittings chafed their shoulders, their belts rubbed their waists raw. Some wrapped cloths around their helmets, most slung the stifling headgear on a horn of their saddle and wore a turban or a broad-brimmed hat. As the days went by, without conscious design, they came more and more to resemble their pretence of mercenary guards of a merchant caravan.

The evening was a blessed relief. With the animals rubbed down, fed and watered, all except the two on sentry duty were free to shrug off the heavy, stifling war gear, to sit and eat in the delicious cool of the night.

Yet it was at this, the best part of the day, that Valens felt most keenly the loneliness of command. In Rome he had been Deputy Tribune of the Horse Guards. He had been able to take problems to his senior, his cousin, and there had been officers of other units in whom to confide, as well as civilian acquaintances at dinner parties or in the baths. He wondered now if perhaps, after the death of his parents, he had strained the patience of his listeners. Misery had encouraged him to drink too much. *Know yourself*, the Delphic Oracle commanded. But in a city of a million souls there had always been someone – if only a passing stranger – to whom he could open his heart.

Oddly, his most pressing concern was not the mission itself, or even his own slim hope of survival, but the attitude of the men. Aulus, the ringleader of the attempted mutiny, remained scowling and aloof. Narses and Zabda, the two easterners from the waterfront bar in Zuegma, often came close to dumb insubordination. On the march, they muttered together as they shepherded the baggage animals; the bushy beard of the Persian and the wispy one of the Palmyrene both nodding. Decimus, the handsome master of horse, and Clemens, the old armourer, were punctilious in obeying orders, replied when spoken to, but seldom volunteered anything. At least Quintus, as if to atone for his role the morning after the death of Severus, was happy to talk, and Hairan, the third easterner, was affable to Valens as to everyone. And then there was always Iudex. His appearance might be slightly disconcerting, and his conversation sometimes unfathomable, but he liked to talk. Yet for Valens it was unthinkable that an equestrian officer should unburden himself to common soldiers under his command, even to those who appeared sympathetic.

They had eaten. Quintus was studying the moonless sky. Iudex was carefully washing his big hands. Clemens and Aulus were out on guard. The rest were already asleep.

Valens watched Iudex. His ritual ablutions complete, the bald man stood facing north. '*Restrain my heart and mind from the turmoil of sin, and let me ascend on the road of peace.*' Iudex said the words reverently. With an agility surprising in such a large man, he got down on bended knee, then prostrated himself full length on the ground. '*May I become perfect in mind, spirit and body, and through your power, Lord, may I conquer the deceitful demons of my soul.*'

Iudex prayed seven times a day. On the march, he would pull his horse out of the line and dismount. Frequently he was left behind, out of sight. Soon after, his sky-blue cloak would appear as he cantered after the column. Resuming his station, his cherubic features were suffused with happiness.

The piety of this strange soldier unsettled Valens. No matter how bizarre the cult to which he belonged, Iudex had a god in which to believe, a beneficent power to look to for succour and guidance. Valens missed the faith of his childhood. He had never felt so alone as he did now. To avoid the temptation of opening a flask of wine, he walked over to talk to Quintus.

'How do you plot a course by the stars?'

'There is no great mystery.' The navigator had large, thoughtful eyes in a delicate face set under wavy, swept-back hair. It gave him a look of youthful and sensitive intelligence.

'I would like to know.'

'We do not follow the stars which wander across the heavens. Instead, the never-setting pole star, the brightest in both the Bears, is the certainty that underpins all calculations.'

Valens looked where Quintus pointed.

'And you see over there . . . the lower Arctophylax sinks, and the nearer to the horizon Cynosura dips, the further east we travel.'

'You know exactly where we are?'

'From the stars, and the height of the sun, I can judge with some accuracy how far we are from north to south.' Quintus smiled, almost apologetically. 'How far east–west is a matter of reckoning, but if we keep going east we must come to the upper reaches of the Tigris.'

'There is no true reckoning to be had from the stars.'

The interruption made Valens jump. For such a bulky man, Iudex moved very quietly.

'They deceive mankind. It is in their nature.' Iudex spoke with certainty.

'What do you mean?' Valens asked.

Iudex tilted his huge, hairless head to one side, as if pondering. Officer or not – was the questioner worthy of an answer? Eventually, he nodded.

'The Living Spirit captured the demons of darkness. He flayed them, and stretched their skins to make the firmament. Their bodies he fixed as the planets and the signs of the zodiac. The stars have a malign influence on humanity.'

Quintus snorted in derision. 'Your religion has addled your mind.'

Iudex spread his hands in benediction. 'The Light shone in Darkness, and Darkness comprehended it not.'

A suspicion slipped into Valens's mind. 'You are not a Christian, are you?'

'*Thou shalt not kill*, so the Christians say. Sometimes killing is necessary. It is the Lord's will. I have no qualms.'

Valens was going to ask further questions about his beliefs, but Iudex forestalled him. 'It is late. We should sleep. Our road is long. There will be better times to put your feet on the path to righteousness.'

In the blue light of pre-dawn, the clouds were gone from the peaks of the Singaras, dispersed by a rising wind out of the east. They watered and fed the animals first: three portions of oats to two of hay, chaff mixed in with the hay to stop them bolting the food unchewed. Some of the men gathered camel thorn for fires to warm their rations. The tough twigs spat and burned fast, and gave little heat. Valens ate his hard tack and bacon cold.

The needs of men and beasts satisfied, Decimus oversaw the loading of the mules. They worked in pairs. Everyone lent a hand – Valens teamed with Iudex. There was no opportunity to talk. *Cinch – take – break – take.* Like the liturgy of a religion, the responses echoed down the line. To properly train a muleteer was said to take a year, but the basics could be learnt in about a month. *Frumentarii* were resourceful, and these men knew what they were about.

They moved out before sunrise. The country was flat, with nothing to obstruct visibility, but there were dry watercourses, some deep, running across their path. Each of these could offer concealment. Mindful of this, they maintained a good order of march. No more than five paces was allowed between each mule. All the horsemen kept in close attendance, except for Hairan riding ahead on point. Valens would not let them be ambushed by bandits or tent-dwellers again.

After an hour at a walk, they stopped to check their girths, smooth the saddle blankets, and adjust the loads on the mules. As they worked, the sun came up. It threw long shadows of men and beasts. The sky was a bowl of the purest blue. It was going to be a hot day.

Remounted, they increased the pace, the horses trotting, the mules going at an amble. Riding at the head of the column, Valens watched Hairan. The bright red robe that the Hatrene wore over his armour billowed in the freshening breeze. Valens noted the little swirls of dust that lifted and snaked towards them. Beyond Hairan, on the horizon, the plain lifted to a low ridge of sand-coloured hills.

They had made no great distance before they had to rein in at a steep wadi. Dismounting, they first led the horses down its crumbling bank, and up the other side, then returned for the mules. Their hooves slipping, the baggage animals jibbed and complained at this unwanted break in their routine. The men sweated and cursed and swore.

Back in the saddle, after they had resumed station, Valens took them straight back into a trot. The hills looked surprisingly near – he had not thought they had travelled so far. Yet, lacking landmarks except the Singaras away to the right, distance was hard to judge in the desert.

'Ahead.' Quintus pointed.

Hairan was coming back, riding fast.

Valens felt a stab of foreboding. He squinted at the incoming rider. Hairan was not holding his cloak aloft, the signal for enemy in sight. Valens scanned the landscape. It was empty, nothing living in sight, not even a bird, although the hills seemed much nearer.

Hairan disappeared as he descended into a watercourse. Waiting for him to re-emerge, Valens held up his hand to halt the column. The day had turned dull, the sky overcast and oppressive. The crest of the hills seemed to move and shift, perhaps a mirage, or some other trick of the hazy light. Quintus had dismounted to check his mount's feet for stones. Facing the horse's tail, the navigator lifted each of its legs in turn, holding them between his own thighs and using a knife to clean the hoof.

Hairan popped back out of the wadi and put his horse into a gallop for the final section. He was waving an arm, shouting. The sighing of the wind, and the noise of his coming, drowned the words.

Valens lifted his gaze again to search for potential threats. For a moment he could not believe what his eyes saw. He must be mistaken. The hills were moving – like a great brown tidal wave, they surged across the plain towards them.

'*Haboo!*' In his alarm, the Hatrene was shouting in his native tongue.

Iudex translated. 'Dust storm.'

'Turn around!' Hairan had reverted to Latin. 'Get back to the last wadi. We can shelter there.'

Valens circled his arm. The order was unnecessary. Already the men were yanking the heads of their mounts around. Decimus and Narses were either side of the bell-mare, turning her, the first mules plodding after. Zabda had set off for the rear with the spare horses on leading reins.

Valens could not take his eyes off the approaching storm. A dark wall of swirling cloud, it raced ever closer. Was it a mile away, two? There was no way to tell.

Hairan rode straight past.

'We best go,' Iudex said.

Quintus's horse was playing up, circling as he tried to mount, hopping after it.

'Let me help,' Valens said.

'I am fine. You get moving.' Quintus's hair was blowing in the wind, flicking across his face. 'Stand still, you fucker!'

Iudex was cantering back towards the baggage train.

A spray of sand was hitting Valens in the face, stinging and gritting his eyes. Pebbles were skittering along the ground.

'Get off, and help with the mules,' Quintus shouted.

Valens turned his gelding. The mule train was stationary, in disarray. Some of the animals had stepped over the traces and become tangled. Decimus was on foot, wrestling with the twisted leather, shoving the recalcitrant beasts. Narses, still on horseback, was leaning over, gripping the bridle of the bell-mare.

Slinging a leg over the horn of his saddle, Valens dropped to the ground.

'Have to cut them loose,' Decimus yelled.

Holding the reins of his horse in one hand, it was near impossible to saw through the thongs.

'*Fuck!*' Decimus was swearing loudly and monotonously. '*Fuck!*'

When the animals were freed, they stood, looking anxious and uncertain.

From the east came a roaring like surf on a shore.

'Go on, Narses,' the horse master bellowed. 'They will follow the bell-mare.'

The Persian needed no further urging, but jammed the heels of his boots into the ribs of his mount. Packs swaying, the mules went after the tinkling bell.

Decimus swung back into the saddle and Valens went to follow his example. He glanced up. The storm loomed over him, no longer a wall, but a high cliff – a hundred foot, or even higher. It roiled with destructive energy, thundered like an avalanche. Stones smacked into his shins. And then it hit.

Valens staggered with the force of the wind. It was as hot as a blast from a furnace. The sand was flaying his exposed skin. The world had narrowed to a few indistinct feet. Without warning, the horse reared. It wrenched the reins from Valens's grasp. He grabbed for the trailing strap, and missed. In a moment the beast had vanished in the swirling murk. The beats of its hooves heard for a moment, then there was just the howling storm.

No one in sight. Valens was alone. He must not panic. Tugging his scarf up to his nose, hunching his back against the wind, he staggered back the way they had come.

The world was full of hurtling, stinging, biting torment. He was breathing sand. His ears rang with a sound like a malevolent giant tearing cloth. He reeled under the impact of the wind.

Disorientated, it would be so easy to become lost. Wander miles away from the others. *Do not panic.* The wind was from the east. The wadi ran right across to the west. Keep going, and he had to reach it. *No need to panic. Just keep going.*

Once he thought he heard horses running, out of sight, in the heart of the storm.

Step by step, gasping for breath, inhaling sand, he tottered on.

Another time in that hellish journey there was a sound like a scream.

Just the wind. Keep going.

Eyes bleared, he did not see the lip of the watercourse until he nearly fell into it. On his arse, he slid down the bank.

Blurred outlines of men and beasts. The quiet down here unnatural.

'Is that you, sir?' It was Decimus.

'Is everyone else here?'

'Clemens just turned up, but Iudex and Quintus are still out there.'

'The animals?'

'Not sure. Some are missing.'

A huge, dark shape above them. Stones rattling down.

They scuttled apart.

Iudex, leaning back in the saddle, his horse almost sitting back on its haunches, skidded to the floor of the wadi.

The great hairless cranium shone in the gloom. With the grace of an acrobat, Iudex vaulted off his mount.

'Are you alright?' Valens shouted. 'Did you see the others?'

'No, they are lost.' Iudex smiled. 'Unbelievers move in darkness, but the Lord guides the path of the Elect.'

CHAPTER 10

Arbayestan

THEY FOUND QUINTUS THE NEXT MORNING. The storm had blown itself out during the night. The navigator was no more than fifty paces from the wadi, half covered in sand. It gritted his wavy hair, dulled the once expressive eyes. His head was twisted at an impossible angle. Obviously his neck was broken.

'Poor bastard,' Decimus said. 'Must have taken a fall. No sign of his horse.'

'Well, that is an end to it,' Aulus said.

Valens rounded on the Gaul. 'What do you mean?'

'You all know what I mean. Without Quintus we are lost. No choice but to go back.'

'We obey our orders.'

'Not what the boys think.' Aulus looked around for support. Narses and Zabda held his eye. The others looked at the ground.

'This is a Roman army unit, not some Greek democracy,' Valens snapped. 'We go where I say.'

'Two men dead, and we are not in enemy territory yet. We must go back while we still can.'

'No.'

'Without Quintus we have no way of plotting our course.' There was an ugly, stubborn and belligerent cast to Aulus's aged and pouched face. 'We could wander these wastes until we die of hunger and thirst, or until the tent-dwellers pick us off one by one.'

'Nonsense.' Valens affected a certainty that he did not feel. 'We have supplies for several days, enough water, the Arabs are nothing to fear, and Quintus taught me to navigate by the stars. We follow the sinking of Arctophylax and Cynosura to the east. Soon we will reach the Tigris. Once we are in the realm of the King of Kings, Narses is a Persian and can guide us.'

Narses cleared his throat. 'I once served in Hyrkania, did a tour of duty at the Castle of Silence – the Lord Mazda be praised for bringing me safe from that lonely place – but I do not know the mountains that we must cross in the province of Matiane to reach the Caspian.'

'Then once across the Tigris, we hire a native guide.' Valens was adamant. 'You and Hairan speak Persian. And money is a universal language.'

Zabda spoke, although somewhat reluctantly. 'I have the Persian tongue as well. The wealth of Palmyra depends on their trade.'

'All mercantile endeavour is trickery and fraud,' Iudex said. 'If I pray, the Demiurge will set my spirit-guide on the right path.'

'Your *spirit-guide*?' Aulus spat, sacrilegiously near to the corpse. 'A human guide might be more reliable.'

'Enough.' Valens drew himself up, tried to radiate authority. 'We will search for the strayed animals, see to those we find and those that remain. Then we will return and bury Quintus. Those are your orders. Carry them out.'

Valens saw Aulus look at Iudex.

'We will do what is ordered, and at every command we will be ready,' Iudex said.

One by one the others repeated the words. Aulus last, and with utmost reluctance.

We will do what is ordered, and at every command we will be ready.

No one had spoken the ritual with any enthusiasm, but they began to walk back to the dry watercourse.

'Did Quintus really teach you?' Hairan spoke quietly to Valens.

'It is not difficult. Anyway, ride into the rising sun, and we will reach the Tigris.'

Hairan twirled the points of his long moustache. 'An open road, the wind in your face, a sword on your hip, a woman in your bed, a poem in your heart – adventure is in the blood of the warriors of Hatra – although there are few women in this desert. Perhaps in Persia . . . Have you ever had a Persian?'

'No.'

'You should, they are very lascivious. And a few nights with a *houri* does wonders for learning a language. Although much of what they say is not polite.'

They had not been searching long when they found Valens's horse and one of the missing mules at no great distance. The horse was sheltering in a small depression. The mule was standing in the open, enduring with the eternal patience of its kind. But Quintus's mount and four of the mules were gone beyond recall. As bad luck would have it, one of the lost mules had been carrying half the trade goods.

'Some tent-dweller will find a fortune,' Hairan said.

'Perhaps the bones and the jewels will lie undisturbed forever,' Valens said.

'Or some traveller will stumble across them in centuries to come.' Iudex narrowed his eyes, as if peering far into the future. 'Long after Rome has fallen, they will hold those artefacts in their hands, and wonder at the pointless ingenuity of the artists who expended such time and skill in carving tiny figures in gemstones, condemn the vanity of those who desired such things.'

'You do not believe Rome to be eternal?' Valens asked.

'Nothing is eternal, except Light and Darkness,' Iudex replied.

As the merchandise was easily portable, Valens decided to redistribute the remainder in the saddle bags of the eight surviving members of the expedition. That an individual might desert crossed his mind for the first time. Once the idea was there, it seemed extraordinary that he had not thought it before. The three easterners could be most tempted. They were closest to home. Although, of course, Hairan's city of Hatra was no longer inhabited. But all *frumentarii* were selected for their resourcefulness. Any of them could decide to vanish. It would not be difficult to make a new life somewhere in the vast expanses of the empire, or even beyond its frontiers. The price of the cameos would set a man up, if not for life, at least for a time. Yet Valens thought sharing out the valuables a risk worth running. If all the trade goods were lost, it would be hard to pretend to be nothing more sinister than a merchant caravan.

Several of the animals had cuts and abrasions from the storm, but from only one of the spare horses did the blood spurt bright scarlet. The incision was high on its thigh. This animal Decimus left aside. From the others the blood ran dull, red and slow. For these the horse master used some of the caravan's precious water to bathe the wounds. Using forceps, he removed every trace of dirt and grit, then, with delicate precision, shaved the hair around the injury. When the blood barely oozed, he applied a plug of clean wool, held in place by a linen bandage.

'The spare horse?' Valens asked.

'An artery is severed.' Decimus brought his face close to that of the injured animal. He talked gently to it, stroked its nose, let it inhale his breath. Then without preamble he drove a blade deep into the horse's neck. It tried to rear up, but he held it down by its soft and tender nostrils. When he withdrew the knife, a stream of blood thick as a man's arm pumped forth. The horse did not fight, but stood trembling. The blood pooled in the dirt. Everyone was silent, as if attending the rites of some deep religious mystery.

When the horse collapsed, Decimus cleaned his arm and blade. Valens saw tears in the eyes of the horse master.

'We must get on,' Valens said.

Leaving Decimus to cut strips of meat from the dead animal's haunches, they went to bury Quintus.

The stiffness of death had gone from the navigator. His corpse slumped, and his hands and feet dragged along the ground as they carried him down into the wadi. They enlarged an overhang in its bank, placed a coin between his teeth, and shovelled dirt and stones into the opening.

May the earth lie lightly upon him.

It was the second makeshift grave in which they had left one of their number. Valens thought water must run at some time of the year in what was now a dry watercourse. A flash flood would drag Quintus from his resting place. Still, they had done what was right. When the waters came, the shade of Quintus would have departed. The coin would have paid Charon, and the ferryman would have taken Quintus over the Styx. The soul of the navigator would have joined the countless dead thronging the dark meadows of Hades. Except, since the death of his parents, Valens no longer had any belief in such things.

On the third day after the storm they reached a watercourse that did not lie across their path, but ran ahead towards the east. There was a small stream in its bed, scrubby vegetation on its banks. They led the animals to the water gratefully, drank themselves, and replenished their flasks. Ordering that two men stand guard at all times, Valens gave the rest permission to strip and wash and take their ease.

Valens took the first sentry duty with Iudex. Below them the others splashed and laughed in the rivulet. Valens forced himself to look away from the cool tempting water, and scan the bare ochre countryside. He was tired, dirty and hot, but he must lead by example. You should never order men to do what you will not do yourself.

Surely this channel must lead down to the Tigris. Their journey across Mesopotamia was nearly at an end. But any sense of accomplishment was undermined by the thought of what was to come. No matter how dangerous the lands between the two rivers, so far they had travelled through territory at least nominally owing allegiance to the Rome. Soon they would be beyond the frontier. Once they crossed into the world of the barbarians, they would be beyond help from any Roman troops.

Perhaps we already are. The unsettling thought struck Valens. In this wilderness, who could tell exactly where was the boundary between Roman and Sassanid? The very idea of Persia frightened him.

Shapur was said to be cruel beyond measure, and certainly the King of Kings was implacably hostile to Rome. Both characteristics would be shared by his subjects. As well as the fear of pain and death, there was the fear of alienation. Not speaking Persian, Valens would be forced to rely on those that did. Narses, of course, was Persian. Coming from the caravan city of Palmyra, Zabda would have grown up hearing the language. If Iudex had not intervened, the two easterners might have murdered Valens at the start in Zeugma. Their evident continuing hostility did not encourage trust. At least there was also Hairan. But it was sobering for Valens to consider how very little he knew about the warrior from Hatra. Not even what fate had befallen his city.

The four westerners brought little comfort. Decimus the horse master and Clemens the armourer appeared dutiful enough, but

Iudex was unaccountable, touched by some god, and Aulus the quartermaster more than reluctant to obey orders or continue the mission. Waiting in the hot sun, Valens turned his problems over until his thoughts became splintered, and the fragments glittered and turned and fell in no order, like a ruined mosaic.

At long, long last Clemens and Narses clambered up the bank, tugging on their armour. Valens and Iudex were free to go down and bathe.

As he lay in the stream, Valens looked at his naked body. His hands and forearms were tanned a deep mahogany, the rest of him was very white. The journey was changing him. He was thinner, and the muscles in his legs more defined.

When he got up, he decided that they had been in the saddle long enough today. After the dangers and privations of the last few days, he was unsure that the men would go on if he ordered them.

Drying himself, Valens ordered the men to pitch camp for the night.

They left at dawn, and by the afternoon any remaining doubts Valens had entertained about not having left Rome wholly behind were dispelled. A multitude of large black birds wheeled around the summit of a lonely hill to the south. At the apex of the outcrop was the silhouette of a curved building.

'Ahuramazda be praised,' Narses said.

With one accord, as if summoned by that deity, they turned their animals away from the stream and up the incline.

The walls shone golden in the sunlight. Twenty or more of the birds sat on the wall like dark sentinels. A ramp ran up to an open gateway at the top of the building. Dismounting at its base, they hobbled the horses. The mules they left standing in a line, the leading reins between them trailing on the ground.

The birds on the wall did not take flight, but watched them without curiosity or alarm as they ascended the walkway. The clean desert air was tainted at the top of the ramp. It was worse in the darkness under the gate. When they got inside, they saw the horror.

They were standing on a sort of viewing platform. The building was round, with a flat roof. A low parapet ran around the edge, and there was a pit in the centre. The corpses were laid out in concentric circles around the pit: the small bodies of children innermost, then women, the men at the outside. There were forty or more, in all stages of decomposition. Some were little more than bones, ready to be shovelled into the pit. Others appeared to have been dead for only a few days.

Valens found himself staring at a nearby corpse. The man was on his back, his legs splayed in a vaguely obscene way. Strips of clothing, just tattered rags, still clung to the putrefying flesh. A vulture was tearing at the meat of his calf. The bird looked up malevolently, as if the intruders might dispute its food.

'*Everywhere, custom is king,*' Valens said.

'What?' Clemens said. The question was peremptory, the armourer's voice tight.

'A story in Herodotus. A Persian king asked some of his Greek subjects what they would take to expose the bodies of their dead. They refused, and begged him not to even say such a thing. He asked some of his own people if they would bury their dead. The response was the same. The moral is that people everywhere believe their own customs are natural.'

'I don't give a fuck about some old Greek.' Clemens's jowls were quivering with disgust. 'No Roman would ever contemplate such a thing. Only savages could treat their own with such inhumanity.'

'This is a holy place, a tower of silence,' Narses said.

'It is revolting,' Clemens almost shouted. 'A crime against the gods and men!'

'It is the will of the Lord of Light, Ahuramazda.' Narses spoke softly.

'No god would command such a thing, only an evil daemon!'

'Careful what you say, it is death to insult Ahuramazda.' There was a fierce gleam in the eyes of the Persian.

'Barbarian!' Clemens spat out the word.

They were facing each other, hands on hilts. Valens knew he should act, but was frozen, captured by the drama, as if at the theatre.

It was Hairan who stepped between the irate men. 'It is not just the Greeks who preach tolerance. Bardaisan, the wise man of Edessa, collected the customs of many peoples. All Indians, when they die, are burnt with fire, and their wives are burnt alive on the pyre. All Germans who do not fall in battle are strangled by their relatives when they get old. They regard it as a kindness. They have been living for thousands of years according to their own laws. Nothing can alter their customs.'

Clemens stopped glowering at Narses, but muttered under his breath.

'Look!' It was Decimus who broke the final strands of anger.

From this high place they could see for miles. Everyone looked where the horse master pointed.

To the east, a river curved through the dun landscape. Its waters flashed silver in the sun. The Tigris – half a day's ride away.

'Let us go,' Valens said.

'Gladly.' Clemens stomped off. The rest moved to follow.

'I will catch you up.' Iudex was sitting cross-legged. He had a stylus and a pot of ink, and was sketching in a notebook.

Valens looked over his shoulder. The drawings were detailed and precise, catching every nuance of the dead.

Iudex glanced up. 'I had heard that Orientals putrefy differently to westerners. Of course these are all easterners . . . a missed opportunity.' He smiled happily. 'Do not worry, sir. I will not be long.' He bent back over his work.

Valens hesitated, feeling he should assert his authority, yet reluctant to intervene.

Frowning with concentration, Iudex spoke, probably to himself. 'The unexamined death, like the unexamined life, is nothing.'

CHAPTER 11

Rome

IT WAS HOT. THE PAVEMENTS and the facades of buildings radiated back the heat of the day. Murena had walked down from the Caelian, through the Forum, and across the Campus Martius. It was not that far, and it was good to get away for a time from the endless reports that his secretary piled on his desk. Murena was fit, but he was out of breath and sweating hard. No wonder that most of the elite left the city in high summer. Those that remained travelled the streets in shaded litters. Murena could have hired a litter, but it would not have suited his purpose. Instead he trudged, red-faced and panting, dressed in nondescript tunic and sandals. Just another of the urban plebs making his weary way through the metropolis.

The Temple of Vulcan was down by the Tiber. It was eight days before the Kalends of September, the Volcanalia, the festival of the lame and ugly blacksmith-god. Vulcan had been married off to Venus, the beautiful goddess of love, much against her inclination. She had wasted no time cuckolding him with Mars, the straight-limbed and virile god of war. Discovering the betrayal, the outraged husband had retired to his forge and hammered out a bronze hunting-net, as thin as gossamer but quite unbreakable. Telling his wife that he would be away, he left the trap suspended above the marital bed. Sure enough, at dawn, Vulcan summoned the other gods to witness the illicit lovers naked and entangled. A man of traditional piety, Murena knew the myth well. It was propitious, he thought, for his task. It was the duty of the *frumentarii* to uncover the secret and the shameful.

The approach to the sanctuary along the embankment smelt of mud and decay and sewage. The yellow-brown waters of the Tiber were low at this time of year. Wide swathes of the sludge of its bed were exposed – the indescribable filth deposited by a city of a million souls.

Suddenly, Murena had the sense that he was being watched. Stopping to tie the laces on his sandles, he surreptitiously studied those in the street. He recognised no one, and there was nothing suspicious. Certainly none of his *frumentarii* were present. Since taking up his office, Murena had made a point of memorising the faces of all those under his command in Rome. The sense was nothing but a trick of his imagination.

Murena followed the crowd into the old, gloomy temple. Tradition held it to have been founded by Romulus, at what was then a remote place outside the city, so that he could consult the senate in privacy. That seclusion had been the downfall of Romulus – it was here that he had been murdered. After the deed, the senators dismembered his corpse, and each carried away a piece hidden in the folds of his toga. Nothing remained, not even a shred of clothing. They gave out to the plebs that he had been snatched away to the heavens.

The senators remained as treacherous today. Given the opportunity, many of them would still turn on their ruler, hack him into bloody hunks of meat. That was why Murena was in this ancient sanctuary. The target was easy to spot: tall, clad in a snowy toga, a broad purple stripe on his tunic, standing in the space reserved for the *Honestiores*, the honest men of wealth and position. This senator would be denied the chance to strike down the Emperor.

'He came here alone.' The unseen speaker whispered in Murena's ear. 'In a litter, he did not stop, talked to no one.'

Murena gave no sign that he had been spoken to. He had been expecting the approach, and he did not look around. The *frumentarius* would have melted back into the crowd.

It had started with an impecunious magician. In a backstreet bar down in the Subura, the down-at-heel charlatan had bragged that he could predict the future. Nothing was hidden from him. His art had divined the nature and time of the death of the Emperor. The drunken boast had been his undoing – the man to whom he spoke was a *frumentarius*. To meddle in such forbidden things carried the death penalty. After his arrest, in a forlorn attempt to avert his fate, the sorcerer claimed that he knew of a conspiracy against the life of the Emperor. The desperate ploy was unwise. All it had brought was the attentions of the torturers. In a cell in the Camp of the Strangers, under the pincers and the claws, through his agony the magician had gasped out that he had been hired by a senator to discover what would kill the Emperor. The revelation, as so often, was enigmatic, poetically vague: *On the Ausonian plains, the sons of Ares, men inured to violence, will ring him around. He will be smitten by gleaming steel, betrayed by companions.* The wizard had named the inquisitive senator as Marcus Acilius Glabrio. The unholy rites he had commissioned to reveal what the gods ordained for the Emperor had been conducted in the dead of night in a secluded corner of the Gardens of Lucullus.

The circumstantial details were accurate. The gardens were owned by the family of Acilius Glabrio. They were deserted after dark. Even so, the sorcerer's confession had been given little credence. Men on the rack always tried to implicate someone. The *frumentarii* heard the like all the time. Nothing had been done, except open a file, and place a spy in the household of Acilius Glabrio. The magician had been burnt alive in the arena, his tongue prudently removed to prevent him saying anything unseemly.

In retrospect, the execution had been a mistake. Subsequently, the informant in Glabrio's household had reported that at a dinner party, during the serious drinking after the food, thinking himself secure in his own home, safe among his own kind, the senator had made treasonous criticisms of the Emperor. Glabrio had mocked Gallienus Augustus as an effeminate and a coward and a fool. No wonder the empire tottered when the throne was occupied by a spendthrift who squandered money needed for the army on lavish buildings to flatter his vanity: a luxurious portico along the Flaminian Way; a statue larger than the Colossus on the Esquiline; Platonopolis, a whole city of philosophers in the Apennines. Was there no end to his profligacy? By all the gods, the majesty of Rome was dragged through the dirt by a degenerate who drank himself into insensibility, dressed as a woman, and was a slave to his lust for a barbarian mistress. Know a ruler by his companions. Gallienus surrounded himself with pimps and prostitutes, Greek philosophers and Syrian dancers. Reviling the Senate, the nobility of Rome, Gallienus gave high office and military commands to common soldiers, men who had started life as peasants or goatherds.

These might have been nothing but inebriated words, and no actual threats had been uttered, but then Acilius Glabrio changed the routine of a lifetime. This summer he had not retired to his villa on the Bay of Naples, but had remained in the swelter of Rome. A man who previously had paid no more than lip service to the demands of traditional religion, now, under the scorching August sun, had taken to traversing the city to attend obscure festivals in out-of-the-way shrines. Either the senator was seeking divine approval for some desperate act, or the ceremonies were a cover for clandestine meetings. Murena had decided it was time he saw for himself.

'Vulcan, God of Fire, hear our prayers.' The sacrifice was about to begin.

The priest held a fish caught in the Tiber. It twisted and gasped in his hands.

'Mulciber, Quietus . . .' The titles of the deity were intoned.

The priest threw the fish alive into the fire. Its silver scales hissed and blackened.

Murena continued to watch Acilius Glabrio, but his thoughts roamed. It was a skill he had learnt early as a *frumentarius*. Nothing must be missed, but if you gave all your attention to the object of your surveillance you drew attention to yourself.

The priest took another fish.

The strange sacrifice made sense to Murena. By offering things usually safe from Vulcan, it might induce the god of conflagrations to spare things that would burn only too easily in the hot season. Rome was largely built of wood, and the fear of fire was a terrible reality.

The next fish was added to the flames. The stench of the river was overlaid with an agreeable kitchen-like smell.

So far, Acilius Glabrio had made no contact. Perhaps, for whatever reason, the senator was communing with the god. *Yet*, Murena reflected, *the time is ripe for treason.*

The news from the north was not good. The public despatches spoke of victories, strategic gains, and a prudent early withdrawal into winter quarters. The private letter from Volusianus told a different story. The Praetorian Prefect urged Murena to added vigilance. The campaign in Gaul had failed. Besieging the rebel Postumus in the city of Autun, Gallienus had been wounded by an arrow. The imperial field army had fallen back across the Alps. The Emperor was in Milan. It was thought he would live. Yet there was no certainty, and Gallienus was incapacitated.

The unsuccessful expedition had given Acilius Glabrio another, very personal grievance. A cavalry column led by the general Ballista had not returned from Gaul. It was thought to have been destroyed or captured by the rebels. Among its number was a cousin of the senator.

More fish were being immolated on the altar. Such a thing would be unimaginable in Murena's home province. Across Syria, fish were widely considered sacred. Many of the great temples had elaborate marble ponds in which swam carp and other prized fish. They lived long lives, were cared for and fed; sometimes they wore jewels like earrings. Killing them was sacrilege. Mankind found innumerable ways to worship the gods. It was no part of the brief of a *frumentarius* to judge the religious beliefs of others. Unless, of course, they were devotees of a proscribed cult, like the Christians.

Acilius Glabrio still stood alone.

The thoughts of Murena continued to dwell on the east. The abortive campaign into Gaul, and the injury to the Emperor, made it ever more necessary that the mission to the Castle of Silence fail. Prince Sasan must remain a Persian prisoner. Events in the west left Rome even more unready for war with the Sassanids. No excuse to invade could be offered to Shapur.

Murena wondered where the caravan had reached. Had it crossed Mesopotamia yet? Was it in Persia? There was no way of telling. Severus was a resourceful commander. Yet, if the traitor had carried out his orders, Severus would be dead, and Valens would have assumed command. Valens was young and inexperienced. The soft and pampered youth owed his commission in the Horse Guards to patronage untouched by merit. And Valens was a heavy drinker. When his parents had been killed he had fallen into maudlin lethargy and drunken self-pity. Murena had appointed Valens to fail. If the gods were kind, Valens, guided by the malign hand of the traitor, would have led his men to disaster, and their bones would already be whitening in some distant desert.

The ceremony was drawing to a close. Acilius Glabrio turned to leave.

Murena slipped out unobtrusively. The reek of the river again assailed his nostrils. He watched the senator stride through the blistering sunshine to where his litter waited. The very way he walked conveyed an air of entitlement. Acilius Glabrio did not pause, and he talked to no one suspicious or otherwise.

As the senator climbed into the litter, Murena scanned the onlookers. A man among the crowd caught his eye. Murena nodded, almost imperceptibly, to the *frumentarius* who would continue the surveillance, then he walked away.

CHAPTER 12

Adiabene

THEY RODE DOWN TO THE TIGRIS. The river curled, sinuous and expansive, across a flat and dusty land. Yet the vegetation and fields along its banks were almost shocking in their vibrant green after the long journey through the high plains.

There was no bridge, but the river was broad and shallow. A rough path led them to a ford. There was a small mudbrick settlement on the far side. The sprays of water glittered like diamonds as they splashed across.

A crowd had gathered, as if summoned by the clanking of the bell on the mare that led the mules. The inhabitants stared silently at the apparition of the travel-stained riders.

Valens raised his hand to halt the column.

The throng parted, and an official stepped forward. Portly, smooth cheeked, full of self-importance, the man was obviously a eunuch. He spoke in Persian.

'A customs officer,' Hairan said.

Even in this fly-blown, out-of-the-way place, taxes had to be paid.

Valens waved Narses forward to deal with the eunuch.

'Who are you who wish to enter the domain of the Mazda-beloved Shapur, King of Kings?' Hairan translated in an undertone for Valens.

'All the Earth is mine, and I have a right to go over it and through it,' Narses replied.

Valens whispered to Hairan. 'Why is he antagonising the eunuch?'

'What else would you expect from a Persian? Arrogance and cruelty are in their blood. Narses comes from the noble clan of the Suren.' Hairan smiled. 'Although perhaps it is necessary in this case. Show weakness to a eunuch, and he will rob you blind.'

'From where have you come, and who sent you?' The eunuch was speaking angrily, drawing himself upright, stiff with the dignity of his petty office.

'We have sent ourselves to see if we can make men of you, whether you like it or not,' Narses said.

'If you do not answer my questions, I will have you tortured.' There was an outraged petulance in the manner of the official.

'By the peasants here?' Narses laughed, his teeth very white in his dark beard. 'It will be good for you do it with your own hands, so that you may be tested by the touchstone of a true man.'

Clemens nudged his horse closer to Valens. 'The Persian fool will get us all killed.'

Valens hushed him.

'By the gods, who are you?' In the face of the armed men, and Narses's assured intransigence, the tone of the eunuch had changed to a whine of entreaty.

'Since you asked me with politeness this time, I will tell you. I am Narses, son of Rastak of the Suren, caravan guard in the service of Marcus Aelius Valens, merchant out of Antioch. We carry carved gemstones and jewellery to trade in Hyrkania.'

As if by magic, the attitude of the eunuch became civil, even obsequious. Although a gleam in his eyes indicated this might have been caused by him scenting his own perquisites on these valuable commodities.

'If you would be so kind as to accompany me to the customs house.'

Inside the building, the merchandise was brought out. In the negotiation, Narses was gracious but firm. The tax across the border was set at twenty-five per cent, the highest known in the world. A contribution to the official brought the sum down.

Even when Valens had handed over the money, the business was far from over. Through Narses the eunuch asked each man his name and family, what was his profession, from where he came, and his reason for travelling. As there was no reason not to, they gave their real names. The official wrote everything down in a book, although all the answers except the names were the same. It seemed to take an inordinately long time.

'He is recording our dress and appearance,' Hairan quietly told Valens. 'They will be passed on to the *Ears of the King* – the Persian King, like the Roman Emperor, has those who watch and listen.'

'One last formality.' The eunuch went to a sort of shrine, and brought back a small statuette. It was made of gold, and looked incongruous in this poor village.

'What is this?' Hairan asked.

The eunuch looked surprised that another in the party spoke his language.

'Shapur the King of Kings has decreed that everyone entering his territory must pay their respects by kissing his image.'

'Romans are exempt from this ceremony.' Hairan said with finality.

The official wrung his hands apologetically. 'Only envoys from the Roman Emperor.'

When Hairan translated the exchange, Clemens bristled. 'A free man only gives such a tribute to a god.'

Unexpectedly, Iudex also refused. 'It is anathema in the eyes of the Lord to venerate idols.'

'They are right,' Hairan said. 'I will not abase myself to an image of that murderous bastard.'

Although unable to follow the Latin words, the eunuch understood their refusal. 'It is the law. Anyone has to be arrested with dishonour unless he pays honour to the image.'

'Never,' Clemens said.

'It is an abomination,' Iudex said.

'There are no soldiers here,' Clemens said. 'We have nothing to fear from this excuse of a man.'

'Fuck the Persian bastard,' Hairan added.

'Have you three lost your minds?' Valens snapped. 'There are no soldiers here, but there are tens of thousands in Persia. We are hundreds of miles from our objective.'

They stared back at him.

Valens rounded on Clemens and Hairan. 'You will have done worse as . . .' he checked himself, avoided the word *frumentarii* '. . . in your *duties*.'

Both men looked at Iudex.

'As for you, Iudex, an oath taken under duress is no oath at all. Your god will absolve you.'

It was difficult to face down the huge bald man.

'We are merchants, not an invading army. We must behave as such.'

The small childlike features regarded Valens with great solemnity.

'Everywhere, custom is king. Kiss the fucking thing!'

With no expression on his face, Iudex did as he was told.

One by one, with more or less evident reluctance, every man did the same.

Last of all, Valens bent and put his lips to the image.

'It is all good, my friends.' The eunuch was beaming with relief. 'All very good. At the edge of the village is a caravanserai. It is basic for such honoured guests, but it is clean, and the food is excellent, and they tell me that the girls are skilled.'

The cameos were wrapped and packed away.

The eunuch quickly wrote a note, recording them as a merchant caravan that had paid the import duties and was bound for Hyrkania, which he presented to Narses.

'You can get provisions in our market – wine, venison and bacon, leavened bread and vegetables, palm dates like amber. You must stock up. The land downstream is full of wormwood, everything that grows there is bitter. There are few villages there, and the people are thieves.'

As the fat official prattled on, Valens still felt the cold press of the metal on his lips. If the gods existed, they had no interest in mankind. There could be no sacrilege. Yet somehow he felt vitiated, as if he had betrayed some part of himself.

Valens lay back on the narrow bed. The cheap, stained sheets were rumpled.

Alexander the Great had said that only sex reminded him that he was mortal.

The girl ran her palm across his chest, murmuring incomprehensible endearments or compliments.

Her skin was brown, smooth like silk, her dark nipples almost as black as her hair. The first coupling had been brief. It was a long time since the girl in Resaina. In the second, she had feigned pleasure.

Now Valens felt an overwhelming urge to get away, to be downstairs drinking with his men. He removed her hand, and got up. Finding his wallet, he gave her a few extra coins as a tip. When she spoke her tone sounded grateful, but he could not tell if she murmured thanks or was cursing him.

'Our officer returns.' Clemens was in fine humour, his air of archaic republican morality set aside for the evening. The armourer flourished his cup, and recited a poem in Greek.

> *Looking at her beauty, I melt like wax before the fire.*
> *And if she is dusky, what is that to me?*
> *So are the coals, but when we light them,*
> *They shine as bright as roses.*

Valens sat down, took the proffered drink. In a crowded room full of good cheer, Iudex alone looked disapproving, as he quietly ate a melon and sipped water.

'Cheer up, you old bugger,' Clemens called over. 'Even stern old Cato said a young man should visit a brothel, as long as he did not – like that whore-chasing Hatrene Hairan – make it his home.'

Iudex stopped eating. With the solemnity of a religious rite, he broke wind loudly.

'Sanctimonious in public, but we know what your cult gets up to behind closed doors – at it like sparrows.' Clemens winked, adopting a conspiratorial air. 'They say you spread a lot of flour over the floor, and hump on top of it. The men pull out, shoot their load, and then you make bread out of the flour.'

'A foolish calumny.'

'A *calumny*? I need a dictionary to talk to you.'

A look of infinite sadness passed across Iudex's features. 'The Lord has spoken, but you are deaf. A man loses the divine light through semen. It is the fault of Eve. She was created for a diabolical purpose. When Adam saw her, garlanded and naked, he gave way to lust. From their copulation was born Seth, the ancestor of the sinful race of mankind. Adam repented, tore his hair, beat his breast. *Woe to the maker of my body, the chainer of my soul, woe to me who is reduced to servitude!*'

Clemens grinned. 'Old Iudex is always such an adornment at a drinking party.'

All the men laughed, except Decimus. The horse master, becoming maudlin with the drink, did not join their merriment. He was hunched over the table, his gaze fixed on something no one else could see. As men often did in their cups, he too turned to verse.

Women are a curse,
They may be good in bed
But they are better off dead.

'Gods below,' Aulus broke in, 'not more fucking poetry.' His watery old eyes expressed utter contempt. 'If a man has something to say, let him say it openly and straightforwardly. Poets are nearly as big liars as philosophers.'

Clemens shook his head. 'You miserable bastards.'

A group of musicians had arrived, and were tuning their instruments.

Valens turned to Iudex. 'You never drink?'

'Wine is the evil bile of daemons.'

'And I have never seen you eat meat.'

'It is wrong to butcher animals.'

'Because they are sacred?'

'No, because they are filth.'

'So you will not kill an animal, but a man?'

'That is different.' The musicians had started playing, and Iudex looked distracted.

Suddenly he leapt to his feet. Beaming, he placed one of his enormous hands on Valens's shoulder. 'Music and dance, nothing is holier in the sight of the Lord.'

His body already swaying to the rhythm, Iudex made his way to the open space at the centre of the room.

'All this talk of Eve and Adam,' Valens said, 'are we sure he is not a Christian?'

'He once told me he followed some prophet called Mani,' Clemens said. 'Whatever, touched by one god or another. Utterly insane, but he does dance well.'

Valens took a drink.

'That eunuch was full of shit,' Aulus said. 'There was no venison at all to be had in the market, but I did get some bacon.'

But Valens was not listening. His eyes followed Iudex as, despite his sobriety, the soldier capered like a Bacchant in time to the music. Could such a strange man be trusted?

At first they thought it was another Tower of Silence. In the distance, the vultures wheeled black against the hot azure sky. When they got nearer, they saw it was not.

The column had spent two further days resting in the caravanserai. They had not drunk as much as the first night, but Hairan looked exhausted by the time they left. Valens had not visited the dark girl again. For three days they had been riding south, the river on their right. On the second they had come to Nineveh. Little remained of the fabled city of the once mighty Assyrian empire, except low humps in the ground and a squalid settlement sprawled among them.

What I have eaten and wantoned, the pleasures I have had
of my loves,
These alone have I now. The rest of my blessings have
vanished.

It was Hairan who had recited the notorious lines. Valens had accompanied the Hatrene in searching the site. But for all their efforts they found no trace of the stone on which the poem was said to be inscribed, nor any of the sculptures with which the last Assyrian king had adorned his ancient capital.

They had spent the night in Nineveh. Setting out the next morning, they expected a long day would bring them to the Lykos River, which they would follow east into the mountains. Somewhere upstream they would hire a local to guide them through the passes.

It was in the afternoon, the sun arcing down, when they spotted the vultures. As before, something unspoken drew them away from their route. Coming closer, they saw the burnt wagon, the scatter of debris about it. Valens sent Hairan and Aulus out to scout the surroundings.

The wagon was still smouldering, occasional little licks of flame running across its planks. Pathetic belongings lay abandoned on the ground: a smashed amphora, a lone shoe, a woman's torn veil. The first corpse was slumped by the wagon. The vultures rose at their approach, ungainly and reluctant. Dressed in a coarse tunic, the man lay on his back. The carrion birds had not been long at their feast. Despite their feeding, the two wounds were still evident in his chest. The tearing of the flesh showed the killers had taken trouble to retrieve their arrows. The other corpse was further off. This victim was stark naked, staked out. He had been tortured. Valens looked in horror at the blackened, burnt soles of his feet, and the bloody mess where his genitals had been.

'Arabs,' Narses said.

Valens gestured at the wagon. 'What hidden treasure could they think he might reveal?'

'Arabs,' Narses said again. 'It gives the tent-dwellers pleasure.'

The scouts clattered back.

'Tracks heading north-east. Camels and horses, a couple of mules, probably from the wagon, a few are going on foot,' Aulus reported.

'How many?' Valens asked.

'In total, more than ten, less than twenty.'

'How long?'

'Recent, an hour, maybe two.'

'We should either bury or cremate the dead,' Decimus said.

'There are no trees,' Aulus said, 'and the wagon is already charcoal.'

'If they were locals, they were followers of Zoroaster,' Narses said. 'We should leave them exposed.'

'We cannot leave them to the vultures.' The idea appalled Valens.

'So custom is only king when it fits your sensibilities?' Narses said.

Although it was repugnant, Valens knew the Persian was right. 'Untie that one, lay them both out respectfully. In case they worshipped the Olympian gods, put a coin in their mouths and sprinkle a pinch of earth on each.'

As they carried out the order, Valens stood respectfully by. But there was something else that had to be done.

'Aulus, can you track the tent-dwellers?'

'I am a Gaul. We are born hunters.'

'You could follow their trail in darkness?'

'Of course.' Aulus looked somewhat affronted. 'Anyone with eyes could, and I was a scout for the Third Augusta in Africa. But why?'

Valens picked up the ripped veil. 'There was a woman with the wagon.'

'She was unlucky.'

'We are going to rescue her.'

'Have you taken leave of your senses, sir?' The last word was an afterthought. 'Our mission is to free some Sassanid princeling, not every woman taken by the nomads.'

Valens steeled himself to face this new challenge to his authority. Before he could speak, unexpected aid came from Narses.

'I would not leave anyone in the hands of the Arabs.'

Aulus, furious and truculent, looked for support from the others.

'The officer is right,' Clemens said.

'But there are more of them than us,' Aulus exclaimed. 'Why put your hand in a nest of rats?'

'We are soldiers,' Valens said, 'and they are nothing but ragged tent-dwellers.'

Aulus turned away. 'Either the sun has addled your minds, or some daemon is leading us to destruction.'

CHAPTER 13

The Castle of Silence

THE WOMAN HAD DANCED SLOWLY and sensuously. Beneath a glittering veil, her robe was sheer and clinging. It revealed all the contours of her body. Barbad had taken her breasts in his hands, felt the nipples harden against his palms.

Only fragments of the dream remained, but his semi-erect member told the story. Barbad smiled: a seventy-five-year-old eunuch with an erection. The good god Mazda be praised. It depended when you were cut. If a boy had reached puberty before the knife, as a eunuch he might achieve an erection, although obviously he would be sterile. Some women sought out certain eunuchs for those qualities.

Barbad half remembered a simile employed by a Greek philosopher. Something or other was as frustrating as a woman attempting to have sex with a eunuch. They could spend the whole night together, and he could do no more than annoy her. Greek philosophers were not always as wise as they claimed.

Barbad had been old to be cut. Later, in his youth, he had lain with women. He was not one of those eunuchs who had run to fat. His muscles had not withered. His voice was not effeminate. He had shared the bed of women into his vigorous middle age. They had not seemed annoyed at all. Some had appeared to enjoy the experience.

It was late summer, warm even here in the mountains. The shutters were wide open. Barbad looked out at the night sky. A garment of stars was stretched across the heavens. The boy was fast asleep in his own bed. The young lived in the moment. Although he still did not want to pass the night alone in his sleeping chamber, it had been more than a month since Sasan had had a nightmare. Perhaps the young were just more resilient, or it could be that life had yet to crush their natural optimism.

Barbad regarded the stars. The Hyades, the Bear, Orion, and the Dolphin; they were as familiar to him by their Greek names as their Persian. As scribe to Prince Papak, Barbad had learnt Greek. It was the language of diplomacy. When a Persian met a Roman, they talked Greek. And some of the prince's tenants were Greek; either prisoners recently taken in the campaigns of Shapur, or the descendants of those settled long ago by Alexander and his successors.

The Greeks and Romans were hypocritical about eunuchs. They condemned them as evidence of eastern cruelty and decadence. Castration was illegal in the Roman empire. Yet they imported them in their thousands. Provided they were cut beyond their frontiers, in out-of-the-way places like Abasgia by the Black Sea, it seemed not to matter. It was said that in their palaces the Caesars and the senators were served by eunuchs. There had always been eunuchs in Persia – their uses had been recognised since the time of Cyrus the Great. Unable to sire a family of their own, they were loyal. If cut young, it was safe for them to guard the women of the family. A pretty young eunuch made a good bed companion for a man. And, if anything went wrong, if scandal touched their master, the blame could be placed upon his eunuchs.

Of course there was another reason that boys, even men, were castrated. Vengeance. Barbad knew the story of Hermotimus. It was in Herodotus, one of the first works that he had read when learning Greek. As a prisoner of war, Hermotimus had fallen into the hands of Panionius, a slave trader. Panionius had castrated Hermotimus, and sold him in the market at Sardis. By chance, or the will of the gods, Hermotimus had been bought for the household of the Persian king. Later, when Hermotimus had become the King's most valued eunuch, he sought out Panionius. Listing all the benefits that had come his way thanks to the slave trader, Hermotimus persuaded Panionius to come with his family to live with him, so that he could do as much good in return. When Hermotimus had Panionius in his power, he dropped the pretence, took him prisoner, and cursed him. For his crimes, the gods had delivered Panionius into his hands. Hermotimus had the four sons of Panionius dragged in. One by one he forced the slave trader to castrate his sons, then the sons to castrate the father.

The sky was paling. It would soon be dawn. It was time to begin the endlessly repeated routine of the day.

Forcing himself not to groan, Barbad levered his old bones from his bed. Having found his slippers and robe, he shuffled quietly to the door. The boy was still sleeping, his dark curls spread across the pillow. The gaolers had given Barbad oil for the hinges. The door opened without a sound. Gently, Barbad pulled it shut behind him.

Overnight, the coals in the brazier had burnt low. With infinite care, Barbad blew them into life. When they were glowing, he placed new coals by hand, one at a time, careful to make no noise that might wake the sleeping boy next door. The fire tended, he washed his hands, then set out the clothes that Sasan would wear that day. The Prince had three changes of costume. It was almost the only thing that demarked one day from another in the Castle of Silence. Once a month the supply convoy came, a wagon and half a dozen outriders climbing the trail to the main gate. Every time Barbad watched them from the high window with a mixture of excitement and utter dread.

The former was a measure of the monotony of their existence. The latter, he knew, was rooted in his cowardice. When the order came from the distant royal court, it would not arrive in a supply cart. Instead it would be carried by a single rider travelling fast. A golden chain on the harness of his horse or dromedary would mark him as a messenger on the business of the King of Kings. A man not to be detained on pain of death.

Barbad heard the key turning in the lock. It was nothing to fear, only the start of yet another monotonous day. A day just like all the others.

The outer door swung open. A guard brought in a tray. Another guard stood on the landing. From his demeanour it was obvious that he had been stationed there for hours. When closed, the door shut out any noise. No footfalls could be heard. It was impossible to tell how often the guard was changed, yet Barbad was sure a soldier was always on duty.

The guard placed the tray on a table and left. The door was locked again. He had not spoken a word. They never did. Even when Barbad made a request – for more oil or coals or whatever – they did not reply. Later the things might appear. Sometimes they did not. The books had never arrived. The warden of the Castle of Silence did not look like a man who would keep a library.

On the tray was flatbread, cheese and fruit, a jug of wine and a pitcher of water. A meagre repast for a prince. Barbad tipped some of the wine into a bowl and set it on the brazier to warm. He had no fear that Sasan would be poisoned. When the order came, it would be something far worse.

Three times a day the door opened. The food varied. Nothing else changed. They had long exhausted their one book of poetry. For long hours Barbad would tell the boy stories: Persian folktales, anecdotes from the many books of the Greeks, gossip from happier days. The latter was carefully selected not to upset the prince. The rest of the time they slept or stared out of the windows, watching the wheeling buzzards, seeing the occasional eagle, noting the play of sunlight on the crags and ravines. Sometimes Barbad wondered if he was going insane.

Barbad had been cut just before his fourteenth birthday. It was when Ardashir, the father of Shapur, had seized the throne. Barbad's family were of the old Persian nobility, and had been faithful supporters of the rightful king. To become King of Kings, the pretender Ardashir had murdered his own brother. It was given out as an accident: a building at Chumai on the road to Darabgerd had collapsed. Nothing but the will of the gods. The persecutions that followed were evidence of the lie.

Many of those who had kept faith with the true king had fled into exile. Barbad's family had not been so lucky. His father, his uncle and two cousins – all his adult male relatives – had been captured. They had been condemned to die slowly in the troughs. As a boy, Barbad had been 'spared' to watch. Then he had been cut. Even now his mind shied away from that day. He tried not to think of his pain, or the terrible suffering of those in the troughs.

For years Barbad had harboured a dream of revenge. Like Hermotimus, he would castrate the man responsible for making him a eunuch, wield the knife on all those the man loved, take the manhood of every man and boy in his family, make Ardashir watch their agony and humiliation. Yet even as it had sustained him, he had known that it was no more than an idle fantasy. A eunuch scribe could never emasculate a King of Kings. Now it was too late. Ardashir was long dead.

The wine was warm. Barbad diluted it with three parts water. With fussy precision, he arranged the boy's morning meal. It was dawn. Almost time to wake Sasan.

Barbad hesitated, reluctant to open the door on another interminable day. There had been no news for months. They knew nothing of the outside world. Confined to two rooms and a privy. No companionship but the silent and watchful guards. Nothing to see but the bare crags of the mountains. Any man might lose his mind.

Nothing remained but duty. Sooner or later, Barbad would perform the last service for Sasan. He would save the boy from torture. The slender knife was still concealed. Before it was too late he would act. Barbad was ready.

CHAPTER 14

Adiabene

T HEY WATCHED THE ARABS FOR HOURS. Valens lay with five of
the men in a shallow scrape about two hundred paces away.
Decimus and Hairan were half a mile back, hidden in a wadi with
the animals.

Aulus had been right that the tent-dwellers would make no effort
to cover their tracks. Their choice of campsite also indicated that
they had no fear of pursuit. They had pitched their shelters at a
watering hole which stood out prominently against the bare, rolling country. Their campfires were kindled in a stand of date palms.
The light reflected from the undersides of the fronds, shining like a
beacon in the dark.

About the numbers of the nomads, Aulus appeared mistaken.
Dressed alike in cloaks and boots, all wearing headbands holding
back their long hair, they were hard to differentiate. They observed
no order, but drifted about haphazardly. Valens had counted and
recounted them. By his calculation, the group was twenty-five strong,
each armed with a spear and a bow. One or two also had swords. They
were too well armed and too many for an open attack in daylight.

As the hours passed, and the evening turned to night, the soldiers
observed the arrangements of the nomads. Their rough shelters
were skins stretched over upright poles. They were open at the sides,
and grouped around the fires. The camels were tethered at one side
of the camp, the horses and mules at the other. The Arabs produced
hunks of meat from sacks of skins. They cooked them in kettles over

the flames. They ignored their usual drink of milk for the wine they had looted from the wagon. Amphorae went from hand to hand. Likewise, the woman was led from one shelter to another. None seemed to feel the need for privacy when they took her, confirming the nomads reputation for lechery. Most of the men raped her more than once. There was nothing the watchers could do to end her suffering and humiliation.

Unaccustomed to the wine, which they drank unmixed with water, one by one the Arabs rolled themselves in their cloaks and went to sleep. Eventually there were just four left awake. They dragged the woman to the bough of a tree in the middle of the camp, tethered her there like another animal, then fell into a loud and heated argument. Roused by the noise, some of their companions also shouted. The outcome was that a young nomad, complaining vociferously, was deputed to stand guard.

Valens measured the course of the moon by the tip of the tallest palm. When he judged that at least half an hour had gone by, he nudged Zabda and Iudex. It had been decided earlier that the three of them would venture into the camp. Zabda was a thief, accustomed to moving surreptitiously, and Iudex, for all his bulk, had the grace of a dancer. Valens did not feel that he could remain behind if he ordered men into danger. Aulus, Clemens and Narses would remain, bows ready to cover their return. Narses, it was agreed, was the best shot in the party.

At first the sentry had walked the perimeter of the camp, stopping frequently to relieve himself. Once he had been sick. Weariness and the wine overcoming his duty, soon he had sat with his back to a palm tree. As the fires burnt low, it was impossible to tell if he was asleep.

Zabda waited for a cloud to pass across the face of the moon, then got to his feet. Valens and Iudex rose up with him. All three had smeared dirt on their faces and hands. No words were spoken.

As the shadow of the cloud shifted across the bare earth, they set off in its gloom. Valens noticed that, out in the open under the ambient light, his own dark cloak, and that of Zabda, stood out more than the sky-blue one of Iudex.

They went in single file: Zabda, then Iudex, with Valens at the rear. Leading them in a wide detour, the Palmyrene made towards the camp using the cover of the horse lines.

Although they had left their helmets, armour and the ornaments from their belts with the baggage train, Valens thought the noise they made enough to wake the dead. His heart was hammering, and his breathing coming in a short, loud panting.

The horses stirred, hooves softly thudding. Ears pitched forward, the animals' huge gentle eyes regarded the approaching men. Curious about their nocturnal movements, one horse called out to them. A restlessness ran through the herd. Going past the other men, Valens went to the nervous beast. As he got near, it jerked up its head and whinnied. Valens stopped. Its head came down. With infinite slowness he moved closer. Still suspicious, it stretched its neck, smelling this stranger. Valens leant forward. The horse's muzzle snuffled over his face. Valens forced himself to relax, to betray no tension. He breathed in its nostrils, the horse calmed, a thoughtful, dreamy look in its eyes.

Zabda stole past between the warm flanks of the horses. Iudex remained.

Time slowed, as if held in the hand of a god.

Valens found that he was murmuring very softly to the horse.

Somewhere out in the desert a fox barked. Valens jumped. The horse ruckled down its nose. Now it was the solid presence of the horse reassuring the man.

Valens peered around the huge head.

In the flicker of the dying fires he could see the outline of the motionless sentry.

Gods below, how much longer?

As if the infernal deities heard the prayer, a patch of darkness rose up behind the palm where the young Arab rested. It lapped around the tree. A flash of silver in the moonlight. A sudden gasp of surprise and horror. A brief scrabble of boots in the dirt. And all was still again.

None of the sleepers had wakened.

The horse stiffened, scenting the blood. Valens leant a little of his weight against its neck.

'We must go,' Iudex whispered.

Valens found himself reluctant to leave the illusory security of his equine companion.

'Now.'

Together, they ghosted into the camp. Like the epiphany of some dark god, Zabda was suddenly in front of them.

They moved deeper into the encampment, down a narrow alleyway between two shelters. Drunken snoring came from either side. The smells of stale wine and rancid goat meat and unwashed men were heavy on the night air.

Suddenly a man spoke. The words were incomprehensible but loud and distinct.

Valens almost blundered into the back of Iudex.

The three men stood motionless. Valens's heart was beating so hard against his ribs that he was shaking.

The Arab muttered again, this time slurred and evidently half asleep.

They remained stock still, waiting for the nomad to fall back into a deep slumber.

Valens looked around with loathing. The tent-dwellers huddled two or three to a shelter. He could almost touch the pair to his right. They lay on their backs, unconscious, without a care. Valens wished he could cut their throats, wished he had enough men that he could cut all their throats. The surge of hatred caused not so much by their cruelty to the woman, as by his own terror.

Iudex touched his arm. They crept onwards.

As they passed one of the fires, Valens was surprised by its warmth on his face. He had not noticed the chill of the night.

A pot shard cracked under his boot. Again the three men froze. By the light of the low fire, the occasional tongues of flame, it looked like some macabre child's game.

Zabda gestured for them to continue.

Valens went slowly, keeping his eyes down, searching for other fragments of discarded and broken amphorae. He placed each foot carefully, the outside of his boot first, in a sweeping motion, feeling for debris, before committing his weight.

Looking up, he saw he was falling behind. A panic seized him that he would be left alone among these savages. Abandoning his caution, he rushed to catch up.

They came out in the small clearing where the woman was tethered to a tree. She was unmoving.

Zabda waved Iudex to keep watch one way, Valens the other, while he went to cut her bonds.

Valens was facing the camel lines. The ungainly-looking beasts regarded him with what appeared to be contempt. Their jaws worked ceaselessly as they chewed regurgitated food. Their stench was overpowering. No wonder horses unaccustomed to them were said to become unsettled, even unmanageable.

What was taking Zabda so long?

The moon had tracked far across the heavens since they set out.

Valens glanced over his shoulder.

Zabda had severed the thongs that held the woman. He had a hand over her mouth, and was talking low and urgently into her ear. Her eyes were wide and very white in the near darkness.

When he turned his head back around, against all expectation Valens saw the outline of a man just four or five paces to his front. Facing away from him, the nomad stretched and yawned. Gripping the scabbard in his left hand, Valens drew his sword with his right. The blade slid free with just a whisper. But it was enough.

The Arab turned, although slowly, and without undue alarm.

Valens hesitated to kill an unarmed man.

Their eyes met, and the tent-dweller started with surprise.

Still Valens could not bring himself to strike.

The Arab opened his mouth to shout.

Valens leapt forward, lunging with his sword.

The nomad yelled as he tried to twist away. The edge of the steel sliced across his half-turned back. The Arab staggered, doubled up with pain. Valens raised his weapon, brought it down in a clumsy two-handed chop, like an unskilled woodsman cutting logs. The impact jarred up through his forearms as the heavy blade bit into the back of the skull.

The camp was full of noise; the camels roaring with anxiety, men grunting and stirring, calling out questions.

Zabda pushed past Valens.

'You and Iudex hold them back.'

The Palmyrene half carried the woman between two shelters off to the south.

Iudex was at Valens's side. The big man bent to pluck a burning brand from the nearest fire.

'Stay with me,' Iudex said. 'Work together, keep our heads, and we will get out of this.'

They backed down the alleyway after Zabda.

Like a disturbed nest of vipers, the camp was stirring. Dark figures flitted here and there, gathered around the dead man. The camels bellowed and stamped.

Iudex swung the smouldering branch through the air. After three or four passes, it blazed fiercely. He ran it along the skin covering one of the shelters. The dry skin caught. In moments it crackled with little licks of flame.

Pounding feet warned them of the approach of the Arabs. Three of them, rushing down the alley.

Training took over, and Valens brought his sword up into a guard, but he could not drag his eyes away from the glittering tip of the Arab's spear. At the last moment, he leapt backwards, swatting ineffectually with his blade. The point of the spear missed. The nomad recovered his balance, and pulled back.

To his left, Valens saw Iudex step forward. With a practised economy of movement, the bald soldier flicked the spears of his two opponents aside, and stepped inside their reach.

Valens had no more time to watch. His assailant thrust again. This time he gave no ground. Balanced on the balls of his feet, he blocked the attack. The nomad's momentum brought him crashing into Valens. Locked together, they tottered a couple of steps. The rank stink of the man was choking. Fingers stiff, Valens drove his nails into the tent-dweller's bearded face. They missed the eyes, but raked the flesh. The nomad reared away, howling. With the strength of desperation, Valens thrust his sword into the man's stomach. A split second of resistance, then the steel slid in easier than into the carcass of a chicken.

The reek of hot blood and faeces filled the air.

Still holding the torch in one hand, Iudex was standing over his two victims.

'More coming,' Iudex said.

By the flickering light of the burning tent, they saw a throng of nomads filling the opening to the alleyway. It would be no time before they thought to work around the shelters, and take the two men from the rear.

'Give me the torch,' Valens said.

Wordlessly, Iudex handed it over.

Valens swished the brand until it flared again. He judged the distance, then, not pausing to think further, ran three or four steps forward. He hurled the torch overhand. It cartwheeled over the nearest tents, trailing sparks.

The throw was good. The torch landed amid the camels, hitting one on the flank as it fell. Maddened by pain and fear, the beast wrenched the peg that secured its tether from the ground. It blundered into the next in the line. At once all the camels were roaring and struggling, boring into each other. One went down. As it went to get up, its legs fouled those still on their feet.

Nothing was more precious to the nomads than their camels. Jabbering with concern, the crowd of men facing the two Romans rushed to their aid.

'Run,' Iudex said.

Holding his scabbard in his left hand to keep it from tangling in his legs, the hilt of his blade still grasped in his right, Valens ran. Terror gave wings to his feet. Even so, Iudex was drawing ahead.

The respite was temporary. All too soon, Valens heard the shouts of his pursuers.

He ran on, his breath torn, rasping from his throat, his lungs scorching.

It was no more than two hundred paces to the depression where Narses and the others waited. It might as well have been miles. There was no sight of them, or even of Zabda and the woman. Just the blue cloak of Iudex swirling in the expanse of the night.

The nomads were gaining. Their unearthly ululating cries echoing in the darkness.

Valens glanced back. They were but thirty paces behind.

The inattention was his undoing. Something caught his boot. Off balance, he ran another four or five steps before crashing to the ground.

His hands and forearms were grazed by the stony desert, his chin gashed, the sword cracked from his grip.

A yell of triumph, of hunters closing in on their prey.

Frantically, Valens grabbed the hilt, and was up and running, oblivious to the pain.

'Get down!'

The fall had knocked the wind out of him. He could not draw breath. He was not going to make it. The Arabs were right behind him.

'Get flat, you fool!' The shout was in Latin.

Valens dived to the earth.

Something whisked above his head.

He rolled, hilt clasped in sweating palm. The nomads were but ten paces distant.

But they had stopped. One of them was looking at his chest. With a look of utmost surprise, he regarded the fletchings of the arrow buried in his body. The others gazed at their companion. Then, like a bad actor on the stage, he toppled.

Three more shafts tore through the night. Two vanished into the dark. But another struck home. It took the tent-dweller in the throat. He was plucked backwards, as if yanked by a rope.

The remainder of the nomads – a dozen or more – hunched down. A couple of the bravest, or most foolhardy, edged towards the prone figure of Valens.

The next volley again yielded a single victim. An arrow hit a nomad in the shoulder. The blow was not fatal, but all the better for that. The injured man spun around, clutching the wound, and screamed in agony. Fear enters by the ears as much as the eyes.

At the ghastly sound of his suffering – a suffering inflicted by an unseen foe – the rest lost their nerve. As if heeding a command, they turned and fled, loose cloaks flapping.

The wounded nomad hobbled in their wake.

No one stopped to aid him. He had made half a dozen steps before three shafts thumped into his back.

CHAPTER 15

Adiabene

AT MIDDAY THERE WAS A COLUMN of dust in the distance on the northern horizon. It was tall and thin and rose straight in the air. Decimus said its shape showed it was raised by a column of mounted men moving fast, three, perhaps four miles away.

Reunited after the raid on the nomad camp, the soldiers had ridden through the remaining hours of darkness. The cool of the night, and the wind of their motion, acted as a tonic. They were in good spirits. They had eaten and drunk in the saddle. Valens was glad to be alive. If the gods had cared, he would have thanked them.

They had ridden on in the morning; in the greyness of predawn, through the long, canted shadows of sunrise, and into the heat of the day. By the fourth hour they came to a watering hole. The horses and mules were very tired, the men hardly less so, and they had halted.

Although hardened by the long journey since Zeugma, Valens was stiff and sore when they dismounted. The woman had ridden pillion, clinging on behind Zabda. The Palmyrene had had to lift her off the horse and place her upon the ground. Her clothes were ruined, and she had not yet spoken a word. Zabda hovered anxiously over her, his receding forehead turned this way and that, like some moulting hen bird, as he regarded her carefully from different angles. The other soldiers had gathered around, offering spare tunics and cloaks, a drink from a flask or a bite to eat. She had sat silent and withdrawn, ignoring their ministrations. There was a simplicity to the soldiers. Usually licentious, often brutal, and capable of terrible cruelty, yet if someone – usually a child or a woman – sparked their sympathy, their solicitude was infinite. After a time Valens had ordered them to their duties; the horses and mules would not see to themselves.

They had left the mules standing in line, the lead reins thrown on the ground. The head of the foremost mule was turned and secured to its pack to prevent it moving. The bell-mare was released from her traces, and led to water with the horses that had been ridden and the spare mounts. They were taken to the watering hole two at a time so they did not cause a commotion. After the horses had drunk, they were hobbled and unsaddled. They were given a little hay as the men brushed their backs and first checked their feet, then cleaned their eyes, nostrils and dock with a damp cloth. Finally, when they had cooled down, they were fed a mixture of oats and hay, and given a salt lick from the stores. After the horses, the mules were fed and watered. Their feet and legs and backs were examined, and their rigging adjusted, but they were not unloaded.

Clemens's horse had gone lame, and he joined Decimus and Valens in selecting a replacement from the remounts. That done, they had worked together to improvise a saddlecloth and tack so that the woman could ride the quietest of the remaining spare horses.

'Need to keep an eye on her,' Decimus said. 'A lot of women commit suicide after they have been raped.'

'How is she going to kill herself out here?' Clemens asked. 'She has not got a knife or anything.'

'Drown herself.'

'In that pond?'

'Throw herself off the horse.'

'Be lucky to die.'

'Wander off into the desert.'

'And risk the tent-dwellers catching her?'

'How should I know?' Decimus had sounded irritated at the intransigence of Clemens. 'The road to freedom is always open, so the philosophers say.'

'Lucretia killed herself,' Valens said. 'Her husband and family begged her not to, but she did.'

Everyone knew the story. Raped by the son of the last King of Rome, her suicide had been the catalyst for the overthrow of the monarchy. Her resolution had brought freedom to Rome, and left her name as a symbol of female courage.

'Like I said,' Decimus concluded, 'it is in their nature.'

The other men lit a fire and prepared a meal. They used the last of the fresh meat and a portion of the onions and peas they had bought in Nineveh to make a stew. The flatbread had gone stale, so some of the men heated it on sticks in the fire.

Valens had taken two bowls and a flask of watered wine over to where the woman sat in the shade of a palm tree. The sun was almost directly overhead.

She looked at the food and drink and him equally without interest.

'Eat,' he said.

Mechanically she had done as she was told. She was wearing a white tunic someone must have given her. It was unbelted. That was one road to freedom closed. No danger of her hanging or strangling herself.

'You speak Greek?'

She had nodded.

'What is your name?'

'Lucia, but I am also known as Al-zabba.'

'Where are you from?'

'Matiane.'

'And what brought you here to the desert?'

'Greed.' Her reply was flat.

'The dead man was your husband?'

She had said nothing.

'The other a slave?'

'I knew it was too dangerous, begged him not to.'

'Your husband was trading wine to the nomads?'

'He said they would pay high prices.'

'They have none of their own.'

'I told him they could not be trusted.' There was an edge of desperation in her voice, an echo of that futile argument. 'He would not believe that they would just take what they wanted.'

An old fable came into Valens's mind. 'The god Hermes was driving across the world in a chariot filled with lies, villainy and fraud. To every people he distributed a little of his cargo. In the desert the chariot broke, and the Arabs stole the remainder of the contents.'

She inclined her head sadly, as if he had done more than repeat a story his nurse had told him.

'Where will you go?'

She'd drawn a shuddering breath, mastered herself. 'Home to Matiane. If I can get there, if the gods relent. I have family there. If no one knows what has happened, our customs ensure that I will be given another husband.'

'It was not your fault.'

'That makes no difference. Would you marry a woman who had been defiled by the tent-dwellers?'

There had been nothing he could say.

'Sir.' Decimus approached. It was midday, and the pall of dust had been spotted to the north.

They saddled up quickly with the efficiency of long practice.

'How many Arabs were left in the camp?' Decimus asked.

Valens calculated. He and Iudex had both killed a pair, and Zabda had dealt with the sentry. The arrows of Narses had accounted for three more. 'No more than seventeen.'

'That cloud is raised by at least thirty.'

'Then it might not be them.'

'Or they have found some friends. These deserts are full of the bastards.'

'We will turn south-east. The mountains we have to cross are in that general direction. Sooner or later we should strike the river we need to follow. At Nineveh they said it ran down from the heights.'

There was no panic. For the first mile they went at a walk to let the animals warm up. As ever they then halted briefly to check the girths of their mounts and the rigging of the mules. After that they proceeded at a trot, the baggage animals ambling. They still made good ground, and their relatively gentle progress left less telltale dust behind them.

After another hour, at the next halt, it was evident the other riders had turned after them. The pursuing column of dust was appreciably closer, perhaps no more than a couple of miles to the rear.

Valens sat his horse, studying the sky, thinking.

'We should get going, ride hard.' Decimus said. 'The mules will not be able to keep up. We must abandon them.'

'Not yet,' Valens said. 'We have a head start. If we alter course south-west, and they turn after our tracks, then we can be certain that they are hunting us.'

'But that is away from the mountains.'

'If we continue south-east, we may reach the foothills before we find the river.'

Decimus looked dubious, but did not argue.

'Without the river to guide us up to the pass, we may be trapped against the mountain wall.'

Decimus gave a curt nod, and circled his horse back to his station.

Within half an hour they knew the worst. Again the hateful column of dust dogged them.

Valens raised his arm to halt the small column.

'Take from the baggage train whatever grain and water your horses can carry. Load some supplies onto the sound spare horses. We will leave the mules, and the lame horse.'

'Why leave the mules for the camel-fuckers?' Aulus said. 'We might as well slaughter them.'

'And the lame horse will recover,' Clemens said. 'I hate to think of a nomad riding him.'

'No,' Valens said firmly. 'They may be satisfied with their booty.'

'And they may not,' Hairan said glumly.

The provisions were speedily stowed on the horses. It would leave them short, but it was no time to worry about that.

'Now we ride due south. There are only some three hours of daylight left. They will never catch us before dark.' Valens spoke with far more certainty than he felt.

They did not set off at a mad gallop. That risked accidents, and would soon exhaust their mounts. Instead Valens kept them to a steady canter which ate up the miles.

For the first hour all went well. Valens reined in, and looked back. The Arabs would have been pushing their mounts for longer than the soldiers. Valens and his men were pulling away. But the column of dust was still following. The mules and what they still carried had not been enough to placate the vengeance of the tent-dwellers.

'Persistent, aren't they?' Valens muttered to no one in particular.

'The nomads live by blood feud,' Hairan said. 'We have killed seven of them, they are bound to kill seven of us.'

'Well, as long as I am the one left alive,' Clemens said in a rare moment of black humour.

'Give the horses a drink, and then we press on,' Valens said. 'Not long until darkness, and we must be getting near the river.'

The ground here was more rock than sand. The hooves rattled in the steady, almost soothing rhythm of a fast canter, the easiest gait for both horse and rider. The noise and the motion lulled Valens into something approaching a reverie. He had the odd impression that they were unmoving, that the sky wheeled overhead, and the desert raced away behind them. In this altered state, his thoughts moved unbidden to dark, unhappy things.

Interfectus a latronibus. You saw the inscriptions all over the empire: *Killed by bandits.* You passed without a thought. Until the victims were those you loved. There were many bandits in Italy. The Apennines were full of them. Many were barbarians, stragglers from the Alamannic invasion five years ago. Had they tortured his father before they killed him? Had they raped his mother before they killed her too?

Killed by bandits. He had set up the stone by the mountain road beside which the bodies had been found. They had lain there for some time. It had been impossible to judge how much they had suffered.

A harsh shout, and a break in the rhythm of the horses, brought him back. Valens pulled on his reins.

The woman had fallen. She was lying, groaning on the ground. Zabda and Clemens were already dismounted at her side.

'I can't go on,' she said. 'Don't let them take me again. Please, put me out of my misery.'

Zabda hushed her, and looked up at Valens. 'She is not badly hurt. She can ride with me.'

'Make sure to switch to a spare horse every half-hour,' Valens said. 'Otherwise the extra weight will slow you down.'

Clemens helped Zabda hoist her up in front of the saddle.

Valens gazed back the way they had travelled. The hard scrabble over which they had ridden raised little dust. There was no sign of pursuit. Something caught his eye. Something out of place in that elemental wasteland. He squinted in the late afternoon sun.

'What fool dropped a water bottle?' Valens rounded on his men in fury.

None avoided his eye. One or two spread their hands in a mime of innocence.

'Why leave a trail for them to follow?'

The anger died out of him. 'Just take more care,' he muttered. 'Check the horses, the saddlebags and stowage as well as the tack, before we move on.'

There was no further indication of pursuit before the light faded. But two more horses, those of Aulus and Decimus, went lame. It was not to be wondered at; the animals had been hard used. Neither was broken down, and both could still run on a lead. It did mean there was only one spare ridable horse left, and a further redistribution of their much diminished stores. After the column pulled out, Valens hung back with Hairan, and checked that nothing had been dropped or cast aside that could mark their sojourn.

After the sun had set, the water of the river still held a faint luminescence of the day. They had reached the Lykos, and the nomads had not caught them. The road to the pass was open before them. All they had to do was follow the river upstream.

The waters would cover their tracks. In the upper reaches they could find a local to take them over the watershed. It felt like a pivotal moment.

'How do we know this is the right river?' Aulus's question crushed Valens's temporary joy.

'What other river can it be?'

'Any number of streams must run down from the mountains to the Tigris.'

'The stars indicate we are at the right latitude.'

'The stars are malign,' Iudex said.

The woman walked up to where they stood. 'It is the Lykos.'

'How do you know?' Aulus asked gently. Like all the men, her suffering was on his mind.

'My husband and I followed it down from Matiane.'

Inwardly Valens cursed himself for a fool. How else could the ill-fated trader have crossed the mountains to meet his fate in the desert? Because she was a woman, it had not occurred to any of them to ask her advice.

'We have our guide,' he said.

The soldiers laughed, although Iudex put his thumb between his fingers to avert evil. In his religion women were as inherently evil as the stars.

'Can we take the horses up the riverbed?' Valens said.

'I do not know. We brought the wagon down the track alongside the river,' she said.

'Well, we will soon find out.'

The bottom of the stream was solid rock, but overlaid by a fine silt. The disturbed sediment bloomed up and streamed away from each step the horses took. It turned the waters milky white in the moonlight.

Again Valens waited behind with Hairan. They stood on the bank watching the surface of the river. The stream was fast. Soon all evidence of the rest of the horsemen had vanished.

They swung into their saddles, and splashed into the stream. The water was shallow, only occasionally reaching the fetlocks of the horses. Valens restrained himself from singing. There was no way the tent-dwellers could track them now.

CHAPTER 16

Adiabene

Two days in the saddle separated by a sleepless night had left them bone tired. For two hours they rode up the bed of the river. Their progress was slow, and it was hard to judge how many miles they had covered. Eventually, when they had climbed onto the bank, at least a third of the night had gone.

The land lifted here, and they could sense the solid mass of the mountains ahead. They made camp in a dry wash that ran down to the river. The depression shielded them from view, and there were no trees on its slopes, but from weariness as much as caution they did not light a fire. They were chilled and their clothes were wet as they saw to their mounts and ate their rations cold. Yet sentries had to be set. Each pair would stand guard for two hours. Although exhausted, he had volunteered for the first watch. He needed time to think.

Valens had earned his grudging respect. The young officer had faced down the mutiny after the death of Severus. He had imposed his will in going after the girl. During the rescue, Valens had played his part with courage, and had overseen the retreat with brisk efficiency. The callow youth of Zeugma had been toughened by the tribulations of the hard journey. He even looked different. He was leaner, stood taller, and moved with the growing assurance of command.

Murena had said that Valens was a broken reed. Young and inexperienced, he had turned to drink after the murder of his parents. There was no doubt that Valens would snap under pressure. Murena had been wrong. For all his experience and cunning, for all the information and contacts at his disposal, Murena was a bad judge of character. How could it be otherwise? The commander of the *frumentarii* lived in a world of lies and suspicion. No disinterested informant ever came forward. Every one denounced others, hoping to be rewarded. The soldiers themselves existed to uncover treachery – and found it wherever they looked. Innocuous conversations and letters were twisted to reveal malign intent. Immersed in a climate of untruth, all thoughts became tainted. Innocence was seen as stupidity, virtue as a condemnation of those in authority.

He had come to detest Murena, loathe the profession in which he himself served. Like a tide of filth, it undermined the foundations of anything good in his character. And now it threatened the only part of his life that had remained inviolate.

Marriage had come belatedly for him. At most weddings the man was in his late twenties, the girl fourteen or fifteen. His bride had been a little older, just turned nineteen. But he had been approaching forty. The days when it was illegal for a soldier to marry had long gone. Yet previously the demands of his service somehow had precluded thoughts of matrimony, and, of course, he had not met the right woman.

Tullia was the daughter of a vintner. The family poor, but respectable. Her father's trade had been their introduction. He had been buying wine – a moderately astringent Sabine white, good for the pain he was beginning to feel in his joints – and she had been helping in the shop. Their courtship had been unhurried and formal. That he was a soldier was obvious, but, to avoid alarming her family, he had given out merely that he was in Rome on detached duty from his legion. After their marriage he had been happy to rent an apartment close to her father's business in the Subura. Of course, some of its streets were unsafe after dark, but it was foolish to venture down many streets in Rome at night. Tullia brought him joy, and had given him a daughter.

To begin with, Murena's threats had been indirect. At the meeting in that cramped, dusty office he had listened with mounting apprehension as Murena had revealed his knowledge of his family: their names and ages, Tullia's relatives, their occupations, where they lived, and the state of their finances. If he undertook this mission, saw it through to success, he would be lavishly rewarded. The family would be financially secure for the next generation. Of course if he refused, things would be different. He had watched in horror as Murena had got out the account books of the camp. The evidence could not be argued away. His career would be over, and Tullia's family ruined.

After he had accepted the mission, and been told what it entailed, Murena was less subtle. Should he either fail or betray his orders, he would be classed as a traitor. The family of a man convicted of *maiestas* were also held to be guilty of treason. The implications of that did not need spelling out.

He huddled his cloak around himself. His boots and trousers were still clammy. A chill wind had got up in the west. It was cold sitting here just below the skyline.

There had been no way out, nothing for it but to betray his comrades. Unlike the bandits, the Arabs had been purely fortuitous. If the raid on their encampment had gone wrong, it could have been the end of the expedition. He had trusted in his horse and his skill at arms to get him clear of the disaster. Last-stand heroics did not feature in his thinking. There was money in his belt, and he spoke

Aramaic. It was not far back to the Tigris. Get across Mesopotamia and he would be back in the empire.

Against the odds, they had all got away unscathed. Once the nomads were on their trail, he had dropped a couple of bits of equipment to mark their route. In retrospect he was glad that Valens had seen the water bottle and had taken the rear, which had prevented him leaving any further signs. Drawing the tent-dwellers down on them might have fulfilled his orders, but what use was that if he himself did not survive?

Now the Arabs were left behind, some new scheme was necessary. What would happen should Valens meet with some misfortune? There was no formal second in command. All of the men thought the whole venture ill-advised. Several openly wished to abandon the mission. With Valens gone, most likely there would be much heated debate, and then the expedition would break up in acrimony. Once separated, it might be possible to ensure that few, if any, of its number made it back to Zeugma.

Someone was scrambling up from the dry watercourse. His watch was over. The hours had passed quickly. He rose, grunting with the effort, and tried to stretch some of the ache out of his muscles and arthritic joints. *Hercules's hairy arse, I'm tired.*

'*Libertas*,' he gave the challenge.

'*Pietas*,' came the response.

As if called by his evil imaginings, Valens walked up the incline.

The sentry felt the hilt in his hand. A couple of rapid movements and the unsuspecting young officer would be dead. There would be no outcry. All finished in a moment.

Not now. He forced himself to relax, release the hold on his weapon. The river was not deep enough to bear away the body. Anyway, the disappearance could not be explained.

'Don't move!' Valens hissed.

Guiltily, his hand moved back to the hilt.

'Quiet!' Valens's head was tipped to one side. 'Hear that?'

The sentry cocked his head, straining to listen. At first there was nothing but the wind singing in his ears. Then he heard a faint sound carried on the breeze. Deep in his reflections, he had not heard it before.

They both stood, as if turned to stone.

It came again. A snatch of guttural conversation.

'The Arabs,' said Valens.

CHAPTER 17

Adiabene

THE CANYON WAS A DEAD END. If the nomads had followed their tracks, and had seen the discreet signs he had left, when they arrived they would know that the Romans were trapped.

The slopes were no more than forty foot at their highest. They were not so steep that an active man could not scale them with care. But the climber, exposed on the rock face, would be an easy target for an archer. For a man on horseback there was only one way in and out. Some forty paces wide at its entrance, the canyon narrowed to just ten paces towards the far end, where a landslide had fallen from one of the walls. Apart from the jumble of rocks, the floor of the canyon was bare of any cover.

The Romans had corralled their animals behind the ramp of tumbled rocks, but their camp was in front, out in the open, unprotected by the terrain. No sentry had been posted at the entrance to the canyon. Valens had issued the instructions. The arrangement was not ideal – obviously it would have been far better had there been some other way out – but it suited his intentions.

When they had realised that the tent-dwellers were still on their trail, they had moved out quietly, and without fuss. They had ridden through that night, and on into the next afternoon. Daylight had revealed the jagged peaks of the Taurus Mountains ranged ahead, until the foothills closed in on the river valley, and blocked the view. The following day Valens had discarded the first piece of equipment to draw the Arabs after them, and sent Hairan in advance to find the sort of position the Romans now occupied.

There was nothing to do but wait. It would be dawn in an hour or two. Valens sat partly concealed by a boulder from the landslide. Shutting one eye, so as to not ruin his night vision, he squinted at the campfire. By its light he could see the huddled shapes wrapped in cloaks, the glint of metal helmets laid aside, little piles of gear and baggage: a defenceless encampment of the exhausted and unsuspecting.

When he had explained his plan, the men had raised no objections. The nomads were not going to give up. Most likely the Arabs were travelling light, and had spare mounts. The Romans could not outrun them. Something else was necessary.

The woman Lucia had asked for a knife. If things went wrong, evidently she had no intention of falling into the hands of the tent-dwellers again. Valens had dithered. Part of his uncertainty stemmed from not having a spare knife. If he lost his sword, selfishly he had no wish to find himself unarmed. And it was a terrible thing that she asked. The decision was taken from him by Zabda. The Palmyrene had produced a blade hidden in his boot. With a courtly bow of his balding head, he had handed it over, hilt first. Since the rescue he had remained close to Lucia, often talking to her reassuringly in Aramaic. The solicitude was unexpected given his normal behaviour.

Valens glanced back to where Lucia was resting by the corral. Surely sleep would be out of the question. The rockfall hid her from view. Decimus was down there too. Certainly the horse master would not be sleeping. The animals were saddled and ready, their tethered reins close to Decimus's grasp. Speed in mounting was essential. Everything would depend on timing.

Peering among the boulders around him, Valens could just make out Iudex, sitting cross-legged, his arms stiffly down at his sides. Valens could not see if his eyes were open. Perhaps he was meditating, or communing with his strange god. More than once Iudex had claimed that his spirit could leave his body, could range far and wide across the world, had even journeyed to the underworld. Possessed of such abilities, it was disappointing that Iudex had been unable to discern just how close behind the nomads had been.

Clemens and Zabda were a little further off, and completely hidden among the rocks. Valens had chosen who was to stay with care. The armourer Clemens was said to be the finest swordsman in the party. Iudex and Zabda had shown their metal in the raid. Decimus was necessary for the horses.

Well before last light, Aulus had led Narses and Hairan away. A trained hunter, brought up in the central highlands of Gaul, Aulus was accustomed to mountains. On his skills, and those of the two easterners, rested the survival of those in the canyon.

Were the stars fading? Valens wanted this night to end. The waiting was hard. He shivered. Without his cloak, he was cold. But he knew he was shivering with fear. With numb fingers, he fumbled a piece of dried meat from the pouch on his belt. To prevent his teeth chattering, he put it in his mouth, and chewed mechanically. For the umpteenth time, he obsessively ran his hands over his weapons.

In his mind's eye he saw the wicked glitter of Zabda's knife as he presented it to Lucia. Not many women killed themselves with a blade. Like slaves, they tended to use poison, or hang themselves. One summer, when Valens had been a child at the family villa on the Bay of Naples, a slave girl had drowned herself in the well. His mother had been upset, and not just by the loss of her property. She had been fond of the girl. The reaction of his father had been anger. He had fulminated against her selfishness. It would be an age before water could be drawn from the well. The foolish superstitions of the other slaves would make them reluctant ever to use it again. He had insisted repeatedly that the girl could have had no reason for the act, no reason whatsoever.

After the murder of his parents, the thought of taking his own life had occurred to Valens in the depths of his misery. Insane sects like the Christians might claim that pre-empting the will of the gods was a sin, but there were many sound Roman precedents. In the old days of the free republic falling on one's sword had been honourable. Facing defeat, rather than endure the shame of being taken prisoner, many a soldier had turned his blade on himself. His initial attempt foiled by his friends, Cato the Younger had ripped out the stitches binding his wounds, and with bare hands had torn out his own innards. Even such agony had been better than the shame of being executed by Caesar, or, much worse, enduring the ignominy of being pardoned.

The rule of the Emperors had raised the rituals of self-inflicted death to the status of a cult. A condemned man invited his friends to a meal. Over the food he calmly discussed weighty and relevant issues, such as the immortality of the soul. After taking leave of his companions, with the same composed and cheerful demeanour, he retired to a bath. There a slave opened his veins. The steam and warm water were said to lessen the pain. Some would order the incisions temporarily bound up, so that they could dictate a short work of improving philosophy, before their lifeblood drained away.

Of course, such deaths were done for the family. If a man pre-empted trial and conviction, it was possible that the Emperor would not confiscate his estate. If you took your own life, your wife and children might not be reduced to destitution, might not be judged implicated in your real or imagined treason.

After he lost his parents, Valens had tried to fortify himself with the principles of Epicurus. If suffering overwhelmed the pleasure of life, it was logical and right to end the misery of existence. But the philosophy had not taken deep root in Valens's soul, and he had come to acknowledge that self-pity was not the same as true pain. There was an irony in looking back. Then he had wanted to kill himself, now he was terrified to die.

The stars were paling, the sky lightening. It should not be long.

What waited after the coin was placed in the dead jaws, after the earth was sprinkled on the corpse, or beyond the flames of the pyre? An eternity of regret, of envy of the living? Perhaps best if the Epicureans were correct, if at last all returned to sleep and quiet.

Something alerted Valens. He saw and heard nothing, but he detected a presence at the mouth of the canyon. He sniffed the air like an animal, but smelt nothing. Despite the chill, he was sweating.

Valens looked over at Iudex. The great domed hairless head had not moved. If his spirit-twin was roaming, it had better return fast.

The blue of the sky was assuming a delicate pink hue. The sun would rise soon. There were no clouds, and not a breath of wind.

A small movement by the cliff at the opening of the ravine, half glimpsed then gone.

They were here.

Let us be men, Valens said to himself.

It had taken no great foresight to judge that the nomads would attack just before dawn, when most men were deeply asleep. *Conticinium*, the time when birds and animals woke, but men still slumbered. If men were awake, they were at their lowest ebb in mind and body. It was the best time to fall on your enemy, perhaps take him unaware.

If it was a scout that Valens had glimpsed, he would have gone back to report. Valens imagined their low and urgent deliberations. All the gods, let them make their move soon.

The sky was getting lighter by the moment, visibility increasing.

If they decided to besiege the Romans in the canyon . . . No, they would not do that. The tent-dwellers lacked the patience and the stamina. One quick rush was the limit of their tactics. Survive that and their courage drained away. Everyone knew that they had no discipline, would not stand close to the steel for long. *Dear gods, let that be true.*

Valens heard them before he saw them. A muted rumble of hooves on the hard ground.

His fingers were clumsy with apprehension as he untied the laces of his bow case. As he fumbled, part of him cursed his caution. Yet the damp of the night air might have loosened the string of his bow had it not been protected. At last the weapon came free. The smooth leather of the grip calmed him a fraction. Opening his quiver, he selected and nocked an arrow.

The noise swelled, echoing back off the walls.

The first rays of the sun struck the western lip of the cliff.

Down in the lingering gloom, a murky shape flowed into the entrance to the canyon a couple of hundred paces from where he waited.

Valens got into position, half screened by the boulders.

They were coming fast. In the gathering light, individual riders emerged from the dark mass; men on horses, taller figures on camels. Thirty, perhaps forty of them, too many to count.

Valens part drew his bow.

A hundred paces. The thunder of their coming filled the canyon.

Surely now they must notice the lack of movement in the camp.

Valens's left arm was trembling with the strain. Everything in his being screamed to shoot, to get this over. He did not move.

Fifty paces out, the nomads yelled their war cry. The ululating and unearthly sound was terrifying. Valens fought the urge to turn and run. Scrambling up the rocks offered no safety, only certain death. A coward dies a thousand times, a brave man only once.

The tent-dwellers swept into the camp. Long lances stabbed down at the humped shapes in cloaks. When they failed to bite into flesh, the Arabs finally realised the deception. They had been duped into slaughtering rocks and sacks masked by cloaks into the forms of sleeping men. Their war cry died to be replaced by a jabber of angry and alarmed shouts. The nomads were hauling on their reins. Horses and camels milled in confusion.

From high above came the call of a hunting horn.

The bearded faces of the tent-dwellers looked up.

The first arrow from the heights took one of them in the shoulder. He reeled, clutching the wound. An incredible shot into the shadowed ravine. It could only be Narses. More shafts hissed down. A horse reared as it was hit. Spear discarded, desperately its rider clung to its mane.

'Now!'

Iudex loosed as he shouted. His arrow plucked a rider to the floor.

Like creatures from the underworld, Clemens and Zabda rose from concealment. While their bows still twanged, they reached for another shaft.

For a moment Valens watched, as if at the arena, a spectator detached from his surroundings.

Two more tent-dwellers howled in pain.

The ache in his arms brought Valens back. He drew his bow, fingers back by his ear, tracked a nomad, and shot. The arrow missed. Automatically his fingers found the fletchings of another. This time the arrowhead punched into the haunches of a horse. It screamed as it spun around. Its rider lost his seat, went crashing to the earth.

Without thought Valens sent arrow after arrow into the wheeling mass.

Recovering from the shock, the tent-dwellers were dropping their unwieldy lances, and yanking their own bows from where they hung over their shoulders. Some may be down, but they were still ready to fight. Although the Romans were in cover, and had the advantage in being on foot to aim, they remained outnumbered by at least four to one. They would lose any prolonged exchange. The first surprise had not broken the Arabs. A more drastic gamble was needed to drive them from the field.

Valens felt a near-compelling reluctance to quit the shelter of the rockslide.

Let us be men. It was all or nothing.

'Horses!'

Letting his bow fall, Valens turned and scrabbled back over the natural barrier. The sharp rocks grazed his hands and arms, tore at his legs.

Decimus was mounted, with difficulty holding the reins of the other four horses. Agitated by the din of battle, the sounds of their own kind in pain, the animals sidled and showed the whites of their eyes.

Valens hurled himself into the saddle. His mount tossed its head, fighting against the bit.

Freed from managing the led horses, Decimus was cutting the ropes of the corral.

'Close up!' Valens unhooked his shield from one of the saddle horns, drew his sword.

Zabda came knee to knee one side, Iudex the other.

Clemens went to form the tip of the wedge with Decimus.

'Hit them as one.'

It had to be now. Any hesitation and the nomads would get over the confusion of the ambush.

They clattered around the end of the landslip at a canter.

Hades, there were a lot of the enemy.

Decimus pushed into a gallop.

There were many tent-dwellers, but they were in no order.

The Romans smashed into their ranks like a stone from a siege engine.

At the heart of the wedge, Valens followed Decimus's armoured back, Iudex and Zabda on either flank. Then, without warning, the formation was dispersed, and he was alone.

A nomad thrust from his left with a knife. Valens just got the edge of his shield in the way. A splinter of wood stung his cheek. The motion of his mount took him clear.

Another Arab struck from the right. This one had a sword. Too slow, Valens parried. The tip of the blade skidded over his mailed chest. Links of mail snapped. Only the four horns of the saddle gripping his thighs kept Valens on his horse. Instinctively, without looking, he slashed backhanded. A satisfying impact ran up his arm. A howl of agony rang loud in his ears.

A tent-dweller on a camel blocked his way. Valens kicked the heels of his boots into the sides of his mount. It leapt forward. But a moment before impact, the camel threw up its great, ugly head and roared. Unnerved by the alien beast, Valens's horse refused. Shying violently, it tripped over its own legs, fouled. Fighting for balance, the horse stumbled a few steps, but it was going to fall.

Releasing sword and shield, Valens grabbed the two front saddle horns, levering himself up. As the horse went down, he jumped clear. The earth rushed up at him. He landed hard, face down. For a terrible moment he thought the horse would crush him. The wind knocked out of him, he felt the enormous weight of the beast thump down right beside him.

As the horse thrashed trying to regain its feet, Valens fought to get up, to drag breath back into his lungs. A hoof caught him in the side, it smashed him sideways and back down. Chest and ribs searing with pain, Valens got to his knees, tugged out his dagger.

With a lurch, the horse was up. Before Valens could grab the reins, it was gone. The Arab, impossibly high on the camel, towered above him, drawing his bow.

Somehow Valens forced himself upright.

The nomad aimed at his chest. Mail would not stop an arrow at twenty paces. Valens was unshielded. There was no cover in reach. Hopelessly, he began to shuffle forward, dagger in hand. The tent-dweller was too far away.

His assailant smiled. Steadied his arm, focused on his target.

Die on your feet, like a soldier. Wracked with pain, Valens put one foot in front of the other. He would never make it.

A blur of movement in the periphery of his vision.

Intent on his prey, the Arab saw nothing.

A flash of steel. A spray of bright blood. The nomad stared with amazement at the fountaining stump where his left arm had been.

Another neat blow, and Zabda cut the Arab from his mount. Braying, the camel padded away as Zabda reined to a halt. But another nomad loomed behind the Palmyrene, with a lance still in hand.

As Zabda grinned and saluted, Valens opened his mouth to shout a warning. But with no air in his lungs, he could make no sound. He pointed wildly.

Zabda started to turn. The tip of the lance speared into his back. Valens ran to the Palmyrene's aid, all pain forgotten. The force of the blow had driven the lance deep into Zabda's body. As the Arab tried to recover his weapon, the two horses circled in a macabre dance. Held by the saddle, Zabda's body jerked as his killer wrenched at the lance.

Plunging his dagger into the nomad's thigh with his right hand, Valens seized his cloak with his left. Throwing himself backwards, he used his weight to haul the man from his mount. The wounded Arab landed on top of him. Valens rolled out from underneath. His fist found a stone. The tent-dweller shouted something, perhaps a plea for mercy. Valens smashed the stone into the man's face. Through broken teeth, the nomad shouted again. After a time he merely made incoherent noises, then fell silent as Valens beat him to death.

A shadow fell across Valens. The sun must be high in the sky. Numbly, he straightened up. His hands and arms were red with blood. He was unarmed, but beyond fear or hope.

'They have had enough,' Iudex said.

Valens looked around, as if observing events that had little bearing on himself.

It was true. Having dropped their lances at the onset of the ambush, the half-naked tent-dwellers, for all their advantage in numbers, had lost the will to continue to face the swords and unbridled ferocity of the armoured and trained Roman soldiers. Some riding two to a mount, they streamed back down the canyon.

'At least a dozen of them are dead.' Iudex's face was seraphic with pleasure. 'Clemens and Decimus are finishing off their wounded. Both have slight cuts, but we have only lost Zabda.'

Valens gazed around until he saw the Palmyrene.

'The tent-dwellers will not return today, probably never. Blood feud will only drive them so far.' Iudex spoke slowly, as if to an infant. 'But we should not tarry.'

Valens knew Iudex was right. There was so much to be done.

'Get me a horse,' Valens said.

While Iudex did that, Valens went among the carnage to find his weapons and shield. Slowly, he managed to gather his thoughts.

He was ready when Iudex returned.

'Signal Narses and the others to come down from the heights. Clemens can make sure there are no survivors. Send Decimus back for the woman and the other horses. Round up the spare horses, put Zabda over one – we will bury him when we are clear of this place – then meet me at the mouth of the canyon.'

Without waiting for an answer, Valens mounted and rode away.

CHAPTER 18

Matiane

THE VILLAGE THAT WAS HOME TO AL-ZABBA, the woman also known as Lucia, was not large, but obviously prosperous enough. Although remote in its upland valley high in the Taurus Mountains, there was a good road. From springs at the base of the nearest cliff, ice-cold water bubbled forth to irrigate fields of grain, and gardens growing pears, apples, plums and apricots. On the higher slopes, above the springs, were extensive vineyards. Higher still were lush meadows for pasturage and forests of poplar and walnut well stocked with game.

The house in which the feast was held was built of stone. Its main room was tall and cool. They sat in a circle, cross-legged on rugs and cushions. Lucia had warned the Romans that it was ill-mannered to point the soles of your feet at another guest.

From Valens's left Lucia translated the conversation of the guest to his right. The farmer was waxing lyrical about the hardiness of the black grapes. Apparently they lay buried under deep snow in the winter, and flourished in the hot dry summer without any watering whatsoever. Certainly the wine they produced was sweet and strong.

They were eating lamb and chicken with flatbread and salad. A musician was playing a stringed instrument a bit like a lyre. Serving girls kept their cups filled, and the cook – his mouth ostentatiously covered, so as not to breathe on the food – made sure their plates were never empty.

The Romans had been well received. There had been mourning for Lucia's murdered husband, but the Romans had been praised both for taking vengeance against the tent-dwellers, and returning his widow unviolated. Hairan and the other Aramaic speakers had given an edited version of her rescue, which – praise the gods! – it was said had been carried out before the nomads could defile her. A compound had been allocated to the Romans, and this feast in the house of the village headman was in their honour.

Unaccustomed to the cross-legged posture, Valens's legs were beginning to ache. His loquacious fellow diner moved on to describing in great detail how the lamb was rubbed with a sour and bitter gruel and thickened buttermilk, and how the best-tasting chicken had to be fed on hemp seed and olive oil and made to run. While nodding attentively, Valens's thoughts began to roam.

It was ten days since they'd left the canyon. There had been no more sight of the tent-dwellers. Presumably their casualties had cooled their commitment to the demands of blood feud. At the end of the first day the Romans had come to a hamlet in the foothills. There they had buried Zabda, and bought all the provisions available. Even so, they had been on short rations for the next couple of days until they reached a more substantial settlement. By then they were high in the mountains.

They had forded fast-flowing mountain streams, moved through the gloom of deep ravines, and edged along tracks that clung to the sides of vertiginous precipices. When there was a fork in the path, Lucia had guided them unerringly. For several days she had led them almost due south, away from their destination, before turning up yet another river valley to the north-east. They had met a few travellers, and the occasional shepherd and charcoal burner. But without the woman they could have wandered for months in that rocky fastness.

Now they had reached her home, and here she would stay. Valens had instructed Hairan to hire a guide from the headman for their onward journey through the remaining mountains, and down to the territory of the Mardoi and the southern shores of the Caspian Sea. There were merchants in the village who had travelled the route. The expedition had plenty of money in Persian coins, and Hairan was amiable in all the many languages in which he was fluent. Valens did not think that the request should prove a problem.

The diners fell silent, even Valens's talkative neighbour, when the musician began to sing a high plaintive song. Unable to understand a word, Valens looked at Hairan and the headman. The two were flanked by the local Zoroastrian priest and a huge bear of a man, who seemed to be the chief of the headman's guard. The leading man of the village kept a numerous body of armed retainers. Despite its idyllic setting, this was still the wild uplands, where every man carried a weapon and had to look to his own protection.

Although still hundreds of miles from their goal, the expedition had done well to get this far. Through all their tribulations only three men had been lost: Severus, Quintus and Zabda. The ten men had become seven. Courage and ingenuity, and a large measure of luck, had ensured their escape from the nomads. For the moment they were safe. While they were fierce, even savage, hospitality was said to be the main virtue of those who lived in these mountains.

Yet some nagging doubt lurked in the dark corners of Valens's thoughts. So many bad things had dogged their steps: the bandits, the dust storm, the tent-dwellers. Of course, he had brought the last down on their heads. Unless you believed in magic, and Valens did not, the storm was just chance. But the more he considered them, the bandits were different. In the Greek novels he had read, the brigands often chose their victims with care. They did not just wait for whoever came along. In one of the stories, an accomplice in the town informed the outlaws who was setting out on a journey. Was it *Chaereas and Callirhoe* or *Leucippe and Clitophon*? In his memory they had all merged into one over the years. The column had hardly left Zeugma before the bandits struck. That could well be chance. But something Quintus had said afterwards had stuck in Valens's mind. It was their behaviour. They had not gone for the rich pickings of the mule train, but attacked the armed men and killed Severus. In retrospect, the killing of the commanding officer seemed almost as if it were deliberate.

And later, in Adiabene, there was the matter of the water bottle dropped in the flight to the River Lykos. It had given Valens the idea to lead the tent-dwellers into the ambush. At the time he had been angry, put the discarded item down to carelessness. But had someone before himself been leaving a trail for their pursuers?

Yet why would anyone in the expedition seek to betray them? Of course all, except himself, were *frumentarii*. They lived in a world of treachery. If there was a traitor, who could it be? Zabda would have been his main suspect. The Palmyrene was a thief, mistrusted by the others, especially by Hairan. Before they had set out, Zabda had drawn a knife on Valens in that bar. But Zabda had given his life to save him.

Nothing had gone wrong since the canyon. Perhaps the traitor was biding his time.

The singer ended, the audience applauded quietly, and the serving girls brought in the sweetmeats.

Perhaps there was no malign hand at the heart of the column. Bad things just happened. Most likely it was all a figment of his own imagination.

As the gourmet on his right was addressing himself to the pastries with a zeal that precluded conversation, Valens turned to make himself agreeable to Lucia. She encouraged him to take a delicacy flavoured with apple juice, honey and cardamom.

'You must be relieved to be back at home,' he said.

She smiled, although without much conviction.

'And your late husband's brother will take you as his wife.'

'Yes.' The smile faded.

'It is not our custom in Rome, but each people have their own.'

She did not reply, but it did not take a physiognomist, or some other expert in the human psyche, to see she was less than delighted.

'The family are not poor. You will have a good home.'

She looked scornful. 'Our customs require that three times a day a wife kneels before her husband and asks him what is his wish, and how she can make him happy.'

She spoke with such bitterness that Valens glanced at their neighbours.

'Only the merchants in the village speak Greek,' she said. 'These are farmers.'

'Among us a woman is subject to the authority of her husband,' Valens said. 'Some say the greatest praise of a woman is that she is never mentioned.'

'Among you, a husband does not lend his wife to the beds of any he chooses.'

Valens had no answer to that.

'The priests preach that if the god Mazda had been able to find any other creature to bear children, he would not have created women.'

Again Valens was silent.

Lucia took a deep breath. Obviously she was preparing to change the conversation. She smiled again.

Until this moment Valens had never really looked at her. On the journey there had never been time. He had been too tired, there had been too much to be done. If anything, she had been a self-inflicted encumbrance. Now he saw her as if for the first time.

She was not beautiful. Her nose and face were too long, her black hair, parted in the centre and dragged back behind her ears, was too flat and without lustre. But there was a knowing intelligence in her dark eyes, and her mouth hinted at a hitherto unnoticed playfulness and sensuality.

Aware of his appraisal, she was unflustered, and spoke as if she had read his thoughts. 'The priests give many instructions to men concerning a wife. Her stature must be neither too tall, or too short, her head and neck well formed, her fingers long, and her waist slender. They go into great detail. Her limbs must be soft and smooth, her buttocks rounded, her breasts like quinces, and her body milky white to her toes.'

Valens knew she was teasing him, but could think of nothing to say.

'Even her pillow talk is regulated. In bed she must have good words for her husband, but never talk shamefully.'

Valens took another pastry to avoid answering.

'My late husband was an avaricious fool. Obviously he lacked religion, as he enjoyed shameful talk.'

As if summoned to rescue Valens from this unexpected flirtation, Hairan came over.

'We need to talk,' Hairan said.

'Lucia can be trusted.'

Hairan flicked a glance at those sitting nearby.

'They have no Greek,' Lucia reassured him.

Only partly mollified, Hairan spoke quietly. 'The headman says that no villager will act as our guide. They are scared to venture away from the settlement alone. It is the fault of a djinn.'

'A djinn?' Valens said.

'A malevolent spirit, like a daemon. Several locals have vanished. The djinn took them.'

Valens grinned. 'Really?'

'It is not a laughing matter.' The Hatrene looked shocked. 'My uncle encountered one out in the desert, south of Singara. Only just got away alive.'

'For the sake of all the gods, you do not believe this stuff?'

Lucia broke in. 'Listen to Hairan. The disappearances had begun before I left with my husband for Adiabene. A labourer in the top meadows and a boy herding goats in the woods both vanished. The lair of the djinn is in the caverns up beyond the treeline.'

Was there no end to superstition? 'If we go up and scour these caves, will it give one of the villagers the courage to come with us as a guide?'

'We cannot all go,' Hairan said.

'Why not?'

'The djinn is a shape-shifter, like an *empusa*. It can transform itself into an animal or bird. We will not find it.'

'These are stories to frighten children.'

Hairan ignored the interruption. 'The djinn never appears if there are more than two men.'

This was ridiculous. 'Then tomorrow I will take just one man with me to chase away your djinn, or *empusa*.'

CHAPTER 19

Matiane

THEY RODE UP ACROSS THE MEADOWS and through the dappled shadows under the walnut trees and the poplars. It was one of those glorious mornings as summer began to turn to autumn. The sun shone from an almost cloudless sky, and a warm breeze whispered through the trees.

Despite the beautiful weather, Valens's head was thick with the fumes of the wine he had drunk the night before. The slave girl he had taken to bed – the headman was a generous host – had seemed distressed when he left. Like the rest of the village, most likely she did not expect him to return. How could people be such fools? Still, the exercise would dispel his hangover. And when he came down from the mountain unharmed, the locals would have no excuse not to furnish them with a guide.

As they came out of the trees, the sun was hot on his shoulders and back. Hairan had tried to persuade him to wear armour. Valens had pointed out that climbing a cliff in a mailcoat would put him in more danger than some imaginary *empusa* or djinn.

They halted at the foot of the rock face. The horses could go no further. Dismounting, Valens handed his reins to Iudex. Valens would go on with Aulus. The others would stay here with the horses, their mounts loaded with food and drink. Although he subscribed to the reality of the daemon, Hairan had suggested they bring a slave girl or two to help pass the time. In the daylight, even he did not seem to be taking the threat with any great earnestness. However, none of the girls had been willing to accompany them. And there was a limit to hospitality – the headman had not ordered them.

An experienced mountaineer, Aulus had been the obvious choice for the expedition. Valens had a good head for heights, but the Gaul might be an aid if the climb was difficult. They had brought ropes and metal spikes to act as pitons. They coiled the former over their shoulders, and secured the latter, along with a torch each, on their sword belts. The long swords themselves would have been an encumbrance, but it was unwise to be entirely unarmed. They kept their daggers. This high in the mountains there was always the chance of encountering a leopard or bear.

'Shout if you see an *empusa*,' Clemens said. 'They do not like loud noises. Philostratus recorded that was how the holy man Apollonius of Tyana scared one away.'

'The *Life of Apollonius* is fiction,' Valens said. 'At one dinner the utensils and serving dishes start moving by themselves.'

'This is a fool's errand,' Iudex said.

At least, Valens thought, *one of the men does not share the general superstition.*

'There is no *empusa* here.' Iudex said with complete certainty. 'Last night, while you all squandered the divine light in your semen on slave girls, my spirit-twin searched the whole mountain. It found nothing.'

Gods below, Iudex was the worst of the lot.

At first the ascent was easy. They were able to step around more of the large boulders that had fallen from above than they had to clamber over. When the rock under their feet was not solid, the scree was bound together by tough mountain grass. Aulus set a fast pace for a man who must have been in his forties, probably approaching retirement from the army. Soon, Valens was sweating and blowing hard.

When they came to the steeper slopes, Aulus called a halt and sat down. He regarded Valens with his rheumy eyes, a smile on his ill-favoured face.

'Tired yourself out with that serving girl,' he said.

Valens shrugged. 'Only inclination held you back.'

Aulus nodded, accepting the truth of the statement. 'It is strange. Among us no one thinks the worse of a man for enjoying a slave boy. No harm done, no one gets hurt. But these Persians call it an unnatural lust or sinful copulation. Their laws are harsh: a whipping or death. Apparently, in their underworld, such sinners are punished with snakes crawling up their arses and out of their mouths. Not a pleasant way to pass eternity.'

'You speak Persian?'

'A little, and some Aramaic. I was stationed in the east for a time. If you are rested, we should get on.'

The cliff was steep, but nowhere close to vertical. The rocks were dry, and fissures offered hand- and footholds. The tall, thin figure of Aulus led the way, taking it slowly. They never needed the pitons or ropes. Only once did Valens slip, when a projecting rock came away in his hand. Gripping with his other hand, his boots wedged in a crevice, he waited for a moment. He did not look down. Soon his heart returned to something near its normal rhythm.

Although the climb was not that demanding, Valens was relieved when they reached a wide ledge. Aulus reached down to help him up. They flopped down on a broad path which graded up to the mouth of the caves.

From where they sprawled, getting their breath back, the enclosed world of the settlement was spread out like a painting. Below were the woods. They could see the horses grazing, but their companions must have retreated to the shade. Beneath the woods were the fields; neat rectangles bounded by loose drystone walls formed by the stones lifted over generations from the thin soil. At the bottom of the valley was the village itself. The houses and the walls of the compounds were bright in the sun. The inhabitants, going about their mundane tasks, were no bigger than ants, but clearly visible. The white line of the road crawled across the vista. Beyond the village the scene was repeated, as the land lifted again. All around, the horizon was limited by the peaks of the towering mountains.

It was, Valens thought, the ideal lookout. Nothing could move in the valley without being seen.

The path on which they sat caught his attention. Its surface was hard, compacted by traffic over the centuries. His gaze followed it to the east, where it was hidden by a shoulder of the rock. Given the high and unbroken crags to the south, it must zigzag down to the floor of the valley. Probably it descended into the woods not that far from the settlement. None of the locals had mentioned its existence.

Valens heard the rasp of Aulus drawing his knife. He turned. Aulus tested the blade on his thumb, then carefully paired a broken nail.

Looking away, Valens gazed up at the entrance to the caves.

'Do you believe in daemons?'

Aulus sheathed the dagger. 'Socrates had a daemon.'

'I thought that was more a philosophical image of the soul.'

'Maybe so, maybe not,' Aulus said. 'Philosophers talk bollocks, but we all worship the genius of our Lord the Emperor. Yet no one seems sure if that is the divine aspect of his soul, or some supernatural guardian that watches over him.'

Talking to a *frumentarius*, even on this remote mountainside, Valens thought that it best not to be drawn into such potentially treasonous speculation. 'When I was a boy, the slave of a neighbour on the Esquiline had these strange marks on his skin: circles, like those made by a cupping glass. My nurse said they were caused by a daemon.'

'Dangerous things, daemons.'

'She always said lots of them lurked in the baths.'

'Maybe they like the dark and the steam.'

'She said they smelt bad.'

'That would account for them making their homes in the baths.'

'You have never seen one?'

'No, but that does not mean they do not exist.' Aulus frowned with thought. It accentuated the sunken cheeks of his tired, pouched face. 'If I meet one, I will try shouting, like Clemens said. If that does not work, I will see how it gets on with a dagger in its guts.'

Valens sat in silence, rather admiring this practicality.

'Where on the Esquiline was your parents' place?' Aulus asked.

'The Carinae.'

'Nice district,' Aulus said.

'We better go and hunt for our daemon.'

The entrance to the caves was as tall as a man, and as wide as a farm gate. The floor sloped upwards, which would keep out the rain and the snow in winter. A short passage opened into a chamber the size of the atrium of a moderately well-to-do house.

Scattered around was evidence of occupation by goats and their herders: a hearth, a rough wooden bench, some hurdles to pen the animals, and piles of their ancient droppings.

'Welcome to the cave of the Cyclops,' Aulus said.

'They were sheep.'

'Eh?'

'Not goats, sheep. Odysseus and his crew escaped by tying themselves under the bellies of sheep.'

'If you say so,' Aulus said. 'I don't care for poetry.'

Valens remembered the lines where Odysseus escaped.

Dear old ram, why last of the flock to leave the cave?
In the good old days you would never lag behind the rest . . .
Are you sick at heart for the eye of your master
Gouged out by a coward and his wicked crew?

Valens put his hand on the hearth. The ashes were cold, but did not look as if they had been there very long.

'The daemon appeared before Lucia and her husband left for Adiabene,' Valens said. 'This fire has been lit since then.'

'Would get chilly up here at night, even in summer,' Aulus said. 'Maybe daemons feel the cold?'

'That would account for their predilection for bathhouses.'

Aulus snuffled the dusty air. 'No feral smell. No bear or the like has made this its den.'

'Is that better or worse than a daemon?'

'Maybe better.'

A passage opened at the rear of the cave. This was low, and they had to go on hands and knees.

To give him his due, Aulus did not hesitate to go first.

Crawling after, Valens noticed that Aulus's knife was again in his hand. In this enclosed tunnel, nothing could get at Valens past Aulus. He left his dagger in its sheath.

The tunnel was long and it was not straight. After a time it divided into two. Aulus looked back for instructions. There was nothing to choose between the passages. Valens shrugged, then pointed to the left. They crawled on over the smooth rock. Eventually the enclosing walls fell back.

Very little light filtered into the next chamber, but they could sense its echoing size. From somewhere in the darkness came the sound of fast-running water. Valens crouched and took the box of fire-making tools from his belt. He struck sparks from the flint and steel into the tinderbox. When they caught, he lit his torch. Aulus lit his from that of Valens.

Standing, they could see the huge extent of the cavern. The flickering light of the torches barely illuminated the vault of the roof. Long stalactites hung down, and there were galleries opening in the rock high above. To their left, a shadowed chasm yawned in the floor. From there issued the roar of rushing water. The gloomy vastness reminded Valens of the interior of a temple.

A shelf, perhaps thirty paces long and some five wide, led past the abyss to an outcrop which partly masked the mouth of another tunnel running deeper into the mountain. Thank the gods they had lit the torches. Without them, one misstep and they would have plunged into the void.

Suddenly they were surrounded by dozens of dark winged shapes. Both ducked and waved their torches as the bats flitted, squeaking fearfully around their heads. Equally suddenly, the bats were gone.

'The air is still good,' Aulus said. The flames of the torches sawed, the smoke streaming back the way they had come. 'Further in there must be a shaft leading to the surface.'

Aulus was right; Valens could feel a cold breeze on his face. It came from yet deeper in the caverns. Aulus led the way to the shelf. Above the noises of the water and their own movements, Valens thought that he half heard a chink of metal on stone.

'Listen,' he hissed.

Aulus stopped.

They cocked their ears, straining to catch any alien sound.

Another chink of steel on rock. It seemed to come from the galleries above.

Then there was nothing but the subterranean river and the rasp of their own breathing.

Valens was beginning to think the noises were nothing but an echo of their own movements, a trick of the cavern walls, when he heard a low grating sound.

'Run!' he shouted.

True to his training, Aulus instantly obeyed.

The noise intensified to a deep grumbling as Valens launched himself after the older man. Small pebbles and a fine rain of dust fell. The noise reverberated around the vast space. Aulus was at the entrance to the next tunnel when the first boulder crashed into the shelf just behind Valens.

The younger man sprinted, arms pumping, as fast as his legs would go. A small rock glanced off his shoulder. He staggered, almost off balance. The lip of the gorge was horribly close. Another stone caught him between the shoulder blades. He stumbled, then gathered himself and dived after Aulus into the shelter of the outcrop by the next passage.

In the confined space, the avalanche deafened them, stunned their senses. A thick wave of dust surged into the tunnel, gritting their eyes, choking them.

The silence that followed was unnaturally deep. The river was muted. Now it sounded very distant.

Aulus helped Valens to his feet. Valens doubled up, coughing. His hands and knees were grazed, and his back hurt. Aulus picked up the torch the officer had dropped. It had gone out, and he relit it from his own before handing it back.

Together they stepped out from the outcrop and looked back. The dust was dispersing. Most of the rockslide had tumbled down into the abyss. Three substantial boulders had lodged on the shelf, although, thankfully, none of them totally blocked the path.

'Do you think . . .'

Through Aulus's words Valens heard a sharp twang. He hurled himself sideways, knocking the soldier to the ground. He felt rather than saw the shaft whip past, heard it snick off the wall of the tunnel.

'Not a daemon then,' Aulus said, once they were safely behind the rocks that stuck out like the jamb of a door.

'Not unless they use a bow and arrow.' Valens gathered their dropped torches, which were thankfully still alight. 'I am no expert, but I have never heard of that.'

They were both laughing with shock or relief.

Valens peeked around the entrance to the tunnel, ducking back before their unseen assailant could get his aim. With a sinking heart, the reality of their position dawned on him.

'There must be a passage down from the galleries. After levering the rocks loose, he has got down between us and the entrance.'

Aulus crawled to glance quickly back along the shelf. Scuttling back, his dusty face was grim. 'From the opening of that tunnel he can shoot us down if we try to cross the ledge.'

'Then we are at his mercy.' Valens heard the note of rising panic in his own voice. 'We are trapped.'

'Maybe not,' Aulus said. He pointed at the flaring torches. The smoke drifted towards the cavern they had left, and ultimately to the entrance to the complex. 'Stay here, and I will go and find the source of that.'

Valens was seized by a great reluctance to be left alone.

Aulus put a hand on his shoulder. 'The bowman is as trapped as us. If we go back, he can shoot us. But if he comes after us, you will put a dagger in his guts.'

'But he can get out any time he likes.'

'Leaving us free to escape, and tell the world there is no daemon. Someone has gone to a lot of trouble to convince the natives that these caves are haunted by some supernatural menace.'

Without further ado, Aulus set off.

This passage through the hillside sloped upwards, running away at an angle to the right. Aulus's torch cast bizarre patterns on the sides and ceiling as he went.

Valens took another quick look around the outcrop into the big cavern. There was no sign of the archer. He must be hidden in the outer tunnel.

Wedging the torch into a crack between himself and the opening, Valens drew his dagger, then sat with his back to the rocks.

The light of Aulus's torch had completely disappeared.

Now his breathing was under control, Valens could hear nothing but the hiss of his torch and the subdued roar of the water. No sooner was he settled than he was up again. What if the man took the initiative? Would he hear the attacker coming? Again he peered out at the ledge. Its surface was covered with a carpet of small stones from the avalanche. That would betray any stealthy approach.

Valens settled himself to wait.

The dark hole in the cavern tugged at his thoughts, like an entrance to the underworld. Valens pictured a fanged daemon, its claws clicking on the rock wall, seeking purchase, as it hauled itself gradually up the side of the chasm.

This was nonsense. He was a rational man. There was no underworld, no realm of the dead, no daemons. The Epicureans were right. Beyond this life there was nothing but eternal unconsciousness.

Anyway, his nurse had said daemons had wings.

A faint glow heralded the return of Aulus. When his ugly features reappeared, he beckoned Valens to leave his torch burning where it was lodged, and follow. They moved quietly, hoping the archer would not hear them depart. Valens could not help looking nervously back over his shoulder.

When they had put some distance between themselves and their attacker, they came out into another hollow chamber. The floor here was thick with mud and bat droppings. Aulus propped his torch in the filth, and pointed upwards. Despite his companion's torch, Valens saw the tiny chink of light.

The shaft was some eight feet up. It was exceedingly narrow, surely too narrow to admit a grown man. Its sides were slippery and covered in moss. Valens's spirit sank. Up there was fresh air and daylight, up there you could move without restriction. It was so close. They could see freedom, but it was out of reach.

'Lift me on your shoulders,' Aulus said.

'You will never fit.'

'There is no fat on me.'

'You will get stuck, or slip and fall.'

'Do you have a better idea?'

Valens did not.

'I have my hunting horn,' Aulus said. 'If I make it, I will get behind him and sound the horn. When you hear its note, rush the bowman. I will take him from the rear. One of us at least should reach him.'

Dumbly, Valens nodded. An ignoble part of him experienced a flood of relief that he did not have to attempt the climb.

'After I am in the shaft, take my torch and go back. I may need to use the pitons. Make some noise. Don't let him hear what I am doing.'

They uncoiled the ropes from their shoulders, then Valens got down in the slime, so that Aulus could clamber onto his back. Grunting with effort, Valens hoisted him aloft. Bits of moss and gravel pattered on his head as Aulus cleared handholds. A titanic lurch, and the weight of his companion's boots was lifted.

'Go now!' Aulus whispered, his voice barely audible from the natural chimney above. 'Sing him a song to cover the sound of me hammering in the spikes.'

Taking the torch, Valens warily retraced his steps. Every moment he expected their unknown attacker to rear up before him.

It was with an incredulous relief that he returned to where his own torch burned. Steeling his nerves, he hastily looked around the outcrop. Nothing had changed in the gloomy expanse.

From far away came the ting of a hammer on metal.

'You still there, Cyclops?' Valens shouted.

His words were swallowed by the silence.

Again the faint ring of metal.

Feeling both unnerved and ridiculous, Valens racked his brains for something to say, anything would do. The lines of Homer's poetry beaten into him by his schoolmaster came to mind.

> *But I was already plotting . . .*
> *What was the best way out? How could I find*
> *Escape from death for my crew, myself as well?*
> *My wits kept weaving, weaving cunning schemes –*
> *Life at stake, monstrous death staring us in the face . . .*

His voice gained strength as the words flooded back. The schoolmaster had made him learn much of the epic by heart.

The torches were burning low. Still reciting, he put one of them out. When the still burning torch guttered, he could relight the other. He had a primordial horror of being left here in the dark.

> *Nobody . . .*
> *Who's not escaped his death, I swear, not yet.*
> *Oh if only you thought like me, had words like me*
> *To tell me where that scoundrel is cringing from my rage!*

On and on went his bizarre recital. Every so often he stopped to listen to the resounding silence. But, when he resumed, was there anyone still listening to him? Did he still have an audience, crouched in the opposite passageway, bow in hand, murder in their heart?

The torch began to fail.

Valens stopped talking. He listened. No sounds but the crackle of the dying torch and the water over the rocks far below. Aulus was inaudible. Either he was wedged fast or had fallen to his death. It seemed impossible that he might be out of the shaft. There was no further need for poetry.

Checking the tinderbox was handy on his belt, Valens stubbed out the glowing torch, without lighting the other.

Let us be men. The darkness itself could not hurt him.

Time lost all meaning. He had no idea how frequently he looked into the dimness of the cavern. Just a glimmer of brightness came from the mouth of the tunnel, where the bowman must be hunched. As his eyes became accustomed to the ambient light, Valens could make out the ledge, and the dark humps of the three boulders that littered its surface.

Most of the while he just sat, blade in hand, listening.

How long would Iudex and the others wait at the foot of the slope? Valens had not thought to set a time. He had entered into this with no thought that he was undertaking something serious. Most likely by the time they became concerned, it would be too late in the evening to venture into the caves. Could he stay here until the next morning? If he did, would he retain his sanity?

His mind wandered. In myth, mountains were the homes of the gods. Virtue lived on a crag. Hercules had been offered the choice between virtue and vice. The path to the former was steep and hard, to the latter broad and tempting. In reality, the high places were wild and dangerous. They were the home of shepherds and brigands, and the two were indistinguishable. It was in the mountains that Valens's parents had been killed.

The sound boomed down the passages under the mountain. For a moment, Valens could not believe his ears. It came again, the confident note of a hunting horn.

Aulus! The thin, ugly old bastard had made it!

As Valens leapt to his feet the muscles in his back and legs twinged with the suddenness of the movement after long inactivity. He knew if he hesitated, he would never force himself into the open, would never dare to face the risk.

Knife in hand, he hurled himself around the outcrop, and along the shelf.

Four or five rushed steps – boots sliding on the gritted surface – then he dived for the cover of the first boulder. He heard the arrow slice through the air and vanish into the dark.

He had to keep moving, not give the man time to notch and draw and aim.

Pushing himself up, he sprinted around the rock. This time the shaft was so close he felt the wind of its passing.

Flat out, his feet all too close to the lip of the chasm, he tore past the second rock.

He did not hear the missile coming, just saw the sparks its tip struck from the wall.

Now no effort of will could have prevented Valens diving into the lee of the final boulder.

He lay, curled up, making himself very small. His chest was heaving, like the flanks of a hound after a long chase.

He could not tell how long he cowered there. He tried telling himself the dimness would foil the aim of the archer. He could not stay here forever. Nothing could force him to move.

The horn sounded a third time, much closer.

Valens scrabbled over the boulder. The arrow flashed by his shoulder.

Ten paces to go.

From the opening, a huge bear of a man arose. Valens saw the glint of the sword. *A knife against a sword?* He would die.

Skidding to a halt, Valens dropped into a fighting crouch.

The big shaggy man laughed, got his long blade out in front.

There was no way Valens's dagger could get past the longer reach. The man said something, the words incomprehensible but the tone mocking. Valens feinted right, near the abyss. The sword covered his movement, but not so far as to leave its wielder open. No room to manoeuvre. Valens was pinned between the rock face and the drop. This could only end one way. The swordsman thrust. Valens jumped back, giving ground. Another pace of two, and he would be trapped against the last boulder.

The thump of boots coming down the passage behind distracted the man. His head half turned. Valens struck. Grabbing his opponent's sword arm with his left hand, he lunged at the face with the dagger in his right. The bearded man jerked away. Lowering the angle as the thrust went in, Valens felt the knife bite into the man's left shoulder. With a savage twist, he yanked it free.

Dropping the sword, the man's right hand instinctively went to the wound.

Valens closed in.

The man stepped back.

Like some primeval fury, Aulus burst from the passageway, screaming a war cry.

The man put up an arm to ward off the blow. The gesture was futile. Aulus's blade sliced deep into his ribs.

Blinded by his agony, the man tottered to the edge of the chasm. He stood sawing, then began to topple backwards. Valens scrabbled forward, clutched the blood-soaked front of his tunic. The weight of the mortally injured man was too much. Valens felt himself being pulled out over the edge.

'Aulus!' he yelled.

The soldier stood, as if rooted to the spot.

Twisting his whole body, never slackening his grip, Valens threw himself backwards.

For a moment the forces were in equilibrium. Then Valens crashed back onto the ledge. The corpse landed heavily on top of him. The beard of the man scratched his face, and the blood ran hot and repulsive over his chest.

CHAPTER 20

Matiane

WHEN THE DOORS WERE FLUNG open from outside, the musicians stopped playing and the buzz of conversation ceased. All eyes were on the those who entered.

Valens marched into the room. Like the men at his back, he was helmeted and wore mail. The soldiers were equipped for any eventuality. Each had a shield in his left hand, a strung bow slung across his back, a sword on one hip, and an open quiver on the other. The right hand of all but Valens rested on the hilt of their blades. The young officer carried an evidently heavy leather sack.

Decimus and Aulus halted at the doors. The other four followed Valens into the centre of the circle of diners. Their boots thudded with a measured tread on the stone floor, the rattle of their martial panoply filling the silence.

Four armed retainers got up and stood behind the village headman. Some of the rest of the diners seemed to shrink back, but all remained cross-legged.

Valens stopped in front of the headman. Hairan closed up on his shoulder. Iudex, with Clemens and Narses, stood watchfully behind.

Valens dropped the sack. It landed with a weighty thump, and the eyes of the headman fixed upon it.

'Tell him we have dealt with his daemon,' Valens said to Hairan.

The translation by the Hatrene was longer than the original. Valens caught just the word 'djinn'.

The headman listened, but appeared incapable of tearing his gaze from the stained leather bag.

'We have brought proof.'

While Hairan spoke, Valens bent and untied the sack. He paused and looked up. The headman met his stare. Some deep and troubled thoughts flickered behind his eyes. Standing, Valens lifted out the contents of the sack.

There was a gasp from the diners.

Valens held the severed head by the hair.

The headman recoiled, unable to hide the horror and anger on his face.

Others at the feast were getting to their feet. Valens half turned, taking in each of them. Under his regard they stopped moving. There were about thirty at the meal, half of them women. All the men were armed, but the odds were no worse than two to one. Valens did not want this to end in bloodshed. Now was the time for careful words.

'Tell him there was no daemon. His servant betrayed him.'

As Hairan translated, the gaze of the headman flitted around the room. He too perhaps was calculating the numbers, trying to predict the outcome of violence.

'Tell him his people are safe again.'

One last glance at the hideous object in Valens's hand, and the headman began to talk to Hairan.

'He says he is in our debt. He could never have imagined such a thing. His soul is shocked.'

'Is it now?'

The headman was talking faster, gaining confidence. His hands spread wide placatingly, his tone was oleaginous and ingratiating.

'We are the saviours of his people. He begs us to accept his hospitality, and dine with him.'

'Tell him it has been a hard day on the mountain, and we will eat and rest in our compound.'

Hairan's translation brought forth a torrent of words from the native.

'He asks if there is anything we need. Can he send us food or wine. Would we care for some of his serving girls to ease our cares.'

Valens placed the gory object on the floor. 'Tell him we have everything we need for tonight.'

Again the reply provoked a vociferous outburst.

'He says his house and goods are ours. If there is anything we want.'

'Tell him, with the daemon dead, there is no barrier to one of his people accompanying us as a guide. We want a reliable man, a merchant who has made the journey down to the Mardoi and the shores of the Caspian.'

Valens did not need to understand the language to know the response was favourable, its expression laudatory. When it had run its course, Valens nodded, and turned to leave.

The soldiers waited, then filed out after him. Decimus and Aulus pulled the doors shut behind them.

'He might not have known,' Aulus said. 'The leader of his guards could have just developed a taste for killing. Some men do, it is a form of madness.'

'Of course the headman fucking knew,' Clemens said. 'The question is what he will do now.'

They were in the main room of the house. Iudex and Hairan were up on the flat roof keeping watch. Decimus was checking the horses. Apart from the house, the compound contained a range of stables and a store shed. The beaten earth of the yard was surrounded by a low wall. There were two gates. The whole area was visible from the roof.

'These hillmen have always been bad subjects,' Narses said. 'They have never heeded the laws of the King of Kings. They are rapacious and untrustworthy.'

'Like all easterners.' The weight of centuries of prejudice lay behind the words of Clemens.

'Unlike you Romans,' Narses said. The big black beard of the Persian bristled with indignation. 'There is no backwater, no desert or mountain range, so remote or poor that it is not coveted by your greed. You ravage the whole world in your insatiable avarice, and claim it is all in the name of good faith and safety. *Fides* and *salus*, my arse!'

'That is a lie!'

'Then what are we doing here?'

'Our duty.'

'And why does *duty* send us to abduct a Sassanid prince?' Narses spoke with venom. 'To give you Romans an excuse to start a *just* war on my people, a *iustum bellum*. Even your gods can see through such a threadbare excuse.'

'Enough!' Valens said. Shared adversity in their long travels had not yet smoothed away the mens' animosities. 'We are hundreds of miles into hostile territory. If we do not stand together, we will all die.'

Aulus broke the charged and uncomfortable silence. 'What reason could the headman have had for having his retainer murder his own people? Robbery?'

'What the fuck does a goat boy or a labourer have that is worth taking?' Clemens asked.

'Clemens is right,' Valens said. 'What matters is what the head-man does now.'

'The village might be able to raise over a hundred able-bodied men,' Narses said. 'We keep watch, and we are harder to kill than untrained levies. It is unlikely they will attack us openly.'

'You think the headman will want us gone, and will send a guide in the morning?' Valens asked.

'They might try and poison us,' Clemens said. 'It is a method much favoured in the Orient.'

Aulus spoke before Narses could respond to this latest insult. 'We already have provisions for four days. We could manage eight on half rations, although the horses would suffer.'

Hairan called down softly from the head of the stairs. 'Someone approaching the back gate.'

'Alone?'

'Yes, on their own.'

'We had better find out what he wants,' Valens said. 'Aulus and Narses, take watch on the roof. Hairan, get Iudex, and come with us.'

By the time they reached the gate, there was a faint knocking. Clemens drew the bolts and pulled the gate open, admitting a fig-ure wrapped in a hooded cloak. The gate was swiftly shut behind them, the bolts shot home. The soldiers had taken off their armour, but as ever had their swords. The muffled figure was ringed by glittering steel.

Lucia pushed back her hood.

Back inside they offered her wine and food, both of which she declined.

'You run a risk coming here,' Valens said. 'Your betrothed would not approve.'

'No one saw me,' she said. 'Anyway, he is a brute, and I will not marry him.'

'Why have you come?'

'To warn you not to trust the headman.'

Valens grinned. 'There was little danger of that.'

'You know he set the leader of his men to kill those villagers?'

'Why?'

'The reasons for which all men kill, power and wealth. Whether they believed in the djinn or not, fear made the peasants reluctant to work the outlying meadows. They sold the land to the headman for next to nothing.'

'You did not tell me this yesterday,' Valens said.

'I was not certain until I saw his reaction this evening.'

'What does the headman intend now?'

'My late husband's brother will be your guide. The family has traded along the Caspian many times. This time he will not go there. The headman has told him to lead you deep into the track-less mountains and abandon you there. He wants you dead for the killing of his retainer.'

Valens thought for a time before he spoke. 'You must hate your husband's brother. Having told us that, you know what will happen to him at our hands. The persuasion will not be gentle, although we will not kill him unless it is essential.'

'I would be happy to see him dead, but it is unnecessary.' She looked into Valens's eyes. 'I also have been to the Caspian with my husband, and know the passes as well as any merchant.'

'No.'

'You must take me with you.'

'It is impossible.'

She looked away. In the lamplight her face appeared longer, the bones more pronounced, like that of a man.

'You *have* to take me with you.'

'We do not.'

'If I go with you, there will be no outcry. But if you leave me here, the whole of Persia will be on your tracks.'

Valens said nothing.

'You see, I know why you are here.'

'We are merchants.'

'No, you have been sent to rescue . . . *someone* . . . from the Castle of Silence.'

'What makes you think that?'

'Zabda told me before he died.'

CHAPTER 21

To the Caspian Sea

The rider was waiting at the head of the pass, where the track ran between towering crags on one side and a vertiginous ravine on the other.

Although it was too far to make out the individual, Valens knew it was her.

'It is not an ambush,' their guide said. 'This is a dangerous place, but brigands would lie concealed up on the heights.'

No, thought Valens, *not an ambush for us, but a most unwelcome turn of events for you.*

They plodded up the long rise. The horses were weary, and their heads were down as they negotiated the incline. It was late in the afternoon, and it had been a long day's ride since they left the village at dawn. They would make camp beyond the pass.

So far the guide had not attempted to lead them astray. That treachery would be planned for deeper into the wild mountains that barred the passage from the Tigris to the Caspian. The brother of Lucia's dead husband was a merchant, and he spoke Greek. He had an abrupt manner and an untrustworthy face. Did not some philosophers say that all trade involved cheating? Merchants bought goods cheap to sell them at a profit. On this journey, the man had a more deadly deceit in mind.

Short of the top, Valens looked along the column. As usual, Hairan was out in front, on point. The track here was wide enough for three horses abreast. The guide rode between Valens and Iudex, with Narses following. Behind them Decimus led the four spare horses carrying the provisions. They had bought two new animals in the village to join the bell-mare and the sole survivor of those with which they had set out. The new beasts were not yet accustomed to the routine, and were playing up. Decimus was a fine horseman, and controlled them with patience and firmness. Clemens and Aulus brought up the rear. At each stop in the day Valens had altered the order of march, so that all except Hairan and Decimus shared in the discomfort of riding at the tail through the clinging dust raised by those in front.

'What are you doing here, woman?' The guide was startled and furious.

Lucia sat her horse across the path. Hairan had gone on ahead.

'Exposing your treachery,' Lucia said.

'What are you talking about?' The guide pushed his horse alongside hers.

'Your secret is uncovered.'

'Have you no shame?'

'Do not talk to me of shame. Your brother was a man. You are a snake.'

'My brother was weak, always too soft on you.' He raised his fist. 'You will learn obedience.'

Before the blow could land, Iudex grabbed the guide by the scruff of the neck and hauled him almost out of the saddle.

'You pollute the light in your soul,' Iudex said, before his huge hand released its grip.

The guide landed hard, but was on his feet in a moment, groping for the hilt of his sword.

'Not a good idea,' Valens said, nudging his mount between the guide and the woman.

Looking up at the grim-faced men, all defiance left the guide. 'Take the bitch, if you want her. She can entertain you all. She will enjoy being on her back. Good riddance – only our customs forced me to marry the whore.'

Iudex swung down, and threw his reins to Narses. With brisk efficiency, he disarmed and searched the guide.

'Where did you plan to abandon us?' Valens said.

'Never! I would not do such a thing.'

Iudex cuffed the man. The guide staggered.

'I have done you no wrong.'

Iudex hit him again, but this time he punched him hard in the kidneys.

From where he had crumpled to the ground on his knees, the man looked up. 'It was not my idea. The headman forced me to take an oath. He would have killed me otherwise.'

'What did he make you swear?' Valens said.

'To take you into the uninhabited wastes, to steal your precious things, leave you to die. But I was going to tell you.'

'Are there others following us?'

'No, just me. But I would never have done it.'

'And what shall we do with you now?' The question had been much on Valens's mind. He had reached no conclusion.

The man spread his hands in supplication. 'I will tell him that I have done what he told me, that you are lost, that you will never find your way out of the mountains.'

'And when he asks for the jewels?'

'I will say they were too well guarded. It is revenge he really wants, revenge for the retainer you killed.'

'You will tell him that we are a day's ride away,' Iudex said, 'and he will send riders after us.'

'I would never do such a thing!'

'Not a man like you.' With one fluid motion, Iudex drew his sword and struck. There was a sound like someone breaking the carcass of a chicken or some other roast fowl as the blade bit into the man's skull.

Lucia gasped.

'You said you would be happy to see him dead.' Iudex smiled. 'Consider yourself divorced.'

'You should have waited for my order,' Valens said.

'Then it would have been on your conscience,' Iudex replied. 'Mine is clear.'

Iudex cleaned his sword on the dead man's tunic before sliding it back into its scabbard. He took the purse from the belt, gathered the guide's sword and knife, and handed them to Lucia. 'Do you want his rings?'

Holding the things she had been given, as if unsure of what to do with them, Lucia shook her head.

Iudex went back and crouched over the corpse. With his dagger he severed two of the fingers, which, after he had removed the rings, he tossed aside.

'In the strict letter of the law, all *manubiae* goes to the Emperor,' Iudex said, again wiping the blade on the dead man's clothes. 'But this booty is a long way from Rome. They might fit you, Narses. You like pretty things.'

The Persian caught them in mid-air and, grinning, examined them before slipping them on his fingers.

Iudex regarded the man's boots. 'Shoddy local workmanship. You would have thought a well-travelled merchant would have owned better.'

Valens thought he ought to reassert his authority. 'Get rid of the body.'

'The dead tell no tales.' Iudex took the man by his unwanted boots and dragged him to the precipice. The ruined head left a trail of gore on the track. A shove and he was gone.

Lucia was as good as her word, and she guided them unerringly. Sometimes they went down in the twisting valley bottoms, where fast streams rushed over pebbles worn round and glassy by the ages. At others they switch-backed up scarred slopes to follow narrow paths along the crests. They came to an wide upland plain with a saline lake. The surface of the water was as smooth as marble and alive with shell ducks and avocets. Its beaches were white with the salt, and its rocks also encrusted, as if thick with the droppings of seabirds. Here the villages were more substantial than the isolated hamlets of the heights. The inhabitants were cautious of the armed men, but accepted Persian coins for what produce they could spare. In this region they were able to purchase replacements for two of the horses that had gone lame. Well mounted and fully provisioned, again they climbed, this time to yet higher ranges, where snow lay on the highest summits.

The season was changing. The sun still shone, but with less ferocity. At night in the mountains the temperature plummeted. Some evenings it rained, and afterwards the air brought the tang of autumn. Valens had lost track of time. He thought it was towards the end of September. As they had gone on, somehow the customary man-made divisions of time – the days and the months – had lost their hold. They had been replaced by the endlessly repeated routine of the march: the four watches of the night, first light and seeing to the horses, feeding themselves, breaking camp, setting out at a walk, then a trot, the first halt to check the girths and relieve themselves, all the way through to making camp again, bedding down the horses, eating their rations, and falling into their bedrolls.

Lucia fitted into the routine. None of the men bothered or importuned her. They seemed, if anything, to have adopted her as something between a cherished pet or a mascot. And, of course, they all knew that without her they would be lost.

Once, not long after the killing, Valens had asked her what she intended to do. She had replied that if the gods did not provide, she was not without resource. The future had not been discussed again on the journey.

Finally, she led them to a river running east. At first it was fast and shallow. Descending, it gathered volume from smaller streams. The rock walls fell back, and it meandered, wide and deep, through a green valley of its own making. Isolated tall outcrops of banded rock testified to its power and its changes of course over time.

When the wind was in the east, it brought the smell of the sea.

Then they came to the bridge.

There were actually two bridges. The older was rickety and wooden, undoubtedly made by the population of the settlement on the far bank. The other was under construction. Its masonry piers jutted from the water, and the first two were spanned by well-proportioned arches of dressed stone. It caught the men unawares. They had viewed its like innumerable times, but had never expected to see such a thing here.

The warriors were waiting a hundred paces in front of the bridges. A dozen horse archers, commanded by an officer in elaborate, chased armour. They had their bows in their hands, but they sat their horses easily, confident in their numbers and skill in the face of these ragged, travel-worn horsemen coming down from the hills.

The sight of them gave Valens an unexpected shock. These were the first Persian soldiers they had seen since entering the realm of the Sassanids. Somehow, in the mountains, although hundreds of miles into enemy territory, Valens had almost forgotten they were in lands ruled by Shapur, the King of Kings. In a sense he had been right. Both empires, Roman and Persian, claimed to rule the mountainous regions within their borders. Yet neither exercised any lasting control. Occasionally they might send in a punitive expedition to burn a few villages. Otherwise, providing the inhabitants paid at least some nominal taxes, and did not too often plunder the neighbouring lowlands, the authorities left them alone.

A worrying thought struck Valens. What if the headman of Lucia's village had sent a fast messenger along some other path? Were these soldiers waiting specifically for them? He was relieved that Hairan would do the talking.

They reined in. Valens forced himself to relax, keep his hand away from the hilt of his sword. His tense posture was mirrored by the rest of the party, and he wondered if the Persians would sense their unease.

Hairan alone seemed unaffected. The Hatrene nudged his mount up to that of the officer, greeted him with effusive formality.

The officer answered with reserve.

Hairan gave him the document written by the eunuch at the border. When he had read it, the officer spoke sharply. Valens had picked up enough Persian to gather that there was something missing or wrong with the document. With a courtly gesture, Hairan produced one of the little cameos, and presented it to the officer. Mollified, the officer slipped it into a purse on his belt.

The main business satisfactorily conducted, the officer surveyed the others. His gaze lingered first on Lucia. Hairan spoke rapidly, and Valens heard his own name and the word Antioch. The officer glanced over, said something dismissive, then turned to Narses.

He snapped a question. Narses answered with a bow. The Persian replied, laughing unpleasantly. Valens caught the word Cilicia. Narses's face went rigid, but he said nothing.

The officer gave Hairan some more instructions, then waved them through.

Those labouring on the stone bridge stopped and stared at the riders when they came close. Dressed in work tunics, the majority were fair skinned, several sunburnt. Valens regarded them in turn, with a sad and mounting certainty. Hairan led the column across the native bridge. Its boards rattled under the hooves of their horses.

When they were trotting towards the settlement, Valens asked what had been said.

Hairan stroked his long moustaches, much amused.

Before he could answer, Narses broke in. 'The officer said I looked Persian. When I told him that I was of the clan Suren, he said my mother must have been some Cilician slave lucky enough to be raped by a Persian warrior, the impudent ill-bred fucker.'

'Very proud, these Persians,' Hairan said. 'He also asked about Lucia. I said she was no slave girl, but the wife of our esteemed leader, Marcus Aelius Valens, the merchant from Antioch. He said you were lucky not to have been at home when the Persians sacked the city.'

'Narses is right, he is a very impudent fucker.'

'And he also said there was no accommodation free in the village, and we must camp outside. Finally he told us not to talk to the prisoners working on the bridge, I think you can work out why.'

* * *

Valens went into the settlement with Aulus and Hairan to buy provisions. Aulus was the quartermaster, and none of the others could haggle, seemingly in any language, as well as Hairan. As had become usual when the party was divided, Valens left Decimus in charge of the camp. The horse master was a sober and reliable man.

When they had made their purchases, Valens thought they could do with a drink. Hairan was always amiable company, and Valens's relations with the previously mulish Aulus had been much improved after their experiences with the 'daemon' in the caves.

As in every village, there was a tavern opening onto the square. The afternoon was cool, with a hint of rain in the air. They left the animals loaded with food and fodder tethered to the rail outside. The bar was small and dark and rudimentary, and smelt of stale wine and old cooking. A bored-looking, slatternly girl stood behind the rough-jointed wooden bar. There were only two customers, sitting side by side at a table by the stairs at the rear of the room, facing the door. One was an older man, the other much younger. Both wore clean and respectable tunics, trousers and boots. On the right forearm of each was a tattoo.

'You are a long way from home, brothers,' the older man said.

Although, since the bridge, he had half expected such an encounter, it took a moment before Valens realised that the man had spoken in Latin.

'And you, brothers,' Aulus replied.

Perhaps the drink had been a mistake, Valens thought. The Persian officer had warned them not to fraternise with the prisoners. Well, it was too late now. To Hades with the Persian.

'Health and great joy,' Valens said. 'Let us get you a drink.'

'That would be most civil.'

Without being asked, Hairan went to the bar and spoke to the girl.

Before Valens and Aulus sat down, the two men got up and shook their hands.

'Marcus Julius Priscus, sometime prefect of the camp of the Third Gallica,' the older man said. 'This is Titus, my nephew. He was just sixteen, a new recruit.'

'Marcus Aelius Valens, a merchant out of Antioch. This is Aulus, and over there is Hairan. They are caravan guards.'

The older man raised an eyebrow. 'If you say so.'

The introductions made, they all sat down together.

'Where were you taken?' Valens asked.

'Beyond Edessa with Valerian.'

'Not good.'

The old soldier shrugged. 'The campaign was ill-fated from the start. After we crossed the Euphrates at Samosata, the first rations issued were lentils and salt, the food of mourning, offerings to the dead.'

The girl brought cups and pitchers of wine and water. As soon as she had put them down, Hairan took her arm and led her to the stairs.

'Excuse me,' the Hatrene said, 'it has been a long time.'

The girl appeared no less bored than before as she went up. As if by magic, an almost identical girl materialised behind the bar.

'You survived the death march,' Valens continued to speak in Latin. It was unlikely the serving girls could eavesdrop.

The older man poured the drinks. 'Once a day they drove us to water like animals. There was never time for all to drink. Those that could not keep up, the Persians killed.'

'I heard that Shapur slaughtered men to fill a ravine, so that he could ride his horse across,' Aulus said.

'So they say, I did not see it myself. Cruel things happen in war.'

'And how are things with you now?' Valens asked.

'They could be worse. Shapur gave us land, told us to build a city. Bishapur, he named it, the "beauty of Shapur".' The old man chuckled. 'We laid it out like a Roman camp.'

'Except the best part is the palace he ordered us to build,' the younger man said with bitterness.

The older man silenced him with a look. 'It is not too bad. We built bathhouses and a circus. There were charioteers and musicians and actors among the civilians captured in Antioch.'

'This season Gallienus is fighting in the west,' Valens said. 'When he has defeated Postumus, it is thought he will march east next year to free his father.'

'There have been such rumours for the last five years,' the older man said.

'You do not want to go home?' Aulus sounded incredulous.

'We surrendered. If we managed to reach the border, our citizenship would be revoked.'

'Surely not,' Valens said. 'Your Emperor ordered you to lay down arms. The fault lies with Valerian, not with you.'

'Maybe so, but I am too old to move. Besides, I have married a Persian woman. Now I have a son and a daughter. The Persians value our skills. We are paid to build roads and dams and bridges, like the one here.'

'They work us like slaves,' the younger man said.

The older one smiled. 'The taxes are lower here.'

'Your new religion has taken your courage,' the younger man snapped.

'Mind what you say, boy.' The older man exhaled noisily. 'But yes, I have come to see the light.'

'The light?' Valens asked.

'No harm here in bearing witness to my faith. It will not bring the pincers and the claws, will not see me burnt or mauled in the arena, as it would at home. For all the Persian priests talk of kindling sacred fires in conquered temples, Shapur tolerates all creeds. Jews, Manicheans, followers of the Olympian gods, all can practice their own rites. No harm in admitting that I have become a Christian.'

Valens and Aulus leant back, as if proximity might bring contagion.

CHAPTER 22

The Southern Shores of the Caspian Sea

'THE SEA! THE SEA!'

There, spread out below them, was the Caspian. Its waters glittered in the sunshine of the autumn afternoon. They extended further than the eye could see.

The men laughed and yelled and hugged each other. *Thalassa! Thalassa!* They capered like children, and shouted like the ten thousand of Xenophon at the end of their long march out of Persia.

It was an achievement to have come so far, yet Valens thought the exuberance misplaced. Xenophon's men had escaped the lands of the Persian king. The ten thousand had reached the Black Sea. Its shores were studded with Greek cities. From any of them a man could take a boat, and sail back to Byzantium in a matter of days. Nowadays there were Roman garrisons around much of its coasts. The Caspian was an altogether different sea. It offered no succour and no passage back to civilisation. In the old days it had been believed to be a gulf opening off the northern ocean, and there was a story that an underground waterway linked the Caspian to Lake Maeotis, and thus to the Black Sea. They were no more than travellers' tales. Even had they been true, neither would have provided an easy voyage home. The men with Valens had not escaped. They were deeper in enemy territory than ever, and their main dangers still lay ahead.

'Mount up.' Valens thought they should get down to the shore and find a campsite before dusk.

They rode down in a mood of easy congeniality.

'Did you know,' Clemens said, 'there are islands out there full of gold? It is only the indolence of the Persians that leaves them unmined.'

Behind his big, square beard, Narses pulled a face. 'Nothing but an avaricious fantasy typical of a Roman,' he said. 'You forget that I went to the south-east coast when I was stationed in Hyrkania. The islands are poor, and their inhabitants primitive. In the summer they live off roots, and in the winter dried fruit. They do not even drink wine. At their feasts they light a bonfire, sit around it, and throw hemp on the flames. They sniff the smoke and become intoxicated. Eventually they stand up and dance, and burst into song.'

'I heard it was full of huge serpents, and strange-coloured fish,' Clemens said.

'It depends what colour you expect of a fish,' Narses said. 'Mind you, the serpents do grow to a prodigious length.'

'It is the women that interest me,' Hairan called back over his shoulder. 'Apparently they copulate out in the open, let anyone have a go.'

'I think that is somewhere else,' Valens said, 'perhaps some tribes in Armenia.'

'Oh well,' said Hairan, not disheartened, 'was it not here that the Queen of the Amazons entertained Alexander for thirteen nights and days? That man had staying power.'

'Not in the more reliable sources,' Valens said.

'There are bound to be some women.' Hairan was not to be deflected.

'You should write a book,' Clemens said. 'The sexual mores of all the peoples of the world.'

'A fine idea,' Hairan said. 'It would take much dedicated practical research.'

They had become so used to Lucia that her presence did nothing to inhibit their talk.

They camped on the beach, and built a fire of driftwood. Having carefully scanned the water to be sure that it was free of the rumoured serpents, the men stripped and swam naked in the sea. Narses volunteered to stand first watch. Like every Persian, he had a prim aversion to public nudity, both his own and that of others. He kept his gaze fixed inland. As the soldiers splashed about, roaring from the cold water, Lucia sat on the beach, tending the fire. If she was offended by the sight, she gave no sign. As with their conversation, the men paid her no more heed than they would a bath attendant or a statue.

With their bows, Aulus and Narses had each shot a brace of duck on the way down. After their swim, when the men were dry and clothed, and safe from any real or imagined water snakes, they plucked and gutted the birds. Valens went to skewer one on his sword, but Decimus produced proper iron spits.

'Use your blade to cook, and the fire will ruin it, make the steel brittle,' Decimus said. 'Isn't that right, Clemens?'

The armourer grunted an affirmative.

'If your sword breaks in combat,' Decimus added, 'you are totally fucked.'

Clemens looked vaguely put out, perhaps at the pronouncement of the horse master on his own area of expertise.

Soon the aroma of cooking meat wafted around the little camp. The duck would make an enticing change from the endless meals of bacon, and would help preserve their rations. Valens was hungry. The dripping fat sizzling in the flames increased his appetite.

Hairan had relieved Narses on sentry. He called that there was someone coming from the west, alone and on foot, seemingly unarmed.

His weapons to hand, Valens could not be bothered to get up. The others shared his disinclination.

The figure appeared, staggering down the beach with exhaustion. But his head was up, and his eyes fixed on them like those of a doomed man gazing at salvation. It was the young man from the bar in the settlement by the bridge. He came to a stop a few paces off.

'What are you doing here?' Valens said.

The fugitive's chest was heaving, and he swayed where he stood.

'Sit down by the fire, before you collapse.'

The youth did as he was told.

'Someone give him a drink.'

He took a gulp and choked. Once he had dragged some air into his lungs, he tipped the wineskin up again. This time his throat worked furiously as he swallowed.

'Does your uncle know you are here?' Valens asked.

The young man stopped drinking, wiped his mouth with the back of his hand.

'The officer asked you a question,' Clemens said.

'No, I slipped away.'

'Why have you followed us?' Valens asked, although he thought he knew the answer.

'We do not all think like my uncle. With his native wife, and his new religion, things are different for him. The Christians always talk about turning the other cheek, enduring suffering in silence.' The words tumbled out of him in a stream.

'What is that to do with us?' Valens interrupted. This was heading in an even worse direction than he had feared.

The youth looked at him, as if baffled by the slowness of his comprehension. 'There are over a hundred Roman prisoners working on the bridge. All of them soldiers. The majority would give anything to return home. There are only twenty guards. We have no weapons, but we have our tools and knives. In the night, we could overpower them with ease. You could lead us back to the empire.'

'We are here to trade, not fight,' Valens said. 'We are a merchant caravan.'

'My uncle said you were soldiers. The two with you in the bar have military tattoos on their arms. He saw them under their sleeves, when they were drinking. And that one,' he pointed at Clemens, 'just called you an officer.'

'It is nothing but a courtesy. I am a trader, these are my guards. Some may be veterans, but what they did previously in life is not my business, and no concern of yours.'

The youth waved a hand in dismissal. 'My uncle said he recognised your sort. He would swear that you were spies, would put money on you being *frumentarii*.'

So much for our disguise, Valens thought. Still, an ex-centurion, after a lifetime in the army, would have sharper insight than any local.

'Christians are forbidden to gamble,' Iudex said. 'They hold it a sin.'

The youth looked at him, as if he had said something incomprehensible.

'It does not matter what we are.' Valens had to put a stop to this. 'The thing is impossible. The road is too long and hard. There are the mountains of Matiene and the deserts of Arbayestan. You have no horses. Every Persian warrior in the realm would be hunting you. None of you would reach Mesopotamia.'

'We would be happy to die in the attempt.'

'It would not only be you that would be dying,' Aulus said. 'There is us to consider.'

The young prisoner looked crushed. Then a spark of renewed hope gleamed on his face. 'Then take me with you.'

'No,' Valens said. This was what he had feared.

'It is a terrible thing to be an exile,' Clemens said.

'Listen to him,' the boy said. 'Please listen to what he says.'

'He is not coming with us,' Valens said. 'The Persians will hunt him down, and us with him.'

'Not for days.' The boy tripped over his words in his eagerness. 'They will not start to search for me for days. As an engineer, my uncle has more freedom than most. If my absence has been noted, he will tell the Persians that he has sent me on some errand. It will be alright.'

'Then it will be safe for you to return to him tomorrow,' Valens said.

'Please do not send me back.' The youth was close to crying. 'You do not know what it is like to live as a slave in an alien land, to have no freedom.'

'What you take for freedom is nothing but a legal fiction.' Iudex was measuring his words, as if ladling something weighty. 'True freedom lies in the soul. Stone walls and iron bars do not make a prison. Mere externals cannot touch the true nature of a man. The lowest captive, although he is whipped and branded, is cruelly beaten and degraded, providing he has a noble and virtuous soul, is as free as any man.'

'Easy to say when you are not a prisoner.' Anger was fast overcoming self-pity. 'How many philosophers are slaves?'

'Epictetus was a slave,' Iudex said. 'He knew of what he spoke.'

'Enough,' Valens said. 'It is time to eat. You can stay here tonight, then in the morning you will go back.'

Valens had taken the last but one watch. The sky was getting light when the sounds of men and horses shifting about, and the smell of cooking, made him reluctantly wake after an all too brief sleep.

He stretched, then turned and lay on his back. His shoulders and hips ached from the hard compacted sand. Last night he had scooped out hollows for each, but it was no substitute for a mattress or a soft bed. The serpents had been on his mind – he had a particular loathing of snakes – and he had placed his bedroll well up the beach from the fire. Now, lying there, gradually surfacing from slumber, fragments of dreams slipped from his grasp like smoke.

In Hades, Odysseus had reached to embrace his father. The insubstantial shade of the old man had slid through his arms. Valens knew that he had dreamt of his parents, but the memory moved tantalisingly and irrecoverably out of reach.

He threw off his blanket and sat up. One at a time he turned his boots upside down, and beat them on the ground to dislodge any scorpions that might have crept in for shelter during the night. His boots on, he clambered stiffly to his feet.

Walking a little away from the camp, he fumbled with his trousers, then relieved himself. Idly he directed the stream of urine into a hole under a bush. Then he remembered the snakes, and pissed elsewhere.

Walking back, he retrieved his sword belt and buckled it tight. Everyone except Clemens, with whom he had shared the watch, was already up, and the endlessly repeated routine of the morning was under way.

'Where is the boy?' Valens asked.

'Gone,' Iudex said.

'Gone?'

'He left before first light.'

Valens felt a rising dread hollowing out his stomach and chest. 'Have you harmed him, without my orders?'

Aulus stopped grooming his horse. 'Far from it.' There was a sardonic smile on his ugly, drooping old face. 'We had a talk to him, while you were asleep, and we gave him one of the spare horses.'

'What is going on?' Valens had thought that the journey had made things better between him and the men. But this ignoring of his authority was as bad as ever.

'Of course *we* would have killed him,' Iudex said. 'In our line of work a certain heartlessness is often necessary. You have not been with us long enough yet to become acclimatised to the required brutality. But in this case it was the wrong option.'

'What are you talking about?'

'We advised him to leave before you woke.' The cherubic features of Iudex, so oddly set in his huge bald head, beamed amiably. 'You are a man of great cruelty. We told him that you intended to do away with him in the morning, and throw his body in the sea for the fishes. After that he needed no further persuasion to return.'

'But I had no such intention!'

'Otherwise he would not have gone back,' Iudex said.

'It is like this,' Aulus said. 'The boy's uncle is no fool. He will have guessed where the lad had gone. But, if his nephew returns unharmed, there is a chance that he will not inform his Persian masters of his suspicions about the nature of our mission.'

'Although,' Iudex said, 'there is no guarantee that he will not set the Persians on our trail.'

CHAPTER 23

Rome

I T WAS DARK IN THE CELL.

The man hung from a hook in the ceiling. He was naked. His feet did not touch the floor, and the heavy weight suspended from one ankle increased his suffering.

'Tell me again the message Acilius Glabrio gave you to take to the pretender across the Alps,' Volusianus said.

There was a pool of blood and urine under the dangling feet.

The terrible pressure on his chest made it hard for the man to speak.

Volusianus dragged the claws down the prisoner's thigh. The skin peeled away, exposing the flesh like that of an overripe fruit.

As the fresh blood ran, the man gasped out a line of poetry. '*Save me, unconquered hero, from evil.*'

'*Eripe me his, invicte, malis,*' the Praetorian Prefect repeated. 'Virgil, the words of the shade of Palinurus to Aeneas on the banks of the Styx.'

Murena admired the thoroughness of Volusianus. The Praetorian Prefect had sent away the torturers, and was conducting the investigation himself.

'And the reply Postumus sent back?'

'Please, I have told you all this. I am just a messenger.'

Volusianus raised the claw, and the prisoner desperately tried to twist away. The swaying motion this caused was enough to escalate his pain, so Volusianus lowered the claw again and waited.

When the prisoner's body had ceased its agonising pendulum, the man spoke again. *'I will not cross to those shores. Cease to hope that fate, once spoken by the gods, can be altered by prayer.'* His voice, little more than a harsh whisper, sank to nothing.

'And the rest?'

'You, set forth on your path, pull the blade from its scabbard.'

'There was nothing else?'

'No, by all the gods. Please, I don't know what any of it means.'

Volusianus went to put down the claws, careful not to step in any of the foul liquids on the floor. 'You should read poetry. It is improving, good for the soul.'

'Please, cut me down.'

Volusianus ignored him, washed his hands, and turned to Murena. 'Two separate passages, also from the descent to the underworld, both these are spoken by the Sibyl. The first has been altered to suit the circumstances.'

Murena's respect for the Praetorian Prefect grew. Volusianus might have started life as a peasant, but he knew his Virgil.

'It is odd,' Volusianus said, 'how some senators seem to believe that epic poetry is a code known only to themselves. But this all seems clear enough.'

It did not to Murena, but he kept quiet.

'*Eripe me* ... Acilius Glabrio sent an invitation to Postumus, pledging his support if the rebel crossed the Alps to overthrow the Emperor.'

'Most likely the death of his cousin in Gaul prompted him to act.' Murena had always been quick to pick things up. 'He blames Gallienus.'

'Quite so,' Volusianus said. 'But Postumus has made repeated public proclamations that he is content to rule what he holds. In his reply he had to adapt the lines of the Sibyl to Palinurus to restate that, for him, Gaul, Britain and Spain are empire enough. But in the final line, the one originally addressed to Aeneas – *pull the blade from its scabbard* – Postumus encourages Acilius Glabrio to assassinate Gallienus, and bid for the throne here in Rome himself.'

'It is more than enough evidence to condemn Acilius Glabrio for treason,' Murena said. 'Ironically, he is at Cumae, consulting the oracle. There are *frumentarii* watching him. Shall I send word to make the arrest?'

'Not yet. Keep him under close observation. Have all his correspondence intercepted, copied, resealed and then delivered. That it has been tampered with must not be detected by the recipients. It is a skill for which the *frumentarii* are notorious,' Volusianus said. 'If Acilius Glabrio has the courage to follow the advice of Postumus, he will first look for support. Most likely he will implicate other malcontents.'

'But is there a danger he might act alone?'

'If he is well watched, we can prevent him getting near enough to the Emperor to strike the blow.' Volusianus thought for a moment. 'Acilius Glabrio has many relatives in high places. If he is condemned, they must share his fate. The scandal might delay next year's campaign.'

'If the Emperor recovers, he intends to cross the Alps again?'

'That is Gallienus's intention. After all, Postumus did murder his son.' A knowing look passed across the bluff features of Volusianus. 'But other things might intervene.'

Murena felt a chill of apprehension that he prayed did not appear on his face.

'Any news from Severus?' Volusianus asked.

'None,' Murena said. 'But none is to be expected. They are deep behind enemy lines.'

'They should be near the Caspian by now. If they succeed, we should get word from the Black Sea by the end of winter.'

Murena said nothing.

Volusianus gazed at the pincers and the claws and the other instruments of torture, as if he were a shrewd farmer at market, wondering which to buy. 'You have heard the rumours that Shapur has threatened to mutilate the Emperor?'

'From a good source,' Murena said, 'one of our spies at Ctesiphon. The King of Kings announced that he might release Valerian from captivity, but that first he would cut off the Emperor's nose. The Persian knows that in Rome no mutilated man can wear the purple.'

'The gods willing, it will not come to that.' Volusianus sighed, dismissing the unhappy train of thought.

'What shall I do with the messenger?'

Volusianus glanced at the man hanging in the middle of the cell. 'Keep him alive, in solitary confinement. Don't let him talk to anyone. We may need him as a witness.'

A bitter wind whipped down the Sacred Way as Murena walked past the Temple of Venus and Rome. The street was nearly deserted. The weather was inclement, but tens of thousands of Romans had thronged to the Colosseum. It was five days before the Nones of October, the opening of the *Ludi Augustales*. The first Emperor Augustus might have taken their political freedom, but the people loved the games held in his honour.

It was mid-afternoon, the courts had been shut for hours, and the Forum was not busy. Murena angled across towards the far corner and the Senate House.

Why had Volusianus asked about Severus and his men? As the Praetorian Prefect had said – assuming that they were not already dead or captured – they should be near the Caspian Sea. There was no possibility that there could be any news. Did Volusianus suspect Murena's hand in the mission? No, it was not that. If Volusianus had been suspicious, Murena would have been the one strung up from the hook. The Praetorian Prefect was thorough, his actions decisive and never hampered by sentiment.

Before he reached the Senate House, Murena turned into the Argiletum that ran between the Curia and the Aemilian Basilica.

It was no more than wishful thinking on the part of Volusianus. The unpremeditated comment about the possible mutilation of the old Emperor gave it away. For all his intelligence, Volusianus was a westerner. They lacked the deep subtlety and cunning of the east. Murena was descended from good Italian stock, but his ancestors had lived in Syria for generations. Climate and geography and the surrounding culture had had their effect. Just as Volusianus could unravel the poetry employed by alienated senators, so Murena could read the preoccupations of the Praetorian Prefect.

Volusianus was determined that Gallienus would campaign in the east. The Praetorian Prefect would move Olympus to secure the release from Persian captivity of his great patron, the old Emperor Valerian. If Volusianus could bring that about, it would secure his influence over the imperial court. But Gallienus was set on marching over the Alps to avenge his son. If Prince Sasan fell into Roman hands, it would precipitate war along the Euphrates. If the King of Kings attacked Syria, Gallienus must march to its defence, and Volusianus would get his wish.

Still, Volusianus's question had unsettled Murena. That was why he was walking down to the Subura, to remind himself that he had power over the lives of others, and thus over his own destiny.

There was only one other pedestrian making his way up the Via Fornicata when Murena turned into the Vicus Caeseris. The wine shop was small and dark, with one side of the single public room occupied by great barrels taller than a man. The air smelt agreeably of the merchandise and the sawdust on the floor.

'Health and great joy, Gaius,' the vintner said. 'Not seen you in some time. I have some of the Raetian you like, a good one, well matured in the vats. Would you care to have a taste?'

'That is most kind.'

The wine was a deep red. It smelt and tasted of the pitch with which the barrels were treated. Tullia came in from the family's quarters at the back to help her father. She too greeted Murena as a valued customer.

'How is your husband?' Murena asked.

A look of concern crossed her face. 'He has been seconded to his old legion in the east.'

'Not for long, I hope?' Murena said politely. Tullia was in her mid-twenties, tall, full bodied, not unattractive.

'We do not expect him to be back until next summer.'

'Then we must pray that his duties do not detain him, and that he makes a safe return.'

She thanked him, and took some empty amphorae through the curtains into the back.

'What do you think of the Raetian?' The wine merchant rubbed his palms on the high-belted leather apron of his calling.

'Very good, but I am in the mood for something stronger, something to unknit the cares of life.'

'I have just the thing, a Thurine from Lucania. The grapes are not harvested until after the first frost, makes it very sweet and strong.'

'That would be ideal. I will take a flask with me.'

There was rain in the wind as Murena walked back to the Caelian.

The visit had achieved its purpose. There was something godlike about knowing the destiny of the wine seller and his family was in his hands. But, even so, he was not totally reassured. It would have been better if he had chosen an easterner for the mission. The necessary subterfuge came more naturally. But there had been no alternative. At the time he had not been long in command, and there had been no other *frumentarius* in the camp on whom he had incriminating evidence. Threats of violence alone, even to loved ones, were seldom enough.

The rain had picked up, and Murena was soaked by the time he got back to his office in the Camp of the Strangers. He dismissed his secretary, sat at his desk, and poured some of the Lucanian wine.

That Tullia was not at all unattractive. Come what may, it would be necessary to have her brought to the camp. Murena did not expect her husband to return. If he did, he could not be allowed to survive. The man knew far too much. A discreet accident would be arranged. And he might have talked to his wife before he departed. Murena would conduct her interrogation himself. There was no denying the erotic charge of having an attractive woman stripped and helpless. She might as well give him some pleasure, before she had to die.

An underling could kill her father and daughter.

CHAPTER 24

The Southern Shores of the Caspian Sea

WITH THE SEA TO THEIR LEFT, they travelled east. Although it was not mentioned again, the possibility of pursuit was on everyone's mind, and they went at a good pace. At times a chill wind blew from the north, lifting whitecaps out on the water. Here summer was long gone, and autumn well advanced. But the going was good and level, and the horses moved easily, as if, like the men, they were glad to be out of high country, at least for a time.

By the end of the first day the mountains had closed in from the south, and ran in a great crescent like a huge rampart almost up against the shore. For four days they followed the narrow track between the waves and the rock wall. Lucia said that the sea level was lower now than in the past. In the time of her father the breakers had beaten directly into the base of the cliffs, and merchants had used another route through the hills. There were no dwellings along the path, and they saw no one. Yet a few times, when the wind dropped, pale-blue coils of smoke showed high above on the heights.

Streams gushed from dark caverns in the rock. Some formed strong wild waterfalls, foaming white and plunging straight down the cliffs. Others, fanning out in numerous rivulets, and flowing more gently over stepped shelves of rock, resembled the sort of elaborate architectural water feature that might grace a wealthy city, like an elaborate fountain or nymphaeum. Where the streams cut the track, the surface of their beds was slippery and treacherous. Men and horses descended cautiously, and both were soaked by the spray and the icy water when they clambered out. One river, however, threw itself from the top of the precipice with such force that its waters arced clear over the track to crash straight into the sea. The column was able to ride, wondering and dry-shod, underneath.

On the fifth morning the mountains fell back, and they emerged onto a wide plain. The land was smooth and rich and well worked. It was dotted with settlements. In the fields the stubble of the harvest lay under vines and fig trees, some still heavy with fruit. Small plots of vegetables were tended in among the main produce. Never put all your eggs in one basket, as the saying went. If a blight or storm hit the plain, with luck not all the crops would be lost. Something should remain to feed the farmer's family, or to be bartered in the village. In Italy, the peasants around Valens's family estate employed the same strategy to survive.

The hamlets through which they passed were peaceful and unfortified. Their inhabitants were happy to sell eggs and chickens, bread and cheese to the travellers, who paid over the odds in good coins. In the evenings the sky to the north, out over the gulf, turned a livid purple and orange on the horizon, below dark, threatening clouds. But the rain held off.

On the third day on the plain they came in sight of the main settlement in these parts. Lucia knew it as Sariya, but Narses called it Zadrakarta. The Persian had been here many years before. He said there was a frontier wall two days beyond, which ran from the sea to the mountains, and closed the approach to the plain from the north-east. There was a second another day beyond, and a third further off, which ran due east from the Caspian. They were all said to have been built by Alexander the Great. Now they were garrisoned by Sassanid soldiers to protect the plain from the nomad tribes of the Steppe, and allow the farmers to continue their bucolic life undisturbed.

From Zadrakarta it was planned that Narses would guide them on the final leg of their quest. Before they reached the first of the fortified walls, they would unobtrusively slip off the road, turn south-east, and follow a river valley up into the mountains, and eventually by unfrequented paths come to the Castle of Silence.

Asked how they would get through the Walls of Alexander to the Steppe on their coming down from the mountains, Narses enigmatically replied that Mazda had inspired him with a plan. As it still seemed unlikely that they would ever return from the Castle of Silence, there was little point in pressing him on the subject.

Not far from the outskirts of Zadrakarta, Valens heard the fierce barking of dogs. Off the path, a pack of a dozen strays ringed a figure on the ground. Whether the man was injured, exhausted or both was initially unclear. Feebly, propped on one elbow, he fended the animals off with a stick. As one, Valens and Hairan at the head of the column turned their mounts, and set off to his aid.

The dogs heard them coming and reluctantly fell back, hackles up and snarling.

They were no distance from the man when Narses galloped past. The Persian skidded his horse to a halt, so violently he almost brought it back on its haunches. Turning the horse, Narses blocked their path.

'Stay back!'

'Why?'

'Don't go any closer. He has the plague.'

'How do you know?'

'It is our custom. When someone has a disease that threatens others, he is driven out.'

'To die on his own? That is inhuman,' Hairan said.

'The outcast is given a lump of bread, water and a stick.'

'But when he gets too weak, the dogs will devour him alive.' Valens was as horrified as Hairan.

'It will be as Mazda wills.'

The rest of the party had approached now.

'We can't just leave him to die,' Decimus said.

'You are all foreigners in this land,' Narses said, 'strangers to our laws.'

'We must take him with us,' Valens said.

'The townsfolk would not accept him. They would turn on us.' Narses was adamant. 'Even if he returns from the Gates of Darkness, his family will shun him as though he is accursed and still in the service of the infernal powers. If he recovers, they will have nothing to do with him until the pollution has been exorcised by the magi.'

The others sat their horses without speaking.

'Narses is right.' Lucia was the first to break the silence. 'It is our custom. There is nothing to be done.'

Valens looked at the pathetic and emaciated victim. He wished that he had not.

'Life is not easy,' Iudex said. 'Sometimes we have to harden our hearts.'

The men were subdued as they ate that evening in a caravanserai. Lucia had taken herself off to the home of some acquaintance in the town.

Feeling the need to justify the practices of his people, Narses was holding forth. 'Dogs or birds, it makes no difference. It is sacrilege to pollute the earth with a corpse. If the birds do not fly down on a body quickly, or if the dogs do not come at once and tear it to pieces, we hold that the dead man was profane in his ways, and that his soul is wicked and doomed, given over to the power of evil. So then his relatives mourn all the more, thinking him truly perished, and with no share in the higher life. But if a man is devoured quickly, they congratulate the dead man on his good fortune and marvel at his soul, believing that it is virtuous and godlike, and destined for the dwelling of the power of good.'

Hairan looked far from convinced, and Clemens, who never had any sympathy for easterners, muttered something derogatory under his breath. There was an air of tension at the table.

Keen to avoid any confrontation, Valens tried to think of something emollient to say. It was not easy. The image of sharp teeth gnawing at the living flesh of a defenceless man not half a mile away was preying on his mind.

'Every people consider any practice to which it is accustomed to be admirable and hallowed. To an outsider they may seem ridiculous and incredible, even dreadful and cruel.'

The sentiments were clichéd, but the best Valens could find. They were far from satisfying Hairan.

'Explanations are not justifications,' Hairan said. 'To understand something is not to condone it.' He had already had several drinks, and now he rounded on Narses. 'You Persians are a cruel race.'

'No crueller than any other.' Narses sounded defensive.

'Only jackals and wild asses now live where Hatra once stood. Those of my people who were not killed were driven off into captivity.'

'A great misfortune for you, brother, but such are the laws of war,' Narses said. 'Once a battering ram touches the wall of a city, the lives of its inhabitants are forfeit.'

Hairan tugged angrily at his long moustache. 'After the Sassanid army left, my home was desolate, my family massacred. Once my father died in exile, I was consigned to a lifetime of solitude. What point is there in marrying and having children when all you will do is grieve when a cruel fate takes them, or leave them to mourn you when you die?'

'Would things have been better if the Romans had taken Hatra? If either of the sieges of the Emperor Septimius Severus had succeeded, your city would have been a desert before you were born. Thanks to the Romans you would never have existed.' Narses was trying to be conciliatory.

'Only treachery breached the double walls of Hatra, whose foundations were like sheets of iron.' Hairan turned to Valens. 'King Daizan had a daughter. Nadira was the most beautiful woman of her time. Her skin was so delicate you could see right through to the marrow of her bones. She gave the troops wine, and, when they were drunk, opened the gates to the enemy. Shapur had promised to marry her, raise her above his other wives. Instead he commanded a man to mount a wild horse – she was tied by her hair to its tail, and the horse was made to gallop until her body was torn to pieces.' He looked back at Narses. 'And you deny cruelty runs deep in Persian blood?'

'Shapur is one man. Not all Persians are like him.' Narses spoke abruptly, his patience wearing thin. 'As you bemoan your fate, remember that I too live in exile.'

'Desert or betray us, and your road home is open.'

There was silence after Hairan's words.

Narses hand was on the hilt of his sword.

'Enough of these old, unhappy things,' Valens said. 'None of us would have chosen the path that has led us here. If any of us are to win through, we must be united.'

The six men regarded him. Even Hairan was sobered.

'Let each of us now take an oath, swear in the name of whatever deity he worships, never to desert or betray our brotherhood.'

Solemnly, one by one, invoking Jupiter Optimus Maximus, Ahuramazda, Bel, the Demiurge, or whatever other divine powers to which they prayed, each man at the table took the oath.

'Now,' Narses said, 'let us get drunk. For once, I will set aside the custom of my ancestors, and not reconsider what we have decided in the morning.'

As ever, Iudex could not be prevailed upon to touch a drop of wine. Instead, as the others drank, then drank some more, he sang to them.

In their inebriation, Hairan and Narses seemed reconciled.

After a time Iudex got up and danced. His feet – so small they seemed unsuited to bearing his weight – measured intricate patterns, his huge hands cut through the air, and his great bald head bobbed and weaved to the rhythm. All the while a beatific smile lit up his childlike features.

Lucia was waiting in Valens's room.

The light of the one lamp softened the long features of her face. Well gone with wine, Valens saw only her knowing eyes, the sensuality of her mouth. He stepped towards her.

Firmly, she placed her hand on his chest, held him away. 'I came to *talk* to you.'

Embarrassed, he moved back, mumbling an incoherent apology.

She smiled, not unkindly.

Silently he cursed his foolishness and, after all she had endured at the hands of men, his insensitivity.

'I came to thank you. Zabda told me that it was your decision to follow the tent-dwellers.'

'I am sorry that we did not arrive sooner.'

'That was fate, or the will of the gods.' The depths of her pain showed in her eyes. But she was too strong to break down at the memory. 'When I was in their camp, I wanted to die. Afterwards I thought I would be content to marry my husband's brother. But suffering changes a person. He was a brute, and – Mazda forgive me – I am glad Iudex killed him.'

The wine fumes were clearing in Valens's mind. 'You are going to stay here in Zadrakarta?'

'Yes.'

'What will you do?'

'There is a merchant in the town. He trades in silk and fine clothing. My husband had dealings with him and I saw him while you were drinking. I am a skilled seamstress. He will take me into his household.'

'Will that be suitable?'

'As I told you once, I am not without resource.'

Valens moved to his baggage. From the saddlebags he took a pouch containing perhaps a dozen of the precious cameos.

'Have these,' he said, holding out the bag. 'Life is not easy for a single woman without means.'

'You make a very unconvincing merchant.' She smiled, but took the proffered gift.

'May your gods hold their hands over you.'

'And yours. Even if you succeed, you know, you will not be able to return this way. The whole countryside will be raised against you.' She looked away into the flame of the lamp. 'I am a Persian, a loyal subject of the King of Kings.'

'You will not betray us?'

'The father of the one you go to rescue is a traitor. But the prisoner is just a child. I would not see the innocent punished.' She looked back at Valens. 'No, I will not betray you. But another might. Zabda was convinced the expedition was cursed, or that you rode with a traitor.'

'Why?'

'The deaths of Severus and Quintus.'

'Quintus's fall was an accident in the storm.'

'There were no witnesses. Zabda said he was a fine horseman.' Lucia shook her head. 'First you lost your commander, then your navigator.'

'And then no matter what we did, we could not shake the Arabs from our trail.' That another had shared his suspicions unsettled Valens. 'Did Zabda know who it was?'

'If he did, he did not tell me.'

CHAPTER 25

The Elburz Mountains

THEY WERE SURE NO ONE had seen them leave the road.
Camped by the river, they had waited until there was a brief
opportunity when there was not a soul in sight, no traveller on
the road or labourer in the fields. To cover their tracks, for the
first miles, they had ridden up the riverbed. By the time the story
got about of a caravan that had left Zadrakarta but never reached
the first of the Walls of Alexander, they should be long gone.
Perhaps they would enter into local mythology. Village mothers
would scare their children with stories of spectral horsemen still
riding the plains on dark nights like these, when the moon was
hidden.

Valens rode now with Narses and Decimus at the front of the
column. Narses knew these mountains. He had hunted across
them when serving with the Satrap of Hyrkania. For these final
approaches, the Persian would be the eyes of the expedition. Back
at Zadrakarta, Valens had formally appointed Decimus second
in command. The risks they had run so far would be as nothing
compared with those to be faced at the Castle of Silence. If Valens
himself was killed or captured, the rest would need undisputed
leadership to have any hope of getting out alive.

It had taken them two days to cross the foothills. Maple and ash
and alder had given way to tall stands of beech and oak. The horses
had gone hock deep through banks of fallen leaves. Yet under the

wide spreading branches it was still warm, and some vestigial trace of summer still lingered. Twice they had had to pull off the path to avoid being seen by the last shepherds driving their flocks down to their winter pastures on the plain. When they had camped on the second night the air was drowsy with the hum of bumblebees. The trees were so full of their hives that honey dripped from the remaining leaves. Clemens had warned them not to take so much as a taste. They should remember the honey eaten by the men with Xenophon. Likewise, they should not eat any roots or vegetables, bearing in mind what happened to the troops under Mark Antony in these parts. Narses had laughed in his face. They had foraged, and everyone but Clemens had eaten what was gathered. Not one of them went mad. No one had become obsessed with turning over every stone as if they were accomplishing something of great importance. No one vomited bile and died. With the morning, the honey evaporated on the leaves.

Three days ago they had come out onto the uplands. It was as if they had ridden into a different season. A cold wind blew down from the north. It fretted at their cloaks, and threw gusts of rain at their backs. The slopes were bare, except for a few stunted junipers, and there was snow on the peaks. It must be getting late in October. Soon winter would come to the mountains.

As the third day in the high mountains drew to a close, Decimus, his handsome face pinched with the cold, turned to Valens. 'Do not think me ungrateful of the honour,' he said, 'but you should not have made me your deputy.'

Valens had noted his unenthusiastic response to the appointment back in the town, but had put it down as a becoming modesty. 'You are not one of those soldiers who shuns responsibility. You have shown that as horse master. Anyway, *frumentarii* are selected for their independence.'

Decimus smiled. 'I trust my own right arm, and my judgement, and yes I am good with horses. But I have never served in the east. I do not know the country or the people. I speak no more of the languages than the smattering of words that I have picked up on the journey. You should have chosen Narses here, or one of the others.'

'The men will follow you,' Narses said. 'We are happy enough. Certainly it was better than when we were landed with an untested young outsider.'

Valens looked sharply at the Persian.

Narses laughed, his teeth very white behind his black beard. 'And even that has not turned out quite as badly as we feared.'

'That fills my heart with unalloyed joy,' Valens said.

'You are not the boy you were three months ago,' Narses said.

'And I am also not dead yet. It was just a precaution. The men might never have to follow Decimus.'

'If they do,' Decimus said, 'I will do my damnedest to get them home. I have no intention of leaving my aged bones whitening on these mountains.'

Valens had never really thought about it, but, for all his good looks, Decimus was far from young. 'How soon do you leave the standards?'

'I prefer not to count the months. It tempts fate. But I am getting too long in the tooth for this life. Like old Aulus and Clemens, I should be sitting by the fire, my children gathered around, my wife tending to my needs. Not stuck on a mountain in the middle of nowhere.'

They rode in silence for a time.

'Are you married, sir?' Decimus asked.

'No.'

'Any family at all?'

'I have a cousin.'

'The Tribune of the Horse Guards?'

'Yes.'

'No one else?'

'A few other distant relatives.' It might have been the wind that made Valens's eyes water. But there was a catch in his throat. 'Five years ago, my parents were travelling through the Apennines. They were murdered. *Interfectus a latronibus*. Perhaps bandits, perhaps stragglers from the Alamanni who marched on Rome. There was no way of knowing.'

Now he had started, the words came of their own volition. 'It was that that made me join up. I wanted revenge. Against anyone, against the world, even against the gods. I had a childish fantasy that one day, in some remote glen, I would hunt down their killers. Ridiculous, no more than the dreams of a drunken youth, or a mere boy.'

Somewhat ashamed of sharing such confidences, Valens asked Narses if he had a family.

'Yes.' The Persian answered curtly, then changed the subject. 'We are getting close. The Castle of Silence lies on the far side of that ridge. We will turn off the track up ahead. There is a sheltered valley with a spring some way to the west. It is well hidden. I found it when I was after a leopard. Unless another hunter happens along, we should not be disturbed. From the heights above we can watch the road up to the fortress. Tonight there is no moon. We can move unobserved. I will take the two of you to reconnoitre the castle by first light.'

The Castle of Silence was set on a razor-backed ridge. A road ran up to its gatehouse from the west. It was steep and utterly exposed, but smooth and wide enough for a wagon. The outer wall of the fortress, roughly oval in shape, was built right on the edge of the two precipices. At the far end from the gatehouse, built into the circuit wall, was a tall round tower. From a postern hidden behind the tower, a narrow track snaked down the slope and vanished to the east.

Every detail was clear in the early morning sun. From the cliff to the north they had a good view across the ravine. And everything they saw was depressing. The gates were kept closed. The battlements above them were patrolled. While the sides of the ravine did not look unclimbable, and a few shrubs would provide a modicum of cover, even at this distance it was clear that the wall, constructed of well-jointed masonry, could not be scaled without a ladder or grappling hooks.

'You once served here, Narses, tell us about the routine.' Valens kept his voice down, even though, with the wind keening over the rocks, there was no way anything but a shout could possibly be heard across the void.

'The guards are replaced every two months,' Narses said. 'Any longer up among these crags, and they would go off their heads. Only the gaolers who do the torturing stay all the time, and they are demented anyway.'

'How many?'

'Twenty guards come up from Hyrkania. There are about half a dozen who wield the hot knives and turn the rack.'

'Domestic staff?'

'A dozen or so stable boys and cooks and the like. They never leave.'

There were far too many either to storm the place or ambush the relief. Access would have to be by some more clandestine method.

'Who else comes and goes?' Valens asked.

'Occasionally the zendanig is summoned to court.'

'The *zendanig*?'

'The warden of the prison. Cruel bastard with a big red beard, always wears black. Even inanimate objects seem to fear Naduk the zendanig.'

Decimus thought of something. 'You said you caught a leopard when you were here.'

'Once in a while the zendanig will give a couple of the men leave to go hunting. The gates are bolted behind them, and they are not let back in until they have been recognised. No one dares open the gates without Naduk's order.'

'What do the soldiers do for women?' Decimus asked.

'Usually four or five whores in the place.' Narses shook his head sadly. 'Poor bitches get melancholy, and their looks start to go. While I was here, one threw herself off the wall.'

'Too much used?' Decimus said sympathetically.

'No, oddly not that. After a month stuck here most of the men lose interest. Actually they lose interest in anything. Nothing to see but the cliffs, nothing to listen to but the mewing of those fucking buzzards, never anything new to do or think about. Confined in those walls, the wind always howling in your ears, nowhere to go. That was why I kept badgering the zendanig to go hunting. Not that I liked having to talk to him.'

'Are the girls replaced?' Valens asked.

'Two times in my tour.'

'Are they escorted?'

'A couple of soldiers.'

Decimus smiled, the white scar by his right eye disappearing in the laughter lines. 'There is a story in Thucydides, or maybe Xeno-phon. A revolution in Thebes, I think it was. The conspirators invited the rulers to dinner, promised them some women, gave them plenty to drink. The women come in all veiled . . .'

'It will never work,' Valens said.

'The numbers are right,' Decimus said.

'Narses and Hairan would have to be the escort. They are the only two that can pass as Persians.' Valens paused. 'But of the rest of us, Aulus would make a very unappealing girl, what with his receding hair, and cadaverous face.'

'We would wear veils.'

'Iudex is damn near seven foot tall.'

'Bald as a coot, and with the biggest hands I have ever seen.' Narses added.

'Do either of you have a better idea?' Decimus demanded.

'Actually, I do.' Narses looked very pleased with himself. 'I have been saving it for last.' The other two said nothing. 'I am surprised that neither of you has asked yet.'

Narses was beginning to remind Valens of his old philosophy tutor, which was not endearing.

'The castle is on top of a mountain,' the Persian said.

'Where does the garrison gets its water?' Decimus asked.

'Not that. There is a well in the courtyard.'

'Food!' Valens said. 'Where do they get their supplies?'

Narses beamed. 'A wagon comes up the road once a month. There is the driver, and there are six outriders. Sometimes in the winter, when the snows are deep, they send a mule train. But the supplies always arrive.'

'When do they come?' Valens felt a surge of excitement.

'About the time of the new moon.'

They grinned at each other.

'Where in Hades are Aulus and Clemens?'

The camp was tucked into a depression in the shoulder of a slope. There was a spring of drinkable water, and around it some undergrowth for cover. It was not overlooked by any obvious tracks. The animals were tethered, the kit squared away. Hairan was on watch. Everything was as it should be, except for the missing men.

'They went hunting after some goats we saw,' Hairan said.

'I gave instructions that no one was to leave the camp!' Valens was furious. 'Wandering around the hillsides, they could be seen by anyone. They are endangering us all.'

'That is what I told them.' Hairan shrugged. 'They told me to go and fuck myself; they wanted some fresh meat.'

'Animals are the miscarriage of evil daemons. It is very dangerous to eat them.' Iudex was sitting cross-legged, drawing in his notebook. The object of his study was something shiny on the ground in front of him.

There was nothing Valens could do but wait. Searching for them doubled the risk of being spotted.

'Vegetables are much better,' Iudex continued. 'Aroused by the beauty of the sun, the daemons ejaculated on the ground. From their seed grew all plants. Violets and roses are particularly rich in light.'

'What is that you are drawing?'

Clemens picked up the small sheet of bronze, which was shaped like part of a man's calf muscle.

'Where did you find it?'

'By the spring. I have cleaned and polished it.'

It was from a greave: a piece of armour designed to snap over the lower leg, and be held in place by its own elasticity. It was broken, and time had thinned it and made it brittle.

'Greek, by the look of it,' Iudex said. 'Very ancient.'

'He was a long way from home.'

'Or it came here by trade, or as plunder.'

Iudex went back to his drawing. Valens looked over his shoulder. The picture was perfect, capturing every detail of the griffins exquisitely chased into the rim of the metal.

Holding up the notebook, Iudex grunted with satisfaction. Then he tore out the page, and ripped it into tiny pieces. With his huge, powerful hands he snapped the artefact into small fragments and carefully ground it to powder under his boot. Finally he scooped a hole in the thin topsoil, and buried the detritus.

'Why?'

Iudex looked up contentedly. 'Once it is known to me, it is known to the Demiurge. And once the Demiurge has taken cognisance of a thing, its corporal existence is no longer necessary. It is the same with some men.'

CHAPTER 26

Rome

IT WAS A COLD, MOONLESS NIGHT. Volusianus was huddled in a thick, hooded cloak, but he felt the cold. A chill breeze moved through the trees and shrubs of the Gardens of Lucullus. It was past midnight, and ahead the villa of Acilius Glabrio was silent.

Volusianus shifted in the darkness under the boughs of the ornamental cypress tree. Murena was next to him, but the rest of his men were hidden in the gloom. Volusianus did not need to see the soldiers, he knew they were there. There was nothing to do but wait for the signal.

The villa had been in the family of Acilius Glabrio for generations. Palatial, and surrounded by the wide gardens that still bore the name of their original designer, it was one of the most splendid houses in Rome – a statement of wealth and status. Yet its history was tragic. Messallina, the wife of the Emperor Claudius, had coveted the gardens, and forced their owner to suicide. Later, her infidelities exposed, it was here she had taken her own life. The property, Volusianus thought, would bring Acilius Glabrio no better fortune.

The growth of a conspiracy was much like that of a plant. At first there was little to be done but carefully observe the tendrils it put out. But there came a time when it must be cut down, its roots grubbed out. Inside the shuttered residence Acilius Glabrio was in treasonous conclave with another disaffected senator and two junior officers, one a Praetorian, the other serving with the Horse Guards. Volusianus was not overly concerned by the disloyal senators. Their kind talked and talked. Even when they finally acted, it was seldom with proficiency. But the involvement of the military demanded decisive measures.

After a month of prevarication, Acilius Glabrio had heeded the poetic advice of the usurper over the Alps. When he tampered with the loyalty of the troops, he had drawn the sword. It was typical patrician arrogance, Volusianus thought, that Acilius Glabrio had not been deterred by the disappearance of the man who had brought the message from Postumus.

A light flashed on the wall of one of the rear courtyards of the villa. The shuttered lantern opened three times. Volusianus heard Murena quietly give the orders. The complex was ringed with troops. Now, above the sussuration of the wind in the trees, came the distinctive sounds of armed men moving into position at the front and rear gates.

It was what every member of the senate feared – the arrival of the Praetorians in the dead of night. But the soldiers approaching the entrances were a diversion. It would take time for the gates to be opened, time in which much incriminating evidence might be destroyed.

'*Open in the name of Gallienus Augustus!*'

The command was followed by a series of heavy blows to the front gate. Moments later, the commotion was repeated at the back gate.

Volusianus started walking to where the light had shown. Murena and three Praetorians followed at his heels.

At the foot of the wall Volusianus softly called the password: *Iustitia.*

A pale circle of a face peered over. Then a rope ladder coiled down. Volusianus sent Murena and the Praetorians up first. He had not lived to his advanced age by taking unnecessary risks.

It was difficult climbing in a mail shirt. Volusianus discarded his cloak to prevent being further encumbered.

At the top, on the walkway, Volusianus took a moment to get his breath back. There was a fountain in the courtyard below. Apart from the splashing water it was empty and quiet. The uproar at the gates was at a distance.

The *frumentarius* who had been placed in the household of Acilius Glabrio led them swiftly through the maze of the huge villa. Once or twice servants peeped out from behind half-open doors, but then vanished. Volusianus followed through opulent halls and libraries, and down mean service corridors, until they came to the dining room. Lights and noise issued from behind the curtains.

As before, Volusianus indicated the others should precede him.

There was an outcry when the armed men burst through the hangings.

Volusianus drew his blade before stepping through.

The conspirators were motionless, like a tableau: the two senators frozen in the act of throwing documents into a brazier, the pair of officers facing the opening with swords in their hands.

For a heartbeat or two no one moved. Then one of the officers shouted something incomprehensible, and both armed men hurled themselves at Murena and the Praetorians.

'Take one of them alive!' Volusianus shouted.

Through the clatter of the fight Volusianus saw Acilius Glabrio drop the papyri in his hands and bolt through a small door at the rear of the room. The other senator did not think to follow, but fell to his knees, holding his hands out in supplication.

Unarmoured and outnumbered two to one, the officers had no chance. One of them was clutching his stomach, trying to hold in his own entrails. The other was being wrestled to the ground.

Volusianus moved to the cowering senator.

'Have no fear, Thrasea. I know what you have done.'

The senator whimpered with terror. Volusianus took his hands, gently raised him up.

'Your loyalty to the Emperor is an example to us all,' Volusianus said. 'It took courage to infiltrate the conspiracy.'

A desperate hope dawned in the senator's eyes. 'Yes, that was it. I did not know who to trust, so I told no one.'

'And now you can tell everything,' Volusianus said gently.

'Everything . . . that was always my intention.'

'Later tonight, my friend.'

Volusianus released the senator's hands, and looked over his shoulder. The Praetorians were still struggling with the officer who was not mortally wounded.

'Where does the passage go?' he asked the *frumentarius*.

'Just to the roof garden.'

'Good. Stay with the senator. Murena, with me.'

Volusianus was blowing hard when he reached the roof garden. After the stairs it was bright in the starlight. Acilius Glabrio was by the balustrade at the far end. Out beyond the villa the grounds were lit by the torches of the troops.

Volusianus put out a hand to stop Murena when he went to apprehend the fugitive.

'It is over,' Volusianus said. 'There is nowhere to run.'

'You jumped-up peasant,' Acilius Glabrio spat. 'You sent my cousin to his death.'

'Men die in war. It happens.'

'If not me, someone will kill the degenerate Gallienus.' Acilius Glabrio drew himself up, as if to address the senate or posterity. 'The tyrant is hated by all his subjects.'

'This is not the time for a speech,' Volusianus said.

'Your master will die, and you will be cast down. Vice brings retribution. The gods—'

'No more words.'

Acilius Glabrio stopped talking. He took a ring from his finger and turned it in his hands.

Again Volusianus restrained Murena.

The secret compartment unscrewed, Acilius Glabrio raised the ring to his lips, and drank the poison.

They stood watching each other, the wind sighing around them.

Acilius Glabrio choked, and staggered back against the balustrade.

Volusianus and Murena did not move.

Acilius Glabrio collapsed to the floor.

'Why?' Murena asked. 'We could have uncovered everything.'

'His family are well connected. A trial, even in the palace, behind closed doors, would have been an embarrassment.'

Acilius Glabrio's body went into convulsions.

'Gods below, it is bitter up here,' Volusianus said to Murena. 'Would you fetch me another cloak?'

Evidently surprised, Murena did as he was bidden. Volusianus made himself comfortable on a nearby bench to watch Acilius Glabrio die. It occurred to Volusianus that the death of Acilius Glabrio removed the need to keep alive the senator's messenger to Postumus. The man would never be called as a witness, and he had no more information to divulge. The messenger had been thoroughly tortured – if anything his death would be a kindness.

The spasms of Acilius Glabrio had ended. Now he was motionless, hardly breathing.

It was right to have sent Murena away. In his agony, Acilius Glabrio might say something best not overheard. Murena had done well pursuing this conspiracy, but he was no longer to be trusted.

When they had been questioning the messenger in the cells, and Volusianus had mentioned the Castle of Silence, Murena had nearly pissed himself. Murena had been watched since, his secretary suborned, his movements followed. Why did Murena visit the family of one of the ten sent to rescue Prince Sasan?

CHAPTER 27

The Elburz Mountains

THEY WAITED IN THE CAMP for three days.

The goats that Aulus and Clemens had shot were butchered and cooked. The men only lit a fire during daylight, taking care that it did not smoke. The depression was sheltered from the wind, but it was cold, and when it rained their spirits flagged. They heated stones in the ashes and placed them in their bedrolls. The stones soon lost their warmth, and did little to help them sleep.

Two men remained on watch night and day at the top of the ridge. They were out of sight of the fortress, a couple of miles from its main gate. From their lookout they could see a long stretch of the road as it toiled up from the plains. They were confident that nothing could pass unobserved.

On the second day, Narses asked to speak with Valens. The duty roster was altered, and they stood watch together.

'There were three thousand of us that surrendered at Corycus,' the Persian said. 'We swore the Roman military oath. They made us leave our horses. We were unhappy about that.'

They were lying close together at the top of the slope. Narses was wearing perfume. It was strong, and had the sweet and spicy aroma of spikenard. Valens had learnt that sometimes it was best to let a man talk. Narses would get to the point eventually.

'And then there was a problem about the boats. We are forbidden to soil water with human waste.' Narses smiled. 'We were given big amphorae. The boats were enormous, several hundred aboard each. Privacy was hard to find in the cramped conditions. It matters to a Persian. Those boats soon stank. The sailors did not love us.'

Narses paused. His dark eyes flicked from the road to the camp and back with the lidless intensity of a bird. He did not look at Valens.

'A thousand were sent to the garrison in Egypt, the rest sailed first to islands in the Aegean. I went to Lemnos. From there, five hundred of us were ordered to join the imperial field army at Milan. Later we were joined by those who had been held on Rhodes. We went north across the Alps when Gallienus recaptured the province of Raetia from Postumus. There were almost a thousand of us at the battle near Curia, high in the mountains. We were led by our own officers. Things were not bad. I was a scout. After that I became a *frumentarius*.'

Narses stopped talking.

Again Valens said nothing.

'The Emperor himself awarded me citizenship. Now I am no longer Narses son of Rastak, but Publius Licinius Narses. I have married a Roman woman. Well, Greek actually. We have a child. They are in Rome. I would return to them.'

For the first time Narses glanced at Valens, but then looked away.

'I have had news from my father. He does not approve. He has disowned me. It is hurtful. I have a new life, but I am still a Persian.'

At last Narses had raised what was troubling him.

'You are worried about fighting your own kind?' Valens said.

Narses fixed his gaze back on the road. His black beard nodded.

'It is rather late to mention your concern,' Valens said. 'You should have told Murena before you left Rome.'

'I did.' Narses bared his teeth in a smile which lacked any humour. 'The little shit told me I had to go – no other soldier in the Roman army had served in the Persian garrison of the Castle of Silence. If my conscience troubled me, I should raise the issue with the Praetorian Prefect. Volusianus himself had instructed Murena to send me on the mission.'

'Did you?'

'Of course not.' Now Narses actually laughed. 'Would you?'

'No.'

'When we surrendered, the general Ballista gave us his word that we would never have to fight our own people.'

'You have sworn the *sacramentum* to the Roman Emperor,' Valens said, 'and at Zadrakarta you took an oath by Mazda never to desert or betray our brotherhood.'

'I need no reminding. We are raised to ride, shoot the bow, and abhor the Lie.'

'What will you do?' Valens asked.

Narses blew out his cheeks, exhaling noisily. 'I will not betray or desert the brotherhood. But, if I can avoid it, I will not take a Persian life.'

'A man cannot go into a fight with one hand tied behind his back,' Valens said. 'You will get yourself killed.'

Narses did not reply.

'You might get one of us killed.'

Narses sighed, but still did not speak.

'An oath taken under duress is not binding,' Valens said. 'Perhaps an action born out of necessity is not blameworthy.'

Narses would have snorted with derision had it not been impolite. 'You sound like one of those hairy Greeks, a sophist or a philosopher.'

Valens grinned. 'Gods below, I loathed my philosophy tutor. All that logic-chopping and convoluted semantics do nothing to prepare a man for life.' He stopped smiling, suddenly very serious.

'You must do what you think is right, but we have to trust one another.'

'We have to trust one another,' Narses repeated.

The convoy plodded slowly up the track between the cliff and the precipice. They had been on the road for days, but in a couple of hours they would reach the Castle of Silence. The eight draught horses were labouring against the incline to pull the heavily loaded wagon. The squeal and rumble of its wheels drowned the sound of the hooves. The men were as tired as the animals, too tired to talk. There was nothing to see but the endless ravines and bare slopes and the little gullies choked with juniper and mountain scrub. It was cold and threatened to rain.

A hot meal and a warm fire were the only good things to anticipate about their arrival. The fortress was a dismal place, its warden feared almost as much by the soldiers as the prisoners. The few whores provided for the troops were pale, sad and listless things. At least the convoy would not remain longer than a few days, just long enough to restore the horses. They were better off than the poor devils of the garrison. Two months cramped in that remote eyrie was a harsh penance, even in summer, and winter was fast approaching.

They crested a rise and saw something on the road at the foot of a gully.

The outriders stiffened in their saddles.

It was a man. He was on his back, unmoving.

The mounted officer looked around. The wagon was piled with supplies. There was always the fear of bandits, and other men, the hungry and the desperate, would kill for food and wine. There was a famine in the province of Bactria. But this was not Bactria. These mountains were empty. The shepherds would have driven their flocks down to pastures in the plains for the winter. At this time of year there was no one at all in this high wasteland.

The officer nudged his horse into a trot. The other five riders followed. The wagon lumbered after them.

The man on the track was a Persian, judging by his square-cut dark beard and hair. His clothes had once been fine, but were stained and torn by hard travel. He wore a sword on his belt, and a bow case and quiver lay near him in the dirt. Evidently the soldier had not been robbed.

The officer swung down from his horse, tossed the reins to a soldier.

The prone man grimaced as he tried to raise himself on one elbow. His face was ashen.

'Rest easy, brother,' the officer said. With a groan the man fell back. He clutched his right leg. 'What happened?'

The injured man tried to speak, but no words came.

'Get him some wine.'

At the command, three of the soldiers dismounted. The two remaining in the saddle held their reins.

'Give him some room.' The officer took one of the proffered flasks. The others fell back a pace. 'Drink.' The officer lifted the man's head, trickled a little wine between his cracked lips.

The man spluttered and coughed. The officer waited, then gave him another drink.

'My thanks.' The voice was little more than a whisper. 'My horse threw me. I think my leg is broken.'

Now he managed to get on one elbow, and reached for the wine. He drank thirstily, his throat working beneath the black beard. He sighed and gave back the flask. There was great pain in his eyes.

'My name is Narses, son of Rastak of the clan Suren. I am a messenger of the King of Kings.'

The soldiers straightened up, the officer too. This was a man of importance. It was their duty to give him assistance.

'You are the supply convoy bound for the Castle of Silence.'

'Yes, *Framadar*.' The officer addressed him by the title due to a superior. 'Can you ride?'

'No, put me on the wagon.'

All eyes turned to the approaching vehicle. The wagoner cracked his whip above the animals' ears, but it was still some way off.

'Let me look at your leg,' the officer bent over. 'I can put it in a splint.'

'Leave it!' The *framadar* spoke sharply.

The officer straightened up, as if rebuked.

'I am so very sorry,' the *framadar* said with utter sincerity.

Suspicion dawned on the face of the officer.

Suddenly the air was filled with awful motion. Like a swarm of bees, the arrows thrummed past. The two soldiers still on horseback were hit. One slumped forward in the saddle, a look of disbelief rather than pain across his features. The other screamed and twisted, hopelessly reaching for the shaft embedded between his shoulders.

'You bastard!' The officer drew his sword.

The man on the ground hooked his supposedly broken leg behind the officer's leading knee, and swept him off balance.

Landing on his back, the officer's hilt was knocked from his grasp. Dragging air back into his chest, he scrabbled for his blade. Clutching it, he hauled himself back to his feet. The impostor was also up, sword out, well balanced, but backing away towards the lip of the precipice. Behind the officer the loose horses were milling, their hooves stamping on the hard surface.

The officer spat at the man's feet; the worst insult for a Persian. 'Whoever is a sinner shall be cast down to Hell.'

Valens could not get a clear shot.

After they had toppled the two mounted men from their saddles, all the horses were loose. Now the beasts sidled, rolling their eyes and throwing their heads up, alarmed by the shouts of the men, the smell of blood and the nervous movements of each other. The horses were between the six concealed archers and the Persians.

'Swords!' Valens yelled.

This had to be done quickly. No one could get away. He dropped his bow, snatched up his shield, and set off.

Bursting through the low shrubs, he drew his sword. Behind him he could hear the others clattering down the gully.

Emerging onto the road, he startled the nearest horse. It spun around and set off back down the way it had come. Obeying the imperative of the herd, most of the others took off after. Valens jumped back as a big chestnut almost ran him down.

The horse flashed past, and, like a warrior sprung from the very rocks of the track, a Persian stood in its place.

For a frozen moment the two men stared at each other.

Valens caught a glimpse of Narses, at the edge of the road, back to the ravine. The officer leading the supply train was attacking Narses hard, unleashing a flurry of blows. Narses was standing his ground, his blade moving like lightning to block and parry.

Then the Persian in front of Valens lunged, and the world narrowed to a circumference of just the reach of a blade.

Valens got his shield across his body. The point of the sword clanged off the metal boss of the shield, ripped through the leather cover, and gouged along its wooden surface. The impact made Valens stagger a couple of paces to regain his balance.

The Persian surged forward to press his advantage. But another horse – the enormous black stallion that had been ridden by the officer – swung around sideways, threatening to dash the puny combatants to the ground with its mountainous shoulders and flanks and haunches. Both men had to scamper out of its way like children.

When the horse was gone, the Persian settled on the balls of his feet, legs close together, sword out two-handed in front.

Leading with his left boot, Valens dropped into the ox guard: half turned, shield well forward of his body, sword held back overhand, its tip level with the rim of the shield.

From all around came the clangour of battle. Off to his right, Valens saw a Persian grabbing at the trailing reins of the black stallion. Steel flashed and rang to his left. This should have been easier. The Persians were outnumbered and surprised. They were unarmoured and had no shields. Yet they were neither running nor being cut down. These warriors were no strangers to standing close to the steel. If they had to die, they intended to sell their lives at a high cost.

Valens advanced cautiously, side on.

The Persian turned slightly, watching his every move.

Two quick, short steps, and Valens rolled his wrist and aimed a high cut at his opponent's head. The long straight Sassanid blade flicked up. Valens slipped to one knee, altering the angle of strike down to the thigh. The Persian got his blade in the way, moving inside the blow.

Tucking his shoulder inside his shield, with all the strength in his legs, Valens surged upwards at the Persian. Too late, the Persian tried to step back. The boss of Valens's shield hit him square in the chest. The Persian tottered backwards, arms circling as he fought to steady himself. Valens punched him in the face with the metal boss. Still the man did not fall. Valens hit him again. Now he went down.

On his hands and knees, the Persian scuttled sideways like a crab. Valens brought the heavy blade slicing down into the back of his head. One blow was enough. Planting his boot on the man's back, Valens wrenched the sword free of the ruined skull.

The back of the officer was just ahead. Narses was still defending himself, but the heels of his boots were right on the edge of the canyon.

The officer must have sensed Valens coming. He sidestepped away from Narses, turning to meet this new threat.

Valens swung first. The officer parried with skill. His riposte got past Valens's shield. Only a wild twist of his whole body prevented it driving through his armour and skewering his stomach.

Both gathered themselves, shifting on their feet, each searching for an opening.

With its hooves smacking into the road, the black stallion pranced behind Valens. It was barely under control, but there was a rider on its back. The Persian must have gathered the reins. The horse was heading up the road.

'Narses, use your bow,' Valens shouted. 'Don't let him escape!'

The break in his concentration was nearly the end of Valens. The officer's blade struck like a serpent scenting blood. Valens tried to hurl himself aside. He was too slow. The sharp steel rasped across his chest, snapping the rings of his mail.

Valens's legs had gone from under him. He sat down hard, pain scorching up his back. The officer retrieved his blade, shaped the final blow. Valens scuttled backwards on his arse, the soles of his boots slipping on the gritty surface of the road.

And then the officer wheeled away. Two Romans came at him from either side. Hairan and Decimus, working as a team, intent on taking him down.

Valens left them to it. There was something more urgent.

The Persian had almost mastered the stallion. It had quit its high-stepping sidle, and was breaking into a trot. Narses had his bow in his hand, an arrow nocked.

'Shoot him!' Valens yelled.

Narses raised the bow, took aim, drew the string back to his ear. But, arm trembling, he held his pose, and did not release.

The horse had reached a canter.

Valens grabbed the bow, arrow and all, from Narses. With one motion he drew and released. The shaft flew wide.

The stallion was galloping, fast disappearing up the road. Fifty paces, sixty, the distance stretching with each heartbeat.

Valens took another arrow from the quiver. His hands were shaking.

Seventy paces, eighty.

Emptying his mind, Valens took a deep breath, and exhaled, then drew a shallower breath, and held it. With no conscious thought, relying on instinct and the memory in his muscles, he raised, drew and loosed in one motion.

The shaft flew as if guided by the hand of a god. The horse and rider were a hundred paces distant. The arrow knocked the man sideways, the horse shied violently, and the man slid to the ground. Freed from its unwanted burden, the stallion eased to a canter, then pulled up. It turned across the road, and regarded the object on the road with suspicion.

Valens looked back.

The road was littered with Persian dead. The Romans stood isolated from each other, motionless, as if stunned by the return of silence. Narses stood a little apart, looking aghast.

'Is anyone hurt?' Valens asked.

Iudex raised a hand like a schoolboy. 'It is nothing.'

'Anyone else?'

No one spoke.

'Hairan, catch that stallion.' Valens handed the Hatrene the bow. 'If you can't, shoot it.'

'That would be a shame,' Hairan said.

'A cruel necessity.' Valens gathered his thoughts. 'Decimus, Aulus, get back to the camp, get your mounts, and round up the other loose horses.'

Now they needed to dispose of the corpses.

'Look!'

Forgotten by everyone, the driver must have hidden under the wagon. Now he ran across the road and started to scramble up the slope.

One of the soldiers started in pursuit, then they stopped. The face of the cliff the wagoner was attempting was sheer and could not be scaled.

An arrow snapped off the rocks above the man's head.

'Come down,' Hairan called.

'Please, don't kill me,' the man pleaded in bad Greek. Another arrow splintered closer to where he hung. 'Don't shoot me. I am coming down.'

'And stop wasting my arrows,' Narses said, retrieving his bow from Hairan.

Clemens and Decimus disarmed the wagoner, then brought him before Valens and pushed him to his knees.

'I am just the driver. By all the gods, don't kill me.'

'Death is the last thing that you have to worry about,' Valens said. The words of crafty Odysseus to the Trojan scout he had captured on the windy plains before Ilion.

'I will drive the wagon wherever you want.'

'We can manage the wagon ourselves.'

'But I can help you. I know things.'

'Such as?'

'A rider passed not long ago. A messenger of the King. He will have riches, even the harness of his horse has a gold chain.'

'We saw him pass.'

'Take me with you.'

'Do you always drive the supplies to the castle?' Valens asked.

'What?' In his fear, he was distracted by the question. 'No, this is my first time.'

'And do the same soldiers always escort the wagon?'

'No, they were complaining about it. They had done it last year. They were moaning that it was not their turn to go to the horrible place again so soon.' A look of cunning came into his eyes. 'You will never get in there without me.'

'Why not?'

'I know the password. I will drive, say the word at the gate. I will not betray you.'

Valens looked at Narses.

The Persian shrugged. 'There were no passwords in my day.'

'It is the warden. The soldiers were saying Naduk is a daemon. Always thinking of new things, making the life of the garrison hell.'

'You had better tell us.'

'Then you will kill me. Please, I don't want to die.'

Valens pointed at Iudex. 'You see this bald man here, the one with the face of a baby.'

The wagoner gazed over fearfully.

'His looks are deceiving. He is skilled with the knife, good at making people tell secrets.'

Iudex smiled, and fished a long, wicked blade from his boot.

'No, not that.'

Iudex stepped forward. Clemens and Decimus tilted up the man's head, gripping him so tight that he could not move.

'He takes pleasure in his work,' Valens said.

'It is a weakness of mine,' Iudex agreed. 'Always start with the nose. Some think the genitals, but I swear by the nose. It is extraordinary how painful a slit nostril is, and so much blood.'

'Things will go better for you, if you tell us,' Valens said.

'I will, if you swear he will not cut me.'

'I swear.'

'Perozshapur, it is Perozshapur.'

'It means the victory of Shapur,' Narses said.

'That is what the officer must say at the gate. Please don't let him hurt me.'

'I gave you my word that he would not,' Valens said. 'Unfortunately that does not bind the rest of us.'

'But you said death was the last of my worries.'

'Yes, and that is true for every man.'

CHAPTER 28

The Castle of Silence

BARBAD HAD SEEN THE RIDER coming up the trail. The man was mounted on a dromedary, the beast staggering with exhaustion. They must have travelled all night. It had still been early, the sun just risen. The slanting autumn sunshine had glinted off the gold chain on the camel's harness. The morning meal had arrived, but the boy had not yet awoken.

Now, elbows propped on the sill, he was staring out of the window, wrapped in a cloak against the cold wind. He had become more withdrawn, and had recently spent much of his time silently looking at the mountains. There was snow on the peaks. It fell in the night, and every morning it had advanced down the slopes. Soon the high passes would be closed.

Barbad wondered what the boy was thinking. Sasan had turned eleven in the summer. Persians made much of birthdays, so Barbad had done what he could. There had been no question of gifts, but he had put his soul into the stories he had told. Under the dark-eyed gaze of the boy, he had recounted the boyhood of Cyrus. How he had been exposed to die, and how, having been saved by a loyal servant, he had returned to claim his kingdom. Now Barbad pondered if the hope implicit in the tale had been cruel.

If only Barbad had not seen the rider. He had been watching for the supply convoy. By his reckoning – a crude scratching of days on the wall of the privy – it was due any time now. If only the messenger had been delayed. It would not be long before the passes were blocked for the winter. Perhaps he had been mistaken?

But Barbad knew his eyes had not been deceived. He had not been mistaken. A lone rider, travelling fast. The golden chain on the bridle of his mount. A messenger of the King of Kings. It was every subject's duty to speed him on his way. To hinder or detain such a messenger brought the death penalty.

Perhaps it was nothing to do with Sasan? For all Barbad knew, there were other prisoners in the Castle of Silence. He had no evidence, but they might exist. Or could it even be the messenger brought the order for the release of the young prince?

No, such thoughts were like a drowning man clutching at a straw. After all these months there would be no pardon for Sasan's father. Most likely he was already dead. Tortured, broken, and dead. Shapur was a man of blood, of infinite cruelty, like Ardashir before him.

Now the time had come, the enormity of his duty pressed down on Barbad. It was a terrible thing to contemplate. To kill in cold blood a child you loved was unthinkable. The eunuch's heart quailed.

Yet if he did not act . . .

Barbad forced himself to think of the day he was cut, and the days before that. Painfully, he dredged up the memory of the troughs.

There was no crueller method of execution. The condemned man was secured inside two tightly lashed together wooden troughs, shaped like small boats. Unable to move, only his head, hands and feet protruded. He was given food. If he refused, they pricked his eyes until he ate. He was given milk and honey to drink. They poured it into his mouth, let it run over his face.

His eyes were turned to the sun. Soon, swarms of flies would hide his face. Inside the troughs he lay in his own filth. Before long, worms and maggots seethed up from the rottenness and corruption, devouring his body and eating their way into his vitals.

Barbad's father had been a strong man. He had taken ten days to die.

Barbad would spare the boy such a fate.

In a sense, the messenger was unimportant. Winter was fast approaching. Barbad had turned seventy-five a couple of months before. He was getting very old, his strength failing. He had a persistent dry cough. The rooms at the top of the tower could be made snug with their shutters and braziers, their hangings and rugs. But Barbad knew he would not survive winter in the mountains. The messenger had merely brought forward what he had to do.

The boy left the window. He sat on the floor by a brazier. On the rug, he spread out the bits of kindling that he used as toys. It was awful to see the prince brought so low.

Sasan arranged the sticks in lines of battle. Frowning with concentration, he began to manoeuvre the blocks of troops. Barbad had had to rack his memory to summon up the details of battles from his reading long ago. This was Issus, from the *Anabasis* of Arrian. Sasan liked to replay the battle, trying to devise strategies which would reverse history, would bring the Persian King Darius victory over the Macedonian Alexander. The last time he had solemnly declared that it was only the cowardly flight of Darius that had lost the battle. Already, the boy had something of the man about him; the man he would not live to become.

The thought almost broke Barbad's heart. He loved the boy. The irony was not lost on him – Prince Sasan was the grandson of Ardashir, the evil king who had forced Barbad to watch his father's slow and repulsive death, the tyrant who had massacred his family, had robbed Barbad of his manhood.

As a eunuch, Barbad had been placed in the household of Prince Papak, one of Ardashir's many sons. For years, as he trained to be a scribe, Barbad had dreamt lurid dreams of revenge. The blade slicing, the gout of blood splashing bright on the thighs, Papak screaming as his life drained away. An eye for an eye, a life for a life.

But Papak was not like his father. Trained to ride, shoot and abhor the Lie, Papak was a Persian nobleman of antique virtue. Brave and compassionate, considerate to others, he resembled Barbad's own father. Having served Papak all his adult life, by the time Sasan was born, Barbad's hatred had turned to love.

That degraded cult that worshipped the crucified magician could not be more wrong. No deity would punish the children for the sins of the fathers. Not the first generation, let alone the third.

The key turned in the lock.

With the manners of good breeding, the boy got to his feet. Barbad rushed to stand behind him. With trembling fingers, Barbad freed the knife, but kept it concealed in the loose folds of his sleeve.

Mazda forgive him. He would strike for the neck. The wicked tip of the slender knife should easily slide into the soft flesh.

The door opened.

The hilt of the dagger was slick with Barbad's sweat. *Mazda, can I do this thing?*

The usual guard entered, holding the tray. Behind him his companion, watchful but bored, stood on the landing.

Barbad did not dare try to return the knife to its hidden sheath. Clumsy with fear and relief, he would drop the weapon. If it clattered to the floor, their path to freedom would be barred.

Without a word, the guard placed the tray on the table. He picked up the one from the morning meal and left. The door was locked behind him.

With unsteady steps, Barbad walked to the privy, pulled the hanging shut. Would he have struck? Could an old eunuch find the courage?

Anxiously, keeping well away from the latrine and the dizzying drop below the small hole, he returned the knife to its place of concealment.

Do your duty. Serve my son until the end. Somehow Barbad had to find the resolve.

Long ago, King Mithradates had entrusted his beloved daughter to the safekeeping of a trusted eunuch. Defeated by the Romans, Mithradates had fled. His daughter and the eunuch had been trapped and besieged in a fortress. With no hope of rescue, the eunuch had not betrayed the King's trust. Knowing the fate of the Princess if she fell into the hands of the Romans, the eunuch had killed her, then turned the knife on himself.

Barbad would make the boy's last hours happy. Tonight, while Sasan slept, the knife would do its duty.

CHAPTER 29

The Castle of Silence

FOR THE LAST MILE UP to the fortress the road was steep. Except for Decimus and Narses, they all dismounted and put their shoulders to the wagon. Decimus led their mounts, and Narses rode a little ahead.

'Halt!'

They wedged stones under the wheels of the wagon.

Head down and pushing, Valens had only been able to form a general impression of the castle. Now he stood and studied it.

The gate was heavy, and bound with iron. It was just wide enough to admit the wagon. The gatehouse was taller than the flanking walls. Like them it was crenellated, but had no projecting bastions from which to enfilade the approach. There were no towers along the curtain wall. The Castle of Silence relied on its natural position for its defence. On this precipitous crag, no enemy could bring to bear regular siege works. No rams or towers could make the ascent, and there was nowhere to site artillery. Set on solid rock, undermining the place was not an option. The masonry of its walls was smooth, and could not be climbed unaided. All approaches were overlooked. Unless the garrison were negligent, a surprise attack would fail. The paths up could be blockaded, and the fortress starved into submission, but otherwise it would only fall to treachery or subterfuge. But, of course, the Castle of Silence was not designed as a secure refuge, but a prison.

Narses rode to the foot of the gatehouse. There were a couple of guards on the battlements.

'Perozshapur,' Narses called up.

One of the guards said something in Persian.

Narses replied in a peremptory tone, and the guard vanished.

Valens had caught the odd word. He had picked up a little Persian on the journey, but it was unsettling not to be able to follow what was said.

They waited.

There was nothing to hear but the wind and the thin mewing of a pair of buzzards high above. Valens watched their flight. They were wheeling, serene on the updrafts, masters of all they surveyed.

The two leaves of the gate swung inwards, making no sound. The hinges must be kept well oiled. A dark passage was revealed, like an entrance to Hades. Valens put away the thought and its foreboding associations as Narses beckoned the wagon forward.

Aulus, up on the box, flicked the whip over the lead horses' ears. Leaning into their harness, they took the strain so the stones could be removed from under the wheels. Even so, the wagon shifted back half a revolution. Valens and the others seized the spokes, put all their strength and weight against them. Aulus wielded the whip in earnest. The hooves of the draught horses fought for purchase on the flinty surface. For a moment the competing forces held the wagon balanced. Then, with a shuddering groan, it began to edge forward.

The noise of the wagon was deafening under the passageway. Shafts of light penetrated the gloom from the ceiling. Murder holes, Valens thought. From up there the defenders could pour boiling oil or heated sand on any attackers who had managed to force the gate. There was a second gate at the end of the passage. It would not be good to be trapped in the dark between the two.

They emerged into an oval courtyard. Thatched stables were built against the outer wall to the left. The buildings to the right had the air of a barracks. The tower was directly opposite. Valens noted the postern that Narses had mentioned between the tower and the barracks.

The tower itself was some four storeys high. On the upper levels were a few slit windows, all barred. The door was on the first floor. Stone steps ran up flush against the wall. At the top of the flight stood a huge man with a big red beard, dressed entirely in black. There could be no doubt that this was the feared Naduk, the warden of this remote place.

Narses dismounted.

The gates closed behind them. Valens heard the bars drop into place.

The warden began to walk down the steps.

This was the moment of greatest danger. If their intentions were going to be unmasked, it would be now.

Trying to appear casual, even bored, Valens surveyed the courtyard. The two guards were back on the gatehouse. There was a soldier on the north wall, another on the south, and at least one lookout up on the flat roof of the tower. Another look revealed a sixth stationed at the postern gate. Narses had said there were twenty in the garrison. More than a quarter had to stand watch at a time. It would be another reason the posting was unpopular. Despite the chill, some of those off duty were lounging around braziers in front of the barracks.

If this went wrong, could they fight their way out? They would be outnumbered three to one. Yet the garrison would not be prepared, and the majority would be unarmoured. Narses had said there were also half a dozen torturers, and twice that number of servants. But they should be of little account, no more than the whores. Under their long robes, the Romans were wearing all their equipment. Their bows and quivers were on their belts. Should they seize the moment, and try and take the place by force of arms?

No, that was the course of last resort. Even if they prevailed, with those odds, there was no way they could prevent some of those in the castle getting away. Once the survivors were down from the mountains, they would raise all the troops in Hyrkania, and the whole of the countryside, against them. The garrisons along the Walls of Alexander barring the Steppe would be alerted. There would be no way out.

Narses greeted the warden affably, as one Persian noble to another.

The two men talked at length. The warden appeared put out, perhaps suspicious. Narses was conciliatory, but firm. Both frequently looked at the men around the wagon.

It had been decided that they would not attempt to hide their origins. Despite their loose eastern robes, the westerners did not look Persian. Valens and Decimus could only manage a few words of the language. Narses would be telling the warden that the men he commanded were Roman soldiers captured with the Emperor Valerian. They had volunteered to serve in the armies of the King of Kings, given their oath to Shapur. Such things were not unknown. Narses had led them to Hyrkania from distant Bactria, where they had been stationed previously. It was best to keep such men well away from the Roman frontiers, where they might be tempted to desert. They had been assigned to the supply wagon because the journey to the Castle of Silence was an unpopular duty with the Persian soldiers.

Everything hinged on Naduk believing the story, and the zendanig of the state prison was not going to be by nature a trusting man. So far he did not appear convinced.

The warden marched past Narses towards the wagon. All the soldiers bowed slightly from the waist, put the fingers of their right hand to their lips, and blew a kiss: the ritual *proskynesis* due to a Persian of superior rank. Valens's heart sank as the zendanig halted in front of him. Naduk was a head taller than him, and as broad as an ox.

The warden barked something in Persian.

Valens smiled apologetically. 'Persian not good yet.'

Naduk looked down at him with contempt, then spoke rapidly over his shoulder to Narses. Valens kept his eyes respectfully down as Narses replied.

'To arms!' Naduk roared.

It was one of the handful of phrases of Persian Valens knew.

Gods below, has is come to this already? He dropped his hand to his hilt. Glancing at the warriors in front of the barracks, he drew his sword.

The enormous bearded officer did not flinch. He was laughing. Even in his good humour there was an undertone of menace. Towering over Valens, he spoke in heavily accented Greek. 'At least you understand that, you son of a whore. Now, all of you, unload the wagon.'

Valens was cleaning and mending armour and tack with Narses and Iudex. They were sitting around a brazier outside the barracks. It was late in the afternoon, and would soon be time to eat.

Today could not have gone better. Valens still felt guilty about killing the wagoner in cold blood. His words – *death is the last thing that you have to worry about* – had been nothing but a sophistry. But it had to be done and, if he himself was reluctant, he could not order one of the men to carry out the execution. After the driver was dead, his corpse had joined those of his companions in the ravine. They had rounded up the loose horses and kept those that seemed in better condition than some of their own. Narses had appropriated the officer's Nisean stallion as appropriate for his role. There was a risk that some of the garrison might recognise the horse of one of the dead men, but they were not branded, and it was a risk worth running to be well mounted, given what was planned. When every man had selected a horse, they set four aside as spares and for their supplies and baggage. It was with the greatest sadness that they slaughtered the remaining animals, and pushed them over to tumble down the precipice. It was good that they had left at once. By the time they had set out, vultures had materialised from nowhere, and were drifting down towards the unexpected bounty.

'It is a pity Zabda is dead,' Narses said.

Valens looked up from sharpening his dagger.

Narses nodded up at the tower. 'The sly old Palmyrene could have opened that locked door with his eyes shut.'

'And the guards inside?' Valens said. They had watched the guard change during the day. There was always one on the roof of the tower, another somewhere behind the locked door.

'Any of us can deal with them,' Iudex said. 'Even you.'

Valens did not reply, but tucked the knife into his boot and set about mending a broken bridle.

'Zabda was a thief, but I liked him.' Narses grinned at Valens. 'Of course you two got off to a bad start, what with him trying to kill you in that bar.'

They spoke in Latin, confident that, while some of the garrison would speak some Greek, none would know that language.

The Persian soldiers had not been overtly hostile, but they were not forthcoming. This morning they had watched as the heavy load of the wagon was carried into the storerooms. None had offered to help. Likewise they had given no help in bedding down the horses, had seemed happy to show the arrivals to the worst rooms in the barracks, and had kept apart when they ate. Narses said that they were resentful that these foreign mercenaries would be free to leave this dismal fortress in a few days.

'It was a stroke of luck, that old man this morning,' Iudex said.

It was a strange phrase to describe what they had seen, but it was true.

They had all been worried about the man they had seen urging his tired dromedary up towards the castle. The wagoneer had confirmed their suspicion that he was a messenger of the King. It would have been too cruel of fate if they had arrived on the same day as Shapur's order to kill Prince Sasan.

So it was with relief that they had watched an elderly Persian nobleman dragged down the steps out of the tower. His public execution in the courtyard had been nothing worse than one saw in the Colosseum. First the torturers had sliced off his ears, then his nose. They had amputated his hands and gouged out his eyes. By the time they had decapitated him, he appeared to be already dead.

'It was fortunate for us, but a pity for the old nobleman,' Iudex added. 'I would not have you think that I am inhumane.'

'I thought you followers of Mani were like Christians, and believed taking a life was a terrible sin,' Narses said. 'Yet you were happy enough to kill the tent-dwellers, and it was you that slaughtered out of hand the brother of Lucia's husband.'

Iudex tipped his bald head to one side, as if considering how much it was prudent to divulge.

'I cannot think your prophet will do well at the court of the King of Kings,' Narses said. 'Imagine instructing Shapur to kill no one, not to touch meat and abstain from sex, let alone embrace poverty?'

'When I was in Ctesiphon, in the palace of the Sassanid, I saw that Shapur was a man of violence, a slave to his appetites. It will end badly for Mani,' Iudex said.

'What were you doing at the Persian court?' Valens tried to keep the sudden suspicion out of his voice.

'The things that are done by a *frumentarius*,' Iudex replied.

'You have never mentioned this.'

'It was a couple of years ago. We have all done things that are best left unsaid.'

'Was it there you met this Mani?' Valens asked.

'It was Mani who put my feet on the road to liberation. He taught me to release my spirit-twin. Since then I have voyaged widely, learnt many things in the other world. Now the pupil has surpassed the teacher.'

'What can go wrong?' Narses said. 'We are serving with a man who visits the underworld and talks to the gods.'

Iudex ignored the Persian's mockery. 'There is divine light in all humanity. When unbelievers die, it is not lost forever as Mani holds. As their corpses decompose, the light is released into the earth, and from there enters the plants. When these are eaten by the elect, it is released into the heavens.'

'Well that accounts for your continual farting.' Narses was laughing openly. 'It is a fine religion that sees flatulence as a sacrament.'

Iudex was undisturbed. 'Those who are deceived by other religions find no escape. They go blindly to destruction. The sooner the unredeemed die the better.'

'And what if you kill someone who is redeemed?' Narses said.

'Then he will go straight to heaven.'

'Enough,' Valens said. 'He is coming.'

A Persian soldier was carrying a tray across the courtyard from the kitchens.

Narses got to his feet, and hailed the man in Persian. They spoke for a time. At first the soldier looked uncertain, but then he laughed.

Narses turned to Valens, and spoke in Greek. 'Get up, you lazy Roman dog. It is unfitting for a Persian warrior to carry things like a servant, while a prisoner sits warming his arse by the brazier.'

Valens got up.

The Persian said something.

'You are not going in there armed,' Narses said.

Reluctantly, Valens unbuckled his sword belt and handed it to Iudex.

'Look lively,' Narses snapped. 'Take the tray and follow the soldier.'

Valens did as he was commanded. There was bread and cheese, some cold meat and fruit, and a metal flagon of wine. It was a lot of food for a child.

Narses spoke again to Valens. Once more the tone was haughty, but this time the words were in Latin. 'Everything will be ready. We will be waiting.'

Valens trudged up the steps. At the top, the Persian unlocked the door. When they had gone through, he locked it behind them and put the keys back on his belt.

It was dark and cold within the tower. Stone stairs ran around the inside wall. Every so often, a lamp burning in a niche gave a feeble light. On the second floor they came out onto a landing. A narrow window, unshuttered but set with iron bars, faced a closed door. They did not stop there, or on the third floor.

The tread of their boots echoed in the gloom as they went up towards the top floor.

A voice called down from above.

The Persian replied.

The guard was leaning on the frame of the final door.

Valens glanced around the landing. It was almost identical to the others. A window faced a door, but this window was shuttered. There was another difference – here a ladder ascended to the roof. Given the inclement weather, the heavy trapdoor to above was shut. The guard on the battlements would be very exposed to the bitter wind.

The guard on the door was in no hurry. He chatted to his colleague before levering himself off the door frame and reaching for his keys.

Odds of two to one against, Valens thought. And there was a third man on the roof. Either Clemens or Iudex would have been a better bet – both were natural killers. But an officer could not send men into danger that he would not face himself.

With luck, the sentinel on the roof would hear nothing above the wind. The trapdoor looked solid.

Strike quickly, take them unaware, and it would be over in moments.

The guard turned the key, and pushed the door open.

The sun was setting over the snow-clad peaks. Its light slanted through the slit window opposite the door. Two figures were silhouetted in the centre of the room. As Valens's eyes adjusted, he saw a young boy. Standing behind the boy, and a little to one side, was a tall man. The man was beardless and very old.

Who in Hades was the man? He was ancient, but still he made the odds yet worse.

'Put the tray on the table,' one of the Persians said.

There were hangings on the wall, and cushions on the rugs on the floor. For some unknowable reason, pieces of kindling were laid out on a rug in almost military precision. A low table stood next to a lit brazier in front of the figures in the middle of the room.

'We don't want to stand here all evening.'

Neither of the guards moved to enter the room.

As Valens moved forward, he noted that the old man was sweating, and his eyes were wild.

'Health and great joy,' Valens said in Greek.

'No one speaks to the prisoners,' one of the guards snapped.

Valens placed the tray on the table.

The aged man was clutching at something under his sleeve. There was a terrible indecision etched on his face.

'Get a move on.'

It was now or never.

Valens straightened up, turned and went back through the door. The Persian he had followed stepped back to let him out. When he had passed, the other leant in to pull the door shut. Valens reached behind his leg, and slid the dagger from his boot. Not stopping to think, Valens lunged at the man in front, his right fist flashing out. The soldier tried to twist aside, but his back collided with the outer wall. It was not a clean strike. The blade sliced deeply across the man's stomach. The Persian grunted with pain. He doubled up, his hands going to the wound.

Valens swung around, dropping into a crouch. The guard by the door was drawing his sword. Valens hurled himself at him. Grabbing his beard, he dragged him close. The long Sassanid blade was trapped between their bodies. Valens plunged the dagger into the man's side. With his free hand, the Persian clawed at Valen's eyes. Ignoring the pain, Valens struck again. Three times the steel punched deep into flesh. The blood was hot on Valens's hand and arm.

The Persian was grievously hurt, perhaps mortally. But he was not giving up, and he was strong. His fingers closed around Valens's throat, crushing his windpipe. Flashes of light danced in Valens's vision. He had to finish this man now, or he would die here.

With a last despairing blow, Valens plunged the dagger into the side of the Persian's neck.

The pressure on Valens's throat was gone. The guard swayed, then toppled sideways, half into the room.

Dragging air into his lungs, Valens used the door frame to push himself upright.

The Persian on the landing was down on his knees. In his hands were blue coils of intestines. With futile urgency he was trying to force them back into place.

Valens moved behind him, yanked his head back by the hair, and slid the blade down into the soft hollow of his throat. The tip of the steel scrapped off bone, but went more than deep enough.

It was quiet. Just the wind coming through the window of the room.

Valens gazed up at the trapdoor.

Had the lookout heard anything?

There was no bolt on the underside of the trapdoor. Why would there be?

Infernal gods! Just come, if you are coming.

Fuck it. He couldn't wait forever. If the sentinel descended, Valens would deal with him like the other two bastards.

Valens went back into the room.

The rug was ruined with blood.

The old man held the boy tight in the crook of his left arm. In his right was a tiny knife, the sort of thing with which you might peel an apple. He shouted something in Persian.

'Easy, grandfather.' Valens moved slowly, calculating his leap.

'Not another step!' The aged Persian knew Greek. 'I will not let you harm him.'

Valens spread his hands wide. 'I have not come to harm him.'

'You will not take us alive.'

Valens looked at the boy. 'You are Prince Sasan, son of Prince Papak?'

The boy nodded.

'I am Marcus Aelius Valens, a soldier of Rome. My men are outside with horses. We have come to rescue you.'

CHAPTER 30

The Castle of Silence

'Naduk,' the old man whispered.

Turning, Valens saw the huge figure filling the doorway.

Naduk the zendanig smiled. 'Never trust a Roman.'

Unlike the guard, the warden was not foolish enough to draw a long sword in a confined space. His dagger only looked small because his hand was so large.

'And never trust the clan of the Suren. Treachery is in their blood.'

Valens stood stock still. His eyes never left Naduk.

'Unfortunate for you that I was standing guard on the battlements. I enjoy watching the sunset. The sunlight on the snow is very beautiful.'

Valens started to back away.

'But you are favoured by Mazda, Roman. Circumstances demand that I kill you quickly. The traitor Narses and the rest of your men will die with every refinement of cruelty.'

Valens's calf bumped into something. The table and brazier were behind him.

'Eunuch, take Prince Sasan into the inner chamber. His time has not come. He should be spared the sight of more death.'

'No,' the boy said. But the old eunuch was dragging him away.

The enormous sombre figure waited until the hanging fell back, obscuring the eunuch and the boy.

'Put down the knife, Roman.'

Valens said nothing.

'Kneel and offer your neck. All your fear will be at an end.'

Valens grinned. 'Are you not so good at killing men who can fight back?'

Behind the immense red beard, the warden smiled. 'If I had time, I would make you beg for me to repeat that offer.' Through the window, from far away, came the sound of men shouting. 'Enough talk,' Naduk said.

Valens stepped forward, then turned and jumped over the table.

Naduk roared with laughter, his massive shoulders shaking. 'There is nowhere to run. Why postpone the inevitable?'

Snatching the flagon from the tray, Valens threw it at the Persian's head.

Naduk ducked. The metal vessel sailed out onto the landing and clanged against the outer wall. Some of the wine spattered on the tunic of the zendanig. He looked at the stains dispassionately. 'A waste. You should have drunk it.'

Naduk stepped carefully over the corpse in the doorway. Once he was in the room he somehow seemed even larger.

Valens kicked the table across the room.

The big man let it hit his legs, then stamped it into splinters. The plates and the food were scattered across the floor.

'Did you think that might stop me?'

'No, but this might.' Valens grabbed the leg of the brazier, and hurled it.

With a speed and agility unexpected in such a bulky man, Naduk leapt aside.

Valens started for the door and Naduk moved to cut him off. Sidestepping, Valens lunged with his knife.

Steel scrapped on steel as the blow was blocked by Naduk's blade. The warden brought the heel of his left hand smashing into Valens's face. Tasting blood, Valens staggered back.

Now Naduk lunged. Somehow Valens twisted inside the attack. The big man's momentum drove them together and across the room. Valens slammed into the wall. The back of his head cracked against the stone. His vision blurred. As if at a great distance, he heard his knife fall to the floor.

Naduk changed his grip on Valens, and smashed him into the wall again. A surge of pain from deep in his stomach made Valens retch. The warden pinned him to the wall with one great paw, and readied the other for the fatal thrust.

'Leave him!'

Not slackening his grip, Naduk looked over his shoulder.

The old eunuch had emerged from behind the hangings. He had the young Prince in a headlock, the minute dagger at his throat.

'What will Shapur do, if you have let Prince Sasan die in your care?'

'Put the knife down, you old fool. Everyone knows a eunuch lacks the courage to do such a thing.'

The eunuch's hands were trembling. The tip of the blade pricked the tender skin. A drop of blood as red as a ruby rolled down.

'Drop the knife! Think of the pincers and the hot knives, Barbad.'

Valens hung, limp as a rag doll, momentarily almost forgotten.

'Think what you will suffer in the cellars.'

No matter how big and tough and strong, every man has a weak point. Valens grabbed Naduk's crotch. His fingers closing, he squeezed and twisted.

The big red mouth in the big red beard bellowed with pain.

Bracing his right boot against the wall, Valens hurled them both to the ground. He landed on top of Naduk. The impact jarred the knife out of the warden's fist and sent it skittering off across the rug.

Now Valens drove the palm of his hand into the other's face. There was a crack as the nose broke. Valens rolled off, and scuttled on all fours like an animal towards his fallen knife. He heard Naduk getting to his knees. As Valens dived, a hand seized his ankle. His fingers closed on the hilt as he was yanked backwards. Twisting, Valens drove the blade down between the huge shoulders. Naduk bellowed like a bull in the arena. Valens wrenched the knife free, stabbed down again and again. Eventually the noise ceased.

The dead weight was heavy on Valens's legs. It took him a moment to summon the strength to push it off.

The eunuch and the boy were standing staring at the dead man. The knife was no longer at the boy's throat.

Valens got unsteadily to his feet, trying to clear his mind and orientate himself. The coals from the overturned brazier smouldered on the rugs. The breeze from the window brought a tang of woodsmoke. There were things to do before he got out of here.

'Gather anything you can't leave behind,' Valens said to the boy.

Prince Sasan and the eunuch just stood there.

Kneeling, Valens found the ring with the seal of the zendanig. He severed the finger it was on, took the ring, and threw the finger away.

'Get your belongings, only the essentials. You are coming with me.'

'Not without Barbad,' the boy replied.

Valens looked at the aged eunuch. 'Can you ride?'

'I am a Persian.'

'You too, then.'

They vanished into the inner chamber.

Valens went to the door and picked up the sword of the dead guard.

The eunuch and the boy reappeared. The eunuch had a small wrapped bundle. The boy was clutching a toy lion. Both wore hooded travelling cloaks.

The first flickers of flame were snaking up one of the wall hangings.

The keys!

Which of the two dead guards was the one from outside?

Valens could not remember. He took the sets of keys from both their belts. Then, for good measure, heaved Naduk over and took his as well.

'We need to go.'

When they reached the bottom of the winding stairs, luck was with Valens. The very first key he tried fitted, the tumblers clicked back, and the lock opened.

Swinging wide the door of the tower revealed a scene of chaos.

Thick smoke billowed around the courtyard. The sun had set, and the gloom of the evening was lit by lurid fires. Horses and men were milling and shouting. The stable block was on fire.

'You took your time,' Narses said.

The Persian was waiting at the foot of the outer steps. The shapes of other men and horses were around him.

'Everyone here?' Valens said.

'Yes. Things went well with you?'

'Never better. And I see you have been busy.'

'Bad idea having the kitchens under the same roof as the hay stalls,' Narses said.

'Oddly, I think the tower might have caught fire too,' Valens said. 'Is the sentry still at the postern?'

'Yes. Shall I deal with him now?'

'Not in that way. Show him this seal stone, and tell him the zendanig has ordered him to open the gate.'

Narses moved off. Decimus led up two spare horses, and gave the boy and the eunuch a leg up.

As Valens swung into the saddle, he looked around the courtyard. Some of the garrison had formed a chain to pass buckets from the well. It was an enterprise doomed to failure.

'The postern is open,' Hairan said. 'It is time we left.'

Before they crested the ridge that would take them out of sight of the castle, they reined in. As if by a prearranged compact, everyone looked back.

The castle was a couple of miles away, etched black against the night by the flames. The north wind lifted great gouts of fire from the tower. They went streaming off into the sky. The walls of the tower were of stone, and might stand, but the floors and rafters were wood. The buildings in the courtyard would be burnt to charred beams and ashes. Despite the strength of the conflagration, at this distance nothing could be heard.

> *For I know this thing well in my heart, and my mind knows it:*
> *There will come a day when sacred Ilion shall perish.*

The lines of Homer that Decimus recited were famous.

'When Scipio said those words watching Carthage burn,' Clemens said, 'he was thinking one day the same fate would fall on Rome.'

'Poetry, always fucking poetry,' Aulus said.

'There is divine truth in the greatest poems,' Iudex said. 'Although the works of men are nothing but the blink of an eye to the Demiurge.'

Hairan laughed. 'The King of Kings will be needing a new prison.'

'And a new gaoler.' Narses clapped Valens on the shoulder. 'None of us would have put money on you.'

'They will never find the bodies in the tower,' Narses continued. 'If the gods are kind, the garrison will suspect nothing. Perhaps they will think the boy died in the fire.'

'He was wearing a cloak, but the guard on the postern may have seen him leave,' Valens said.

Narses smacked his hand to his forehead. 'You should have let me kill him.'

'I was not thinking far enough ahead,' Valens said. 'I was beguiled by my own cunning in taking the seal of the warden. It was a mistake.'

'It makes little odds,' Decimus said. 'When they realise that we are truly departed, not cowering from the fire somewhere on the ridge, suspicion will fall on us.'

'The confusion should give us a head start of a day or two,' Valens said. 'By the time they send out messengers, we will be well on our way. Narses, take point, and lead us out of these mountains.'

For a day they remained on the track, then Narses turned them onto a hunters' trail running alongside a mountain stream. For two days they followed the bright water. At times the descent was precipitous, and they dismounted to lead the horses down in a shower of dust and sliding stones. The old eunuch was very frail, and had a persistent racking cough. Others had to lead his mount on the difficult stretches. But some indomitable spirit kept him going, and he never complained.

They waited until darkness on the third day to come out onto the plains.

Some miles off to the east, where the track down from the castle reached the low ground, were pinpricks of fires. Narses had said that a town called Varoshag was near that place. Valens asked him if these were its lights. Wordlessly, the Persian pointed to the north-east, where its fainter lights glimmered. They did not speak of this when they camped in a wood for the rest of the night. But they had no campfires, and they kept the horses bridled and close.

The morning dawned clear and cold, but there were rain clouds building up to the north-east where they were headed. The countryside here was open, and already assuming the flatness of the Steppe. Narses said that the Walls of Alexander were two easy days' ride to the north.

They rode through wide pastures with many sheep. The flocks regarded them until they were close, then ran away bleating. Narses and Hairan spoke affably to the shepherds, but the herdsmen were uncommunicative and suspicious. Valens hoped it was caused by nothing more than their lonely calling on the margins of society.

About midday they spotted a dust cloud coming down from the north. It was tall and thin, and none of the soldiers doubted it was raised by a column of mounted men.

At least the plain was cut by many watercourses coming down from the mountains. They took shelter in one deep enough to conceal them from anyone not actually on its bank.

The stream was no more than a trickle. But its bed was wide. In the spring, when the snows melted on the heights, it would be full. Valens and Narses lay in the reeds at the top of the slope. They were bareheaded and their faces and hair were plastered with dust.

Slowly the pillar of dust crept across the plain.

They did not speak, and the only sounds were the wind moving through the reeds and the muffled coughing of the eunuch.

Narses broke the silence. 'The westerners are unhappy about the eunuch.'

'Unless the cavalry come very close they will not hear him over the noise of their own movement,' Valens said.

'They think eunuchs are ill-omened, that they bring bad luck, like monkeys. Aulus suggested they might smother him quietly one night.'

'I will speak to them,' Valens said. 'The eunuch is useful to look after the boy, and I owe my life to his intervention.'

Now the mounted men were closer, the hidden watchers could hear the thud of their hooves, and clearly make out the individual riders. A troop of Persian horse archers, fifty men in columns of twos, led by an officer in magnificent armour and a standard-bearer carrying a large banner embroidered with an image of a panther or some other big cat.

Marching fast, alternating between a canter and a trot, they passed about a hundred paces away from the watercourse, and headed south. If they remained on that bearing, they would reach the foothills roughly where the Romans had emerged.

'Warriors from the clan Karen,' Narses said. 'Good fighters, not as good as the Suren.'

'A routine patrol?' Valens asked.

Narses shook his head. 'When I was stationed here, the only patrols were north of the wall, keeping an eye on the nomads. Of course, they could be looking for a raid from the Steppe that has slipped across the frontier. But, with the camp at the foot of the main track, it does not look good.'

They went down to join the others. Valens told Aulus to take some food, and go up to keep watch. The rest he ordered to see to the horses – including the mounts of Aulus, the boy and the eunuch, as well as the spares – and then gather to eat a cold meal. While they chewed hard tack and bacon, he briefed them on what had been seen. He spoke in Latin to avoid alarming Prince Sasan and Barbad. When he had finished, Iudex went off to one side to pray. Today, Iudex scooped some water from the stream into his mess tin, and then sat cross-legged, staring at its surface, seemingly lost in meditation. The rest remained sitting in a circle. The anxiety was evident on every soldier's face.

It was Decimus who voiced their concern. 'It looks like they are expecting us.'

'There has been no time for a rider to get down from the Castle of Silence.' Valens hoped the words sounded more confident than he felt.

'Then they already knew we were coming,' Decimus said.

'If they did, I know who told them,' Clemens spoke as weightily as a senator in the Curia.

Everyone looked at Clemens.

'Narses here is a Persian,' Clemens said. 'They are his kin.'

'When have I betrayed our brotherhood?' Narses spoke with quiet anger.

'You made sure you did not kill any of your own at the supply convoy.'

Narses looked disconcerted.

'And now you are leading us straight to the Persian troops on the Walls of Alexander, promising us some cunning way of getting through the defences that you will not tell us.'

Narses rallied. 'I am no traitor. Put me to the test. Place a hot iron on my tongue, have me drink sulphur, pour molten metal on my chest; if I do not lie, it will run off me like milk.'

Valens noted that Decimus seemed not to disapprove of this ghastly and divisive procedure.

It was Hairan who put an end to talk of an ordeal. 'The gods know, as a man of Hatra, no one has more reason to hate the Persians than me. But Narses has faithfully guided us to the Castle of Silence and then out of the mountains. Without him we would have been lost, as helpless as children. If he were a traitor, he could have deserted us at any time. When he returned with Persian warriors, we would have been at their mercy.'

Gravely, Narses put his fingers to his lips, and blew Hairan a kiss.

The handsome young Hatrene bowed in return. 'Not all Persians are cruel, untrustworthy bastards. Even if they do fuck their own daughters.'

Clemens was not quite finished. 'Then how exactly are we going to slip through the walls manned by thousands of Sassanid warriors?'

'We are not.'

'What?'

Narses told them his plan. They looked at each other, then burst out laughing.

'It is insane,' Hairan said, 'but brilliant. I have always loved you – although not in the way your mother did.'

'We have to leave.' Iudex took a last look into the water, then tipped it away. 'Now. We are in danger.'

The laughter had died.

'Anything?' Valens called up to Aulus.

'Nothing.'

Valens hesitated. Better to look foolish than to die. 'Mount up, quickly, no noise.'

They rode down the river, keeping their horses in the stream, hoping the waters might obliterate their tracks. Two smaller watercourses ran off from the river to the west, and after a quarter of an hour a larger one opened into it from the east. They turned into the latter. After no great distance, a grove of willows stood on its banks. They hobbled the horses and left them drinking. Climbing out under the trees, they established a perimeter defence, with the majority of men facing back the way they had come.

They had not long to wait.

A trumpet rang across the plain. At its command, Persian warriors erupted from both banks of the river just south of where they had been camped. Yelling high, thin war cries, the Sassanid horse archers raced to encircle the campsite. Drawing near, they loosed volleys of arrows to drop near vertical down into the riverbed.

'They will be most disappointed,' Hairan said.

'What do we do now?' Clemens said. 'We can see them, and when we move they will spot us.'

Valens turned to Narses. 'How far to the sea?'

'A long day in the saddle.'

CHAPTER 31

The Walls of Alexander

THE NEW MOON HUNG LOW over the Caspian. The storm of the day had blown itself out, but the wind was still cold from the north.

From his post on watch, the westernmost fortress stood stark against the night sky. The great wall itself stretched eastwards across the featureless plain until it was lost in the gloom. No one knew when the Walls of Alexander had first been erected. The name of the Macedonian was often given to any structures that were impressive, and whose origins were lost in time. Whoever first designed them, their intention was to keep out the nomad tribes of the Steppe, but they also formed a formidable barrier to anyone attempting to leave the realm of the King of Kings.

Shifting his position on the damp ground – all his joints ached – he studied the fortress with the eyes of a professional soldier. It was large and rectangular, raised on an earth platform, and set behind a wide ditch filled with water. The mud-brick curtain walls were tall and broad. Even so, it would not hold out long against a besieging Roman army. The corners of the fort were not rounded, but square. Stone-throwing artillery would soon expose that weakness and bring them tumbling down. There were no projecting towers along the walls. Once the moat had been filled in, attackers with siege ladders could reach the wall without being exposed to any missiles except from ahead. If archers and bolt-throwers kept the defenders' heads down, a storming party should reach the breach almost unscathed. Of course, after that, it would be the usual terrible work, step by step up the rubble, close to the steel.

The deficiencies of the fortress would make little difference against the nomads. The tribes on the Steppe were far too primitive to ever undertake regular siege works. Yet somehow the slipshod construction offended his sensibilities. It was typical of Persian indolence.

His gaze tracked west. Some four miles of reed beds and marshes separated the fortress from the Caspian. Narses had said a levee linked two wooden lookouts to the walls. The Persian claimed that when the sea had retreated, the land left behind was too soft to support heavier defences. That was another example of eastern idleness. A good Roman engineer would have sunk deep pilings, poured concrete in reinforced foundations, and extended the barrier to the waters' edge.

Gods below, he was tired. He was too old for this life. They had been a long time in the saddle.

The enemy swarming over their hastily abandoned camp had indeed seen them when they left the cover of the willows. That damned trumpet had rung out, and shrill, ululating calls had come across the plain.

They had gone north at a gallop, flat out.

There had been nothing else for it. They could not have made much speed down in the bed of the river, and, racing down the banks, the Persians would have soon run them down.

The going was good. Their horses were fresh, and those of the Persians already worn by half a day's forced march. Soon they had opened a lead of almost a mile. The cries of easterners were as faint as distant birds. Only the note of the trumpet had cut clear above the thunder of their own horses.

And then the storm had descended. Huge black clouds trailing tendrils of rain rolled down from the north. In an instant they were soaked to the skin, but the visibility was cut to no more than two hundred paces, and the trumpet could be heard no longer.

They had slackened their pace to a fast canter to preserve the horses.

With the sun obscured, it was hard to judge the passing of time.

They came to a forest of ancient oaks. In its depths, moving carefully at a walk, they had altered course to the west.

Once out of the partial shelter of the trees, they had moved back to a canter. The rain had lashed across their path. There was the danger of a horse falling – some slipped, but none went down. Not even the hardiest peasant or shepherd was abroad in the downpour. No one had seen them go, as they fled like creatures of myth from some primordial flood.

As the day ended, the rain slackened but the murk thickened. Narses had turned them once more towards the north, going again at a walk. At the head of the column, the Persian twisted this way and that in his saddle, peering through the spitting rain and the gathering darkness. Sometimes he raised a hand to bring them to a halt. Then he would sit, head titled, listening and sniffing the air.

Fatigue had dulled their thoughts. They sat apathetically in silence, apart from the old eunuch coughing. When Narses moved on, they followed him blindly in the darkness. Few of them noticed when it stopped raining.

It was approaching midnight when the Persian had led the sodden and bedraggled riders through a fringe of reeds and into a grassy hollow, screened from prying eyes. The ground underfoot was damp but firm enough. Narses had urged them to be silent. The Walls of Alexander were less than half a mile away. There were six hours until dawn. They would rest here for four hours, then make their attempt.

The familiar routine of rubbing down his horse – his weight behind the strokes as the brush dried and cleaned its coat, massaged the skin beneath – somehow refreshed his body and cleared his mind. He had sponged its eyes, nose and dock, checked its feet. After he had fed and watered both the animal and himself, Valens had placed him on sentry here at the edge of the reeds.

It was a miracle that the expedition had got this far. None of his plans had come to fruition. Once Valens had appointed Decimus second in command, there had been no point in killing the young officer. In the mountains before the Castle of Silence he had written a warning, in both Greek and Persian, betraying everything he knew about the mission. He had tied it to an arrow. Setting off to hunt those wild goats, he had intended to shoot it over the wall. It would have been difficult to approach the walls unseen by either the garrison or his own companions, yet he was sure it could have been managed. Once inside, the others would have been taken, and he would have been rewarded. And then that fool had insisted on accompanying him. At the ambush of the supply wagon there had been nothing at all to be done. Inside the castle, the enforced intimacy of the barracks had left him unable to find an excuse to slip away from the watchful eyes of the others. As they rode out of the postern, he had dropped the arrow with the writing still attached to its shaft, but doubtless it would have been consumed in the fire.

Yet the Persian cavalry patrols out on the plains indicated that one of his schemes had not failed utterly. The expedition would have outrun the news from the Castle of Silence, but the garrison of the Walls of Alexander had been alerted. The local he had paid back in Zadrakarta had not played him false, but had delivered the letter. The garrison was watching for them. The problem was that the Walls of Alexander stretched for hundreds of miles. In Zadrakarta he had not known where or how Narses intended to get them across the border.

A torch flared in the distance as a sentinel walked out onto the battlements of the fortress.

For a moment he had the urge just to run towards the light, shouting, to get this treachery over with. The notion was ridiculous. Narses was crouched a few paces away in the reeds. He had never seen a better shot than the Persian. And there was no point in bringing destruction down on the mission, if he himself did not survive.

How had it come to this?

It was his own fault. His position of trust in the Camp of the Strangers had made it easy to take the money. Tullia's family were poor, her father's business not doing well. They needed the money. A few strokes in the ledgers and the money had vanished from the army. Everything had been fine until that shrewd little bastard Murena had been appointed.

No, it was not his own fault. It was Murena. Even had the commander of the *frumentarii* not uncovered the fraud, his threats would have been more than enough. Murena knew that rather than see Tullia hurt, he would betray the entire world.

The halo of torchlight flitted along the wall walk, tiny and alone, like a lost soul in the Stygian darkness.

Of course, now that they had escaped the Castle of Silence there was a simple solution. No need to involve the Persians, no harsh necessity of doing harm to his sworn companions. Just kill the young boy. Get close to him, get him on his own, make it look like an accident.

Up on the wall, the light of the torch went out.

CHAPTER 32

The Walls of Alexander

THE WIND STIRRED THE REEDS over their heads. The mud sucked at their boots. Out in the swamp, invisible creatures slithered and plopped into the water.

Of all the wildernesses in the world none was worse than a marsh. For a Roman, no desert or mountain felt so alien and frightening. Roman arms always failed where water and earth came together in a quagmire. At Abrittus, an entire imperial field army had become bogged down and was slaughtered. The body of the Emperor Decius had never been found. It was no wonder that Septimius Severus had failed to conquer Caledonia. How could it have been otherwise in a place where sea and earth could not be distinguished, where you could neither sail nor stand? How could you catch and defeat naked barbarians who could remain for days under the surface of the bog, breathing through a hollow reed?

The marshes themselves were threat enough. They bred fevers and poisonous animals. Without warning the mud could suck you down and smother you in its depths. For Valens, the greatest terror of all was snakes. Swamps abounded in venomous serpents, and Narses had said those of the Caspian were particularly large and deadly.

The sickle moon overhead shone from a cloudless sky. It had been too much to hope that the storm that had saved them yesterday would continue. The night was bright, but the feathery tops of the reeds offered cover. They were taller than a dismounted man and his horse.

Narses took them along muddy trails and embankments. The Persian had hunted wildfowl here. But that was long ago, and the nature of swamps was treacherous. From one year to another channels changed course, mudbanks shifted, and solid ground dissolved. Sometimes the path he was following vanished, and they had to lead their horses belly deep through foul-smelling standing water. Twice they had come to a bottomless black pool. Their progress was slow anyway, and they lost yet more time probing for an alternative route.

They went in single file, as quietly as they could. The reeds rustled overhead, and they had wrapped cloths around their weapons, the ornaments on their belts and the horses' tack to muffle them. Yet the squelch of mud and the slop of water, the creak of leather and rasp of laboured breathing were painfully loud. Barbad the old eunuch had a scarf around his mouth, but it did not totally muffle his persistent coughing. Once they put up a skein of geese. They took to the air honking with a clatter of wings. The men stood, hardly daring to breathe, covering the muzzles of the horses, willing them to make no sound. Valens felt something brush against his boot. In a moment it was gone. It took all his willpower not to cry out or leap away.

As the geese arrowed away low across the moon, Valens saw with dismay the first hint of the false dawn in the eastern sky. They had had but two hours to slip across the levee and vanish into the marshes north of the wall, and much of that precious time had elapsed.

No outcry followed the flight of the wild geese. Narses led them on through the endless fen.

A terrible doubt surfaced in Valens's mind. Was the Persian lost? How could any man find his way through this damp desolation? The swaying banks of reeds all looked the same. The place would have changed out of all recognition since Narses hunted here. Were they wandering in circles? Even Hercules had been defeated by the marshes of Stymphalia and had had to shoot down its murderous inhabitants from dry ground.

Above all, would they blunder into an enemy patrol or outpost? The Sassanids were alerted. The cavalry out on the plain the day before left no doubt of that. For a long time Valens had half suspected there was a traitor among the ten that had ridden out of Zeugma. Too much had gone wrong. The bandits killing Severus, the death of Quintus the navigator in the dust storm – so suspicious in retrospect – the trail left for the tent-dwellers to follow. Now the Sassanid horsemen waiting for them to come down from the mountains had near convinced him. How in Hades had the news preceded them down from the Castle of Silence? And who was the malignant presence in the surviving members of the brotherhood? It was not Narses. Of that Valens was quite certain. The Persian could have betrayed them at any point. All he would have needed to do was inform Naduk when they rode into the fortress-prison. Surely it was not Hairan? The young Hatrene had every reason to loathe everything Persian. They had killed his family, laid waste his home. There was Iudex. He was mad. There was no telling what his god might put into his mind. What possible reason might have inspired the other three? That ugly old pederast Aulus had an insubordinate nature. The no younger or better-favoured Clemens was likewise unruly, and was far more aggressive. Decimus, better preserved and more handsome, gave no reason to think that he was unsatisfied with the world. Valens would have thought Zabda the likeliest candidate. But Zabda, of course, was dead. And he had died saving Valens's life.

In the ambient light, Valens saw Narses raise his hand to call a halt. The Persian turned his horse, and handed the reins to Valens.

'Pass the word to wait,' Narses hissed, his mouth so close to Valens that the Persian's beard tickled his face. 'The levee is just ahead. I will go and look.'

As he went, Narses made no more noise than a fox would going along the narrow track slightly raised above the water.

Soon there was nothing to hear but the wind soughing through the reeds.

Narses's big Nisean stallion lifted its feet unhappily from the mud. Valens went to quiet it, but the black horse tried to bite his arm. Valens growled quietly. The stallion eyed him warily, but stopped playing up.

A gasping, choking sound, then a paroxysm of coughing rent the air.

At once the peace of the night was shattered. Persian voices shouted. A trumpet rang out. A light flared ahead. Then more appeared, one after another, running in a line like fire along a row of stubble.

The levee was less than a hundred paces to the north. By the light of the torches, Valens could see the Sassanids on top of it. There were dozens of them spaced in a cordon along the walkway. They were on foot, their horses picketed.

The coughing did not stop.

A Persian officer, mounted and gorgeous in silks, shouted, obviously for silence.

The noise from the levee dropped.

Silence from the marsh. Then another burst of racking coughing.

It seemed to Valens that the Sassanid officer pointed directly at him through the darkness. From back down the column came a commotion. A rider was scrambling into the saddle.

'Get down!' someone snapped.

Barbad was mounted. With a savage kick, the old eunuch forced his horse off the track. It landed belly down in the stagnant pool with a terrible splash. Half swimming, half running, it breasted the surface. The glossy black water foamed white in its wake.

'No, Barbad!'

Just behind Valens, the boy was yelling as he heaved himself up into the saddle.

Dropping the reins, Valens lunged at the boy. Catching him by the scruff of the neck, he hauled him back to the ground.

The eunuch's horse was floundering east towards an islet with a stand of trees.

Prince Sasan filled his lungs to shout. Valens clapped a hand over his mouth.

The three loose horses were sidling, thinking about bolting.

'Someone catch them,' Valens said.

Hairan moved past.

Sasan bit Valen's hand. The sharp little teeth sank into his palm. Instinctively, Valens let go. The boy darted after the eunuch.

Valens went into the fen a moment after Sasan. The water was up to the boy's chest. Undeterred, he was forcing his way through. Longer legged, Valens closed the distance in a couple of strides. He dived to tackle the child. They both went under.

The cold black sludge enveloped Valens. It forced its way into his mouth and ears. He could see nothing. For a hideous moment, neither his hands or his feet touched the bottom. Then a boot hit something solid, and he came up into the air.

The boy was nowhere in sight.

Looking round wildly, Valens saw a disturbance on the surface. He reached down, groping. His hand closed on something. He hauled Sasan out of the swamp.

Gasping, the boy was going to shout again.

Valens cuffed him hard around the ear. 'Be silent, you fool. The old man is sacrificing his life for yours.'

A flash of movement in the moonlight, and Barbad raced into the deep shade of the trees. A shout of command from the levee was followed by the sound of men wading down into the swamp.

'Do not move,' Valens whispered.

He and the boy stood in the stinking mire.

The others were frozen under the reeds along the track.

More splashing and crashing indicated Barbad's mad flight had crossed the tiny island and re-entered the marsh.

A jabber of Persian voices. The bobbing light of torches trailing after the eunuch.

It was cold in the water. Valens felt Sasan shivering. He put his arms around the boy.

The torches swarmed up onto the islet and disappeared under the trees.

Valens helped Sasan back up onto the track.

'The levee is clear.' Narses had returned. 'The old eunuch did well. But we must hurry.'

When they crossed the deserted levee, Valens thought about turning the Persian horses free, stampeding them. But that would make a noise. There would be other Sassanids nearby in the watchtowers, and it would give them proof that the Romans had slipped past. If the hunters took Barbad alive, Valens doubted the eunuch would tell them anything.

Narses navigated them to a spit of firm ground running into the fens from the north-east. They took it at a walk. When they reached the plain, they moved to a trot, then a gentle canter.

Sunrise found them still in the saddle. Its low, slanting light threw their shadows far out across the plain. Everyone was relieved that the Walls of Alexander were out of sight over the horizon.

The Steppe here rolled like a sea in a gentle swell. It was cut by little watercourses running off to the west. By the third hour of daylight the horses were stumbling with weariness, and roped in sweat. They stopped and watered them at a stream. Although no one had slept in the night, Valens set a watch, and Decimus chivvied those not on that duty to see to the horses.

Despite the cold, men and animals were glad to get into the rivulet and have its bracing water wash away the foul and clinging black mud of the swamp. The men put on clean tunics from their saddlebags, and rubbed the horses dry. They were down to the last of their rations – some hard tack and a morsel of bacon – and there was no food for their mounts. But the autumn rains had revived the grass, and they hobbled the horses and let them graze. Supplies should not be a problem. The Steppe was nothing but thousands of miles of grass, and the men could live off what they caught hunting.

Young Prince Sasan did not want to eat. He was desolate at the loss of the old eunuch. Clemens sat close to him, and tried to offer consolation in Greek. There was a tenderness about his actions. The severe, time-worn face – so very like a sculpture of a senator from the stern time of the ancient republic – bent over that of the boy, showing the concern of a father.

All Clemens's efforts were in vain. The boy continued to sob.

Narses, resplendent in a tunic embroidered with the heraldry of the Suren clan, went over. He pulled the child to his feet. Gripping Sasan's shoulders, Narses spoke to him sharply in Persian. The boy wiped the tears from his eyes with his knuckles, took several deep and shuddering breaths, and stopped crying. Narses passed him a biscuit, and he ate.

'What did you say?' Valens asked.

'I reminded him that he was a Persian: born to ride, shoot and abhor the Lie. I told him that Barbad had died for him, and that of the ten of us who had come to rescue him, three had already given their lives. He owed the dead the dignity of silent grief.'

Before they slept, they resaddled their horses.

The boy moved off to relieve himself. Clemens went to follow. Narses said Persian decorum demanded privacy. Someone should keep an eye on the child, Clemens said. Narses assured him that Sasan would do nothing foolish. Anyway, Aulus was on watch, and out on the Steppe the old hunter could see anything coming twelve miles off.

Valens was woken by someone shaking him. He had not been asleep long, and it was hard to drag himself awake, to force his tired eyes to focus.

It was Aulus. Fatigue had further sunken his cheeks. The skin under his eyes was veined and purple, like bruises.

'They are coming,' Aulus said.

'Who?' Valens was still stupid with sleep.

'The Kindly Ones. Who the fuck do you think?' Aulus said. 'Sassanid horsemen, three columns of them spread out across the Steppe.'

'How far?' Valens ached all over from sleeping in his mail.

'A couple of miles. The rain laid the dust. I caught a flash of sunlight on steel. When I knew the first column was there, I could find the others. There may be more further east. They are dragging the Steppe for us.'

'Wake the others. We will move out straight away.'

Valens went over to Decimus. The horse master was already awake. 'We will fit a blanket and girths on the two spare horses. If a mount goes lame, there will be no time to change saddles.'

As he tacked up the horse, Valens looked at the sun. It was directly overhead. Noon, the horses had had three hours rest. It was not enough. Six hours until darkness. That was too long. Despair seized his mind and limbs. All this way to end in failure on this featureless, empty plain. Severus, Quintus and Zabda had died for nothing. Unless some god intervened, the rest would soon be joining them. But if at last it all ends in sleep and quiet, why worry?

'We are ready.'

Narses's words jolted him back to his surroundings.

'Is the boy enough of a horseman for this?'

'He is a Persian.'

'Mount up.'

As they came up out of the watercourse, they were seen. The Sassanids were much closer, little over a mile. They had been going at a trot. Now, spying their quarry, a trumpet brayed from the nearest column and they went straight up to a gallop. Other trumpets took up the call. The notes were repeated across the face of the Steppe.

The fugitives rode hard, in a clump, in no human order, but like a herd of wild horses.

The Steppe stretched away. It was flatter to the north, utterly without features. There was no cover, just isolated scrubs of wormwood. Nowhere at all to hide. Along the horizon was a series of low, round oddly regular hillocks. They would never reach them.

Their mounts were worn out with hard travel and little rest. Those of the Sassanids must be fresh. Within half an hour the hunters had closed the gap to less than half a mile. They were gaining hand over fist.

Valens could feel the energy dying out of his mount. It was running with its head held to one side, the rhythm of its legs faltering. He bent low over its neck, driving it forward with hands and heels.

There was a shout, then an awful crash from the rear. Valens looked back over his shoulder. Aulus's horse had fallen. The Gaul had jumped clear. He was down in the dirt. The horse was struggling to rise. One of its front legs was broken.

Decimus, with the spares, was near the front. He did not slacken stride, did not appear to have noticed. Every moment was taking them all further away from Aulus.

High and exultant cries came from the Sassanids just a couple of hundred paces behind.

Valens yanked on his reins, sat back in his seat. He would not leave Aulus alone to die.

The first arrow whistled past to embed itself in the turf.

Suddenly Valens's mount leapt forward again. The unexpectedness rammed him backwards. Were it not for the rear horns of the saddle, he would have disappeared over the horse's tail.

'There is nothing you can do.' Iudex brought the flat of his sword across the rump of Valen's mount again. The beast set off, ignoring its rider.

Valens regained his balance, again reined in, and looked back.

Aulus was on his feet, sword drawn.

The Sassanids were almost upon him.

Iudex grabbed Valens's bridle. 'Leave him.'

The enemy horsemen were lapping around the solitary man.

'We will share his fate soon enough.' Iudex kicked his own horse forward, dragging Valens's along.

Torn with indecision, Valens let himself be led away.

'Aulus will buy us a few moments,' Iudex bellowed. 'Now ride!'

Doing as he was bidden, Valens gazed over his shoulder. Aulus was like a beast at bay. The Gaul turned this way and that. He made little rushes. The horsemen surrounding him wheeled out of range of his blade. The Sassanids did not close with Aulus. Instead they shot him down from a safe distance. The first shaft to hit took him in the back of his thigh. Aulus staggered. The next struck his right arm. He shifted his sword to his left. The third and fourth thumped between his shoulder blades.

Valens looked away, over his horse's head.

Those strange round hills were not that far away now. But they were bare, and offered nothing except a last stand.

The Sassanids were so close Valens could hear the jingle of their armour and weapons, hear them call encouragement to each other.

Brightly feathered arrows were falling thicker.

It is hard to aim a bow from a galloping horse, but it was only a matter of time until the first Roman rider or horse was brought down. Valens was tensed for the searing pain as an arrowhead punched into his back. A tiny part of him willed it to happen, to bring this torment to an end.

And then it was over. No more sounds of pursuit. No arrows falling.

Valens looked back. The Sassanids had reined to a ragged halt. As he watched, they wheeled their horses and rode away to the south.

Valens looked ahead. There, in front of the mounds, was a line of the strangest horsemen he had ever seen.

CHAPTER 33

The Steppe

N O ONE WAS PREPARED TO meet the Heruli.

The rumour was that they were not as other men. Rumour did not know the half of it.

Valens sat on his horse, open mouthed, oblivious to everything except the men in front of him.

The Heruli were dressed much as you would expect of nomads. They wore thick fur coats. The furs were luxurious – sable and marten and ermine – and their ornaments were gold. They rode small Steppe ponies. Each had a richly embroidered *gorytus*, a combined bow case and quiver, and had a long straight sword on their hip. Most carried a small round shield. From the tack of their ponies fluttered what looked suspiciously like human scalps.

That was where normality ended.

The faces of almost all the riders were covered in intricate tattoos. The hair and beards of many were dyed a bright red. But it was the heads of the red-haired warriors that were truly shocking. Their skulls were long – perhaps half as long again as that of a man – and they were pointed, like that of some predatory animal, or creature from a nightmare.

A tall rider nudged his pony forward.

'*Zirin*,' he said, and placed his right palm flat to his forehead.

Not knowing what the word meant, Valens saluted.

The rider smiled. Without the tattoos and the red dye and the deformed skull, he would have been handsome.

'I am Andonnoballus, son of Naulobates who rules all the grass-lands from the Sea of Azov to the Volga. My father would have come to meet you himself, but he is . . . *away*.'

Andonnoballus spoke Greek with a slight accent.

'Health and great joy,' Valens replied in the same language. 'My name is Marcus Aelius Valens.'

'We were warned to expect an officer called Severus,' Andon-noballus said.

'He is dead.'

'My condolences.' Three more nomads came forward. 'These are my brothers – Aruth, Uligagus and Artemidorus.'

They looked nothing like either Andonnoballus or each other. Aruth was short and stocky, Uligagus a great bear of a man. The last indicated – the one with the Greek name – had tattoos, but his hair was not dyed red, nor was his skull misshapen.

Seeing the surprise on Valens's face, Andonoballus laughed. 'All Heruli warriors are brothers. You people from the Middle Sea find it shocking that we hold our wives in common. Among us maternity is a matter of fact, paternity merely opinion.'

'Then how can Naulobates know that you are his son?' As soon as the words left his mouth, Valens regretted asking what might be an awkward question.

The young warrior was unconcerned. 'The custom with our wives is not ancestral. My father introduced it some years ago.'

Valens was relieved that his ill-considered words had caused no offence. The safety of the expedition now rested entirely in the hands of these strange tribesmen.

'The gods told my father that the Heruli should adopt the prac-tice from the Agathyrsi, one of our subject tribes. If the woman is willing, any one of us may lie with the wife of another. It is much better than the system of Plato. In the *Republic* the family was to be abolished. How cruel was the Athenian? What is more natural than the family?'

Valens was speechless. Andonnoballus's conversation was even more unlikely than his cranial deformation.

Without leave, Artemidorus interrupted the son of his king. 'That is enough, Andonnoballus. Our guests are tired. Philosophy and discussion of our customs can wait.'

Artemidorus spoke in the pure Attic dialect of Plato or Demosthenes. Its use was now confined to the elite in Greek cities.

'Do not be surprised at my accent.' The swirling patterns of ink on Artemidorus's face came alive when he smiled. 'I was a member of the Boule in the city of Trapezus on the Black Sea. When the Heruli sacked the *polis* seven years ago, I was enslaved. Among the Heruli, courage in battle wins freedom and good advice brings high rank. Look at me now.'

Apart from being blue, not red, the designs on Artemidorus's bow case were not dissimilar to those on his face. The realisation dawned on Valens that the *gorytus* was not embroidered, but covered in human skin.

'My brother is right,' Andonnoballus said. 'Come, our camp is just beyond the burial mounds. Let us make you welcome. Tomorrow we will ride to my father. He is very keen to entertain Prince Sasan.'

The main encampment of Naulobates was a day's ride to the north. It was pitched under tall trees on the far bank of a steep-sided river that cut across the Steppe. The tents were set in the shelter of the wood. There were many of them, but their number was dwarfed by the thousands of ponies grazing across the Steppe.

Andonnoballus had told Valens that this was a hunting expedition. Naulobates had not wished to arouse suspicion among the

Persians at his long journey to their frontier, at the very south-east of his domains. When the King of the Heruli went hunting, it was not a matter of a few friends and dogs. Naulobates was accompanied by ten thousand warriors, and each of them had brought at least five remounts.

As they approached, Valens spotted a lookout stationed high in a tree. It seemed an unnecessary precaution, given that Andonnoballus had left half his troop – no fewer than a thousand riders – strung out across the Steppe south of the burial mounds. Nothing could leave the Walls of Alexander without the Heruli being informed. All the tribes between the Caspian and the Aral Sea were subject to Naulobates. Perhaps their allegiance was uncertain.

There were only a few places where a rider could descend with safety into the bed of the river. Andonnoballus led them down a sandy, well-trodden draw, and called in his native tongue to the man perched among the topmost branches. The warrior replied in a sorrowful tone. Andonnoballus and the other Heruli laughed with little sympathy.

'He will stay there until dawn tomorrow,' Artemidorus explained to Valens.

'Why not relieve the sentry more often?'

This provoked a gale of merriment among the tribesmen.

'He is not a sentry.' Artemidorus could hardly talk for laughing. 'It is a punishment. He must cling there from one dawn until the next.'

'What was his crime?'

'Before we left our winter grazing, he attacked Uligagus.'

'Nothing wrong done by me.' The Greek of the big shaggy Uligagus was not as good as the others. 'Hung *gorytus* outside tent. Enjoying his wife. All quite proper. Come in and attacks me, unproven.'

'Unprovoked,' Artemidorus corrected.

'Yes, that. Gave him good beating.'

'My father showed clemency,' Andonnoballus said. 'In the past, Naulobates has had men torn apart for such a thing.'

'Torn apart?'

'Two saplings are bent down. One of the criminal's legs is tied to each. Then you let them go.'

'There can be no jealousy or mistrust among the brothers,' Artemidorus added.

'What if he falls from the tree?' Valens asked.

'It is a long way down.'

They were shown to their quarters. Three tents at the north-western edge of the camp away from the river had been assigned to them. One was for Valens, the second for the other officer, Decimus, the final tent for the four soldiers. The shelters were made of felt stretched over a round wooden frame. There was a hearth in the centre, and a hole at the top. If the smoke got too much, drawstrings could raise the sides. Although their design was unusual to the Romans, the tents were clean and well appointed. The mission stacked their saddles and tack, as well as what little baggage remained to them, against the walls opposite the entrances.

'When will your father receive us?'

'That is for him to decide. When he *returns*.'

'From where?'

'That is for him to explain, if he wishes. Until Naulobates formally accepts you into our camp, you will stay around your tents. Your horses will be turned out with the herds. Food and drink will be sent, slave girls too. Do not pollute the running water of the river. That is a great crime with us. Use the pots provided. Slaves will empty them. The boy Sasan will come with me.'

'No,' Valens said. Without their mounts they were at the mercy of the tribesmen. If they no longer had the boy, the Heruli might have no further need of them.

'My father instructed me to show Prince Sasan the hospitality due to a member of Shapur's dynasty.'

'We have taken an oath to defend him. He must stay with us. He can take my tent, and I will share with Decimus.'

Narses and Clemens moved to stand on either side of the boy.

The other Heruli looked to Andonnoballus.

It was the child that dispelled the tension. 'Thank your father for his kindness. These men have suffered much for me. It is right that I do not leave them.'

Andonnoballus put his palm to his forehead. 'My father wishes nothing but your safety and happiness. Sacred oaths are not to be broken.'

The summons came the next day.

Assiduous in all their duties, the slave girls had washed the best tunics of the Romans. After some debate, the men decided it would appear too untrusting to attend the feast in armour. Weapons were another matter. Even in Rome, the favoured officers dined with the Emperor wearing their swords.

The pavilion of Naulobates was at the centre of the camp. As the weather was wintry, the feasting would be done inside.

There were no guards at the entrance, although a couple of slaves were present. The latter made no attempt to disarm the guests, but wordlessly pulled back the hangings instead.

Some thirty guests sprawled on rugs and cushions in a rough circle. The hum of conversation dropped, but did not cease, when the Romans entered.

Naulobates sat on a plain wooden chair at the back of the tent. He was dressed in a snow-white tunic and toga. His tunic had the broad purple stripe of a Roman senator, and he wore the boots that were the symbol of that order. Embedded in the ground behind him were twelve axes bound with rods: the fasces of a consul of Rome.

Valens led Prince Sasan and the others to stand in front of the King. Everyone in the party placed their right palm to their forehead.

Naulobates studied each of them in turn without speaking.

The King had the high, pointed head and the red beard and tattoos of the Rosomoni. One of the slave girls lent to the Romans had been taken by the nomads out of a Greek city. Valens had assigned her to look after Prince Sasan. From her Valens had learnt that the 'Red Ones' had been the ruling clan of the Heruli until Naulobates had seized sole power. Even now wives were shared, children of Rosomoni women had their skulls bound.

Naulobates was a slight man, his hair and beard wispy. But his grey eyes shone with deep thoughts untrammelled by conventional morality or pity.

'You.' The King pointed at Iudex. 'I have met before.'

For once Iudex was at a loss. 'Perhaps, Lord, someone who has the misfortune to look like me. This is the first time that I have ventured onto the Steppe.'

'You know a man called Mar Ammo.' It was less a question than a statement.

'Yes, My Lord. I knew him in Ctesiphon, a disciple of the prophet Mani.'

'He wears the same clothes as you: the blue cloak and striped trousers.'

'They are the apparel of the Elect.'

'Mar Ammo was here a couple of years ago. He came to convert the Heruli.'

Iudex said nothing.

'Mar Ammo is a true disciple. You are not. You have betrayed the teachings of your prophet. *Thou shalt not kill*, said Mani. Yet you are a man steeped in blood.'

Iudex accepted this as if a compliment. 'Mani put my feet on the path to the Light. But I have walked further than Mani.'

Now there was tense silence in the tent.

Suddenly Naulobates beamed at Iudex. 'You are a far better man than Mar Ammo or your former master. *Thou shalt not kill* – what nonsense.'

A low murmur of conversation began again. Valens had heard that the nomads showed little respect for their rulers.

'Have you seen the divine twin of Mani, what he calls his *zyzygos*?'

'I have, My Lord.'

'So have I. Brachus, my *tauma*, hunted it through the other world. The *zyzygos* of Mani tried to hide. How it fled! But it was no use. Brachus followed, and Brachus caught him. For nine days and nights Brachus tried to enlighten him. Brachus did not spare himself; he reasoned with him, and beat him without mercy.' Naulobates shook his head sadly. 'Mani was right, the Kingdom of Light is in the north, and working the soil is for lesser men. Yet in his stubborn blindness he could not see that the Kingdom was already to be found here among the Heruli.'

Even Iudex seemed startled by this reworking of the teaching of Mani.

Naulobates smiled at Iudex. 'Brachus saw your spirit-twin the other day, when it had left your body south of the Walls of Alexander. Your spirit-twin was searching for the Persian horsemen, and

did not see Brachus. At once I knew you as a man after the heart of
Naulobates, a pious man who does not flinch to kill.'

'Thank you, My Lord.'

'And then there is you.' The hypnotic eyes of Naulobates fixed on
Valens, then on something no one else could see beyond him. 'My
brother, Gallienus, sent me the ornaments of a consul. They were
brought by your general Ballista. Now there is a man with a strong
daemon. I made him my son-in-arms. I would rather he were here
than you. But Ballista and I will meet again, in the empire. It will
not go well for one of us.' Naulobates stretched, like a man waking
from a dream. 'Still, you are here, Marcus Aelius Valens, and you
bring me this sweet child of my enemies.'

Automatically, Valens put a hand on Sasan's shoulder.

'Have no fear, Valens. My *tauma* has told me this boy will have
the longest and strangest life. He will see things none in this tent
can imagine – a new Earth, a new Heaven.'

There seemed no answer that could be appropriate.

'Now enough of the future. Sit, eat and drink. You are welcome.
By the end of this feast we will have more to celebrate.'

Andonnoballus gestured for the Romans to come and sit with
him and the other three Heruli who had first met them.

Great piles of roast meats and flatbread were brought in. There
were no vegetables. They ate off silver plates. Valens's was worked
with images of naked Greeks killing barbarians: more plunder from
the empire, like the slave girl, or perhaps a diplomatic gift. He noted
that Naulobates ate from a plain wooden platter.

'Great power must be accompanied by great humility,' Andonnoballus said. 'In our winter camp by the Don we have cooks from
Ionia, but this is a hunting camp. My father has brought wine from
the Aegean for you. Our kumis is an acquired taste.'

Feeling it polite, Valens tried the fermented mares' milk. He quickly acquired the taste. It was like a thin, sharp yoghurt with an aftertaste of bitter almonds. Soon his head was buzzing. The kumis was stronger than it seemed.

'Wonder how the man in the tree is getting on?' Valens said.

'Oh, he will be fine,' Uligagus said. 'Aruth here hung in a cage for nine days.'

'With no food and water?'

'No, we are not savages,' Artemidorus said. 'He had three loaves and a jug of water.'

'Why?'

'I had led a charge when Naulobates had ordered no one to leave the battle line.' Aruth had a fetching red snake tattooed on his forearm. 'My three blood brothers chose to share my punishment.'

'And you all survived?'

'Of course, we are Heruli. And Naulobates also allowed them three loaves and a jug each.'

The hangings were thrown back, and a mud-spattered Herul entered. He said something in their language. Many of the tribesmen cheered. They slapped each other on the back, obviously delighted with the news.

Naulobates merely smiled contentedly.

When the uproar subsided, Naulobates looked at Valens and spoke in Greek. 'I prophesied that before the feast was over we would have cause for celebration. The Sassanids have marched out from the Walls of Alexander.'

CHAPTER 34

The Steppe

THE SASSANID ARMY WAS STATIONARY and drawn up to the south across the plain. The brisk and chill north wind whipped the banners above their heads. Embroidered leopards and lions, serpents and dragons, fierce beasts and abstract designs invoking Mazda and other gods writhed and snapped.

Some three hundred paces away, although out of effective bow-shot, every detail was revealed. The Persians were arrayed in three divisions. To spare their mounts, the horse archers on the flanks waited dismounted. All were lithe and slim men with long hair and beards, and wore loose tunics and baggy trousers. They were unencumbered except for their bows, and could leap onto the backs of their horses in a moment. Their quivers and long straight swords hung ready from their saddles. Like the nomads they faced, they wore no armour. Their numbers were difficult to judge, but Decimus told Valens that there were some eight thousand on each wing.

In the centre, under a huge banner bearing the emblem of a bear, stood the *clibanarii*: four thousand armoured Persian noblemen on huge armoured chargers. They were more cumbersome, so to avoid the danger of being taken by surprise, they waited mounted. Some were encased in steel, man and beast. With masks covering their faces, they could have been statues. Many wore bright surcoats over their armour: scarlet and green, yellow and blue silk, bearing the heraldic devices of their clans. The motifs were repeated on those whose horses were caparisoned. The mounts of others were protected by armour of green-blue horn or red leather. Although the majority had a bow case strapped to their saddles, these were shock cavalry. The proud *clibanarii* would rely on the tall lances in their hands. If the lances broke, they would draw the swords on their hips.

Last night, Naulobates had held an impromptu council at the feast. Valens had been surprised at the freedom of speech allowed. Against the obvious wishes of Naulobates, an older warrior called Pharas had argued that they should not fight. They had everything they wanted. The hunting had been good, and Prince Sasan was in their hands. The Emperor Gallienus would pay much gold for the boy. Was it not promised in the letter from the Praetorian Prefect Volusianus? They should break camp, saddle up, and ride away into the vastness of the Steppe.

A few pointed heads nodded at the words of Pharas. But the majority shouted against them. This was cowardice. Had the old man lost his balls? It was time he climbed the funeral pyre. How dare these Sassanids trespass into the realm of the Heruli? They would make the grass run red with Persian blood.

Pharas was not cowed. The Persians would not follow far. If they did, then the Heruli would turn on them. But even if they defeated the Sassanids, that would not force a passage through the Walls of Alexander. They still could not plunder the rich lands beyond.

Fuelled by much kumis, many diners abused Pharas. Too old to satisfy a woman, he should ask a friend to cut his throat. His wife would be glad to hang herself by his ashes. If he wanted a long peaceful life, he should go and live in some Greek city – one the Heruli would not visit! Fuck off, you aged coward!

Naulobates had had a servant beat a drum for silence. When he spoke, his high, thin voice was heard by all.

'We are not Persians who grovel before a despot. We are not Romans who hold their tongues before a dictator. We are free Heruli. Pharas has spoken his mind. Others have unveiled their thoughts. I am the elected war leader. I have listened, and now I will decide.' Naulobates paused, his eyes suddenly unfocused, perhaps hearing voices others could not make out. 'We will meet the Sassanids four miles south of the river. I will lead the centre, Andonnoballus the left, Artemidorus the right. My blood brothers Aruth, Uligagus and Pharas will ride by my side. As an honour, our Roman guests can join my band.'

There had been no choice for Valens. If they had refused to fight, the Heruli would have deemed them cowards. The future was not promising for those so regarded in the camp of Naulobates. If they remained in their tents, and the Heruli lost, the Persians would kill them anyway. It had been best to accept with an air of gratitude.

Valens stood, holding his horse's bridle, with the other five survivors of his mission. At least even the Heruli had deemed the boy Sasan too young to fight. He remained safe in their tent. The Greek slave girl could look after him. Unless the Persians won, in which case his fate was uncertain. If he was not killed when the camp was sacked, presumably he would return as a prisoner to the Castle of Silence.

Valens regarded the standard with the bear and the massed ranks of the Persians. He had enlisted in the army to see battle. Now it was imminent, he was not so sure. A great part of him wished he was back in the tent with Prince Sasan. A distant war is a glorious thing.

To go to war like a nomad was unsettling. Naulobates had told them not to wear armour. Dressed in the quilted jacket of a tribesman, Valens felt naked. They had been offered Heruli ponies, but these were bad-tempered beasts, intractable to those who did not know them. They had brought their own horses. Narses was mounted on his black Nisean stallion. In the light of what was to come, Valens hoped they had not made a fatal mistake.

Taller than the nomads, Valens looked up and down their lines.

There were just over three thousand light horsemen to the east with Andonnoballus. These were warriors from subject tribes. The Eutes had followed the Heruli all the way from the Northern Ocean. The wife-sharing Agathyrsi were more recent adherents. The blue tattoos of the latter made a contrast to those of their overlords.

The same number of riders waited on the right wing under Artemidorus. All those from here to the west were Heruli.

Each flank was outnumbered by more than two to one.

The odds were not so bad in the centre, under the standards of Naulobates. Those with the war leader almost matched their opponents. The majority here were Rosomoni. Their elongated skulls, dyed hair and tattoos, pronounced the Red Ones the elite warriors of the tribe. Also among the throng were their bravest slaves. To prove their valour, the latter were not allowed a shield. Otherwise they were equipped like their owners: bow and long sword, fur or quilted jacket. No matter the courage of masters and slaves, they and their small ponies could never withstand a charge from the terrible *clibanarii* on their huge horses.

A veteran had once told Valens that all pitched battles on an open field happen by mutual consent. Like a festival or a chorus in the theatre, they had their rhythms and pauses. This morning Valens saw the truth of the statement. It was three hours since dawn. Both sides had watched each other for the last hour. Neither had moved. The Persians had sacrificed a kid. The omens could not have been good. They brought out a second, then a third, before they were satisfied.

Now a Sassanid nobleman rode out alone from the centre of their line. His armour and that of his horse was chased with gold, and shone like a flame in the autumn sunshine. A low murmur of admiration, or perhaps greed, ran through the Heruli.

Perfectly calmly, the Persian reined in some thirty paces in front of Naulobates.

'Gondofarr, Satrap of Hyrkania, by the grace of the Mazda-beloved Shapur, King of Kings, bids me tell you to heat the water and prepare his food. He would bathe and eat in your camp tonight.'

Naulobates nudged his pony forward. 'There is no need. Gondofarr will never wash or taste food again. Tonight I will drink my kumis from his skull. Tomorrow his scalp will hang from my bridle, and his skin decorate my *gorytus*.'

The Sassanid drew his bow.

Naulobates made no move to defend himself. None of the Heruli moved to protect him.

The Persian selected a long cane arrow from his quiver. With slow deliberation, he nocked it, raised the bow, and drew the string to his ear.

Valens watched, frozen with incomprehension.

The Sassanid aimed at Naulobates's chest. No fur jacket would deflect the missile.

The King watched the archer.

The Persian lifted the bow to the skies, and loosed. The arrow flew high over the Heruli hoard.

'We have fought the Sassanids before,' Aruth said. 'It is their way. Now we will show them ours.'

As the nobleman cantered back towards the bear standard of the Satrap of Hyrkania, the lines of the Heruli parted. Two tribesmen trotted their ponies out. Behind and between them stumbled a naked man. He had the malformed skull and red-inked skin of one of the Rosomoni. A rope was tied around each of his wrists. The end of one rope was secured to the horns of the pony on the left, the other the one on the right. The riders kicked on to a canter. The naked man was jerked off his feet. For a time they dragged him about between the two armies. Valens winced as the ground tore the man's flesh.

'Spare him no sympathy,' Aruth said. 'In the hunt we drove a boar from its lair. That man dropped his spear. He endangered the brothers around him. Already his suffering brings the favour of the gods.'

Naulobates uttered a thin, high command.

The riders moved to a gallop, then peeled off right and left. The ropes snapped taut. The momentum of the ponies was halted. The riders whipped them on. With a horrible wet rending sound, one of the prisoner's arms was torn from its socket, and ripped away from his torso.

The horsemen cut the ropes, left the severed limb and the man bleeding his life away.

Naulobates turned to Valens. His grey eyes were untroubled. 'Good weather for the fight.'

Valens looked at the heavens. A bank of dark clouds were coming down from the north. 'Will the rain not dampen your bowstrings?'

'Oh, yes.' Naulobates beamed. 'But that is nothing. The gods draw close. On the Steppe there is nothing better than to fight under a storm, while the sky above your enemies is clear. There is no doubt we will be victorious.'

Valens wished he shared the confidence of the Heruli king.

Trumpets sounded along the Persian lines. The Sassanid light horse jumped into their saddles. At a walk, the whole host began to advance.

Naulobates threw back his head, and made an unearthly sound. *Yip-yip-yip*. The weird war cry was taken up by all the Heruli.

As one, the nomads mounted. Valens and the other Romans scrambled onto their horses.

The nomads milled for a moment. Every eye was fixed on the standard above Naulobates. The King gave an order, and the banner with the running wolf inclined towards the Sassanids. *Yip-yipping*, the Heruli raced forward in no order a civilised soldier could discern.

Valens rode just behind Naulobates and his blood brothers.

When the distance between the armies had narrowed to about a hundred paces, bowstrings thrummed. Both sides loosed at the same time. The sky was so full of shafts that Valens saw some collide in the air. Then the first missiles began to fall, and all his attention was focused on dodging and guarding himself with his shield. The Romans had been given small, round nomad shields, which strapped to their arms. Valens wished he was wielding a big Roman cavalry shield. But that had to be held in the left hand, and made it difficult to use a bow.

Suddenly the Heruli wheeled around, with no more warning than a school of fish. Valens sawed on his reins, dragged his mount around after them. Now the Heruli were cantering away from the Sassanids. All the while they plied their bows over their horses' rumps. Busy keeping close to Naulobates, managing his horse, and avoiding the Persian shafts from behind and those of the Heruli ahead, Valens had yet to draw his bow.

A nomad was transfixed by an arrow. Valens stared, fascinated by the bright feathers protruding from his back. The pony did not break stride, but the Herul slid from its back.

The Sassanid heavy horse came after the division of Naulobates, still at a walk. Some men and animals in their front rank had several arrows lodged in their armour. The steel and leather and horn was hard for any nomad shaft to penetrate. Valens saw that more Heruli were falling than *clibanarii*. The Persians were winning this fight.

A great roar came from both wings. The Sassanid horse archers had slung their bows over their shoulders, and unsheathed their swords. They spurred into an all-out charge. Outnumbering these savages by more than two to one, like their betters, they would settle this with cold steel.

The *yip-yipping* on the nomad flanks faltered, then gave way to shouts of alarm. The divisions of both Artemidorus and Andonnoballus were fleeing. They raced away to the north with howls of distress, not even turning to shoot at the pursuers close on their heels.

That was too much for the pride of the Sassanid nobles. The arrows had stopped coming from behind. Valens looked over his shoulder. The *clibanarii* had replaced their bows in their cases. Now they were unslinging the long lances from the loops over their shoulders.

Unnoticed by Valens, the Rosomoni had slacked their pace. Now he found himself out in front of Naulobates, leading the retreat. He was happy enough to ride in this place of comparative safety. The clouds had covered the sun, and the first spits of rain pattered his face.

The *clibanarii* were still walking, but now they gripped their lances two-handed, and brought them down. A wicked wall of sharp steel glittered for a moment, until the shadows swept over the Sassanid horsemen.

A trumpet called, and the Persian nobility urged their warhorses to a trot.

No more than thirty paces separated the fighters. Yet Naulobates kept to a sedate pace.

The Sassanid trumpet sounded again, and the armoured knights moved to a canter.

The ground shook with the thunder of their coming. The air itself seemed to tremble.

Naulobates and his men nudged their ponies to keep just out of reach.

Now the storm front hit. Curtains of rain streamed down from the north, flattening the grass, stinging Valens's face.

Through the murk, he saw that the pursuit on the two flanks was drawing away fast. The riders of neither Artemidorus or Andonnoballus were making for the camp. Instead both were angling away across the limitless Steppe. Soon they would be lost from sight.

Squinting ahead through the driving rain, Valens was amazed to see how far they had come. The trees along the river were no more than a mile away. The day would be decided soon.

Maddened by their quarry always remaining just out of reach, and goaded by the gadfly arrows of their elusive foe, the Persian nobility could take no more. With or without orders they charged at the gallop.

Now the Heruli rode hard. The small shaggy ponies surged past Valens and his men. The thousands of horrible spear tips were almost at Valens's back. He bent low over the neck of his horse, driving it forward with all his strength. Drawing his bow, he used it as a whip.

As they pounded across the plain, the Sassanid ranks broke. The better mounted pulled ahead. They bellowed the names of their clans, riding for the honour of first striking down these cowardly barbarians. Gaps opened in their frontage. But still they came.

Suddenly Naulobates and the riders in front of Valens vanished, as if swallowed by the earth.

Terrified as he was of the Persian spears so close to his shoulder blades, Valens reined back. They were at the river. Thank all the gods, Naulobates had ridden down one of the draws. Leaning back in the saddle, Valens followed him down, his mount almost on its hocks.

The Rosomoni to either side had to jump from the high bank. Valens saw one pony fall. But these nomads had been in the saddle before they could walk. Riding was more natural to them than walking. They and their ponies could negotiate almost anything.

The track up from the riverbed was muddy from the rain, trampled by the hooves of those who had gone before. Valens's mount slipped and staggered up the far side.

Emerging at the top of the bank, he swung away to the right. His men were still with him.

Somehow, like mountain goats, the ugly little Steppe ponies swarmed up the steep and treacherous slope, and reined in around the Romans.

The Sassanids were blinkered by bloodlust, their vision limited by the narrow slits in the masks of their helmets. They did not see the drop until too late. The bravest set their mounts to make the leap. The fainter hearted yanked back on their reins. Those behind collided with them, sending the foremost over the edge, and themselves tumbling after. Even those who had jumped cleanly were often undone by the weight of their armour, their mounts crumpling on landing. In a heartbeat the riverbed was transformed into a welter of thrashing and struggling injured men and horses.

Up on the north bank, the Heruli poured arrows into the chaos. Their bowstrings might be slackened by the rain, but at this range they found any exposed flesh, human or animal.

The *clibanarii*, lucky enough to have reached the river at the track, urged their mounts up against the defenders. The first wave headed by the bear standard went for Naulobates and his three blood brothers. Those following came at Valens and the Romans.

A razor-sharp lance thrust at Valens's face, and almost lost him his seat as he ducked to one side. The big Sassanid charger went chest to chest with his mount. Driven back, Valens's horse sat down on its haunches. Dropping his bow, Valens drew his sword. The Persian thrust again. Valens batted it aside with his blade. The impact knocked the hilt from his grip. Desperately, he grabbed the shaft of the lance with both hands. The two horses circled as their riders wrestled for the weapon, all writhing together like one hellish beast.

A second Sassanid was looming on Valens's left. Clemens got in the way. The two men traded blows. Beyond them, all principles cast aside, Narses was also fighting for his life against another Persian. Yet another Sassanid approached from the right, half behind Valens. Out of the corner of his eye, Valens saw the warrior ready himself to plant his lance in the unprotected target.

Die like a man.

The Sassanid reeled. His head jerked around. He looked stupidly at the blood spreading over his surcoat. Decimus hacked again. Not a clean strike, but enough to drive the warrior down to the ground under the trampling hooves.

The Persian fighting Valens let go of the lance, went for his sword. Left in possession of the lance, Valens instinctively swung it like a staff. The wood clanged on metal as it hit the warrior's helmet. Valens battered with it again and again. Stunned, the Sassanid ineffectually tried to fend off the blows with his sword.

As he recovered the ungainly weapon, Valens saw Decimus fall. Unable to aid him, Valens concentrated on punching the tip of the lance through the armour that shielded his opponent's chest. The first thrust skidded off. On the second the scales of metal snapped, and the point struck deep.

Yip-yip-yip. The Heruli were exulting.

The great bear standard of the Satrap of Hyrkania was down.

There was a gasp of horror from the Sassanids.

There, on the lip of the river, was Naulobates. Like some malformed god of war, the King of the Heruli held aloft his grizzly trophy. No one could doubt that Naulobates had fulfilled his prophesy. Here was the severed head of Gondofarr, the Satrap of Hyrkania.

That was the end of the fight. But far from the end of the killing.

The Sassanid *clibanarii*, all pride forgotten, fought each other to escape from the riverbed. *Yip-yipping*, the Heruli massacred them.

As the Persians fled away to the south, the nomads followed.

The others in Valens's command, even Narses, streamed after the rout.

Suddenly Valens was alone except for the injured and the dead.

Wearily, he dismounted. Decimus was lying a few paces away.

'Rest easy, let me get at the wound.'

Decimus's handsome face was contorted with pain. 'Leave it.' His words were little above a whisper. 'A gut wound, I am done for.'

'Let me look.'

'No point. Put a coin in my mouth for the ferryman.' The horse master tried to smile. 'But before that, some water would be good.'

Valens went back to where his horse stood. All the others had run, either after the rout or off to the herds grazing to the north of the camp. There was a great gash on the horse's near foreleg. In the heat of battle Valens had not noticed it take the wound. The beast would have to be put down.

Valens took his water flask from the saddle, and went back to Decimus.

The pursuit was receding away to the south. There would be much work for Charon at his ferry.

Valens unstoppered the flask, lifted Decimus's head, and tried to trickle the water between his lips.

Decimus was dead.

Valens was unsure how long he sat cradling the head of the dead man. Not long, because the rider had not reached the edge of the camp and the vicinity of their tents when Valens saw him.

The man was mounted on a horse, not a pony, and he was riding west, heading purposefully along the riverbank.

CHAPTER 35

The Steppe

THERE WAS NO GOOD REASON for a Roman to go to the tents. None of them was a coward. But one was a traitor.

Valens looked around for his sword. It was lost somewhere in the debris of battle. He snatched up a discarded Sassanid blade. Only when he reached his mount did he remember that it was injured. All the others in sight were dead or also grievously hurt. He turned and started to run.

Their tents were pitched away from the river at the north-west corner of the encampment, a little apart from those of the Heruli. Valens left the riverbank and cut into the heart of the camp.

The nomads had laid out their shelters in neat, ordered streets. They were well spaced so there was no danger of tripping over guy ropes or other impediments. Valens ran as fast as his tired legs would carry him. By the time he turned into the last thoroughfare, he was bathed in sweat, and the breath was beginning to burn in his lungs.

There were only serving women left in the camp. They stared, silent and round-eyed and wondering, as he raced past.

The thick quilted jacket and sword belt were getting in the way, slowing him down. Not stopping, he peeled off the jacket, unbuckled the belt, and left them lying in the dirt.

The Persian cavalry had been waiting when they came down from the Castle of Silence. Valens had been right. There was a traitor. He was after Prince Sasan. Why he wanted the boy, why he had betrayed his companions, Valens still could not imagine.

The man's horse was cropping the grass off to one side.

The Greek slave girl was outside Sasan's tent. Her throat had been cut. No attempt had been made to conceal her body. She had been cast aside as a thing of no importance.

Without stopping to think, Valens pulled back the hangings and burst through.

The interior of the tent was gloomy, wreathed in smoke.

Sasan was cowering amidst the baggage by the back wall.

Clemens was by the hearth in the centre of the tent. There was blood on his sword and his forearms.

As Valens entered, Clemens half turned, keeping an eye on the boy.

'You should not have come,' Clemens said.

'Why?'

'I have no wish to kill you.'

'And Severus and Quintus, did you not want to kill them?'

'No. It was necessary.'

'We swore an oath. Why have you broken your word?'

'Orders.' Clemens smiled mirthlessly. The deep furrows on his face were like lines incised in marble. '*We will do what is ordered, and at every command we will be ready.*'

'Whose orders?' The longer Valens could keep Clemens talking, the better chance he could take him off guard.

'You do not need to know.'

'Why the boy?'

Clemens glanced at Sasan. 'There are those in Rome who want a war with Persia, and there are those who do not. If this child lives, thousands will die: soldiers on the battlefield, women and other children in the sack of towns.'

Before Valens could strike, Clemens looked back.

'There has to be another way to save them,' Valens said.

Clemens made a small gesture with his sword, as if to dismiss all the horror and pity of war. 'Not to save the ones I love.'

'Your family?'

'Yes, my family.' Despite his age, and the bulk of the nomad jacket, Clemens was quick.

A hand's breadth from his face, Valens blocked the thrust. The force sent him staggering. Clemens thrust again, low to the stomach. Again Valens got his sword in the way, backing off around the wall of the tent.

Clemens followed, feet close together, balanced, feinting and probing. The armourer was a master at arms: he knew his trade. There was nothing Valens could do but retreat, try and stay alive. The unfamiliar Sassanid blade felt awkward in his grip.

Slowly they circled around the hearth. There were no sounds but the pad and stamp of their boots, their panting breath, and the sharp clangour of steel on steel. There was no one to hear. None but women in the camp. No one to intervene.

The smoke was smarting Valens's eyes. His arms and legs were beginning to tire. There was a tight band of pain around his chest. He had to end this soon, before the experience of the old swordsman wore him down. Stepping forward, Valens aimed a cut at Clemen's head, but in mid-air he altered the angle down towards his thigh.

As if he had long expected the move, Clemens stepped inside the blow, and chopped his sword into Valens's right wrist. The long Sassanid blade dropped into the hearth, as agony lanced up Valens's arm. Clemens's elbow smashed into Valens's face, sent him sprawling on his back, head almost out of the entrance.

With calm assurance, Clemens placed his boots on either side of the prone and defenceless figure, readying his weapon.

A flash of movement from the rear of the tent, something coming through the whirls of smoke.

Clemens swung backhanded.

The boy fell back in a spray of blood. The old eunuch's little knife flew across the tent.

With his left hand, Valens tugged the dagger from his right boot. Clemens started to turn back, shifting the hilt of his sword to a double-handed grip. He was going to put his weight behind it, and punch down, skewering his victim to the floor. Still on his back, Valens drove the dagger up into Clemens's crotch.

Clemens grunted, but did not go down. He raised his blade. If he had to die, he would take Valens with him to the darkness. Valens twisted the dagger, forcing it deeper. Now Clemens swayed. The sword clattered close by Valens's head. Clemens's knees buckled. Like a felled tree, he crashed on top of Valens.

Trying to ignore the sickening pain from his wrist, Valens heaved the corpse of Clemens to one side. A wave of nausea forced him to lie still, left hand clamped to right wrist. He attempted to gather himself.

He rolled on one side, drew himself to his knees. Hunched over, he forced himself to release his wrist and look at the injury. There was a deep cut, a lot of blood, but it was not severed. Tentatively, he flexed his fingers. A surge of pain, more blood, but they moved. If the wound was cleaned, it might not fester. He might yet not die.

Valens might live, but the traitor had won. So many hard miles travelled, so much hardship, so many deaths, all to end in failure.

A small sob dragged Valens out of his maze of despair.

Like a crab, he scuttled on all fours to the back of the tent.

The boy was covered in blood, but he was alive. Valens found a pitcher of water and a cloth. He bathed the child's face. There was a terrible gash across his forehead, a flap of skin hung down and would have to be stitched. But he was alive.

'Don't cry, you will be alright.'

Holding the cloth to his wound, the boy sat up. 'I thought you were dead. It was you I was mourning. My father did not lament his fate, and nor will I. You saved my life. A Prince of the House of Sasan does not forget.'

CHAPTER 36

Aquileia

Tomorrow would decide their fate. They were in a bar down by the docks on the river. It was pleasant with the sunshine on the water. May was a kind month in northern Italy.

'I should have suspected the bastard,' Narses said. 'Clemens was always trying to stir up dissension in the mission, attempting to cast doubt on the loyalty of those from the east.'

'When he accused you,' Valens said, 'I should have realised.'

'None of us are to blame.' Iudex was eating melon, while the others ate steak. 'His treachery was well hidden, even in the spirit-world.'

Haïran laughed. 'I am far too trusting for our line of work. I never suspected anything – in this world or another – just thought we were unlucky. And I still do not understand why he broke his oath.'

'Do any of us?' Valens shrugged. 'At the end he spoke of following orders and saving his family. Although I was a little distracted, as he was trying to kill me.'

They had talked about it for months without reaching a conclusion.

The journey had been long. After the battle, and the death of Clemens, they had ridden through the winter, across the entire extent of the domain of Naulobates: around the northern shore of the Caspian, across the Volga, and down the Tanais; endless miles of windswept grassland. The Heruli had been generous hosts, if eccentric. The soldiers had become accustomed to a diet of meat and milk and kumis. From the town of Tanais they had taken passage on a ship across Lake Maeotis to the city of Panticapaeum, and from there across the Black Sea to the Bosporus. The regular sailing season had not opened, but the gods had been kind. At Byzantium the governor had issued diplomatic passes to requisition horses, food and lodgings. They had not hired a carriage. Sasan, as a Persian, preferred to go on horseback. Following the great military road through Serdica and Naissus and Mursa, they crossed the Balkans. At long last they had negotiated the Alpine passes, and descended to the north Italian plains.

Today, the Praetorian Prefect had formally welcomed Prince Sasan with a ceremony in the Forum of Aquileia. Tomorrow, Volusianus would see the four survivors of the mission in private. Valens hoped he had made the right decision back in Byzantium. None of them knew anything about the family of Clemens, but they all knew who had issued the orders that had sent them to the Castle of Silence. Valens had sent a message by the fast imperial posting service direct to Volusianus. The danger was that Murena, as head of the *frumentarii*, took his instructions from the Praetorian Prefect.

'Another drink.' Hairan waved the girl over. 'For who knows what tomorrow holds.'

Valens waited in the big basilica off the Forum. Through the open doors came the noise of the market: traders selling wine and olive oil, slaves and cattle and hides. His head ached from last night's wine, but he did not regret the indulgence. The mission had changed him. Nowdays he drank for the camaraderie, to prolong the evening, not to drown his misery. His parents were long dead. It had not been his fault. Eventually a man has to look things in the face, has to shoulder the unhappiness life brings.

Valens flexed the wrist of his right hand. The wound had healed, but sometimes it still pained him.

Narses came out through the hangings that screened the private room.

Valens felt his heart lift. The Persian had been the first summoned by the Praetorian Prefect, and he was leaving as a free man.

'Volusianus wants you next,' Narses said to Valens.

The Praetorian Prefect was seated behind an inlaid desk. Although clad in a fine tunic, Volusianus's face looked as if it should have been following a plough. But he was alone, and unarmed. That was what mattered. This was going to be alright. Valens had made the correct choice.

Volusianus gestured Valens to a chair. 'A drink?'

'No thank you, sir.'

'Make your report.'

Valens told everything that he could remember – from Rome to the Castle of Silence and back to Italy. Sometimes Volusianus asked questions, sought clarification or expansion. Now and then he jotted notes. All the time the broad peasant face was impassive.

Finally, it was done.

'May I ask a question, sir?'

'Of course.'

'What will happen to Sasan?'

'The prince is an honoured guest. For now he will be educated here in Aquileia.'

'Will it not mean war with the Persians?'

Volusianus ran his hand over his face. He looked old and care-worn. 'War is coming anyway.'

'My men, sir, what will happen to them?'

'They will be promoted, and you will be rewarded.' A shrewd look passed over the bucolic features. 'But first you have another task to perform.'

CHAPTER 37

Rome

MURENA SQUINTED AT THE SUN. He was early. The message he had sent said that he would arrive at noon, and it would not do to be there too much beforehand. It was essential they were alone.

Turning aside, Murena loitered. The Forum was busy. He wore the boots and sword belt of an off-duty soldier. They would draw no attention; Rome was full of troops. Glancing around he saw several in the crowd. Murena half recognised one with long hair and a moustache, vanishing around the Senate House.

Having bought a pastry from a street vendor, Murena sat to eat it on the balustrade that surrounded the Lacus Curtius. He took a bite, but his appetite had gone since the news that morning.

There had been nothing out of the ordinary about Volusianus going north. The imperial field army was still quartered around Milan. But the Praetorian Prefect's diversion to Aquileia had been unexpected. The report had come from a member of Volusianus's staff suborned by Murena. Unfortunately, the informant had not accompanied the Praetorian Prefect, and had not known the reason for the trip.

A ragged child was staring at the hardly touched pastry.

'Hungry?' Murena held out the snack.

'What do you want?' The urchin was suspicious.

'Nothing.'

The boy snatched the food and disappeared into the crowd without a word of thanks.

The news had been waiting on Murena's desk at dawn. Volusianus had returned to Rome late last night. With him were four named survivors from the mission to the Castle of Silence. Prince Sasan had been rescued, and was lodged for the time being in Aquileia. Reading the report, Murena felt as if an abyss had opened under his feet.

At least Clemens had not been among those who had made it back. There was still a chance that this was not the end. If Clemens had revealed his secret instructions to the survivors, the Praetorians would have come in the night, and by now Murena would be in the cellars under the palace.

Murena leant over and washed his hands in the water feature.

The possibility remained that Clemens had told his family before he left. That avenue of danger had to be closed today.

Drying his hands on his trousers, Murena looked at the relief sculpture behind the ornamental basin. An armoured warrior was riding his mount into a marsh. One of the tales was that long ago a chasm had appeared at this place. The soothsayers had said a sacrifice was necessary. A young Roman – Marcus Curtius – had offered himself. The fissure had closed over his head. Not a good omen. Murena had done what was right for Rome. Now would he also pay the ultimate penalty?

There was another story. Once there had been a marsh here in the Forum. A Sabine cavalryman – Mettius Curtius – hard pressed by the Romans of Romulus, had braved its dangers, and escaped. That was more encouraging.

Murena looked again at the sun. It was time to go.

* * *

The Vicus Caeseris was quiet – just a couple of pedestrians and a vagrant with a blanket pulled over his head sleeping rough in a doorway. The latter was big and looked well fed for a beggar; perhaps not a tramp, but a day labourer sleeping off a drinking season.

Murena took station across and down the street, and watched the closed door and shuttered windows of the wine shop. A few more people wandered past; none went to the shop. The slumberer did not stir.

When the sun was almost directly overhead, Murena moved to the door. He listened intently. Once, he thought he caught the murmur of a voice from behind the boards. That was no cause for concern. They were both expecting him.

A final glance up and down the street, and Murena knocked on the door. The sounds of bolts being drawn, and the vintner opened the door.

'Gaius.' The wine seller spoke as if something was wrong with the name.

'Health and great joy.' Murena went inside.

The tradesman shut the door.

'Bolt it,' Murena said.

The man seemed uncertain.

'As my message said, we need to talk undisturbed.'

The vintner shot the bolts.

The room was dark. The single small lamp on the counter barely illuminated the nearby racks of amphorae. The big barrels standing along the left-hand wall were in deep gloom. As ever, the shop smelt agreeably of wine and sawdust. Today there was a hint of spikenard. There was no end to the ingenuity men invested in flavouring wines.

'Is Tullia here?' Murena asked.

'She is in the back.'

'What I have to say concerns her husband.'

'Tullia!' The vintner moved back behind his counter. He was rubbing his palms down the front of his leather apron.

She emerged from behind the curtain with her arms tight across her body, as if holding herself together.

'Health and great joy,' Murena said.

Tullia did not reply, but moved quickly to stand by her father.

'It is about Clemens.' Murena moved between them and the entrance to their living quarters.

'You bastard!' Tullia spat. 'You sent him to his death!'

That answered Murena's question. There was no further need for words. He drew his sword.

'Help!'

Murena smiled. No one would hear their cries. They were trapped behind the counter. He moved forward. Finish them, then quickly check there was no one in the back, and be gone before the alarm was raised. Nothing incriminating left behind.

'Help us now!'

Above the shouts, Murena heard hurried footsteps. The hanging was torn open. A soldier with shoulder-length hair and luxuriant moustaches stood there, sword in hand.

Now someone was pounding on the front door.

Shifting away from the newcomer, Murena flicked a glance towards the sound. In the corner of his eye he saw two figures slide out from behind the huge barrels. He knew them at once. The big Persian Narses and the young officer Valens. Of course, the one with the moustache was Hairan.

The Hatrene was blocking the rear exit.

'Throw down the weapon,' Valens said.

Murena backed into a corner, covering himself with his blade.

Narses went and unbolted the door. The bald figure of that mad bastard Iudex entered.

'It is finished.' Valens spoke softly, as if calming a horse.

Odds of four to one; Murena knew he was right. Hairan ushered Tullia and her father out of the room. The other three spread out and watched Murena.

An image came into Murena's mind of Acilius Glabrio cornered on that dark, windswept roof. He envied the senator the poison concealed in the ring. Like Acilius Glabrio, he would not be taken alive.

Still, it was a hard thing to do. Murena thought of the cells, and the pincers and the claws.

Without warning, he turned and dropped to his knees. Wedging the hilt of his sword against a barrel, he threw himself forward.

At first it was little worse than a punch in the stomach. Then the pain overwhelmed him. As his body toppled sideways, he felt the blade twisting in his guts.

Murena lay very still, clutching the steel, as if that might ease his last agonies. His lifeblood was hot on his hands.

He was dimly aware of the men standing over him.

His face was in the sawdust. His shallow breaths lifted flakes from the floor.

'Why?' someone asked from far away.

Murena could not answer.

EPILOGUE

Constantinople

I call upon thee, O Lord; make
haste to me!
Give ear to my voice, when I call
to thee!
Let my prayer be counted as incense
before thee,
And the lifting up of my hands as
an evening sacrifice!

THE OLD SENATOR DID NOT lift his hands very high. God and man allowed a certain latitude when you were in your eighty-third year. At least it was Sunday, and one did not have to kneel.

The Church of the Holy Apostles smelt of paint and sawdust. As the others senses failed, his sense of smell seemed to have become more acute. It was no great recompense. He could barely make out the rotunda at the end of the nave and its thirteen sarcophagi. Three of them were occupied by the skulls of Luke, Andrew and Timothy. Relics had not been found of the other nine Apostles, and, of course, the Emperor was not dead yet.

'Take, eat; this is my body, which shall be broken for you.'

Declining the supporting hand of his eldest grandson, he approached the Eucharist as he had been taught. Not with his arm extended, or his fingers parted, he made his left hand a throne for his right to welcome the King. He cupped his palm, and received Christ's body.

'Amen.'

Carefully he blessed his eyes with a touch of the holy body, then, careful not to drop a morsel, he put it in his mouth and ate.

'This is my blood, which is shed for you; when you do this, you make my remembrance.'

He did not stretch out his hand for the chalice, but bowed his head in homage and reverence, and sanctified himself by partaking of Christ's blood. While his lips were still moist, he touched them with his fingers, and blessed his eyes, his scarred old forehead, his nose and ears.

Returning to his seat, he leant upon his grandson's arm.

It was wise to appear pious. The imperial edict banning traditional sacrifices had been widely ignored. But the Emperor was not young and he looked far from well. A comet had been seen in the night sky. That presaged the death of a king. Constantine had three sons and two nephews. There would be a struggle for the succession, and all five candidates were Christians. For an octogenarian the future mattered little, but it was important that his family had every chance to weather the coming storm.

The conversion of Lucius Domitius Sasan to the new religion of the Emperor had involved no inner struggle nor revelation. It had been a matter of quiet policy, like so much in his life. He had never been an aficionado of gladiatorial fights, and the public executioners could always find different ways, equally cruel, to dispatch criminals other than crucifixion. Resting on the seventh day struck him as a sensible idea.

Of course, if the Christian god was as all-seeing as his priests claimed, he would not be deceived by such subterfuge. Sasan

would be condemned to an eternity of hellfire. The Psalms made
that clear.

> *Let the mischief of their lips*
> > *overwhelm them!*
> *Let burning coals fall upon them!*
> *Let them be cast into pits, no*
> > *more to rise!*

And Sasan might have exalted company. It was whispered that
Constantine had turned to the Christians only because their priests
had offered him the hope of absolution. Beheading your eldest son,
and having your wife suffocated in a hot bath, would weigh on any
conscience. It would be a strange deity that overlooked such sins in
his judgement of a soul.

Thank God, the service was over. Sasan was hungry. Fasting did
not agree with him.

Outside, the late evening sunshine fell in bands under the portico. Sasan's grandson led him to the litter that would convey
him back to his house overlooking the Bosporus. It was pleasant
there by the water. The house had been one of those gifts offered
by Constantine to those senators prepared to leave Rome for his
new capital. Sasan's domicile, like his piety, was a result of worldly
calculation.

The summons to the *consilium* of the Emperor just before Easter
had been an unexpected honour. Constantine was preparing for
war with Persia. Quite what advice Sasan might have been expected
to proffer was a mystery. He had been an eleven-year-old child
when he had left Persia seventy-two years before. His role as a diplomatic hostage had been eclipsed long ago when Hormisdas, the
brother of the King of Kings Shapur II, had fled to Rome.

Sasan had been grateful that Hormisdas further removed him from attention. Until recently he had enjoyed the company of Hormisdas. But now he kept his distance. Constantine had proclaimed his own nephew Hannibalianus King of Kings. The projected campaign in the east was to place Hannibalianus on the throne in Ctesiphon. Hormisdas had become unnecessary, perhaps something of an embarrassment, and had not been invited to the *consilium*. Perhaps Sasan, as a member of the Persian royal house, had been thought to give some spurious legitimacy to the whole affair.

Truth be told – and one must abhor the Lie – Sasan knew his effect on relations between Rome and Persia had always been negligible. The year after he had been rescued from the Castle of Silence there had indeed been a war. Thousands of men, women and children had suffered and died. Roman troops had sacked Ctesiphon. But the war had been fought by Odenaethus, the ambitious Lord of Palmyra, who had commanded Rome's eastern provinces. It had not dragged the Emperor Gallienus from the west. Odenaethus had campaigned alone to free Valerian from Persian captivity. The Lord of Palmyra had failed. There had been no attempt to set up the young Prince Sasan as King of Kings. The war would have been fought if Sasan had remained a prisoner in the Castle of Silence.

When first brought into the empire, Sasan had been provided with a household and ordered to live in Aquileia. For four years he had enjoyed growing up in the elegant northern Italian town with its views of the Alps and the gulf of Tergeste. He had been glad to be alive, and content to be schooled as if he were a scion of some obscure but wealthy Roman family. Above all he had hoped to be forgotten.

That hope had been disabused when the army of the newly proclaimed Emperor Aurelian had marched through Aquileia.

Aurelian had taken him to Rome, given Sasan citizenship, awarded him the toga of manhood, then declared him a senator. Imperial generosity had provided a house on the Esquiline, and a wife from a senatorial family. Whatever calculation had provoked Sasan's brief return to the public gaze had died with the assassination of Aurelian.

As Emperor succeeded Emperor, Sasan devoted himself to books and the arts. History was his passion, but he had no desire to make it himself. A dutiful husband, he had fathered four children: three sons and a daughter. He had seen them grow, marry, produce eight grandchildren. Apart from an annual trip to the Bay of Naples, he had hardly left Rome until he decided to take advantage of the largess of Constantine, and come to live by the Bosporus. Two sons had predeceased him, but their deaths apart, it had been a long and thankfully uneventful life.

As the litter made its stately way through the streets, Sasan thought of that wilder journey long ago down from the Elburz Mountains and across the Steppe. The wound of Valens, the young officer who had saved his life, had healed. After Aquileia he had never seen any of them again. Not Valens or the odd Manichaean Iudex, not his fellow Persian Narses or Hairan the handsome young man from a desolate city. Ten men had ridden out of Zeugma to rescue him. Six had died in the attempt, including the traitor. They would all be long dead now.

When he still publicly worshipped the traditional gods of Rome, he had made libations to their shades. Even now, in the privacy of his home, occasionally he tipped a little wine on the ground.

But the one who most often haunted his dreams had not been a man at all. He would wake in the dead of night, thinking of an old eunuch and a young boy in a tall tower on a remote mountain crag. Sometimes he woke sweating as the old eunuch was hunted through the marshes by the Caspian Sea.

Tell us about the Castle of Silence, his children had often asked, as had his grandchildren in their turn.

His reticence had only encouraged them.

Tell us about the Castle of Silence.

AD337

HISTORICAL AFTERWORD

The Castle of Silence

'FOR IF ANYONE IS CAST into it, the law permits no mention of him to be made thereafter, but death is the penalty for the man who speaks his name.' Many years ago, when I first read Procopius (1.5.7–6.10), I knew the castle of silence had to be the basis of a novel.

The only specific modern study of which I am aware is G. Traina, 'La forteresse de l'oubli', *Muséon* 115 (2002), 399–422.

The historical fortress-prison was not in the Elburz Mountains. The events of this novel suggest why the King of Kings was wise not to locate it near a frontier, although in Procopius a fugitive manages to make his escape to the Steppe.

Sassanid Persia

Good places to begin to learn about Sassanid Persia are: J. Wiese-höfer, *Ancient Persia from 550 BC to 650 AD* (London and New York, 1996); M. Brosius, *The Persians: An Introduction* (London and New York, 2006); and T. Daryaee, *Sasanian Persia: The Rise and Fall of an Empire* (London and New York, 2009).

The translated documents and commentary in B. Dignas and E. Winter, *Rome and Persia in Late Antiquity* (Eng. tr., Cambridge, 2007), offers a stimulating and different approach.

On the Sassanid army, see: M. Whitby, 'The Persian King at War', in E. Dabrowa (ed.), *The Roman and Byzantine Army in the East* (Cracow, 1994), 227–63; and two articles in B. Campbell and

L. A. Trittle (eds.), *The Oxford Handbook of Warfare in the Classical World* (Oxford, 2013) – S. McDonough, 'Military and Society in Sasanian Iran' (601–20) and A. D. Lee, 'Roman Warfare with Sasanian Persia' (708–25). A splendidly illustrated guide for the non-specialist is D. Nicolle, *Sassanian Armies* (Stockport, 1996). Some of Nicolle's attribution of images are corrected by St. J. Simpson in a review in *Antiquity* 71 (1997), 242–5.

The *Frumentarii*

The *frumentarii* were the closest thing the Roman Emperor had to a secret service. Soldiers seconded from other units, with a base on the Caelian Hill in Rome, they were his confidential messengers, spies and assassins. Their obscurity in scholarship is so profound that they lack an entry in the fourth edition of *The Oxford Classical Dictionary* (2012), but since the publication of my novel *Fire in the East* (2008), they seem to have become almost ubiquitous in Roman historical fiction. A cautious introduction to the historical *frumentarii* is C. J. Fuhrmann, *Policing the Roman Empire* (Oxford, 2012), 152–5.

Mesopotamia and the Roman East

F. Millar, *The Roman Near East 31 BC–AD 337* (Cambridge, Mass. and London, 1993) remains the best one-volume study.

The Walls of Alexander

The dating of these defensive structures, the longest of which stretches for over 120 miles, has long been controversial. For the purposes of this story I have blithely ignored the recent archaeological study that dates them to the fifth century AD: E. Sauer et al., 'Linear Barriers of Northern Iran: The Great Wall of Gorgan and the Wall of Tammishe', *Journal of the British Institute of Persian*

Studies 44 (2006), 121–73; available online at https://www.research. ed.ac.uk/portal/files/.../Linear_Barriers_of_Northern_Iran.pdf

Manichaeism

Ancient Manichaeism was a pacificist religion, and does not seem to have encouraged even its elect to follow the prophet Mani into the spirit-world. These apart, the bizarre religious views of Iudex in this novel are authentic.

An enjoyable way into the religion is via its most famous some-time follower, as analysed by Robin Lane Fox in *Augustine: Conversions and Confessions* (London, 2015). More conventional, and harder going, is N. J. Baker-Brian, *Manichaeism: An Ancient Faith Rediscovered* (London and New York, 2011).

The Heruli

A short essay on this obscure but fascinating and extraordinary tribe can be found in the Historical Afterword to my novel *The Wolves of the North* (2012).

Quotes

The poem that ends Chapter 8 is an extract from an anonymous epigram in *The Greek Anthology* (Harmondsworth, revised edition, 1981), no. 772 (10.118), translated by Peter Jay.

The conversation between Narses and the customs official in Chapter 12 is adapted from *The Life of Apollonius* by Philostratus (1.21; and 27).

The two poems recited in Chapter 12 are by Asklepiades and Palladas, and can be found in *The Greek Anthology*: no. 61 (5.210); and Appendix 2 (11.381); both translations are by K. Rexroth, although the latter is from M. Grant (ed.), *Greek Literature* (Harmondsworth, 1976), 310.

In Chapter 19, when Valens recalls Book 9 of the *Odyssey*, I have used the translation of Robert Fagles (London, 1997), here and there slightly altered.

When Narses justifies Persian exposure of the dead and ill in Chapter 24 he is echoing Agathias, as translated by Averil Cameron in *Dumbarton Oaks Papers* 23/24 (1969/1970), 67–183.

The famous lines of the *Iliad* (6.447–8) in Chapter 30 are from the translation by Richmond Lattimore (Chicago and London, 1951).

ACKNOWLEDGEMENTS

In every novel the cast of characters changes, but those who are thanked remains much the same. Without the encouragement and support, as well as the criticism and forbearance, of the following this novel would not have been written or published.

Family: my wife Lisa, my sons Tom and Jack, my mother Frances and my aunt Terry.

Professionals and friends: Kate Parkin, James Horobin, Stephen Dumughn, Francesca Russell, Clare Kelly, and Claire Johnson-Creek at Bonnier Zaffre; and James Gill at United Agents.

Friends: in Oxfordshire Peter and Rachel Cosgrove, Jeremy Tinton, and Maria Stamatopoulou; in Suffolk Jack Ringer and Sandra Haines, Fiona and Michael Dunne. This novel is dedicated to the latter.

Dear Reader,

Thank you very much for reading *The Lost Ten*. I very much hope that you enjoyed it. This is a story that I have wanted to tell for a long time. Reading the Byzantine historian Procopius many years ago, I first came across the sinister and exotic Persian prison-fortress called The Castle of Silence. Straight away I knew it had to form the basis of a novel. It would be the goal of a desperate rescue mission far behind enemy lines.

In *The Lost Ten* I set out to recreate the excitement and suspense of the classic thrillers of John Buchan and Alastair MacLean that I loved in my youth and still reread for pure pleasure. But I also wanted to introduce the tougher, hard-edged realities of contemporary tales of adventure such as *Bravo Two Zero*.

While the plot of *The Lost Ten* is fiction, the historical background is as accurate as the ancient sources and modern scholarship allow. Historical novelists owe it to their readers to do the research, and to get things right. The reader of *The Lost Ten* is taken on a journey across the Euphrates to the Tigris and beyond, far outside the settled frontiers of the Roman empire. Mesopotamia in the Third Century was a war ravaged borderland between Rome and Persia. The 'Land between the Rivers' was a melting pot of competing cultures and religions, where a Roman from the west would find some things familiar, but others as alien as does a modern reader. *The Lost Ten* aims to bring to life this fascinating and unsettling region.

If you enjoyed *The Lost Ten*, please do look out for my next novel, as yet untitled, which will be out in 2020. A soldier returns home from the sack of Corinth to find a killer stalking the hills of his native Calabria. The veteran has to unmask the culprit, and free his isolated community from the reign of terror. But suspicion soon falls upon himself, and he is haunted by some terrible secret from the destruction of the city. I'm thinking to blend together the fear and darkness of Scandi noir with the explosive action of my *Warrior of Rome* novels.

If you would like to hear more from me about this and my other future books, you can get in touch with me at www.bit.ly/ HarrySidebottom where you can join the HARRY SIDEBOTTOM READERS' CLUB. It only takes a few minutes, there is no catch and new members will automatically receive an exclusive e-book short story. Your data is private and confidential and will never be passed on to a third party, and I promise that I will only be in touch now and again with book news. If you want to unsubscribe, you can of course do that at any time.

You can also get in touch by following me on Facebook, where I frequently post about forthcoming books: https://www.facebook.com/ pages/category/Writer/Harry-Sidebottom-608697059226497/

I'm always grateful, however, to readers who spread the word. If you have enjoyed *The Lost Ten*, I would love you to leave a review on Amazon or GoodReads, on any other e-store, on your own blogs and social media accounts – or even tell another human being directly! You'll help other readers if you share your thoughts, and you'll help me too: I love hearing what people think about my books – and I always read any comments.

But for now, thank you again for travelling with *The Lost Ten* across the deserts of the East – I'm glad you came along for the ride.

Best wishes,

Harry